NANTUCKET
DREAMS

SEASIDE HARMONY

PATTI BERG

D0061513

Guideposts
New York, New York

Nantucket Dreams is a trademark of Guideposts.

Published by Guideposts
16 East 34th Street
New York, New York 10016
Guideposts.org

Cover design by Gretchen Schuler-Dandridge
Cover illustration by Marilyn Chamberlain
Interior design by Müllerhaus
Typeset by Aptara

Printed and bound in the United States of America
10 9 8 7 6 5 4 3 2 1

CHAPTER
One

Caroline Marris remembered this view. She'd dreamed about it for years. But still, seeing it now, it took her breath away.

She stood at the top of the dune. From here, blue-gray ocean stretched as far as she could see. At her feet, the golden sand was laced with delicate but sturdy ocean grasses, and it sloped down to a pale strip of beach. Waves splashed onto the shore, leaving behind a trace of frothy white foam.

Caroline drew in a deep breath, basking in the scent of salty air and the calming sound of the gentle surf. She'd spent so many years away, but it was just like she remembered. Her memories were as fresh and alive as the warm breeze and the midday sun that kissed her face.

She hadn't been sure she wanted to come back to Nantucket, but standing here now—her sisters Gracie and Sam toiling up the dune and her cocker spaniel Max playfully chasing butterflies and bees—she was glad they'd talked her into coming. They needed these two weeks together.

"I think I'd better hit the gym when I get back home!" Gracie's cheeks were red from sun and effort, and her breath came in gasps as she trudged up the sandy knoll. "I can't believe I've let myself get so out of shape."

"I thought I was in better shape too," their youngest sister Sam called out. Sam was fifty-two, and though she carried a few extra pounds from sampling too much of her own delicious cooking, she still looked trim and younger than her years.

Laughing, Caroline pushed her short, windblown blonde hair from her face. The scene was playing out as it always had when they'd arrived on Nantucket for their family's two-week summer vacation as children. Back then, the last one up the dune had to buy a hot fudge sundae for the others. Caroline usually won—after all, she was the oldest, the biggest, and the strongest. It hadn't been quite fair for her to always claim victory, but now that she'd celebrated her sixty-first birthday, she considered it something of a coup to best her sisters.

Sam puffed, and the wind tousled her sleek, shoulder-length hair, as she and Gracie joined Caroline on the crest of the hill. "Guess I'm buying the hot fudge sundaes this time around. I'm getting them with extra whipped cream, a cherry, and nuts on top. Anything to fatten the two of you up so next time it'll be harder for either one of you to win the race."

Caroline reached for her sisters, drawing one close with each arm. Gracie slid a hand around Caroline's waist, and Sam threw arm over Caroline's shoulder. As their laughter subsided, they gazed in silence at the horizon, where the morning sun shattered on the waves in a million golden shards.

"Mom sure loved this place," Sam murmured, saying what each of them had no doubt been thinking.

"Yes, she did." Tears stung Caroline's eyes. They had lost their mother six months ago, just two weeks after Christmas. This was the first summer vacation the three of them had spent on Nantucket without her. They hadn't been here in decades, but this year, it seemed like a good way to honor her.

Caroline could easily picture Rosalie Marris sitting on the beach in a cherry-print sundress, the straight blonde hair her daughters had all inherited pulled back in a ponytail. She would always spread out multicolored Tupperware tubs on the beach blanket, and the family would feast on chicken, potato salad, watermelon, and her special chocolate chip cookies—their dad's favorite summertime meal— while her daughters and husband raced in and out of the surf and built castles in the sand.

Caroline hugged her sisters tighter, wishing—not for the first time since their mother had passed away—that she'd stayed closer through the years. She should have visited them more often, called once a week instead of once every month or so. Of course, all the regrets in the world couldn't turn back time.

"Remember when Mom taught us how to find sand dollars?" Gracie asked, her shoulder-length bob engaged in a losing battle with the breeze.

"She told us they were long-lost pirate treasure." Caroline smiled at the memory. "And we'd look and look, and then as soon as we found one, we had to scoop it up quick, before the next wave washed it away."

"Except she said we had to grab it before a dastardly pirate swooped in and stole it," Gracie said.

"It was years before I learned what *dastardly* meant," Caroline laughed.

"I always wanted to hunt them. But"—Sam winked at Caroline— "it was my job to carry the pail."

"And an important job it was!" Caroline said. "If we'd tried to carry them around in our pockets, they wouldn't have made it home in one piece."

"I know that now." Sam elbowed her older sister playfully. "But back then, the two of you treated me like a baby."

"You were the baby," Caroline teased, "and always willing to please."

"Only because I wanted to pal around with you and Gracie." Sam smiled warmly. "I still do."

The waves crashed against the shore, churning up surf in gorgeous shades of aqua and turquoise and the palest cream. Far down the beach, a young family was spreading out towels down by the water's edge.

Their mother would have loved to see them like this, all lined up on the dunes again. *Why didn't we do this before?* Sam thought. She was on the road so much for her work as a travel writer, and when she wasn't working, she had just wanted to hole up in Briar Rose, the little cottage in the English countryside she called home. But maybe she could have made more of an effort. They all had busy lives, but they could have found time to bring Mother here one last time before she got too frail. If only she could go back and do it all differently... but of course, she couldn't. She shook her head.

"Race you guys to the bottom," Caroline said, and took off, digging her feet into the loose sand as she raced down the dune. Behind her, she could hear her sisters shriek and start to follow her. Max scampered to the head of the pack, barking and running around them playfully. As if they were children again—still Rosalie and Cliff Marris' three blonde stairsteps—they chased each other across the beach, kicking up sand, laughing and giggling. Finally, they stopped and pressed three sets of footprints and one set of paws side by side into the wet sand. Their footprints were much the same size now— no longer small, medium, and large. They'd changed so much through the years; they'd each chosen different paths in life and had spent far too many years apart. This could be an interesting two weeks, as these three very different women, each set in her own ways, tried to recapture the closeness that they once shared so easily. *Even if there are a few little spats, it will be worth it,* Caroline told herself. *Mother would have wanted it this way.*

"Hey! Check out the Misty Harbor." Sam pointed down the beach to the splash of pale buttercup yellow high on the bluff.

Caroline shaded her eyes from the sun, frowning as she stared at the imposing colonial structure perched on the dunes just up ahead. It was still surrounded by a white picket fence, and had lush pink and red roses growing everywhere. "It looks different, doesn't it? Not nearly as big as it looked way back when, but—"

"Everything looked big when we were kids," Gracie teased.

But it was more than the size that seemed different. Caroline just couldn't put her finger on it. She needed to see it close up. "Come on." Caroline headed up the beach, Max prancing at her side.

"You can't just go up to the inn," Gracie said, catching up with Caroline. She tried to smooth her hair down, but the breeze picked it up again. "I'm not dressed for tea—"

"And there might be guests hanging around," Sam added. "We can't barge in."

Caroline stopped. She turned slowly, frowning at her sisters. "We're not going for tea, and we're not going to barge in," she said, starting toward the bluff again. Tiny bits of sand kicked up behind her as she walked. "We're just going to climb the stairs to the top of the bluff, like any summer vacationers would do, and walk by the place. If no one's around, we can stroll through the garden. Remember how Mom loved the Old English roses that climbed the trellises—"

"And the birdbath," Sam added, skipping to catch up with her older sister. "Mom had us toss coins into it and make a wish."

"She was such a dreamer," Gracie said, shaking her head as she followed after Caroline. "You're so much like her in that way."

Caroline shrugged. She thought of herself more as a wanderer, a woman interested in anything and everything. That's what made her such a good travel writer. And anyway, what was wrong with being a dreamer? "You know," Caroline said, "if Mom was with us, we'd be up at the inn by now." Caroline slipped off her flip-flops and started up the hill that separated the old inn from the beach.

"Or we could be inside the place scrubbing floors and washing windows," Gracie added, laughing in her familiar, no-nonsense way. "Remember how she used to talk about buying the Misty Harbor? She had this grand idea that the three of us could work with her to make it the best B and B in Nantucket."

Gracie and Sam started up the sand dune after their sister.

"She already knew how she'd decorate the rooms and what kind of food she'd serve," Sam said, before allowing her voice to mimic their mom's. "'If I owned the Misty Harbor Inn,' she'd say, 'I'd serve nothing but my very own special recipe cranberry and blueberry jams, made from berries I gathered myself.'"

"And she'd have crocheted doilies everywhere," Caroline added, the laughter in her voice softening. "I must have boxed up two or three dozen before we put her house on the market."

Caroline's thighs had started to burn, but she kept pushing toward the top of the bluff. She thought about her mother standing at the ironing board in a pretty pink dress, singing along with Doris Day or Rosemary Clooney, while she pressed the white doilies she'd spent hour upon hour crocheting. Caroline could almost smell Rosalie's favorite Chanel No. 5 cologne wrapping around her, could almost hear her laugh. But all that was left of their mother were memories.

"Remember her crazy stories about celebrities who'd stayed here, and about hidden rooms and mysterious disappearances in the inn?" Caroline said. "I always wanted to hear more."

"There was probably not a grain of truth in any of them." Gracie took in a deep breath and tried to keep up.

"How about the time Mom took us to the Misty Harbor for tea?" Sam said, pretending she was drinking from a delicate china cup, her pinky finger extended, just as Mom had instructed. She huffed a little from the exertion.

"She made us wear those horrible white gloves and pillbox hats, like Jackie Kennedy," Caroline said, laughing at the memory. "And those flowery dresses with the starched slips. I felt silly, like I was too old for such things."

"They weren't so bad," Gracie said. But then, Gracie had liked dressing up and playing house and all the things Caroline couldn't stand.

Caroline shook her head, still mystified to think her mother ever believed her oldest daughter could be anything but a tomboy. She'd hated to dress up then, and nothing had changed. Total comfort was her idea of style. "I wanted to die when she paraded us into the inn, all three of us with our hair curled so tight we looked like Shirley Temple. I was just thankful that none of my friends could see me!"

"I didn't care how I was dressed," Sam said, "but I remember walking into the inn and seeing the tall trays filled with finger sandwiches and minidesserts, and all I wanted to do was eat. Afterward, I wanted Mom to teach me how to make petit fours."

"It was pretty special that she did that for us," Gracie said. "You have to admit that, Caroline. We may not have been as well-off as everyone else in that tearoom, but for that one afternoon, Mother made sure we felt like royalty."

Caroline gave a reluctant nod. Nantucket was a playground for the country's wealthiest families, but the Marris family had never felt out of place here, even though they stayed in budget accommodations and cooked most of their meals in their little rented kitchenette. Their mother probably had to scrimp and save just to afford that afternoon tea, but she had done it to make sure her girls felt special.

Sam snapped a wild pink rose from one of the bushes scattered across the bluff. "I wonder if they still serve tea."

"Only one way to find out," Caroline said, slipping on the flip-flops that had been dangling from her fingers. "Let's check it out."

Gracie, who'd never been one for adventure, sighed. "Oh, all right. But if there's anyone at all around, let's walk by and keep on walking."

With memories wrapping around her as warmly as the breeze, Caroline struck out again, calling out to Max, reminding him that if he didn't leave the bees alone, he'd get stung. But as they neared the old colonial inn, Caroline could see that something definitely wasn't right. The yellow paint that had always been so cheery was weather-beaten and faded. A faded banner that had hung from the pole in the back yard was tattered and listless. And the lilacs were growing over nearly everything in sight. What on earth had happened to the place their mother had so dearly loved?

"It looks closed," Sam said.

"Abandoned," Gracie said, "and that appears to be an understatement."

"Let's get closer." Without waiting for her sisters, Caroline marched through the open gate at edge of the garden and walked along the crushed shell path that meandered around the garden. It was tangled with pink, yellow, white, and purple blossoms, and dark green vines that could trip you if you weren't careful. A hummingbird zipped in front of her, flitting from one mass of flowers to another. It was all so incredibly wild—and beautiful.

Behind her she could hear Gracie comment on how overgrown the yard was, but she kept following the path around to the front of the house. When she reached the front of the inn, she put her foot on the first of three steps leading up to the porch. She tried to imagine the white marble urns, each filled with dark red and glistening white geraniums that used to sit at the top of the stairs. It was an absolute shame there were no flower-filled urns standing there now. She wasn't a gardener, and she found the overgrown garden incredibly beautiful in its wild state, but that didn't mean she didn't love having a garden done up right.

Caroline placed a foot on the second step. It creaked. The third squealed. When she reached the heavy wooden planks of the porch, they felt wobbly beneath her feet.

How could anyone let this fabulous old inn fall apart?

The tall, dark green front door beckoned. There was a yellowed piece of paper taped to the pane of glass in the middle of the door. She walked toward it. She read the hand-lettered note.

Thank you for all the wonderful memories.

Misty Harbor Inn is closed for the season.

She heard the sound of footsteps, and Caroline turned to see Gracie coming up behind her. "Look at this," Caroline said, tapping on the glass.

Gracie frowned as she read the message out loud. "Closed for the season?" She chuckled. "Looks like it's been more than just a season."

"I'd say at least five or six, considering the shape of things," Sam added, her voice carrying toward them on the breeze. She wandered through the garden that had grown so wild that it was encroaching on the circular drive and taking over most everything in sight.

Caroline stood at the edge of the porch, gripped the handrail that needed sanding and fresh paint, and watched Sam stroll beneath a trellis choked with morning glories. Sam stopped when she reached a bronze birdbath with a pensive cupid holding a scalloped shell over his head. It was the birdbath their mother had had them toss coins into so many years ago.

"What's this?" Sam said, parting the vines. She dug out a black and orange sign that said For Sale.

"It can't be!" Caroline tried to wrap her mind around the idea. The old inn had been a landmark in her life. She'd stayed there only once, the summer before their father died from a heart attack, yet through her mother's dreams and wistful tales, the inn—like Nantucket itself—had become a constant in her life. Visiting it was a part of every summer. She couldn't imagine its being for sale like any other property.

"Hang on. There's something else under all the vines." Sam tore out a few deeply rooted weeds, and Max put his nose down beside her, his paws setting to work at the dirt. A moment later they dug out a clear plastic box. She straightened up, brandishing a brittle sheet of water-warped paper she'd taken from inside, waded through the garden, and handed it up to Caroline on the porch.

Caroline scanned the one-page For Sale flyer quickly and then read: "Nantucket Whaler's Mansion overlooking the sea. Extensive lawns and long, meandering driveway lead to the front porch of this 1840s colonial. Cherry woodwork shines in the library, parlor, and dining room; updated, modern kitchen; sunlit rooms to relax in on cold winter days; four guest rooms with en suite baths and living quarters for owner, should the discriminating buyer wish to keep the mansion as an inn. Watch the tides roll in and out from the expansive back porch, or laze the day away in the glorious garden."

"How much?" Sam asked.

Caroline's gaze hovered for a moment over the faded colored pictures taken inside the inn, down to the dollar figure at the bottom of the flyer. She gulped, looked at Sam, then Gracie, and then back at Sam again. She nearly stuttered when she announced the price.

"Well, that explains why it hasn't sold," Gracie said, ever practical. Her eyes narrowed. "No one would pay that…for this."

"Oh, I don't know." Caroline stared out at the jungle that had once been a garden. At the trellises that someone had lovingly built for roses to climb over in summer and early fall. She thought about the view from the back of the house, which was perched right at the edge of the ocean. "My guess is that beneath this wild morass are the remains of something gorgeous. And who knows what's still inside? It might very well be worth every penny."

"Maybe for someone with a strong back and a lot of money," Gracie said.

Gracie was probably right. But Caroline looked down at the sales flyer again and then back at the covered-up window in the door that hid the inn's foyer from view. Was it her imagination, or could she see through it now, all the way to the distant horizon? As she stared, her imagination transformed the shuttered inn, just the way her mother's mind always had: adding a fresh coat of paint, throwing open the windows to let in the scent of salt air and the cool breeze, trimming back the garden, cooking up and canning local jams and jellies to serve her guests.

It is folly, she thought. *But who knows. The old, run-down inn might be just the right place for someone with wide-eyed dreams.*

CHAPTER
Two

"Come on, Caroline," Gracie Gold urged. "We don't belong here. Someone could be watching. If we don't leave now, the cops might show up and make us leave." She rushed down the steps and across the garden, stopping at last when she stood under the rickety arbor that led to the walkway down to the beach.

"Or they might urge us to go inside and take a look around, thinking we might want to buy it," Caroline said, stepping down from the porch. She moved to a window and tried to peer through the closed white shutters that had been beaten by wind, sand, and sea for far too many years.

"We're not here with a real estate agent," Gracie said, edging closer to the walkway. Her sister didn't understand boundaries. She never had. "We don't have a key or permission to be here. I'm sure if the cops came by they'd think we were casing the place, looking for something to steal."

"I'll take the birdbath." Sam pinched a crimson rosebud from a bush and tucked it in her hair. "I have the perfect place for it in my garden."

Gracie looked around uncomfortably, hoping no one was within hearing distance to misinterpret Sam's comment about stealing the birdbath. The only people around were a man and a young boy running along the beach, trailing after the kite they were flying high in the air. She wished she were down there with them. Caroline was bound to get them in trouble before their vacation was over.

"Did you try the doorknob to see if the front door's unlocked?" Gracie heard Sam ask Caroline as her younger sister bounded up the stairs, Max hot on her heels.

Caroline spun away from one of the shuttered windows, looking at Sam. "Would you go inside with me if it was unlocked?"

"Of course she wouldn't," Gracie stated flatly, walking back toward the porch, hoping her sisters would pay attention to what she was saying. "That would be trespassing."

"It's locked anyway," Sam said as she pushed against the door handle. It didn't budge. She pulled a Kleenex from her pants pocket and attempted to wipe some of the film off the door's etched glass and peered inside. "I'd love to know if the owners left behind the furniture and paintings."

"The paintings?" Gracie cringed. "The times we came here with Mom, I felt like the people in those paintings were watching our every move. They reminded me of those creepy portraits hanging inside the Haunted Mansion at Disneyland. If this place were mine, I'd take them down and store them up in the attic."

"But they gave the inn an extra dose of character," Caroline said. "If Mom owned the inn, she would have known the history of each person in the portraits so she could tell her guests stories about their lives."

"Wouldn't it be fun to know if any of the people in those paintings had nefarious backgrounds?" Sam asked. "Maybe a robber baron? A Union or Confederate spy?"

"Or an assassin," Caroline added with a laugh. "They were probably just stodgy old goats with bad breath and gout."

"All the more reason to get away from here." Gracie latched on to the newel post at the bottom of the front porch steps. "I don't believe in ghosts, but if the souls of any of those stodgy old goats are still hanging around, they might not take kindly to our messing with their property."

"Oh, Gracie!" Sam bounced down the creaky steps and hugged her sister. "Lighten up and have some fun."

Gracie blew out a long breath. She rolled her shoulders, trying to let go of the tension that had built up in the last few minutes. There was something about the inn that bothered her, and it wasn't ghosts or stodgy old souls or even getting caught snooping around. It was more a feeling of foreboding. Obviously Sam and Caroline didn't share her feelings. They were laughing and running around the place as if they were kids all over again.

"Let's see if we can get a look through any of the other windows." Caroline tucked a rosebud she'd pinched from one of the bushes into Gracie's hair and kissed her on the cheek. "I promise neither Sam nor I will try to climb inside even if we do find an open window or door."

Gracie sighed heavily. "Oh, okay."

She followed Caroline and Sam, weaving through overgrown English roses in need of a good pruning, as well as purple and pink hibiscus, towering lilac, and lavender wisteria that had rambled everywhere. She hoped her own garden would never end up in a mess like this. Her late husband Art had had the greenest thumb in all of Portland, Maine. He'd won awards for his flowers at all the fairs. He would love overhauling this garden, but he wasn't here to do it. And Gracie sure wasn't interested.

"Over here," Sam called out. "You can just barely see inside…into the parlor, I think."

Caroline rushed to Sam's side. Gracie snagged her thumb on the thorn of a salt spray rose. A speck of blood dripped onto her yellow T-shirt. She made a mental note to scrub the spot with cold water and soap before throwing it in the washer.

"*Ooh*, look at that," Caroline said, her forehead pressed against a shutter. She peered through a knothole in the wood. "That table has to be original to the house."

"Let me see." Sam nudged Caroline aside with her hip. "Oh, it's beautiful. Gracie, come see."

Gracie knew they were goading her. She loved antiques, and was a sucker for old-fashioned furniture. She and Art had filled their home with antique store finds, and they had read up on many of their favorite time periods. But they weren't supposed to be here, and—

"There's a fabulous old square piano. Baroque, I think."

Gracie sighed. If she just took a quick peek, maybe her sisters would be satisfied and she could drag them away. Gracie rejoined her sisters on the porch and nudged them aside. "Let me look."

She had to stand on her tiptoes to see through the shutter's knothole, and if not for a beam of light shining into the room from the other side, she wouldn't have been able to see much at all. The room was far too dark. But the piano was lit up brightly, and specks of dust fluttered all about. She squinted to get a better look. It was a grand piano, all right, but a square grand, a type you rarely saw anymore. They were very popular in the Victorian era, and were typically ornately carved and exquisitely detailed, as with most furniture of the period. This piano's legs and music stand were created of elegantly carved scrolls.

"Fabulous is an understatement," Gracie said, her heart beating rapidly at the sight of something so magnificent, "but it's not Baroque. It's probably American, mid-nineteenth century. There was one of these things in every Victorian parlor for a while, but then the uprights edged them out. It's quite rare to find one these days."

"Is it worth a lot of money?" Sam asked, gently shoving Gracie aside.

"That depends on what kind of shape it's in, how it sounds, and whether or not it can be tuned. Whether the soundboard is cracked or not," Gracie said, but once her heart stilled and she came back to reality, she shrugged. "But why would anyone abandon a piano like that if it were valuable?"

"Why would anyone abandon the inn in the first place?" Caroline asked, bumping Sam aside to take another look through the window.

"Maybe it's haunted." Sam grinned. "Wouldn't that be a kick?"

"I for one wouldn't want to wake up in the middle of the night and find Marley's ghost rattling his chains in the middle of my bedroom," Gracie said, smiling at her sisters, before taking the lead and heading off to the next window. If she couldn't get her sisters to leave, she might as well try to see more of the inside. As much as she'd wanted to get away from the inn, she had to admit, she was finally having fun, joking with her sisters, laughing with them in a way they hadn't done in years. Gracie tried wresting a loose shutter from the next window and… She stumbled backward, the shutter still in her hands. "Oh! I didn't mean to pull it all the way off."

"Of course you didn't," Caroline said, laughing. "But since you did, we might as well take advantage of it and get a good look inside."

"We'd better put the shutter back up before we leave," Gracie said, the muscles in her neck tensing as she once again looked around to make sure no one had seen what she'd done.

"Oh, Gracie, we're not criminals." Caroline picked up the torn-down shutter and leaned it up against the inn. "If the police come by—"

"Don't even bring up that possibility." Gracie shook her head at her sister. *Why does Caroline always have to be so cavalier?*

Gracie stood on tiptoes again and peered through the window. Even more sunlight filtered into this room. Empty bookshelves lined three walls, and sheets covered what appeared to be a couple of wingback chairs. Were they covered in chintz? A heavy brocade? Maybe cut velvet?

"Is it beautiful inside, or what?" Sam asked, brushing against Gracie's shoulder, trying to take a look.

"Dusty," Gracie told her, "but a lot of lemon oil and elbow grease could probably turn the room into a showpiece."

"Let me see," Sam said, as Gracie stepped aside and let Sam peer in too. "There's a stained glass panel over the double doors, and two wall sconces—"

"Are they crystal?" Caroline asked. "Waterford, maybe?"

Gracie shook her head. "Bronze, I think."

"It's really ornate," Sam added, "not in a gaudy way, just, well, flamboyantly elegant, if that makes sense."

"My turn." Caroline squeezed in next to Sam and Gracie stepped back.

"This would be the perfect room for you to sit in and read," Caroline said, turning back and smiling at Gracie. "And Sam, you could sit next to one of the windows, all comfy in your favorite chair, cross-stitching to your heart's content."

Caroline was dreaming again.

Gracie's dreams didn't involve old houses or bronze chandeliers—flamboyantly elegant or otherwise—that would have to be polished far too often. Her own dreams were back in Portland, in the small Cape Cod house she and Art had bought when he'd come home from Vietnam in 1975. It was their first house, the home they'd always shared. Her memories were there. Her heart.

She slipped away from Caroline and Sam and swept the dirt from an ornate white wrought iron patio bench. There was a time when she'd wanted to be an architect, and nineteenth-century houses like this one would have fascinated her. But she'd gotten married instead. She'd given up her dreams—no, switched dreams, from designing fabulous buildings to keeping house for the husband and children she loved. She hadn't become a female Frank Lloyd Wright, but she had been available to be a room monitor when Brandon and Paige were in elementary school, to cheer at Brandon's football and basketball games and Paige's swim meets. Now she had her grandchildren, who were the light of her life. She'd never regretted the decision to give up architecture—not for a moment.

"Penny for your thoughts." Caroline plopped down beside her on the bench. She looked bright and lovely in a white eyelet peasant blouse, khaki shorts, and a chunky amber necklace. She was smiling, always smiling. *Caroline's life is so carefree*, she thought.

"Nothing important." Gracie offered her sister a smile, and switched her thoughts from Art and their home to the overgrown, uncared for jungle of a garden surrounding the rundown inn. "I was just thinking about the kids. I hope they'll be okay while I'm gone."

"They'll be fine. They're perfectly capable of surviving two weeks without you." Caroline nudged her with her elbow.

Gracie gave her a halfhearted smile. She knew Caroline meant well, but the closest thing Caroline had ever had to children was Max. She had no idea what it was like to put other people first. Gracie saw her grandkids several times a week, and Brandon and his wife Stacy depended on her for child care.

"This place is pretty amazing, isn't it?" Caroline asked, turning her head back toward the house.

"It makes me think of *Arsenic and Old Lace*. Maybe I've watched that movie too many times, but I can't help but wonder if there are a couple of crazy old ladies living inside the Misty Harbor Inn who have a penchant for bumping off little old men and burying them out here in the garden."

"And maybe a loony old guy who thinks he's Teddy Roosevelt running up and down the stairs!" Sam said, coming up beside them. "Let's stop at the video store in town and see if they have a copy we can rent. We can pop popcorn and chow down on Milk Duds and M&Ms."

"Does that mean you're finally ready to leave?" Gracie asked. She stood up and brushed off the back of her capris. "I don't know about the two of you, but the ferry ride to the island was enough excitement for me today, and our long walk has done me in."

"But there's still so much to explore around here," Caroline said. "We could spend a good hour or more—"

"What on earth are the three of you doing?"

Gracie spun around to find a little old woman with snowy white hair framing a once-pretty face. She was brandishing a cane and a menacing frown. Gracie started to speak, but her worst fears had suddenly come to life—they'd been caught—and her words stuck in her throat.

"We're just having a look around," Caroline said with an infectious smile. "Our mother brought us here when we were children, and we wanted to see if it had changed."

The woman's eyes narrowed. She was short and pudgy and looked like Mrs. Santa Claus, except she was decked out in a pale pink polyester pantsuit with a large rhinestone peacock pinned to the wide lapel. "This place has definitely changed for the worse, no thanks to the present owners, I dare say. But be that as it may"— she wagged her cane at Gracie, Sam, and Caroline—"this is still private property, and I don't take kindly to strangers fussing about where they're not supposed to be."

"We were just leaving," Gracie finally managed to utter. She smiled weakly, thinking again about *Arsenic and Old Lace* and Cary Grant's dotty old aunts. "You don't live here, do you?"

The old lady fixed her with a steely glare. "I beg your pardon?"

"I was just wondering...," Gracie sputtered, but the old lady moved toward them with surprising speed.

"If I lived here, I'd never let this place get into this kind of shape. I live next door." She gestured at a large and well-kept gray home surrounded by lush lawns. "But I keep an eye on this place, make sure no one breaks in or vandalizes it."

"Are there many people trying to get inside?"

"Wasn't all that long ago that I called the cops on a bunch of vagrants who'd been living inside, and just last week a couple of kids tried to break in, but I called the cops on them too," the woman said. "Who knows what they might have done if they'd been able to get inside. As far as that goes"—her eyes narrowed—"there's no telling what you might do."

"We were just looking around, nothing more," Caroline interrupted, pleading her case. "Honestly."

"You could be casing the place for all I know. I watch TV. I read true crime and suspense. Not every robber looks like a bad guy. In fact, some are blonde and pretty, just like you. And you all are acting pretty guilty, if you ask me."

"We're not guilty," Sam said quickly. "You just surprised us. We didn't think anyone was here."

"Which, I suppose, led you to believe that you could snoop around." The woman planted her cane on the ground in front of her and leaned on it. "You're trespassing."

Suddenly, out of nowhere, Max appeared, yapping up a storm. His long buff fur was splattered with mud, and he made a beeline straight for the little old lady. He skidded to a stop, his nose just inches from her cane. He bared his teeth and growled, and then, as he did so often when he knew he was being bad, he rolled over on his back and played dead.

Caroline laughed uncomfortably. "Max is harmless. And truth be told, if we'd come here hoping to sneak inside without being seen by anyone, we wouldn't have brought Max along. He's not all that good at covert affairs."

"Well—" The woman waved her cane again. "You should probably be going then. Come back with an agent if you want to see more."

Gracie backed toward the rickety, overgrown archway that separated the garden from dunes, ocean grass, and wild, meandering pink roses. Sam followed a little behind, but Caroline—brave to the very end—stayed put and stuck out her hand. "I'm Caroline Marris. Those are my sisters, Gracie Gold and Sam Carter. It's been a pleasure meeting you."

The woman ignored Caroline's hand.

"All right. We'll be on our way then." Caroline patted the top of Max's head. "Come on, boy. Let's head back to the beach and find some seagulls to chase."

The dog barked and ran toward Gracie and Sam, and a moment later, Gracie, Sam, Caroline, and Max were practically skipping down the path, all the way to the beach. When they hit soft sand, Caroline dropped down on the beach, pulled her knees up close to her chest, wrapped her arms around them, and began to laugh. Sam followed suit, and slowly Gracie allowed herself to chuckle.

"That was a close one." Caroline kicked off her flip-flops, stretched her legs out in front of her and wiggled her toes. "I'm sure that cane could have been lethal if given half a chance."

"I wonder how long she'd been watching us." Sam drew in a deep breath.

"Oh dear." Gracie felt her throat tighten again. "Please tell me you put the shutter back in place."

Caroline's eyes opened wide. Her hand flew to her mouth. "Oh no!"

"Oh, Caroline, you didn't forget, did you?" Gracie asked, a knot settling uncomfortably in her throat. "If that lady sees it's been taken down, she'll call the cops on us for sure."

Caroline shook her head, smiling. "Of course we didn't forget."

Gracie felt her shoulders relax.

Caroline slung an arm around Gracie's shoulder. "Gosh, it's great to be with the two of you again. It's just like old times."

Gracie sighed. Just like old times was right, with Caroline leading them into trouble.

CHAPTER
Three

"Who wants the last crab cake?" Sam asked Gracie and Caroline that evening as they sat out on the deck of the two-story cottage they'd rented on India Street, just a few blocks from Nantucket's town square. The sun was just starting to vanish over the horizon, and the early-summer breeze drifted over the yard, bringing the salty smell of the ocean and the sweet scent of hydrangeas. The sisters sat around a sturdy wooden table, and the citronella candles they'd lit to keep bugs away cast a soft glow over the scene.

"I ate four already," Gracie said, leaning back in her chair, her hands on her stomach, "and that's already one over my limit."

"They were delicious." Caroline picked the last bits of crab off her plate with her fingers, ready to pop them into her mouth, until Max sat up on his haunches at her side and begged for a taste. "Even Max thinks so," she said, letting the pup lick her fingers. "But you did all the hard work, Sam. You eat it."

"They weren't hard to make," Sam said, scooping the crab cake onto her plate. "It's one of Mom's recipes: a little Old Bay seasoning, saltine crackers, and fresh crab."

"I don't remember them tasting so good when Mom made them," Caroline said.

"Our tastes change over time," Sam said. She slid the last crab cake onto her plate. "Oh, and I used more butter than she did, so that probably helped." She surrounded it with one last scoop of salad from the wooden bowl in the middle of the table.

"No doubt." Gracie smirked as she finished the last of the fresh-squeezed lemonade in her glass. Sam knew her sisters probably used powdered or frozen mix at home, but fresh tasted so much better.

"Do you ever wonder if Mom made up all the stories she told us about the Misty Harbor?" Caroline asked, stabbing a plump red grape with her fork. "You know, about the secret rooms and the famous people who stayed there."

"I should have known you'd turn the conversation back to the old inn," Gracie said. "You've been fixated on that place all day."

"Goodness, Gracie!" Caroline winked at her sister. "It drives you crazy when I bounce from one interest to the next, and here I am staying totally focused on the inn, and that's driving you up a wall too."

Gracie rolled her eyes. "It just seems to me that you're becoming a bit obsessed with the place."

"You can't possibly tell me you haven't given it any thought."

"Not for a second," Gracie said, with a defiant shake of her head. "My mind's been on buying Nantucket T-shirts for the kids, and I was trying to figure out whether to buy that seashell bracelet we saw this afternoon."

"You could make a bracelet like that," Sam said. The overpriced trinket was one of many exorbitantly priced objects they'd seen on Main Street after their excursion to the ramshackle inn. Sam didn't think of herself as particularly artsy, but after several decades of teaching elementary school, she had gotten good at crafts of all kinds. "I can show you how, if you're really interested. But that whaling ship's figurehead that we saw in the antique shop—now that was something you don't see every day."

"It's not exactly a souvenir," Gracie said, laughing. "And besides, it wouldn't fit in with the rest of your home's décor."

"Not to mention my pocketbook. Be still my heart." Sam patted her chest. "Did you see the price tag? Two hundred fifty thousand, and they threw in ninety-nine cents for good measure. Can you believe that?"

"If I'd had two-hundred-and-fifty grand to spare," Caroline said, "I'd snatch it up in a minute. Of course, I'd have to have the right place to mount it."

"That cottage of yours is awfully small. It might not even fit through the front door," Gracie reminded her.

"I wasn't thinking about displaying it inside Briar Rose. I was thinking about the Misty Harbor. The masthead would go nicely with all those Haunted Mansion portraits." Caroline chuckled. "Of course, for all we know, there might already be a masthead hanging on one of the walls or stuffed upstairs in the attic."

"There could be any number of things hidden up there collecting dust, including trapdoors leading to secret rooms," Gracie said, "and I, for one, don't want to know about any of them."

Sam shook her head. Gracie was turning into such a fussbudget. "Where's your sense of adventure, Gracie?"

"What little I had flew the coop when that old lady came at us with her cane. But"—Gracie peered at Caroline—"what is it with you and that inn?"

Sam couldn't help but wonder the same thing. Several times today Caroline had pulled the folded-up sales flyer from her back pocket and looked at the pictures. Her expression would change every second or so from awe, to puzzlement, to uncertainty, and then she'd smile, as if she was hatching a plan.

"Well…" Caroline looked pensive now. She seemed to be contemplating, wondering if she should admit what was on her mind. At long last she said, "I think we should buy it."

Sam nearly choked on a sip of lemonade. "What?"

"You heard me." Caroline drew the wrinkled sales flyer from her back pocket and smoothed it out on top of the round patio table. "We should buy the inn, turn it back to its former glory, and make it a place tourists will long to stay."

Sam coughed as she tried to regain her composure.

Gracie shook her head.

"With what?" Sam finally managed to say. "We could never afford that place."

"It's actually not that much more than what Mom left us," Caroline said. "We could probably offer less. If we pooled our inheritance money—"

"No," Gracie said quickly. "That money is going to the kids."

Sam wished Gracie hadn't reacted so quickly or so forcefully, but she understood her sister's point. Their mother had managed to squirrel away a substantial amount of money in sixty years, and that plus her life insurance meant that the sisters had each inherited a healthy sum when she died. If they put their money together, it would come close to the asking price, but Sam had assumed she would save her portion. She was retired, after all, and it made her feel better to have something in the bank for a rainy day.

"Don't look at me that way, Gracie," Caroline said.

"What way?"

"With that full-of-doubt face. It's the same one you were wearing right after I graduated from high school and I told you I was going to hitchhike to Hollywood."

"You'd never acted in your life!"

"But I had dreams."

"Pipe dreams. If they had been more than that, you might have gotten to Hollywood instead of stopping at the end of our street and coming home again with a change of heart. And then suddenly you wanted to be an archaeologist."

"Okay, so Hollywood might have been a little far-fetched—"

"And I had to give up my dream to move into your bedroom and no longer share with Sam." Gracie attempted to laugh, but Sam knew it was halfhearted. "Hollywood was completely impulsive. So was archaeology, like so many other things you've done in life."

"If I wasn't impulsive, I wouldn't have traveled to nearly every corner of the earth. I wouldn't have done things or seen things that most human beings will never do or see in their lifetime."

"But they weren't long-term endeavors. You can pick up and travel to Timbuktu for one or two days and never get tired of where you are. But would you still be fascinated with Timbuktu if you had to stay there, sweeping out a dirt hut or whatever they do there, for months at a time? Maybe years?"

"I know what you're getting at Gracie. You think I have zero stick-to-itiveness."

"I don't think, Caroline. I know."

Sam stood up quickly and started gathering the plates. "Who's ready for some dessert? I made a blueberry crisp, with berries fresh from the farmers' market."

Neither of her sisters responded. Caroline's short blonde hair, so different from the long blonde braid she'd had the last time they'd seen each other, whipped around when she looked up at Sam.

Sam supposed it had to have happened sometime. Those two had fought like cats and dogs when they were kids. Maybe this fight had been building for a long time. But she also knew it was a ridiculous fight. Caroline was just dreaming. She wasn't serious about buying the inn—not serious enough to see such a huge project through anyway. Surely Gracie could see that.

"There's nothing wrong with dreaming, Gracie," Caroline said quietly.

"No," Gracie finally exhaled. "I guess there's not."

At long last, Caroline laughed. Gracie stared at the table and slowly but surely, as Sam had hoped, managed a smile.

"There. That's much better." Sam dropped the dirty plates on the granite counter just inside the French doors and came back out with a dish of warm blueberry crisp. "Now, please tell me you have all of the aggression completely out of your system, and that I won't wake up tomorrow morning having to clean up blood," she said as she used a big spoon to scoop the crisp onto fresh dessert plates.

Caroline brushed a lock of hair behind her ear. "It's a promise."

Gracie was a little more reluctant, but at last she came around. "Sorry." She reached across the table and squeezed Caroline's hand. "I guess it's just hard…" She let her voice trail off.

"What do you mean?" Caroline asked.

Sam readied herself to play peacemaker again. "This blueberry crisp is delicious, if I do say so myself," she said. Then she noticed that neither Caroline nor Gracie had touched theirs.

Finally, Gracie spoke up. "What do you say we go in and watch the movie?"

"You can't make a statement like that, Gracie, and then ignore me when I ask what you're talking about," Caroline said.

"It's nothing," Gracie said, picking up her dessert plate. "I'll finish this inside."

"Do you know what she's talking about?" Caroline asked Sam, after Gracie slipped through the French doors and went into the house.

"I don't know," Sam admitted, "although..." She shrugged.

"Oh, no you don't," Caroline said. "Gracie might have gotten away with ignoring me, but you can't start a sentence with *although* and then drop it. Although what?"

Sam sighed. She hated to tell tales, especially about Gracie, but it was high time Caroline knew some of what was going on in Gracie's head. "She had a really tough time after Mom was diagnosed with cancer. I was still teaching, and even if I hadn't been, I would have had a ten-hour drive to get to Portland, so most of the burden fell to Gracie. She had to do everything for Mom. The last couple of months were especially bad—"

"I would have come sooner if I'd known."

"Yes, but Mom didn't want you to know."

"Why not?"

"Because you had such a tough time handling Dad's death."

"So did you; so did Gracie."

Sam remembered picking Caroline up from the airport two days after their father passed away. She'd flown in from Prague. She'd spent the hours before her flight inside St. Vitus Cathedral, praying for their father to survive. She hadn't slept a wink since their mother had called her with the news. Caroline's once-pretty blue eyes were rimmed with dark circles, and her cheeks were hollow. She looked like she'd aged ten years in the six months since they'd seen each other. And then she couldn't eat; she wouldn't eat.

"You were a mess, Caroline." Sam took a bite of the warm crisp.

"Yeah, I guess I was. Not just during the funeral, but for the next few months. But we were a lot younger then, and Dad and I had been so close when I was little. Still"—Caroline sighed—"I loved Mom. I would have done anything for her. I should have been given the chance to come back to the States to help out. Gracie should have told me she was so sick." Caroline stabbed at her dessert with her fork.

"You were there the last month. That's all that matters."

"But if Gracie resents—"

"No, Caroline, that's not it at all. Gracie doesn't resent you, but really... I'm the wrong person to explain Gracie's comment. That's between the two of you. Now come on"—Sam picked up the plates left on the table—"help me clean up this mess. Then let's get into our pj's and watch *Arsenic and Old Lace*. It's been a long day, and I think we all need a good laugh."

It was nearly ten thirty that night when Sam's cell phone rang. She'd just climbed under the crisp floral sheets on one of the two twin beds in her room at the cottage. She was comfy and cozy, but she rolled over to grab the phone off the nightstand and answered it quickly. She smiled when she heard her daughter Jamie's voice at the other end. Jamie's father had been out of the picture for a long time, and Sam had always been especially close to her daughter.

"I didn't wake you, did I?"

"Oh no. We just finished watching an old Cary Grant movie and I'm stuffed on extra buttery popcorn and M&Ms. I'll probably have a headache in the morning, and I'm sure my ribs are going to ache from laughing so hard."

"Sounds like a great way to start your vacation."

Except for the argument between Caroline and Gracie, but Sam wasn't about to tell Jamie about that.

"Is Aunt Gracie relaxing?" Jamie asked. "Or at least trying to relax?"

"You know that doesn't come all that easily for her."

"She hasn't kicked back since Grandma got sick." Sam could hear the worry in Jamie's voice. "She runs herself ragged taking care of Evelyn, Zachary, and Jacob, when really, Mom, Brandon and Stacy could afford day care."

"But she enjoys it, Jamie. Her grandchildren are her life."

Jamie laughed, a bit too cynically. "Then remind me not to have any children, because I don't want you becoming a glorified babysitter—"

"I want grandchildren. Lots of them. But you know I'm in no hurry. You also know that I like living my own life. I'm enjoying retirement," she said emphatically, although she still missed teaching first and second graders. She just didn't want Jamie to know how much. "And you know I'd do anything in the world for you. That includes babysitting. Of course, I'd rather have you raise your children the way I raised you. If I wanted to go somewhere, I took you along—"

"Unlike Aunt Gracie who still doesn't go anywhere."

"I promise. I'll try to get her to relax while we're here."

"Don't let her make any lists."

Sam smiled. "She already has. Gracie and I are going antiquing tomorrow, right after I make breakfast for the three of us. She has bicycle rides planned, museum tickets bought, and beach days slotted in."

"What about Aunt Caroline? Isn't she going antiquing with you?"

"She bowed out. Said she has an article to work on and thought she'd hole up in the cottage by herself to get it done and out of the way."

"Have you asked her to stay in the States yet?"

"I have to figure out how to bring it up."

"If you don't work up the nerve, she'll end up right back on a plane to England."

"I know. I just don't want to make her uncomfortable. I don't want to make her feel guilty for living so far away from us."

But she so wanted her sister to stay in the States. She adored Caroline. She'd idolized her when they were growing up, and now she wanted her closer than a phone call away.

Sam tried to stifle a yawn and then gave up. She snuggled her head into a comfortable position on the big down pillow, listening to Jamie talk about her latest research. Jamie was working on a master's degree in American history and was focusing on early American myths and legends, and though she was done with classes for the summer, she was working hard on her thesis. When her daughter grew quiet, Sam asked, "Are you still planning to come to the island for a few days?"

"Actually, that's what I called about. I've managed to rearrange my schedule, so I'm going to come next Monday. Will that work?"

"It'll work perfectly. And Cory is okay with you leaving?" Sam asked out of politeness, not because she cared what her daughter's snooty boyfriend thought.

"He wishes I would stay, but I wouldn't miss it."

"I'd ask you to bring him along, but this is an all-girls' house and a girls' getaway."

"He's so busy studying for the bar that about all we do together anymore is grab a cup of coffee close to his apartment—if he can squeeze me into his day."

Jamie deserved so much more than a twenty-seven-year-old up-and-comer who yearned for a corner office in a tall building on Fifth Avenue. Cory was tall and tan and good-looking—a product of an Upper West Side New York upbringing. He thought Jamie's flat in Brooklyn was a shabby hole-in-the-wall. Truthfully, Sam felt the same way, but Jamie loved her apartment and the mishmash of treasures she'd found in one thrift shop after another. Sam knew, with all her heart, that she'd raised her daughter right. She'd make the right decision about Cory when the time came.

"Mom." Jamie said, her voice soft, barely a whisper.

"What, hon?"

"I can't wait to see you."

"Ditto," Sam said. They disconnected, but as she burrowed down into the pillow again, she was kept awake counting worries instead of sheep. Something was troubling her daughter, but what? Why was Gracie so prickly? And what on earth had possessed Caroline to suggest they buy the Misty Harbor Inn? It was such a ridiculous idea. Then again, she thought of all the wonderful dessert recipes she could try out on guests. At last she had something sweet to think about as she fell asleep.

CHAPTER
Four

Max trotted at Caroline's side the next afternoon, weaving in and out of hundreds of other tourists who strolled along Main Street's cobbled road, buying souvenirs, licking ice cream cones, and enjoying the azure blue sky and the hint of a breeze.

"I'm so glad the two of you dragged me away from the article I was working on," Caroline said to Sam and Gracie, who'd insisted she join them for a jaunt through antique stores. "Just remind me to get it finished tonight. My deadline's a week away, but I'd like to send it off so I can spend time with you."

Gracious oaks arched above the brick sidewalk, and dappled sunlight filtered down onto the sisters as they walked. Caroline breathed in the sea air and took in the sights and sounds around them.

"Working late at night is the only thing I haven't missed since I retired," Sam said. She wore a flowing, calf-length white skirt, a poppy-pink T-shirt, and a necklace made of gleaming pearl-white seashells. "I do miss my first and second graders. Still, I'm glad I retired. If I hadn't, right now I'd be teaching a summer school class and wishing I was at the beach. And I definitely wouldn't be with the two of you."

"No doubt you'll be tired of us long before the first week of our vacation's gone by," Gracie said, turning off of Main onto Center. The shops on this street were housed in small, quaint old buildings, brick and wood with large paned windows. They were headed toward India Street, where there was an antique store Gracie wanted to check out.

"I'd never get tired of the two of you," Sam said, the sun shining on her smile. "Listening to you bicker makes me feel like a kid all over again."

"And being here makes me feel like a kid all over again," Gracie said pausing at the window of a stationery store. Gracie seemed taken with a set of letterpressed cards, but all Caroline could see was really expensive paper. Who sent handwritten notes these days anyway? She sighed, and they moved on. Max watched, transfixed, as Sam licked a drip on her ice cream cone that threatened to spill over.

"Wouldn't it be amazing to live here?" Caroline said, drinking in the scents of hydrangeas and fresh sea air.

"You'd never leave your cottage. You love living in Chipping Campden."

Caroline smiled as a little boy rode past them on a red two-wheeler. His parents followed several steps behind. "I've been thinking of giving it up."

Sam stopped so quickly she might have run into an invisible brick wall. Gracie's steps slowed and finally she turned to stare at Caroline. "But...you love that place."

"I do," Caroline said, already feeling a lump building in her throat and tears welling up in her eyes, "but it's never going to be mine, not really. Every time I've talked with the owners about buying it, they give me the same old song and dance and say 'Someday...maybe.'" Caroline shrugged. "I'm tired of waiting for someday to come."

"Are you serious?" Sam wanted to believe it, but she knew her sister too well.

"I think so. For the first time in my life, I feel like settling down." Caroline couldn't miss the roll of Gracie's eyes. "I know you don't believe me," Caroline said, nudging Gracie's arm, "but it's true. I've felt that urge more and more since Mom passed away."

Sam leaned over a picket fence to inhale the heady perfume of a delicate white rose. She turned toward Caroline, looking a touch troubled. "Are you coming back to the States?"

"You should come back to Maine," Gracie said. "Not that I can imagine you living there again, after all the times you used to tell me that when you grew up you were going to split, leaving humdrum old Maine behind."

"Maine's beautiful, but, no, I don't think I'll be going back there."

"There's a townhouse for sale down the street from mine," Sam said, smiling again. "The housing prices in Upstate New York are the lowest they've been in ages."

"Whoa! Slow down!" Caroline said. "Right now, nothing's settled. I might go to Annapolis, at least for a little while. George's boat building business is doing well, and he has a small yacht he said I could live in until I find something permanent."

Sam gave Gracie a meaningful look.

"Oh, stop it. George is just a friend. Always has been, always will be."

"If you say so," Sam said, her eyebrows raised.

"Could you really live on a boat?" Gracie asked. "Wouldn't you feel cramped?"

Caroline chuckled. "Obviously you've never lived in a five-hundred-year-old English cottage. I have to bend over to walk through the doors. But... I'm not all that sure that's what I want."

"You're not really thinking about Nantucket, are you?" Gracie asked.

"And what? Live in a cranberry bog? That might be one of the few things you could afford on the island." Sam had always been good with money, and Caroline knew she was probably right, but she wasn't looking for practical advice right now.

"Now don't come all unglued, but I'm thinking the Misty Harbor Inn."

"And I want to live in Buckingham Palace!" Gracie grinned. She grabbed Caroline's arm, and they continued their stroll toward Quince Street. "Come on, let's check out some antiques and see if we can find something to buy that might actually fit our pocketbooks."

If Gracie thought she'd put an end to Caroline's musings about the inn, she was sorely mistaken. People had told her more than once in life that her ideas were half-baked, that she couldn't settle down to just one thing, that she was a dilettante and a flake, but she'd refused to listen. Maybe she did get caught up in a lot of grandiose schemes; maybe she had far too many interests; but she'd designed her life around who she was and what she liked. *So far*, she thought with some satisfaction, *it has worked fairly well.*

Gracie might think she could snap her fingers and make all thoughts about the inn disappear from Caroline's head, but that wasn't going to happen.

Sam aimed her camera at her sisters, snapping their pictures—
and Max's, of course—as they posed in front of hydrangea bushes
loaded with fat blue flowers and hanging baskets of red and white
geraniums. Quince Street was lined with old homes—a pristine
white Greek Revival, a red brick Federal, and an endless number
of colonials, most of which were painted yellow, pale blue, or
white, others with washed gray shingles. The eclectic houses
edged a street lined with ancient trees that shaded the tiny front
yards.

Her townhouse in Saratoga Springs didn't have much of a
front yard either; but it definitely didn't exude character like these
homes did. They made her think of the Misty Harbor Inn again. She
understood how Caroline could have fallen under the spell of that
old rundown place.

But could Caroline really want to buy it? She'd always needed
coaching to make her own bed. Dusting was on her list of banned
words. And she couldn't even cook. How could she possibly think
about opening a bed-and-breakfast if she couldn't serve her guests
something scrumptious for breakfast?

It was such a crazy idea, but it really did pique Sam's curiosity.

At last they reached a wisteria-draped bungalow with worn
shingle siding and an elegantly painted sign out front that read "Into
the Past."

"This is it," Gracie said, stopping in front of the path that led to
a quaint, three-story antique shop. Its door was propped open with
an old ship's anchor, inviting customers to step inside. "I hope it's as
beautiful on the inside as it is out."

Sam waited while Caroline fastened Max's leash to one of the
posts at the bottom of the stairs and told the rambunctious pup to

stay. He wouldn't go very far, but that didn't mean he wouldn't start howling or barking.

They stepped into the antique shop, and Sam was instantly captured by its charm. The scents of vanilla and coconut emanated from candles burning in crystal sconces and hurricane lamps. A rustic, dark wood cabinet just inside the entry was draped with heirloom lace, sterling silver napkin rings, flatware, and several small chests, all carved in elegant designs.

"It's beautiful," Sam whispered, turning in a slow circle, trying to take in all of her surroundings.

"Look at this dresser." Gracie's words were soft and breathy. Sam thought the cabinet was rather ostentatious, but she nodded.

Sam picked up the tented card sitting discreetly at the back of the dresser, right beneath its overly ornate mirror. English oak: that was nice. $8,250. She coughed, put down the card, and grabbed Gracie's arm. "Come on, Sis, there's bound to be something in here that's more your style."

"How about this?" Caroline asked, as if she'd heard Sam's words. She stood next to a lovely china cabinet holding a cobalt blue bowl that was a lighter aquamarine on the inside. There was a hand-painted figure of a mermaid reclining on a seashell raised and molded so it surrounded nearly the entire circumference of the dish. "Pretty, isn't it?"

"It's English Majolica." A woman with carrot-red curls that flowed over her back and almost all the way down to her waist made her way toward them. "Made in 1860, and I must admit, it's one of the loveliest pieces of Majolica I've ever seen. I have a matching cup too. It should be here with the bowl, but my son, bless his heart, doesn't quite agree with me on how antiques should be displayed."

The woman turned and walked away, showing off long and slender legs encased in skinny blue jeans. She had to be at least six feet tall—a good half a head taller than Caroline, Gracie, or Sam. She stopped, took a matching cobalt blue cup out a glass-fronted china closet and then turned back and smiled. "Right where I imagined Dustin would put it."

She crossed the room again, handing the tiny cup to Caroline. And then she did the oddest thing. She peered at Gracie and then Sam and then Caroline, as if she'd seen them somewhere before. "You wouldn't by any chance be the women who were looking at the Misty Harbor Inn yesterday, would you?"

Sam was stunned by the question. "We were there, but"—she frowned—"how did you know? We only saw one other person—"

"Shirley Addison." The woman pushed an out-of-control, curly lock of hair behind her ear. "Short? Wavy white hair?"

"Looks a bit like Mrs. Claus?" Caroline added.

The woman, obviously the proprietor of the shop, chuckled and nodded. "That's Shirley in a nutshell. She lives next door to the inn and keeps an eye on it."

"And calls everyone in town to tell them what she's seen?" Gracie asked, one eyebrow raised.

"We have Bible study together on Monday nights. She told me you're planning to buy the old place."

"She's wrong there," Gracie said quickly. "We visited the place a few times when we were young and simply wanted to see if it had changed."

"Boy, has it," Caroline added, "but if you close your eyes and picture the garden when it's carefully manicured, and imagine the sun shining down on the windows instead of closed up shutters, you can easily see how beautiful it was once upon a time."

"It was beautiful once. I hope it'll be that way again sometime soon." The woman stuck out her hand to shake Caroline's. "I'm Megan Folger-Wildes. You're visitors to the island, right?"

Caroline nodded, and introduced herself and her sisters. "I have to admit, I do want to buy the inn, although my sisters don't seem to be as interested in it as I am."

Megan nodded. "There are a lot of stories about that old place."

Sam leaned forward. "Like what?"

"Oh well, you know," she waved off the question. "Just the usual. Hidden rooms, secret passages, mysterious disappearances, that sort of thing. With a town this old, every building has a story."

"Mysterious disappearances?" Sam thought she saw Gracie shudder.

"Just rumors." Megan shrugged, like maybe she'd said too much. "Probably invented to sell rooms back when it was a hotel."

Max let out his first howl and then started to bark—more than likely upset that he'd been left outside, leashed to a post for far, far too long.

"That's Max, my cocker spaniel," Caroline said, inching toward the door. "I'm afraid we'd better get going or there's no telling what kind of mischief he'll get into."

"What about the Majolica?" Megan said, staring at the bowl and cup Caroline and Gracie were holding. "Are you interested?"

"I'm afraid they're out of our price range," Sam said, "but—"

Megan held up a hand. "I understand." She smiled as Gracie and Caroline set the beautiful pieces of pottery on the china cabinet. "I know all too well that not everyone who comes in here is going to buy. It was nice to meet you, though."

Max howled again, even louder this time, a plaintive cry for help.

"I know you have to get going," Megan said, "but if you're going to be here over the weekend, you should check out my church, Harvest Chapel." She held out a flyer with her church's information. Sam didn't move to take it. Her sisters were both into church, and their mother had always taken them when they were young, but Sam didn't see much use for it herself.

"Thank you," Gracie said, looking at the flyer for a moment, before sliding it into her purse. "I was hoping to find a welcoming church to attend Sunday."

"And we're having a clambake out at Madaket Beach Saturday night. If you've never been to one, you don't know what you've missed. Grandpa Folger will be there, and goodness me, he sure knows how to tell a tale." She winked. "Some people think Grandpa knows where all the skeletons on Nantucket are hidden."

Sam didn't miss the sudden sparkle in Caroline's eyes or the roll of Gracie's. She herself smiled. Skeletons in closets! Oh my!

She had a sneaking suspicion she knew where they'd be Saturday night.

CHAPTER
Five

I don't know about you," Caroline said later that evening, dropping down into the fluffy cushion on the patio chair next to Gracie's, "but I can't wait for Saturday night." It was another perfect evening, with the crisp sea breeze starting to cool the warm June air. The sky was slowly changing from a deep cerulean to a warm amber, and fireflies danced and twinkled in the quiet. "Just think, lobster, steamed clams, thick and creamy chowder, and a ghost story or two. Maybe Grandpa Folger has some tales to share about the inn."

Gracie squeezed a wedge of lemon into her tall glass of iced tea. "Tall tales are nothing but myth and innuendo, Caroline," she said flatly. "I have the feeling that any truth about the Misty Harbor Inn has faded into oblivion, just like the inn."

"But doesn't the possibility of learning more about the inn intrigue you?" Caroline asked. She'd brought her laptop out and flipped it open. The screen blinked to life.

"All right, yes, I admit I'm intrigued," Gracie said, "but not for the same reasons as you, I'm sure. You want to learn more about the inn. I'm interested solely because anything of historical significance fascinates me."

"I thought you were done with work for the day," Sam said, stepping out of the cottage carrying a platter full of finger foods for them to snack on. She glared at Caroline.

"I'm not working. I'm doing some research of my own on the inn." Caroline logged in and typed in the cottage's wireless password.

"Oh, good. Don't shoot me for saying this, Gracie, but the inn fascinates me too. I don't have the foggiest idea why, but it does."

"You've always gotten caught up in things that excite Caroline," Gracie said, grinning as she reached for a cracker. Gracie was flipping through a home décor magazine, and seemed absorbed in an article about mixing antiques with modern pieces.

Sam shook her head. "I think it has more to do with the fact that Mom loved it." She chose a goat cheese and honey bruschetta from the tray. "It makes me feel close to her to explore the things that she loved."

Caroline grinned, and typed "Misty Harbor Inn, Nantucket," into the search engine. "Let's see if we can find any history online. There's got to be something. Who knows? We might even end up with our own tall tales to share at the clambake."

The first link that popped up looked like the inn's Web site, but when she clicked on it, an error message popped up. She went back to the search page and clicked on the next link, but that led to a travel site where the inn had been reviewed—poorly, it seemed—by guests. She clicked through the first page of links, but all she could find was out-of-date information about making reservations. No information about the inn's history. Caroline clicked on a link about places to stay on Nantucket, and that led her to another page about an old insane asylum on the other side of the island.

An insane asylum? Now this was interesting. She would just read a little bit and then get back to searching for more about the inn.

"Have you found anything yet?" Gracie looked up a while later. The sky had darkened into a deep indigo, and it was now too dark to read. The glow from Caroline's laptop and the flicker of the occasional firefly provided the only light on the patio. Gracie flipped her magazine closed and scooted her chair closer to her sister. Sam had stepped inside to put away the food.

"Totally." Caroline nodded. "Did you know that there is a lot of controversy about the night the Quaise asylum burned down in 1844? It seems the fire crews from town didn't even try to get out there to save it. We should go out this week and see it. Apparently you can sometimes hear ghostly screams there."

Gracie blinked in the darkness "How on earth did you get from Misty Harbor to an old asylum fire?"

"It's Nantucket history," Caroline said. Gracie could see her click on another link on the page.

"You're supposed to be focusing on the history of the inn." Gracie should have expected this. She knew how easy it was for Caroline to start a project and move on to the next without finishing anything. She could feel her jaw tightening. Time and time again when they were young, Caroline would get Gracie excited about something—a dance she promised to take her to, even though Gracie was really too young; introducing her to the cutest guy in school; a long-awaited trip to an amusement park; the thought of sharing a secret that nobody could or should ever know about—and then she'd bail on her. Caroline would lose interest and not care at all that Gracie was on pins and needles, waiting for something big to take place.

She took a deep breath. She'd already made way too many waves with Caroline on this trip and she didn't want to come unglued now. Instead, she flipped over her magazine and smiled. Calmly, she said, "I'll add the Quaise asylum site to my list of things to do while we're here. But have you found out anything else about the inn?"

Caroline clicked away at the keyboard.

"Why don't you start with property records?" Gracie asked.

Caroline stopped typing and looked up at Gracie. "What do you mean?"

"Here, let me show you."

Caroline gently pushed the computer toward Gracie.

"Do you have that real estate flyer?"

Caroline pulled the Realtor's listing from her pocket and smoothed it against the table. Gracie scanned the flyer, found the inn's address at the top of the page, and typed it in to a real estate Web page.

"When Art died, I looked at putting the house on the market," Gracie explained as the page loaded. "I used this site to see what comparable houses were selling for in the neighborhood. When I saw what other people were actually getting, I decided it wasn't worth giving up my home. But here, see"—she tilted the screen so Caroline could see it—"this site lists not only the sales history for the address, it also lists who was involved in each sale."

Gracie scanned the page. The records for the inn were not complete, but they could see a list of most of the owners. The house had changed owners several times in the past few decades, and before that, it had been owned by a hotel group. But the person who was listed as the original owner was a Jedediah Montague.

Montague. Caroline pulled the computer back toward her and typed "Montague Nantucket" into the search bar. There was Caroline, taking over again, but Gracie didn't really mind. It was kind of nice to be working with her on this.

The first couple links led to more sites geared toward tourists to the island, but then a site about genealogy came up. She clicked around on the page and then stopped.

"I think I may have found something," Caroline said. She pointed to the screen. A black and white photo of a man in a long coat, tight dark pants, and a matching vest stared out of her screen. He was hawk-nosed, and had dark receding hair and sideburns that stretched out along his jaw. He was standing next to a woman in a fitted dress with a wide skirt. "This is Jedediah and Mehitabel, or Hettie, Montague."

"Who are they?" Gracie asked.

"Let me read this to you." Caroline looked at the text beside the photo. "'Jedediah Montague. Born 1824; died 1878. One of several hundred ship's captains who successfully plied the oceans in search of sperm whale, and expanded his family's fortune by bringing whale oil, ambergris, which was used for perfume, whalebone, and other whale products home to Nantucket.'"

Gracie shoved her reading glasses a little higher on her nose. "She's so tiny. Goodness, she barely reaches his shoulders, and look at that waist. Can you imagine your waist cinched up in a corset and wearing whalebone stays to keep your back straight?"

"That's got to be half the reason women in those days always looked so stern in their pictures—they were inches from crying," Caroline said.

"Or dying," Gracie added. "I might like to read history, but I wouldn't have wanted to live it."

"Jedediah looks rather formidable, doesn't he?" Caroline said. "Definitely not someone I'd want to do business with, let alone marry. But"—Caroline clicked on another link and again tapped the screen with the tip of her index finger—"this says Jedediah and Hettie had two children, Lachlan and Fitzwalter, who inherited Montague Manor when their father died."

"What happened to Hettie?" Sam asked.

Caroline trailed her finger down the article. "She died in 1865, the same day as President Lincoln. Jedediah married again, later in life, but there's no mention of his second wife's name, whether they had any children, where she was from, or anything."

"Is that it?"

"That's all that's on this page." She clicked back to the main search page. "But let's see if we can find anything else."

She tried a few links, but none told them anything they hadn't already learned. Then, Caroline clicked on another link, and it led to a page on the Nantucket Historical Society Web site.

"Now why didn't we think to start there in the first place?" she asked, and Gracie smiled. It was a good point.

The Web page listed the society's hours and location, and the main page outlined the island's history as a whaling center until the mid-nineteenth century. But when Gracie pointed out a link labeled "Important Sites in Nantucket," Caroline clicked on it and they were taken to a page with photos and short blurbs on some of the sights in town. There was a paragraph on the Brant Point Light, the Basket Museum, the Quaker Meeting House, several original homes, and... Gracie leaned in closer. "Caroline, that looks like—"

"It does." Caroline was already clicking on the picture of a grand house perched on a bluff. The photo was in black and white, and the exterior had been altered, as had the gardens, but when the enlarged photo appeared on the screen, Gracie could see it was definitely the Misty Harbor Inn.

"That's it!" Gracie didn't mean to shriek, but somehow the noise she made came close to one.

Sam popped her head out the French doors. "Find something?" she said.

"I think we did," Gracie said, smiling at her sister. Sam wiped her hands on a dish towel, dropped it on the counter, stepped back out onto the deck, and pulled her patio chair up close to the table where Gracie and Caroline were sitting.

"This says it was called Montague Manor," Caroline said.

"Montague Manor was built by Jedediah Montague," Gracie read. She leaned closer, pushing her reading glasses up on her nose. "It seems like the print on everything is getting smaller and smaller these days." Caroline tilted the screen so she could get a better view. "A whaling baron. Born in 1824, he was son of a ship's captain who found fame and fortune exploring the Pacific. We already know all that." She kept reading. "Montague Manor was built as a gift from Jedediah Montague to his wife, Mehitabel 'Hettie' Montague, in 1852. Let's see"—her finger trailed across the words on the screen—"Their sons Lachlan and Fitzwalter inherited the house, and owned and lived in Montague Manor until the stock market crash of 1929. 'The house, like the brothers, had fallen on rough times,'" Gracie read. "'It was sold for a pittance to Ezra and Mabel Fortescue, well-known Philadelphia artists. In 1950, Ezra and Mabel sold Montague Manor to the Grace Brothers Hotel Group. In addition to its historical significance as an early example of colonial architecture on the island, the house is notable as the last site Jedediah Montague's second wife Hannah was seen alive before she mysteriously disappeared in 1880.'"

For a moment, the only sounds Gracie heard were the soft breeze rustling through the trees and the happy shrieks of children somewhere off in the distance.

"Is that it?" Sam finally asked.

Gracie squinted at the screen. "That's all it says here."

"There's got to be more," Caroline said, and clicked back to the historical society's main page. Gracie leaned back in her chair, watching Caroline search through page after page. Max came out of his hiding place behind a purple hydrangea planted in the corner of the small backyard and sprawled on the patio between Gracie's and Caroline's legs. Fog started to roll in.

"Maybe we should call it quits for the night," Sam said at last, "and look some more tomorrow."

Gracie was getting tired, but she had to admit, she was now more than a little curious. She was not at all interested in buying the inn, but she sure would like to find out what happened to Hannah Montague.

CHAPTER
Six

Caroline stood under the rose-covered arbor, mesmerized by the buttercup yellow inn and its garden in spite of their fading beauty. Max lay on the crushed shell path at her feet, panting after their run on the beach. After goofing off all day yesterday, hitting up one antique shop after another, staying up until too late looking for information about the inn, and sleeping away most of the morning, Caroline really should have stayed back at the cottage to work on her article. But she wanted to check out the town library, and she couldn't stop thinking about the inn.

Last night, Caroline thought for sure Gracie and Sam would want to come see it again after what they had learned, but her sisters had wanted to laze about today—Gracie reading in the overstuffed chairs in the cottage's living room, Sam doing counted cross-stitch and watching cooking shows. She'd promised to be back in time for dinner at six and had headed out, taking Max with her. She headed straight for the Misty Harbor.

Caroline couldn't have stayed away even if she'd wanted to. The last time she'd been this intrigued by a place was when she set eyes on the twelfth-century Norman tower of St. James Church in Chipping Campden. Caroline sighed. She'd miss Briar Rose if she moved away, but something told her this would be a whole new adventure.

She held Max's leash loosely in her right hand and let her canine companion lead her around the garden. She steered him clear of the thorny English roses. They reminded her of her own garden back in Chipping Campden, and she drew in a deep breath.

"You know, Max, this could make an awfully nice home for you and me."

Max barked twice and danced around a few times, but then with his attention caught by a butterfly fluttering from flower to flower, headed for a periwinkle-colored hydrangea, overgrown but incredibly beautiful.

Caroline's foot caught on a vine, and she stumbled. She grabbed the arm of a marble Grecian goddess mostly wrapped in ivy to catch her fall. Was this Aphrodite? Athena? Persephone? Whoever she was, she was beautiful, even though the marble was cracked and chipped in a few places.

Oh, how she wanted to buy this place. It felt magical; it had wrapped around her, making her feel as warm as her own Briar Rose Cottage had. She'd thought she'd never find another place that could give her that sense of home, but the Misty Harbor Inn was inching its way into her heart.

She and Max headed for the porch that crossed the entire back of the house. They climbed the creaking steps and stopped, stunned once again by the view. The afternoon sun splintered across the deep blue ocean. A couple of boats in full sail raced across the water, and the waves rolled gently back and forth. The soft roar sounded almost like a lullaby. If there'd been a hammock hanging out here, she could easily stretch out and fall asleep.

It was heaven here. The scents of salt water and overgrown flowers wafted around her.

The shutters on this side of the house had been closed up tight, nailed or screwed into place, just as they had been in the front. As Max went sniffing around the yard, she jiggled one shutter after another, looking for one that might be a little bit loose, and found one at last. She jiggled it again and again, trying to get the shutter open far enough so she could see what room this window looked in on.

"Back again, I see."

Caroline spun around. She hadn't heard any footsteps, but the woman with the Gibson Girl hairdo was standing right behind her. Her hands were on her hips. She wore a pale blue polyester pantsuit today; the black rhinestone brooch fastened to her wide lapel looked like a leopard. Its red rhinestone eyes glared at Caroline.

"This old place seems to have a hold on me," Caroline said, smiling warmly, hoping to ease the woman's suspicions. "I couldn't help but come back. I just wish I could get inside, or at least peek through the windows."

"A simple call to the real estate agent would remedy that," the woman said. She cautiously eyed Caroline up and down. Then, she slowly stuck out one hand, while her other hand held on tightly to her cane. "I'm Shirley Addison."

Caroline reached for her hand. It was cool and dry, like old paper.

She had lost some of the bluster from their first encounter, but Caroline was still cautious. "My mom brought my sisters and me here nearly fifty years ago," she ventured. Shirley watched her carefully. "But I still remember the wallpaper in the parlor. It looked like a million peacocks were marching around with their colorful feathers spread out for everyone to admire."

"Yes, I suppose the old wallpaper did look like that. The company that turned the house into an inn back in the 1950s had a thing for peacocks. They even had a few real ones here. 1960, I think it was."

The woman looked around the yard, as if imagining them parading around the garden today.

"It liked to have scared me to death the first time I heard them. They were quiet as cotton blowing in the breeze during the day, but in the middle of the night, when their tail feathers got ruffled, they'd start their screeching. Mr. Addison, my husband, God rest his soul, might have taken a shotgun to them if they hadn't been so pretty. Don't know what the owners ended up doing with those birds, but one day they were gone, and they've never been back."

Max chose that moment to barrel up the stairs, nearly knocking over Mrs. Addison. He started to run circles around her. He liked attention, and he wanted Mrs. Addison's. "This is Max," Caroline said, grabbing the rambunctious cocker spaniel by the collar. After ordering him four times to sit, Max finally plopped down on the porch.

Mrs. Addison eyed him, and then she turned her stare from Max back to Caroline and gripped her cane with both hands.

"You're going to buy this old place, aren't you?"

Mrs. Addison said it with so much conviction that Caroline wondered if she had some sort of sixth sense. Caroline didn't know if it was possible, but she wanted to. She'd need both of her sisters to go in with her, and Gracie was so set against it, but she would keep trying to convince her.

"I've thought about it." Caroline chuckled. "My sisters think I'm out of my mind."

"The people who are out of their minds are the ones who walked away from this place. I don't see how they could just let it get in this condition." Shirley shook her head, tsking her disgust. "I've seen a lot of changes here over the years. Mr. Addison and I bought our place, Quincy Court, in 1952. Takes a lot of work to keep up a home built in 1799, but when you love a place, you do what you have to do."

"It doesn't look like the owners of the inn were in love with the place."

Mrs. Addison *tsked*. "The current owners had one spat after another with the historical society and the buildings department. They wanted to paint the place red, which would have been fine and dandy if they'd opted for Cottage Red." Caroline nodded. She knew that there were only eleven colors a building in Nantucket could be painted. The Nantucket Historic District Commission had determined the handful of shades that were historically accurate for the island, and it was against code to paint a home or business anything else. Cottage Red was one of the approved colors.

"But no," Shirley continued. "They wanted something that looked like the candy apple red Mr. Addison painted our fifty-seven Chevy, and that was an absolute no-no."

"That's it? The issue of paint colors caused them to walk away from the inn?"

Shirley tucked an errant strand of long white hair back into the pouf of her bun. "Oh no. They also wanted to add false dormers to the outside and put a brass weathervane on top. It would have looked like a barn by the time they were finished, instead of a nineteenth-century colonial." Shirley shook her head, *tsking* again. "Plus, the inn had been going downhill for a while. I've talked with many a guest over the years, and found out that the mattresses were hard, the plumbing creaked, the pillows were polyester instead of the down that was advertised. And the food! I could tell you stories about the food that would set your stomach to churning. Suffice it to say, the number of guests dwindled."

This information was no surprise. It jibed with the reviews Caroline had found online. "So the new owners gave up?"

"It was the previous owners who had trouble keeping it up. In way over their heads, if you ask me. They sold it to the California couple who had issues with the historical society. They were rather snooty, to say the least. Thought they could turn this place around by turning it into a unique property, something very un-Nantucket-like. That didn't go over well, and while they fought against the commission, they just let the building fade. Absolute shame, if you ask me."

"It is a shame," Caroline added. She leaned against the white railing around the edge of the porch. "So the California couple still own the building?"

"As far as I know. I haven't seen them in a few summers, and nothing's been done to the inn since then."

"Do you know if anyone's tried to buy it?"

"Oh, there's been interest, or so the real estate agent says, but it's going to take a lot of time and money to get it back in ship's shape," Shirley said. "Whoever buys the inn this time around will have to work hard. It won't be easy to rebuild the place's reputation."

"No, I imagine it won't."

"Do you know much about the history of the inn? I mean, older history, like from the last century?"

Shirley stared at her. "Exactly how old do you think I am?"

Caroline laughed, "Oh, I didn't mean that you'd remember the history, of course." She gave Shirley a grin. "But we've heard that the original owner's wife disappeared from this house, and we're interested to know more."

"I don't know about all that." Shirley waved her hand dismissively. "They never did find poor Hannah. It was such a shame. She was a good girl—" Caroline suppressed a laugh as she heard Shirley talk about the second Mrs. Montague as if they were friends—"but I've always assumed the stories about her disappearance and the hidden rooms and all that were just wild speculation."

"So you don't know anything about it?"

"That's what I just said, isn't it?"

Caroline choked back a smile. If they ended up buying this place, it was going to be fun to try to win over the neighbor.

Caroline looked at her watch, remembering her promise to be back at the cottage before six. She still wanted to go to the library, get a visitor's card, and check out books on Nantucket history. She had just a couple of hours to spare. She'd better not be late. Gracie and Sam would never forgive her.

"I've got to run, but it's been really nice talking with you, Shirley." Caroline smiled. "You don't mind me calling you Shirley, do you?"

"I prefer young people calling me Mrs. Addison." She sniffed. "But for you"—she eyed Caroline up and down—"Shirley will do."

"I'll be sure to call the real estate agent if I can talk my sisters into coming out here to look inside the inn," Caroline said, clipping the leash back on Max. "I have a flyer with her name and phone number."

"Good. Good." Shirley nodded and then grasped her cane and started heading toward the porch steps.

Caroline and Max practically skipped down the stairs. She felt a new lightness in her step as they made their way through the unkempt garden. When she got under the arbor, she snagged an Old English rose from the vines and tucked it behind her ear, captivated by the scent that reminded her so much of her Cotswolds home. She waved good-bye to Shirley Addison, who stood on the porch, watching her every move. "I hope we meet again, Shirley."

Shirley shrugged and then slowly allowed herself to smile softly. "I hope so too."

CHAPTER
Seven

*T*hat smells absolutely delicious." Gracie lowered the paperback she'd been devouring for the past few hours and looked at Sam over the reading glasses precariously balanced on the end of her nose. "What are you making?"

"Well, these are rolls," Sam said as she pulled a baking tray out of the oven. The sweet, yeasty scent of fresh-baked bread filled the room. She set the tray down on the counter and pulled the oven mitts off her hands. "And I made a green salad and asparagus and corn on the cob, but I suspect what you're smelling is the scallops."

Gracie inhaled deeply. "Is that just butter and garlic you're cooking them in?"

"And shallots, with a bit of fresh lemon juice." Sam wiped her hand across her forehead and surveyed the platters of food splayed across the table. She had set it with the cottage's clean white dishware, and Gracie had filled a large glass vase with fresh flowers from the garden. They had decided to eat inside tonight because the sky had clouded over, but so far there was no rain. "These are about done, so as soon as Caroline gets home, we can eat." Sam aimed the controller at the TV, watched Paula Deen drop a stick of butter into her mixing bowl, and then turned the sound off on Paula's infectious laugh and looked at Gracie again.

"It's almost six."

"Have a little faith in her, Gracie. She said she'd be here."

Gracie set down her book and rubbed the bridge of her nose. "If I had to venture a guess, I'd say she's at the Misty Harbor Inn right now, snooping around again." Gracie shook her head in frustration. "She's obsessed with that place, but she's being totally unrealistic. Even if we technically do have enough, I have other plans for my share of the money."

"Such as?" Sam used a hot pad to slide the rolls off the baking sheet and into a basket lined with a pretty linen napkin.

"Such as"—Gracie shrugged—"Brandon and Stacy have had to borrow money a time or two. I want to have it on hand in case they need more. And the grandkids have to go to college, and there's no way Brandon will be able to afford that without my help."

Sam pressed her lips together. Gracie knew what she was thinking, but she pretended she didn't see the knowing look in her sister's eyes. She felt no shame about putting her family first.

"Plus," Gracie continued, "I don't really want to spend my retirement years washing endless amounts of linen, laying out a gourmet breakfast, and making up other people's beds every morning."

"I'm not all that fond of that idea either, but I have to admit I have given an ounce or two of thought to buying the place."

"It's just one of Caroline's whims," Gracie said.

"Buying the inn was originally Mom's whim," Sam reminded Gracie. "She talked about it whenever we came to Nantucket, and she filled notebook after notebook with B and B ideas." Sam checked her watch and turned off the heat under the scallops. "You know, Caroline and mom were two peas in a pod."

"With a lot of big differences. Mom didn't rush from one idea to another; she always tried to finish what she started."

"Maybe Caroline's trying to change. Maybe she really has decided to settle down," Sam said. She could see Gracie's point, but she really didn't want to be caught between her two sisters. She had always been the peacemaker; sometimes she wished she could just stay out of the fray.

"I wish I could have faith in her," Gracie said, glancing at her watch, "but tonight's a perfect example of Caroline's flightiness. She promised to be here in time for dinner, yet—"

The front door of the cottage flew open, a gust of sea air blowing Caroline and Max into the cozy sitting room. "Sorry I didn't get home sooner, but I popped into Homer's Pet Shop to get a couple of toys and some special treats for Max, and I got to talking to Skip Roderick, Homer's son, who knows everything there is to know about dogs, and then, when I couldn't get into the library, because I had Max with me—"

"Oh, Caroline, you should have known the library wouldn't let Max inside," Gracie said.

"Of course I knew it, but I had to try, and since they flat out said no, I went to the Rarest Books—"

"Is it as wonderful as I imagine?" Gracie asked.

"You'll love it, Gracie. Make sure you put it on one of your lists. Chad Douglas was so helpful, showing me books on Nantucket's history and eighteenth- and nineteenth-century American furniture."

"Great," Sam said. She aimed the remote at the TV and turned off the set. "You can tell us all about it over dinner."

Caroline looked down at her shorts and one of her many colorful gauzy shirts. "I've been all over town in this and I could definitely stand to put on some clean clothes. Can I have a few minutes to change?"

"We'll finish setting the table while you're getting freshened up," Sam said, scooping the scallops onto a charming chipped china platter. She set the dish on the worn oak table and surveyed the meal. It looked as good as it smelled. She took a glad pitcher from the counter and started to fill it with water.

The moment they heard Caroline's bedroom door slam, Sam grinned at Gracie. "See, what did I tell you? I might not completely share your faith in the man upstairs, but I certainly have faith in Caroline."

"So, Caroline, you said you went to Rarest Books?" Gracie asked after they were all seated around the kitchen table and had said grace. The soft light from the hanging lamp cast a warm glow over the meal. The bookstore was on Gracie's list for later in the week, but she had been looking forward to seeing the shop and was eager to hear what Caroline thought.

"It was a beautiful little shop," Caroline said. She cut one of her plump creamy white scallops in half and was about to put it in her mouth before continuing. "It's small, but it's got these gorgeous plank floors and antique shelves and comfy couches you just want to plop down in and the sweetest little children's nook. They even serve free coffee and tea. I wanted to stay there forever."

Gracie tried to stifle a smile. The idea of Caroline staying in any place forever was hard to imagine.

Sam glared at Gracie and then quickly said, "Did you say you got into a discussion with the owner?"

Caroline nodded. "I told him I wanted to see what they had on old Nantucket homes, and he showed me a whole section on local history."

Gracie felt tension building in her shoulders. So Caroline had not yet given up on her scheme to buy the Misty Harbor Inn. She could tell by her sister's tone of voice and the dreamy look on her face. Sam must have known it too, because her younger sister kicked her lightly under the table. That was a warning. *Be nice!*

"Did you find anything interesting?" Sam asked, spearing a bite of lettuce.

"Less than we learned all on our own last night." Caroline shook her head. "Chad, the owner, was nice and helpful, but he's just bought the Rarest Books, and he's new to Nantucket. He knows books, but he doesn't know any more than we do about the island's past."

"That's too bad," Gracie offered, slicing a spear of asparagus in half.

"I'm sure we'll find out something, though. Someone has to know more about the old building. I'll see if I can find out anything from Grandpa Folger on Saturday night."

Sam kicked Gracie again, as if she knew full well that Gracie was about to say something she shouldn't. Somehow Gracie bit her tongue, but what she really wanted to do was tell Caroline enough was enough. She didn't want to hear anything more about the inn.

"What do you want to know about it?" Sam asked, her eyes sparkling. Oh dear, she was definitely falling into Caroline's trap, getting excited about Caroline's latest passing fancy.

"If he knows anything about secret rooms, for one," Caroline said. "Does he know what happened to Hannah Montague? You know, all the nitty gritty stuff, especially the tales that could make the inn even more interesting."

"Is that really how you want to spend our vacation? Researching the history of an old, rundown inn? Didn't we do enough of that last night?" Gracie asked, feeling Sam once again kick her lightly under the table. She pretended she didn't notice. "What about our bike rides? Building sand castles? Reading books just for fun?"

"What about learning more about the inn before we make the decision to buy it?" Caroline tossed back. "The more we know—"

"I'm not interested in buying the place," Gracie said. Suddenly the meal Sam had spent all afternoon cooking seemed unappetizing.

"But it has so much going for it, Gracie. I went back there today and took a closer look at the gardens—"

"You didn't! That woman told us to stay away."

"I ran into her again today too, and she's all bluff and bluster. Something tells me she'd do anything for the right neighbors."

"We're not the right neighbors, Caroline. I live in Maine; Sam lives in New York; you live…wherever the mood suits. We don't live in Nantucket, and even if we had the money to buy the place, I don't want to leave my home and move here."

Caroline's back stiffened. "Maybe I should buy it on my own."

"That's a lot of money," Sam said, her voice calm, trying to reason with Caroline. "Do you have that much?"

"No, but if I used my inheritance from Mom, plus my savings as a down payment, I could probably get a loan for the rest."

Gracie was stunned. She'd never heard anything so ridiculous. That place was a money pit. Sam might have been thinking the same thing, but she put her hand on Caroline's. "Please, Caroline, don't rush into this. Let's talk about it more. Later."

"Maybe you and I can talk about it later, but it's pretty apparent Gracie's mind is closed."

Under the table, Gracie could feel Sam's hand come to a rest on her knee. She felt her sister squeeze lightly, offering her some comfort. Across the table she heard Caroline sigh.

Gracie hadn't wanted to ruin their evening, but it had suddenly come to an abrupt and distressful end.

CHAPTER
Eight

Sam kept a close eye on Caroline as they sat across from each other at the kitchen table later that night. Gracie had disappeared into her room as soon as the dishes were done, and now the two of them worked together on a jigsaw puzzle of the Brant Point lighthouse and munched on cinnamon and sugar-toasted walnuts that she'd roasted.

After the dinner, she wished she had never come up with the idea for the three of them to vacation together on Nantucket. Caroline and Gracie had two completely different personalities and had always clashed with each other. On the other hand, she knew they needed to be together. They needed to come to terms with their differences, accept them, and find a way to get along in spite of them.

Sam plucked a puzzle piece from the table and snapped it into place. She wished everything else going on in the cottage could be solved so easily.

Caroline was too quiet. So was Max, who was sprawled on the cool hardwood floor, eyes closed, twitching every once in a while. He must be having a bad dream; if things didn't get better, Sam imagined she'd end up with bad dreams too.

"I wish I knew why Gracie's so dead set against buying the inn," Caroline said, absently touching and inspecting one puzzle piece after another. Sam wasn't sure if she was looking for one piece in particular or just needed something to do with her hands.

"She enjoys her life just as it is," Sam offered. She couldn't possibly tell Caroline the truth. She knew Gracie didn't trust Caroline, that she was afraid Caroline would end up hurting both sisters if they went along with her scheme to buy the inn.

"Other than babysitting her grandchildren, she doesn't do anything other than read, watch old movies, and listen to her Beatles and Dave Clark 5 records, as if she were still living in the sixties—"

"It makes her happy, Caroline. She's not like me and she's definitely not like you."

Caroline frowned. "You say that as if there's something wrong with me."

Sam laughed. "Do you have any idea how much I wanted to be just like you when I was growing up?"

From the incredulous look on Caroline's face, Sam could see she didn't. "Now you're just trying to placate me."

"I'm not. It's true. When you dropped out of college and took off for San Francisco to become a hippie—"

"It was Hawaii, and I was never a hippie, just a free spirit." Caroline snapped a puzzle piece into place. "And don't forget, I got a job running errands for a travel agent and worked my way up until I was running the place." She turned back to the box and began sifting through the pieces again.

Sam popped a sugary walnut into her mouth and chewed thoughtfully. "I thought you were the luckiest person on the face of the earth, traveling the world, seeing places I could only dream about."

"You were only ten or eleven. You should have been dreaming about birthday parties, or at the very least, David Cassidy. Ten-year-olds don't dream about traveling the world."

"That shows how little you know about me."

A touch of sadness crept into Caroline's face. She picked up a new puzzle piece and tried to fit it into the picture that was slowly forming on the table, turning it around and around, but she couldn't find the right spot. She sighed. "I should have come home more, or at the very least picked up the phone to call you all more often."

Sam reached across the table and clasped her older sister's hand. "We all could have kept in touch more. It wasn't just you, Caroline. I was busy with Jamie and teaching, and when I had free time, all I wanted to do was hole up in my living room and cross-stitch or watch cooking shows. Mom kept busy with her gardening, and sewing, and reading clubs. And Gracie, well, Gracie was involved in the kids' sports and helping out in their classrooms, and now she's completely wrapped up in her grandchildren."

Caroline picked up another puzzle piece and fitted it into a puffy cloud hanging over the lighthouse. "Even though Gracie's upset with me tonight, I'm glad we're all together. It's been far too long."

"I just wish Mom could be here with us."

Caroline nodded. "Me too. Of course, she'd probably tell Gracie and me that we're acting like children, and that we should get over ourselves."

"And then she'd make you kiss and make up." Sam laughed. "And Mom would give me a cookie on the sly."

"You're kidding. Why would she do that?"

"Because I was such a good girl. Always."

Max rolled onto his back. He wanted his belly rubbed, and Sam leaned down to give him exactly what he wanted. It must be nice to have such a laid-back life.

Caroline's chair scraped across the floor as she pushed up from the table and headed toward the kitchen. She peeked down the hall, probably looking to see if Gracie's bedroom door was opened even a crack, but when she sighed, Sam knew the door was still closed tight.

"I'm going to make some tea. Would you like some?"

"Sounds great…Just add two tablespoons of honey." That's the way their mother had always taken hers, and always in a dainty teacup, never in a mug.

Sam rose from the table, pressed her hands into the curve of her spine and stretched out the kinks. Max scratched at the French doors, and she let him out into the backyard. "If you did buy the inn," Sam said, "what would you do with it?"

Sam couldn't help but notice Caroline's eyes light up. She leaned against the counter that separated the small kitchen from the sitting room, and watched Caroline set two cups and saucers on the countertop.

"I'd do exactly what Mom wanted to do. Turn it into a B and B."

"Do you know how to do that? I mean, as cool as that sounds, you can't just snap your fingers and find it transformed from a run-down inn to glistening B and B."

Caroline winked at Sam. "I may be free-spirited, and I may have a tendency to rush into things, but I know I'd have a lot of homework to do."

"A whole lot," Sam added. "The garden would have to be—"

"Pretty much gutted," Caroline interrupted. "The woodwork outside would have to be stripped of paint, sanded, and repainted.

The inside would need endless amounts of cleaning, redecorating, and probably remodeling."

"And there's no telling what condition the wiring's in, not to mention the plumbing."

"Think of all the fun we could have making the inn look picture-perfect again."

"We?" Sam felt one of her eyebrows raise. She had to admit she was tempted by the idea of owning a B and B. She loved to cook, and now that Jamie was out of the house, she rarely made elaborate meals anymore. It would be kind of fun to come up with interesting and delicious breakfasts for guests all the time. But she wasn't about to rush into anything.

"Of course, 'we.' Maybe I could do it on my own, but I don't want to. I want you and Gracie to be a part of the inn. I want it to be ours, not mine. I want it to be Mom's too."

Caroline made it sound so easy, so idyllic. A place filled with memories. But she was overlooking the hard work that it would take. And she no doubt wasn't being realistic, especially when it came to money. The inn would cost a small fortune; fixing it up would cost even more; and running it…well, there was no guarantee the rooms would ever be filled with guests.

Sam spooned honey into her teacup, just as their mother had always done. She took a sip and thought about what it would be like to sit on the inn's back porch on a warm night like this, with a billion stars twinkling overhead, listening to the surf rolling back and forth on the beach. It did sound wonderful.

"You know," Sam said, "it might be a good idea to sit down and seriously discuss costs—what we'd have to spend up front to buy the inn, plus what it would cost to make repairs, clean it up, and make it habitable. There are bound to be permits too, and I'm sure there are rules and restrictions on preserving a historical property."

Caroline's face broke out into a smile. "So you're interested?"

"Not so fast. I—we—need to see the inside first. Let's not put the cart before the horse, okay?"

"I'll call the agent first thing in the morning. We can—"

"Going to see the inn isn't on Gracie's list for tomorrow. Why don't we wait a bit. A day or two, maybe."

"Oh, all right," Caroline said with a sigh, "but let's not wait too long. I'd hate for someone else to come in and snatch the inn out from under us."

Sam hated to hear the note of disappointment in her sister's voice, but knew she had to be completely honest. "If that happens, then buying the Misty Harbor Inn wasn't meant to be."

Gracie pulled the soft duvet up around her shoulders and squinted to see the time on the alarm clock next to the twin bed in her small room. It was nearly half past two. She hadn't slept a wink. How could she do anything more than toss and turn when she'd acted so childishly? She hadn't meant to hurt Caroline's feelings, but she obviously had.

Pale, silvery moonlight filtered in through the gingham curtains that hung over the room's small window. She could see the outline of the nightstand, the tall dresser, and the foot of the narrow twin bed. She closed her eyes and tried to stay perfectly still, but she couldn't stop the whirling in her mind.

She'd felt such tension when they'd been wandering around the inn's overgrown garden a few days ago. Now she knew why. The inn was destined to drive her and Caroline further apart.

She couldn't let that happen.

Rubbing her eyes, she sat up on the edge of the bed and yawned. She'd had plenty of sleepless nights throughout her life: when her children were newborns and she continually sneaked into their rooms to peek into their cribs to make sure they were breathing; when her son and daughter, Brandon and Paige, stayed out past curfew; when Art was in the hospital, and she felt more alone than she ever had in her life. But this was different. This was her fault.

She and Caroline had been so different growing up, and the six-year difference in their ages hadn't helped. She loved her though. She always had. If she was honest, Gracie had always been a tad jealous of how Caroline could throw responsibility to the wind and do whatever she wanted, but mostly she had seen how that thoughtlessness had affected other people. She'd been hurt by it too many times.

Still, Caroline seemed to suffer more than anyone else when their mother had died. She'd felt guilty for not coming home sooner, and it wasn't even her fault. Gracie thought now that she should have ignored her mother's plea not to tell Caroline she was ill. She should have called Caroline and asked her to come home. She knew Caroline would have been on the next plane. Instead, she'd arrived after their mother had slipped into a coma. She hadn't been able to really and truly say good-bye. But Caroline had never once blamed Gracie. That wasn't Caroline's style. She was loving and kind and exuberant in all she did. And now Gracie had hurt her again.

Gracie climbed out of bed and drew a soft terrycloth robe around her. As she stood up, she felt the touch of arthritis in her hip that plagued her every now and then. It was only two short steps from the bed to the door, and she opened it quietly, trying not to wake her sisters or Max.

She crept down the short hallway toward the kitchen. Her head hurt; the pain at the back of her neck had tormented her since the argument, and she needed something hot to drink and a couple of aspirin. If she could get rid of the headache, she might be able to sleep.

She saw a flicker of blue light from the TV reflecting on the hallway wall. Caroline's bedroom door was closed and the light was out. Was Sam still up?

Gracie padded down the hallway and stepped into the living room. Caroline was curled up on the sofa with Max, who was lying on his back, his four furry legs sticking up in the air. His eyes flew open when one of the floorboards squealed. He rolled over, his tail wagged wildly, and trotted toward Gracie, nudging her hand with a cold nose.

"Enjoying the movie?" Gracie asked softly.

Caroline smiled. "In between dozing off."

"How can you possibly sleep through *Notorious*?" Gracie pulled an afghan from the back of an overstuffed easy chair and curled up at the far end of the sofa. She covered her bare feet and Caroline's with the blanket. "You've seen it before, haven't you?"

"Once, I think. Probably with you."

"That's no surprise. It's one of my favorites, especially when Ingrid Bergman's on the phone and Cary Grant's kissing her." Gracie found herself sighing. It wasn't much of an apology, but maybe talking about something as nonconfrontational as an old black and white movie could ease the strain she'd caused between them.

"I like the beginning, when they're in the car and Bergman's driving like a maniac," Caroline said, tucking the afghan around her feet. "Cary's so calm and cool and looks handsome and sophisticated in his tux." Caroline swept her hands through her hair. "You don't still have a crush on him, do you?"

Gracie wrapped her arms around her knees and stared at the handsome man on the screen. "Till the day I die, I'm afraid."

"Well, I have to admit, there aren't many men like him around these days."

"What about George?" Gracie asked, thinking about Caroline's longtime friend. She'd heard about him for years and met him at their mother's funeral, and she'd liked him instantly. "Don't you find him dashing and daring and devastatingly handsome?"

"I don't normally think of George as dashing or daring or devastatingly handsome, but"—a slow grin touched Caroline's face—"he's a mighty attractive best friend."

"I never forgot the day you called me from Istanbul and told me that you'd met this gorgeous guy inside the Hagia Sophia. 'He was studying one of the mosaics of Christ,' you said, and I could hear the thrill in your voice when you added, 'he was studying me too.'"

"That seems a thousand years ago," Caroline said wistfully. "That first day, I liked what I saw. He was humble and quiet, so different from other men I knew. I thought he was going to be the love of my life. But somehow, over the years, we've just stayed the best of friends, nothing more."

"Art was my best friend, but he was also the love of my life. The two can go together, you know."

Caroline tugged the afghan up over her knees. "I'll settle for friendship. Falling in love is easy and staying in love is far too risky."

"Don't you ever want to get married?"

"That's even more risky than falling in love. I guess I'm not the marrying kind."

"Is George the marrying kind?"

Caroline frowned, as if she'd never given the question much thought. "We've never talked about it," she said finally. "We're usually off in our own worlds. He's got a business to run in Annapolis, and you know me—I rarely stay put for more than a couple of weeks at a time."

"But you're giving up the traveling, aren't you? Isn't that all a part of your moving back to the States and spending more time with family?"

Caroline avoided Gracie's gaze for the longest time. She seemed deep in thought. "I love to travel, but I want to spend more time with you and Sam—and George. And," she said, knocking lightly on her head, "I have thousands of travel tales stored in my brain. I could write articles and make money off them from now until doomsday."

Would she really stay put? Gracie wanted to give Caroline the benefit of the doubt, but she'd witnessed her sister change her mind about big, important things far too often. Still, she smiled at Caroline. "I'm glad you're coming home." She swallowed the emotion that had been building up for far too long. "I've missed you."

Caroline wiped away a tear racing down her cheek. "Me too."

The flickering light from the TV caused shadows to dance around the room.

Caroline pushed up from the sofa. "Want some cocoa? I picked up a can of instant stuff at the store yesterday. Might help us both get to sleep."

"No, I'm fine. Thanks." But she stood up and followed Caroline into the compact kitchen.

"So what do you have planned for all of us to do tomorrow?" Caroline asked, taking a freshly washed mug from the drain rack next to the sink. "Bike rides? Sport fishing? Whale watching?"

"Actually, we're going to climb the Unitarian church's bell tower."

Caroline dropped the spoon she'd just taken from a drawer. She stared at Gracie as if she'd lost her mind. "Aren't there something like a hundred stairs?"

"Ninety-four, and they're pretty steep, but all the tour books say the view from the top is phenomenal."

"The drifting sand in the middle of the Sahara is beautiful too, if you're crazy enough to brave the hundred-and-thirty-degree heat."

Gracie grinned, easily imagining her sister traveling an ancient caravan route, oblivious to the shifting sands and the blazing sun. "You braved it."

"I was a lot younger then."

"Well, it's on the list. And... I've added something else to the list." Gracie took in a deep breath. She didn't want Caroline to get the wrong idea, but she knew what she had to do to make amends with her sister. "Why don't you call the Realtor to make an appointment to tour the Misty Harbor Inn. Just don't get it in your head that I want to buy it or even go in halves or thirds on the place with you and Sam. I'm just trying to—"

Gracie couldn't get out another word because Caroline threw her arms around her and nearly smothered her with hugs. She might live to regret putting the Misty Harbor Inn on her list of things to do tomorrow, but she'd never regret the love she was feeling from and for her big sister right this minute.

CHAPTER
Nine

Caroline rolled over in the comfy queen-sized bed and stared at the clock through bleary eyes. Why couldn't it be 4:30 instead of 5:45, so she could sleep for another half hour or so, before having to make her phone call? She rubbed her eyes, wishing they didn't feel like they were crusted with sand. She also wished she'd gone to bed at a reasonable hour, instead of talking with Gracie until 3:30. But she couldn't change any of that now. She needed to make her phone call.

A few hours from now, she'd make another call—to the real estate agent. Even though she was half asleep, she managed to smile. It was going to be a great day.

She grabbed her cell phone from the nightstand, scrunched down in the bed, fluffing her pillow under her head, and punched the button that would automatically dial George.

George subscribed to the theory that the early bird catches the worm. He rarely—in fact, almost never—rose later than four thirty in the morning. He did fifty sit-ups, drank a tall glass of freshly squeezed orange juice, ate a piece of toast slathered with chunky peanut butter, grabbed a tall cup of plain black coffee on his way to work, and was in the office by five thirty. George built custom yachts and had a lot of customers in Europe.

He should be drinking his second or third cup of coffee right about now, Caroline thought, as she heard the ring of the phone at the other end. She liked the sound of his voice in the morning and smiled when he answered with his usual, "Hi, hon." He'd called her "hon" for years; it was simply a familiar habit he'd fallen into. Gracie might not understand that a man and woman who were just friends could call each other by an endearing term, but it worked for George. He loved her; she loved him—but not in an in-love kind of way.

"Morning."

"You sound awful."

"Late night," Caroline said, her voice a bit rough. "Gracie and I were up talking till, oh, just a couple of hours ago."

"Then why call so early? You're on vacation. You're supposed to sleep late."

"I could easily sleep until noon." Caroline stifled a yawn. "But I wanted to catch you before your day gets too busy."

"Everything okay?" She could hear a touch of worry in George's voice. "Did you tell Gracie and Sam you're moving back to the States?"

"Yes, although I don't think Gracie believes me. She's sure I'll change my mind."

George was silent a moment. She heard him sigh. "Can you blame her?"

"No, I suppose I can't. If Briar Rose was for sale, I'd snap it up in a second and not even think about moving back to the States. I'd ask Sam and Gracie to come visit me, instead of the other way around.

But it's not for sale, it never will be for sale, and I am moving back here. In fact, that's what I want to talk to you about."

"The *Mary Claire*'s sitting in the harbor waiting for you. Eighty-nine feet with a sky lounge and a galley that's the perfect size for someone who doesn't like to cook. There's enough storage for your wardrobe. It's roomy and comfortable and—"

"You know I wouldn't mind living on a boat. It's bound to be far more comfortable than some of the hostels I've stayed in. But I've found somewhere else to live...maybe."

"Maybe?"

She could so easily imagine George's right eyebrow raise, the way it so often did when he questioned one of her schemes. The Misty Harbor was rather a sudden urge, but it had stuck with her for days now. She simply wanted George's blessing.

"Oh, George, you have to see this place. It's absolutely magical. From the first moment I saw it, it seemed to wrap its arms around me and made me feel all warm inside."

He was silent again. Pensive. Always thinking. Never rushing into anything. "I take it this place is in Nantucket?"

"On the west side of the island, on a bluff overlooking the ocean. I haven't yet seen the sunset from the back porch, but I can only imagine how beautiful it is, bright red and orange, like a wildfire streaking across the sky. And the garden's just as glorious, or it will be, once a gardener's gotten his or her hands on it and gets it under control."

"Hold it, Caroline. Why isn't the garden under control?"

"Well...," she dragged out the word. "Actually, it's an inn—the Misty Harbor, and it's been closed for a few years."

"Why?" The skepticism in his voice deepened.

"Any number of reasons. One set of owners got in over their heads and couldn't afford the place. The current owners had numerous fights over the historical preservation regulations."

"How old is this inn?"

"A hundred and sixty years. Maybe a little older."

George nearly groaned out a sigh. "Have you had it inspected? Are there termites? What's the wiring like? The plumbing?"

"No, I haven't had an inspection yet, but I haven't made an offer. In fact, I haven't been inside it since the sixties. My sisters and I went there with our mom when we were kids but—"

"Please don't tell me you want me to put my stamp of approval on this idea of yours?"

"As a matter of fact, I do."

"You know I can't do that without seeing the place."

"But if you see it, you might tell me I'm crazy. Gracie thinks I've lost my mind. But, you know I've done crazy things before and I've come out totally unscathed."

"Most of the time—not always."

"This feels right, George. I don't know why. It was my mom who always dreamed of owning a bed-and-breakfast. Doing something like that never entered my mind. Not once, until the day we arrived on the island and I saw it again...and I just sort of fell in love."

There was that silence again. She could hear George breathing. She thought she heard him take a sip of coffee. A phone rang in the background. He cleared his throat. "I can't get away for a few days, but as soon as I can, I'll be there."

"I knew I could count on you."

Caroline could envision George's smile at the other end of the phone. "Just do me a favor, hon."

"Anything. Just name it."

"Don't make an offer until I've seen it."

"I won't, unless someone comes along and tries to snatch it out from under me."

"Ninety-two, ninety-three, ninety-four. At last!" Gracie spun around breathlessly when she reached the top of the Unitarian church's tower, taking in the incredible view. Every speck of pain she'd felt in her knees and all of the strain in each and every muscle in her legs had been worth it.

"Oh my." Sam's cheeks were pink, she was breathing hard, but her bright-eyed gaze showed her awe. "It's beautiful."

They had a full view of Nantucket in every direction. The sky was a bright azure, and a few puffy white clouds floated about in the gentle breeze. Off in the distance, Gracie could see the dark reddish tint of cranberry bogs, long stretches of sandy beach, an endless number of expansive homes, and a handful of smaller, quaint cottages. Over the canopy of lush green trees, she could see steeples rising all around town.

"There's the Old Mill," Caroline said, pointing south. "And that's Nantucket Sound off to the north."

"You're sure?" Sam asked, snapping one picture after another.

"Positive. I may have a lot of faults," Caroline said, "but I know how to read a map and tell north from south."

Gracie watched Caroline as she pointed out many of the landmarks she'd read about in the tour books and some they'd passed on their walks. Out in the harbor, they saw sailing ships and motor yachts. Some were elegant and streamlined and obviously belonged to the wealthier islanders or visitors, and some were smaller and had no doubt been plying these waters for many years. There were old out-of-service Coast Guard cutters that had been turned into floating homes, small sailboats bobbing on the water, and hundreds upon hundreds of seagulls floating on the air current, keeping a keen eye out for scraps.

"That's Madaket way, way out there in the west. Can you see it?" Caroline asked. "They say some of the prettiest sunsets in the world can be seen from there."

"Actually, Madaket's right about there," a man's voice came from the steps. Gracie jumped. The man was dressed in a T-shirt, gym shorts, and running shoes. He wiped sweat from his brow and then pointed a little bit southwest.

"Sorry if I startled you," he said. "I try to run up and down the tower twice a week. It's good exercise. Gets the heart pumping. But I'm getting the distinct feeling that I've got your hearts pumping too, for all the wrong reasons." He ran a hand through his shaggy gray hair. "If you'd like, I'll run back down right now and leave the three of you to point out all the tourist destinations, even though you're pointing in all the wrong directions."

Gracie couldn't help herself. She chuckled. He seemed nice enough, and the blue eyes that peered out from behind his wire-rimmed glasses looked kind. Truth be told, he was kind of handsome.

"No, no, don't run back down on our account, not yet anyway," Gracie said. "We'll just go back to checking out the sights, and you can catch your breath."

"What kind of born-and-bred Nantucketer would I be if I didn't give you the 360-degree tour?" he said, stepping up and in between Gracie and Caroline. "Over there, that white Greek Revival building with the columns, is our library, the Atheneum. Some people might tell you we've spelled it wrong, but we haven't. If a Nantucket islander leaves out a letter or two, that's just the way it is. Anyway, that's the best and also the only library on the island. And over there"—he pointed off to what Gracie now could see was the north—"is the Brant Point Lighthouse. Not the first one, of course. This one's number nine. First one was actually a bonfire set on a hogshead. That's not what you think, of course. It's really just a big old barrel. That was in used back in 1700. The lighthouse is white now, but it was painted black until 1895."

"You don't by any chance know all there is to know about Nantucket, do you?" Caroline asked.

The man laughed. "Not quite. But I'm getting there."

Gracie could tell where Caroline was going with this, but she forced herself to not react. She needed to support Caroline, even if her interest was bordering on obsessive.

"I'm interested in the history of the Misty Harbor Inn," Caroline said.

"I like to pride myself on knowing a little bit about a lot of things, but all I know about the Misty Harbor is that it's been sitting empty for far too long." The man rested his hands on the railing and smiled at Caroline. "Of course, when I was a kid, my mom insisted on taking my sister and me there for tea. She was trying to teach us manners and provide us with some of the culture we were lacking." He grinned, his smile a touch lopsided but somehow familiar to Gracie. "I'm afraid the inn hasn't been that upscale in a very long time."

"It's on the verge of falling down," Gracie said. "It probably has wood rot and—"

"It's not that bad," Caroline interrupted. "It simply needs a little loving care, which I fully intend to give it."

The gray-haired man scratched his head. "You're buying it?"

"She thinks she is," Gracie said.

"Well, in that case"—he reached into his well-worn wallet and pulled out a card, handing it to Caroline—"I'm one of Nantucket's many odd-job specialists, which pays the rent when my artwork doesn't." He smiled. "If you're seriously thinking about buying the Misty Harbor, give me a call. I'm also a licensed and bonded building inspector. I'd be happy to give you an unbiased opinion on whether or not it'll stand for another hundred and fifty years."

"Thank you so much." Caroline stuck out her hand. "I'm Caroline Marris and these are my sisters, Gracie Gold and Sam Carter."

"Bill Dekker," he said, shaking Caroline's and Sam's hands quickly and then taking Gracie's. "Nice to meet you."

Gracie played the name over and over in her mind. For some reason it sounded familiar.

Gracie suddenly realized that Bill Dekker was still holding her hand. His was warm and very big and she could feel the calluses on his fingers and palms. Slowly, she slipped her hand out of his and looked at her watch. "It's getting late, and we really need to be going."

"I'm guessing you're here on vacation."

Sam nodded. "Two weeks, and the time's going by much too fast."

"Well, if you're going to be here Saturday, my church is having a clambake. It's an all-day affair, but most people will show up around dusk. It's out on Madaket Beach." He hooked his thumb in the direction he'd pointed out earlier. "We can't build bonfires like we could back in the day because of safety concerns, but we make it look like an authentic clambake, charcoal grills and all."

"Oh, we heard about that," Sam said. "The antique store lady told us about it."

"Megan," Caroline clarified.

"That's right," Bill said. "Megan Folger-Wildes. I'm glad she invited you."

"I hope it'll be okay for us to bring a salad," Sam said. "And a dessert and bread maybe?"

"Dessert's always welcome, but don't worry about anything else. We'll have music, corn on the cob, and the best chowder you ever ate. Do you know how to find Madaket?"

Gracie nodded. "Megan gave us a flyer a couple of days ago. You know her, I suppose?"

Bill nodded. "Her father-in-law's our minister, and her late father was a friend of mine. We were in 'Nam together, but that's a story for another day."

That had always been a story for another day with Art too. Vietnam was a nightmare he'd wanted to stop visiting, but never had.

"It's awfully nice to meet you," Bill said, and looked at his wristwatch and then plowed a hand through his windblown hair. "I've got to get cleaned up for a board meeting at church." He took a few steps to the stairs. "Hope to see you at the clambake, but if you need me to look at the inn for you before then, just give me a call."

He was gone in an instant, the smile and blue eyes that sparkled in the sunlight disappearing from view.

"He seems awfully nice," Caroline said, raising an eyebrow at Gracie.

Gracie could see the wheels turning in Caroline's head. And she was right. He was nice. But Gracie had no plans to ever again fall for a man. Art had been the only man in her life, and he was the only man she ever wanted in her heart.

Sam turned and headed back toward the stairs. They probably had time for a quick lunch back at the cottage before their appointment to see the inn. As her sisters started back down, Gracie turned and looked out over the island again. Off in the distance, she immediately spotted the pale yellow inn sitting on a bluff overlooking the ocean. From their lofty vantage, it looked small and rather forlorn, and in a little over an hour they'd be wandering around inside it. She wished she hadn't changed her mind about touring the place. The Misty Harbor Inn was Caroline's dream, not hers. But she had a sneaking suspicion their appointment this afternoon was going to change everything.

CHAPTER
Ten

Caroline could hear the gravel crunching beneath the wheels as Sam turned the small rental car onto Misty Harbor Road. She had a lump in her throat, her stomach was in knots, and her breath was shallow and rapid.

Sam came to a stop where the drive widened into a circle at the front of the inn, and Caroline was the first to unfold out of the cramped vehicle. Next to their car sat a gold Mercedes with a magnetic sign on the door that read "Deborah Greenleaf Real Estate." A woman wearing red-framed sunglasses, a crisp white blouse, and white capris waited for them on the porch.

She walked briskly toward Caroline, her hand extended in greeting. "Hello. I'm Deborah Greenleaf. And you must be—"

"Caroline Marris." Caroline shook her hand, trying not to stare at the big red rubies in Deborah's ears. "And these are my sisters, Gracie Gold and Sam Carter."

Everyone smiled and shook hands. They chatted about the usual things: the weather, how they were enjoying their stay on Nantucket, where they had eaten. Deborah recommended they not miss going out to 'Sconset. "It's one of my favorite places on the island, especially when I'm looking for something unique. A piece of metal art, an inexpensive oil painting by a local just learning his or her craft," Deborah smiled. "There are also quite a number of lovely homes for sale in that area, if you decide the Misty Harbor isn't quite what you have in mind."

"Actually," Gracie said, and Caroline knew exactly what her sister was going to say, "we didn't come here looking for a place to buy. It's just that Caroline's intrigued by the inn and is dying to see the inside."

Deborah's smile fell. "I see."

"Actually," Caroline corrected, before Deborah decided she'd wasted her time, "I'm more than just intrigued."

"Me too," Sam said, taking Caroline by surprise. "Although the price on the flyer seems high, considering all the work that needs to be done. Granted, we haven't seen the inside yet, but I've looked at quite a few Nantucket homes on the Internet, and it seems to be listed for around the same price as other homes that are pristine, and this place needs an overhaul."

Deborah's smile returned. "I'm not sure which homes you looked at, but not every home on the island comes complete with antiques like this one does. The furniture that comes with this home could bring quite a sum if sold at auction."

Sam's brow puckered. She was the detail person, the sensible one who dotted all the *i*'s and crossed every *t*. She'd obviously done her homework, and now it appeared she had a lot of questions. Though Caroline was grateful for her sister's thoroughness, she was dying to get inside.

"The inn has been for sale for quite some time," Sam said. "If it's not the price that's keeping it on the market, what is? And if the antiques are so valuable, why hasn't the owner tried to sell them individually, rather than include them in the price of the inn?"

Deborah raised her shoulders a little. "The owners are very busy, and they decided not to spend the time to go through the pieces individually. They decided they would prefer to just sell everything together." She smiled conspiratorially. "It's not how I would have chosen to handle it, but they have other properties and business ventures, and at this point, they just want to be rid of it."

Caroline couldn't imagine how anyone could want to be rid of this magnificent home.

"That could work out very well for the buyer," Deborah added.

"We would need to have it inspected, of course," Gracie said. "To see if there are any structural issues."

"Of course." Deborah seem unfazed by the questions. "Why don't I show you around. I'll give you a complete tour, and if you're interested and still feel the price is too high, I can show you similar properties that are on the market so you can see a comparison."

"Fair enough," Sam said, marching toward the front door. Caroline knew her sister was a terrific negotiator, and she trusted Sam to handle that element of the process. But that would never happen if they didn't get inside the house.

"The garden definitely needs work," Deborah said, entering her key code into the lock box affixed to a water spigot hidden behind an overgrown blue hydrangea. "Fortunately the fine bones of the landscaping are still there. I'm sure you noticed that."

"It's a beautiful garden," Caroline said, hoping to smooth over any rough feelings that might have come about from Sam's exchange with Deborah. "I love the birdbath."

"Sadly," Sam said, "the arbors are falling down under the weight of all the vines, and the weather over the years hasn't helped them at all. The siding on the inn has suffered as well."

"That's to be expected in homes that were built in the mid-1800s, and thankfully, we have several contractors here in Nantucket who specialize in refurbishing old houses."

"Another cost to factor in to the purchase." Sam took a notebook from her backpack and started jotting down tidbits of information.

Deborah put the key in the lock. "There are three things you must remember when it comes to real estate purchases. Location. Location. Location." Deborah grinned, even though the key refused to turn in the lock. "I mean, look around you. The ocean's stunning. A sandy beach is mere steps away. You're within walking distance of a wonderful town with fine restaurants, fabulous shops, and"— she struggled more with the key, until the door finally flew open—"a steady stream of tourists, who would love to stay in a place like the Misty Harbor, should you decide to keep it as an inn."

Caroline coughed as a thin cloud of dust billowed out of the inn.

"I'm so sorry about that," Deborah said, stepping into the foyer and holding the door open for Sam, Gracie, and Caroline to enter. "The inn's owners no longer live on the island and haven't paid anyone to keep it up. In the beginning I came out every couple of weeks to dust, but it's a big job."

"Yes, I imagine a place like this would be a big job." Gracie aimed a sardonic I-told-you-so gaze at Caroline.

Caroline walked right past Deborah, pushing Gracie's pessimism out of her mind, and stepped into the center of what could be a beautifully welcoming foyer. Even through the dust she could see the exquisite woodwork in the crown molding and wainscoting. "It's cherrywood isn't it?" Caroline asked, looking back at Gracie, as her fingers whispered over the elegant panels, molding and rails.

Gracie pulled a tissue from the pocket of her pink capris and rubbed a circle of dust from the trim, exposing the deep and rich reddish-brown wood. "Definitely cherry. You can tell by just how smooth the wood is." Gracie smiled softly. "It was probably a yellowish pink when the inn was built, but it changes with age, and this wood has darkened beautifully."

"A touch of lemon oil and a soft cloth will bring out its luster," Deborah added. "It's the same wood that's on the banister."

Caroline turned to look at the stairs and smiled when she saw how they curved gently toward the second-floor landing. She'd seen dozens of elegant staircases in her travels, most far more dramatic than this one. Still, as she skimmed her fingers along the dusty cherry wood, she could easily imagine a Victorian woman dressed in burgundy taffeta and white lace sweeping down the staircase, twirling a frilly parasol as she headed out for the day to make calls on her friends. That image turned to a modern bride in white satin, a wreath of rosebuds in her hair, a nosegay of pink, yellow, and red roses clasped in her hands.

"Are the stairs structurally sound?" Sam asked.

"Oh, can't you see the banister draped with evergreen garland and red velvet bows at Christmas? Or the grandchildren—your Zachary, Jacob, and Evelyn," Caroline said to Gracie, "sliding down from the second floor?"

"Their mother would have my head if I let them slide down a banister. You know what a mama bear Stacy can be at times."

"But wouldn't it be fun?" Caroline raced halfway up the steps and then glided down the stairs. "If I weren't"—she cleared her throat—"the age I am, I might give it a shot."

"I believe I slid down it a time or two," Deborah said, her businesslike demeanor easing just a little. "Back in the sixties my friends and I used to sneak into the inn to see what kind of cookies and other treats were laid out for the guests. When no one was watching, we'd use the banister as a slide." She smiled. "I'd almost forgotten what a good time I'd had back then. But come on, there's so much more to see."

Caroline trailed her fingers over the peeling wallpaper on the foyer walls, imagining just how welcoming the entry would be with crisp paint and a soft, flowery wallpaper that reflected what visitors saw in the garden. And Gracie was so good at flower arranging. She could work wonders in each room with a freshly picked bouquet.

Deborah led them into a large, open room just off the foyer.

"This was once a ballroom," Deborah said, interrupting Caroline's musing. "In more recent years, it's been used as a parlor or sort of formal living room. As you can see, the previous owners took advantage of its size"— she gestured around the room—"but, sadly, I don't believe they took advantage of the windows that look out across the garden."

"These aren't the original windows," Gracie said, walking straight to the back of the room, which was lit only by the artificial lights, since the windows had been shuttered tight, blocking the view.

"When the home was turned into an inn back in the fifties, the original windows were removed and replaced with more expansive panes of glass to afford the guests the very best view of the ocean and the sunsets," said Deborah.

"Did they get rid of the old windows?" Gracie asked, her architect's mind concerned about the integrity of the original building.

"I don't know for sure," Deborah said, "but if my guess is correct, they were stored in the basement or out in the carriage house, should a new owner wish to restore the home to the original."

"As lovely as that would be," Caroline said, "I can't imagine living here without having full access to the view." She wished she could see it now from where she stood, but she'd seen it a couple of days before when she'd stood on the veranda. It was definitely a sight to behold.

"And all of these antiques stay with the inn?" Sam asked. She peeked under a white sheet to reveal a plush sofa covered in what was now a dingy jacquard print, all dirty pink roses and lackluster green leaves.

"Yes, everything here stays." Deborah carefully unfolded a dusty white cover from an elaborately carved table sitting at the back of the sofa. "Even the Majolica, like this piece," she said, lightly caressing a colorful large tabletop figurine of dolphins and seashells, "not to mention the tableware, the linens and lace, and my favorite piece in the inn—the piano."

They'd seen the piano when peeking through the windows, and Caroline had barely been able to take her eyes off of it when they'd entered the parlor. Her fingers were already stroking the keys, which were made from genuine ivory and ebony. She'd taken endless hours of piano lessons when she was young, but was less than proficient. She could maybe play "Chopsticks" with a partner and peck out simple pieces, but what she really wished she could play was *Rhapsody in Blue*. Right now, though, she was afraid to plunk the keys, positive she'd hear dull thuds instead of the glorious melody an antique like this should produce.

"It's gorgeous," Sam said, the pads of her fingers whispering over the dusty, dark reddish-brown rosewood. "This must have cost a small fortune back in its day."

"It would probably be worth quite a bit now," Deborah said, circling the piano slowly, "though I'm sure it would benefit from some restoration."

Caroline gingerly touched the ancient ivories, hesitantly picking out the first few melancholy notes of Beethoven's *Moonlight Sonata*. It was out of tune, but it played.

Sam clapped when Caroline finished and then sat next to her sister and—as they'd done when they were kids—plunked out a bit of "Heart and Soul," their fingers moving over the keyboard perfectly in time with each other.

Gracie folding her arms atop the ornate, old-fashioned, square grand. "On the other hand, the carving on this thing is a mass of nooks and crannies. Can you imagine how many hours you'd have to spend each week dusting it?"

"It would be worth it," Caroline said. "Just imagine what it would sound like if it was tuned." Caroline offered a little trill on the keys. "Can't you imagine sitting around this piano on a cold winter's night, with a fire flickering?"

"Drinking hot cocoa," Sam added. "With homemade snickerdoodles."

It certainly needed work. Specks of ivory and ebony were chipped off some of the keys, though they were mostly intact. But that didn't make it any less beautiful. Caroline tried not to think about the expense involved in having it tuned and restored. "I can't believe they just left all this," Sam said, rising from the piano bench and turning in a full circle to taking in the full view of the room. "It's like the inn, the antiques, and everything else inside didn't matter to them at all."

"As I mentioned, they had other business ventures they were interested in." Deborah removed another dust cover, revealing yet another antique table and another piece of brightly colored Majolica pottery. "They were frustrated in their efforts to remodel the inn and simply gave up and moved on to something more their style—a contemporary hotel in Miami."

Caroline couldn't imagine anyone leaving the inn. She was ready to move in right then and there, without an inspection, without George taking a look and giving her his blessing. It seemed to be calling out her name, and she knew she had to buy it.

If only Gracie and Sam would go in on it with her. She wasn't quite sure she could refurbish the place and run it as a B and B all on her own.

"Why don't the three of you wander around and take a peek at the library off to your right. The dining room, kitchen, and owners' quarters are to the left of the foyer, and when you're through down here, we'll move on up to the second-floor bedrooms."

On their way into the library, Caroline, Gracie, and Sam left flip-flop prints on the dusty wooden floorboards. Deborah walked in behind them, flicked on the overhead light, and the room brightened to reveal the rich wood the sales flyer had mentioned. Empty bookcases lined three walls. A lovely, ornately carved fireplace occupied part of another wall, with a bronze light sconce on either side. A massive desk sat atop a nearly threadbare Oriental rug. That would definitely have to go, but Caroline couldn't miss the sparkle in Gracie's eyes. Reading was one of her passions. The tabletops in her home were piled high with books.

"If—and that's a huge if," Gracie said, "the three of us were insane enough to purchase this place, I can picture myself sitting in here reading biographies about everyone imaginable. I could go haunting garage sales and the Rarest Books shop downtown to fill the shelves, and—"

"And picking flowers from the garden outside and arranging grand bouquets to fill the room with their fragrance and color." Caroline slung an arm around Gracie's shoulder. "You're warming up to the inn, aren't you?"

"Actually"—Gracie slipped away from Caroline to inspect the desk—"I've been thinking about the dusting, the window washing, and keeping these floors clean. It'll take a lot more than just running a vacuum cleaner over them once a day. They'll need buffing and—"

"And new carpets to replace the old ones," Sam interrupted. "Wouldn't it be fun checking out the carpet stores in Boston to see what we can find? Hopefully we can get a few at a bargain price."

Caroline's heart was feeling a little lighter. Sam seemed to be warming to the idea of buying the inn, and Gracie, even though she still balked at it, was showing hints of interest.

"You know," Caroline said, "the three of us complement each other really well. Gracie worries about how much work the place will be; Sam puts everything in perspective; and I'm ready to throw a party, no matter the cost, no matter the work involved. In fact—"

Caroline grabbed Gracie's hand and pulled her back into the parlor. Once Sam joined them, Caroline walked to the center of the room and twirled around. "Can't you just imagine what this room was like filled with men in tuxes, women in satin and taffeta and feathers dancing around to the strains of Mozart played on vio—"

She sneezed. The air was filled with dust. It smelled musty, and like something was rotting. But Caroline was captivated. "If you can't imagine it in the past, think of it a year from now, once we've got this room cleaned up and refurbished. Picture this table over here"— she peeled the yellowed dust cover off yet another antique—"with a four-tiered wedding cake, all white frosting and pink roses, and a lovely bride gliding into the room on her father's arm, with a man—her husband-to-be—smiling at her with so much love in his eyes that you find yourself crying.

"And then the music begins, something soft, maybe Some Enchanted Evening. The groom sweeps the bride into his arms, and they dance their first dance as husband and wife." Caroline sighed. "If I were in my twenties again, if I had ever had any thoughts of getting married, I'd hold the ceremony right here."

"No you wouldn't." Sam plunked a few jaunted keys on the piano. "You'd be down on the beach, barefoot, and carrying one simple rose."

"Okay, so maybe my dreams are too grandiose—"

"No they're not," Gracie said solemnly. "They're the same dreams Mom would have shared with us if she were here right now."

Caroline felt tears well up at this unexpected gift from Gracie.

"She'd be happy, wouldn't she?" Sam said. "All smiles, dreaming up menus for the wedding feast yet to come."

"And she'd be in the kitchen right now checking it out," Caroline said, latching on to her sisters' hands. "Let's see if it's as perfect as it sounds in the sales flyer."

"Oh dear." Sam stood in the center of the kitchen. She was not quite horrified, but she wasn't encouraged by what she saw. "It looks like some of the wildlife of Nantucket has taken up residence in here."

"Actually, it was a couple of vagrants," Deborah said, picking up the one lonely business card left by an agent who'd shown the inn, or at least visited it. "Fortunately, someone saw them coming and going from the inn far too often and called the police. We've boarded it up tight since then."

"They didn't steal anything, I hope?" Sam said.

"No, they simply left behind a lot of filth."

"Is there a security system?" Gracie asked, opening the white pebbled refrigerator. A forlorn-looking box of baking soda its sole occupant. "Yes," Deborah said, "but, as I'm sure you've guessed, the current owners don't want to spend the money to keep it activated."

"If they had"—Caroline chuckled—"we could have been caught trying to peek through the shutters and hauled off to jail."

"All that aside," Deborah continued, "the kitchen isn't fancy, but it is fairly up-to-date."

A good kitchen doesn't need sleek modern counters and cabinets to function well, Sam thought, checking out the 1980s era white painted cabinetry and laminate work surfaces. Everything needed a good scrubbing, and the stove and oven might need servicing, but all in all, it would work.

Still, there was so much work to do around the inn to make it shine. She hoped the rest of the rooms wouldn't leave a sour taste in her mouth.

They toured the owners' quarters next. There were two bedrooms and a shared bathroom, but the rooms were good-sized and had large windows that looked out over the garden and let in a lot of light. They would need to figure out who would have to share if they did end up buying the inn. They then headed upstairs and started touring the second floor. The upstairs hall was lined with a thick, dusty carpet and painted a dingy yellow-beige that had scuff marks all along the walls. "As it says in the sales brochure, each guest room comes with its own bath." Deborah opened the door to the first guest room to the right of the stairs, and Sam followed her sisters inside.

"What do you think, ladies?"

"Beautiful," Sam whispered. The walls were a light pink, and the trim was painted a cheery white, and there was a fireplace with a wide mantle. The floors were scuffed and would need to be refinished, but they were a light, wide-plank hardwood. There were two windows, one looking toward Shirley Addison's house, and the other facing the back of the house, looking out directly onto the beach. The windows were shuttered, but she could imagine the view.

She suddenly found herself caught up in Caroline's dream world, picturing a Victorian woman in a ruffled white cotton nightgown that covered her from neck to wrist to toe letting her dark wavy hair down for the night. Sam could almost see her standing at the window, looking out at the ocean, wondering when her mariner husband would be coming home from sea.

"Once a lot of elbow grease is applied," Gracie added. Sam's vision burst like a bubble. Gracie seemed determined to find a complaint about everything, but finally a smile pushed away her frown. "Of course, that four-poster bed is amazing." It was a dark wood—Sam wasn't sure what, but surely Gracie would know—and the headboard was carved with an elaborate fleur-de-lis. "I can just imagine what it would look like with a canopy of lace."

"Battenburg lace." Caroline said. "With crisp white linens and a down comforter."

"And locally made chocolates resting on the pillow when the guests turn in for the night," Sam added. "Or I could make them myself. I have the perfect recipe, and I could get candy molds shaped like whales or seashells."

The other two guest rooms were in similar shape. One looked out over the front of the house, and the other would have a view of the ocean and the coastline up to the north. The bathrooms in each room were dated, with pink tiles and fixtures, and would need to be redone. But all the work appeared to be cosmetic. There were no cracks or mold spots or any indication that there were structural problems.

They laughed and chatted all the way through the rest of the house—the linen closets, the dining room, the basement, even the attic, piled high with boxes that no doubt had been there for decades. They wished they could rip away all the shutters so they could see what the rooms would look like with sunshine pouring in. Finally, Deborah ushered them outside.

"Should you decide you want to make an offer—a serious offer," Deborah emphasized, closing the door behind them when they stepped out onto the front porch, "I'll talk to the owner about having the shutters removed. It's amazing the difference natural light can make."

"You don't by any chance have estimates from contractors giving approximate costs for making repairs, do you?" Sam asked, knowing they'd have to take that into consideration before making any kind of offer. If they made an offer.

"I do, as a matter of fact. I can copy them for you if you'd like to drop by my office to pick them up." Deborah looked at her watch again. "I can't get them for you until tomorrow, I'm afraid, and I do have another appointment to get to in just a little while, but I'd like to show you the carriage house before we leave."

"Tomorrow's fine," Sam said, following Deborah along the crushed-shell-and-gravel drive that wound its way past the garden to a two-story clapboard building painted the same faded and peeling buttercup yellow.

"I've always thought this carriage house could be turned into a charming rental, if anyone was willing to empty out the contents. I'm afraid a lot has been shoved inside by many different owners. Grace Brothers, the hotel company that bought the inn back in the fifties, did a rather quick remodel of the inn, adding the bathrooms to the guest rooms upstairs, replacing a few doors and windows, but as far as I know, the attic and the inside of the carriage house were never touched."

Deborah stopped in front of the carriage house's double sliding doors. They were warped from wind and rain and snow, not to mention time. "The carriage house, like the inn, was built in the 1850s," Deborah said, jiggling a key in the rusty padlock, proving once again that the inn and the carriage house hadn't been shown to interested buyers in a very long time.

"Do you know much about the history of the inn?" Gracie asked as Deborah struggled with the lock.

"Not much beyond its recent history. There's not as much about it in the history books as you would find if it had belonged to one of Nantucket's original founders, people like the Folgers, Macys, and Starbucks. But I believe it was built with whaling money originally."

Gracie glanced at Caroline and then asked, "We heard that the original owner's wife disappeared. Have you heard anything about that?"

"I've heard that rumor, but it's such ancient history that I never really paid attention." She put her body weight into turning the key in the lock, but it didn't budge. "There are also rumors about hidden rooms. I don't know if that's true either. However, if you wanted to play up that history in your inn's advertising, you might be able to attract some guests that way. A lot of people are drawn to places with mysterious pasts."

Sam wasn't sure she wanted people like that staying at their inn—not that it was their inn yet, or ever would be. Just then, her cell phone rang with Jamie's familiar ring. She pulled it from her backpack. Then she excused herself for just a moment, sensing it might be some time before Deborah was able to open the carriage house doors.

"Hi, sweetheart. What's up?"

"Not much. Kind of quiet here, so I thought I'd give you a quick call to see what you're up to."

But Jamie's voice was strained, and Sam sensed that something far more than just some downtime had led to the call. "Everything okay? You haven't changed your mind about coming to the island, have you?"

"Oh no, I'm still coming. In fact, Mom, I'm wondering if it would be okay for me to come early. Tomorrow maybe?"

"Of course that's okay." She'd ask Jamie what was troubling her, what had prompted her to make such a sudden change in her plans, but if something dreadful had happened, Jamie would tell her immediately. If it could wait, it might be best to talk face to face, so Sam could hug her daughter if she needed it. "Are you flying in?"

"Driving to Hyannis and taking the ferry. I'll call you in the morning to let you know what time I'll be in."

They chatted for another moment or two, and Sam couldn't help but worry when she ended the call. Something was wrong. She just knew it. And Sam had a strong suspicion whatever was wrong had to do with Cory Lippincott.

"Everything okay?" Gracie asked, when Sam joined her sisters again.

Sam nodded, giving Gracie a quick rundown. "I'll pick her up at the ferry—"

"At last!"

Deborah removed the padlock, fanned her face, which had broken out into a bit of a sweat, and with Caroline's help, the two of them pushed open the doors to the carriage house, letting the sun pour inside.

"You weren't kidding about a lot of stuff being piled up in here." Gracie stepped inside, attempting to wind through boxes stacked from wood plank floor to ceiling. "Is there a second floor up there?"

"Yes," Deborah said. "An apartment actually, and the stairs are outside. And—so the story goes—there's a secret entrance to a hidden room in here somewhere, although where it could be is beyond me. Of course, as I said before, tales like that give the inn a little more mystique, a little more charm. They draw guests to a B and B, which, again, makes the place more valuable."

Deborah was doing her best to sell the inn. Sam jotted down another entry in her notebook, yet another reason for the owners to accept a much lower price: Ghosts? Although intriguing, they could scare off some guests.

Caroline pulled a box down from one of the stacks, opened it up, and she and Sam peered inside to find an endless number of old *National Geographic* magazines. "These are from back in the thirties." Caroline grinned. "So much has changed since then."

"Think they're worth anything?" Sam asked, making another note to check out the magazines on eBay to see what kind of prices sellers were getting.

"Depends on who's interested," Deborah stated. "I see them in antique stores quite often. They'd also look nice on the library shelves. Something for the inn's guests to peruse on a stormy day."

"Sam! Caroline!" Gracie called out from somewhere deep inside the carriage house. "Come see what I've found."

Squeezing through the boxes and inhaling mold and mildew and who knows what else, made breathing downright difficult. Sam coughed and sputtered as she followed Caroline and the sound of Gracie's voice.

Suddenly, Caroline stopped dead in her tracks. "Oh my!"

"What is it?" Sam asked, but Caroline and Gracie didn't need to answer. Over Caroline's shoulder, Sam saw it—an old car. A very big, old car.

Gracie tugged the cloth partially covering it the rest of the way off, revealing empty mousetraps atop the cherry red hood. The paint had been dulled by time, but Sam imagined it would shine bright with a lot of Turtle Wax. The person who'd stored the car must have known what they were doing, because it seemed to be in impeccable condition—no gashes or gouges and no apparent rust on the body, although there was no telling what it might look like underneath. "Does this come with the inn too?" Sam shouted back at Deborah, who hadn't ventured inside.

"Everything inside the inn, everything inside the carriage house, and everything on the property is part of the price."

Sam wondered if Deborah even knew there was an old car hidden away. The tires were flat, but with their wide white sidewalls, they looked original. There was no telling if the car would run, or if it even had an engine or anything at all under the hood, but what a find. Their dad had always loved old cars. He might have even ridden in or owned one like this once upon a time.

"Do you know what kind of car it is?" Sam whispered to Gracie and Caroline.

"Packard," Caroline said, using the hem of her shirt to rub away the built-up grime on the logo above the oversized front fender. "Can you see through the windows, Gracie? Does the upholstery look good?"

"The glass is a bit murky, but everything appears to be in good condition, even the leather upholstery."

"No rat nests?" Sam asked. "No other creatures living inside?"

"Not that I can see," Gracie said. If this car was in decent condition, Sam suspected it could finance a year's college tuition at a good school. If they bought the inn, there was no telling how much they could make selling off this, and a lot of the antiques. They could then furnish their B and B with pieces that would be easier to clean and would look fresh and up-to-date. But then the inn would lose too much of its charm. Its magic.

"Caroline! Sam! Gracie! I need to get going," Deborah called out to them. "Next time you can look till your heart's content, but right now, I need to lock up."

"Be there in just a minute," Sam hollered back. Next time. Somehow, Deborah seemed certain they would be back. And Sam was beginning to think that maybe she was right.

CHAPTER
Eleven

*T*here must have been a hundred or more seagulls circling the docks when the ferry from Hyannis pulled into the harbor on Friday. From where Sam stood in the waiting area, she could see the passengers packed in like sardines, eager to disembark after the hour-long ride from the mainland to the island. She was even more eager to hit the shops, the restaurants, and the beaches with Jamie.

As long as Jamie was up to it. She'd halfway expected her daughter to call last night, but she hadn't, and now she anticipated a tearful reunion. If Cory had broken Jamie's heart, Sam just might have to hunt him down in Manhattan and wring his neck.

But for now, all Sam wanted to do was hug her daughter. Sam shaded her eyes with her right hand, watching the ferry's passengers disembark. Slowly but surely, the crowd thinned, and at long last she spotted her daughter. Jamie was tall like her dad, the man who'd turned out to be far too controlling for Sam to stay married to. He'd disappeared from Jamie's life when she was barely a year old, and Sam had played mom and dad ever since.

Jamie's strawberry blonde ponytail bounced up and down as she made her way off the ferry, carrying a duffel bag, a backpack slung over her shoulders, and wearing jeans and a fitted cotton top.

"Hey, Mom!"

Jamie had her arms around Sam in an instant. She dropped her duffel bag on the ground at her feet so she could use both arms. She hugged Sam extra tight. That's when Sam first heard Jamie sniff. She held her daughter out to arm's length and saw the tears in her red-rimmed eyes.

"Oh, honey, I knew something was wrong." Sam smoothed away Jamie's tears. "Let's get in the car, and you can tell me what's wrong."

Rather than head for their cottage, which was only a few blocks away, they rode in near silence for three miles and pulled into the parking lot at Dionis Beach. The early afternoon sky was a clear, breathtaking sapphire, and the silver sand was dotted with colorful towels and striped umbrellas. Children ran up and down the shore, and lifeguards in tall stands watched over the people playing in the surf. Arm in arm, they walked down to the shore, where the water was calm and they were sheltered by dunes.

Jamie sat at the base of a dune, where sea grass grew all around, and hugged her knees close to her. She looked out at the westerly sky and the colorful sails on the boats lazing on the water. Sam sat beside her, quiet, waiting for Jamie to open up.

"How's your research going?" Sam said to fill the silence.

Jamie acted as if she hadn't even heard. She was focused on the horizon.

"I called it quits with Cory yesterday," Jamie finally said.

That wasn't exactly what Sam had expected to hear, but she was relieved. Thrilled. Yet so, so sorry for her daughter's pain. "Want to tell me what happened?"

"It all seems rather trivial now."

"Breakups are never trivial, honey."

"Cory and I were supposed to get together for dinner the other night, but an hour before, he canceled. Apparently he'd been invited to a networking event with one of his friends from law school, and some people were going to be there from a firm he really wants to work for."

"I thought he had a job lined up?" Sam was fuzzy on the details, but she thought Jamie had said he would be working for a small firm after he passed the bar.

"He does." Jamie pulled off her sandal and buried her toes in the sand. "But this is a big corporate firm with offices all over the world. Apparently if he got a job there, he could work on bigger, more important cases."

"And make more money." That seemed to be what motivated most of Cory's decisions, from what she'd seen.

"Exactly. And I guess I was just tired of coming last in his life. He assumed it was okay to cancel on me because I was less important than his career. I'd been feeling like that for a while, and this was just the last straw." Jamie turned her head and looked at her mom. "So last night, I told him we were finished."

"I'm sorry, honey." Sam tried to choose her words carefully. She didn't want to make Jamie feel any worse than she already did. "But I think you did the right thing."

Jamie nodded. "I can't believe I put up with everything for so long. He sometimes canceled on me to play handball with the guys, or forgot about our dates because he got so wrapped up in his studying. He criticized my apartment and the fact that I lived in Brooklyn over and over, and laughed about it in front of me and his friends. But the other night was the last straw."

"I'd been telling myself that things would get better once Cory passed the bar, but the other day I realized things weren't going to get better."

"It must have been hard to do it."

"Sometimes the right thing is hard."

"That's true." Sam linked her arm through Jamie's and looked out at the ocean. "How'd you get to be so smart?"

"I always figured I'd been switched at birth," Jamie said, and laughed. Sam tossed a handful of sand at her.

"Just don't ever sell yourself short, Jamie. You deserve someone far, far better than Cory could ever dream of being. It's his loss that he didn't see that."

Jamie drew in a deep breath, and another tear slid down her face. "I know I did the right thing, Mom, but"—she let out a sigh—"it hurts. A lot."

"Then you've come to the right place. We'll have popcorn tonight, with loads of butter; we'll take a long walk on the beach. And Gracie insists we watch another Cary Grant movie tonight— *Bringing Up Baby*."

"Is that the one with Katharine Hepburn and the leopard?"

Sam nodded. "And Cary running around in Hepburn's silky nightgown. You've got to love a guy like that. One who can make you laugh."

"I definitely need a good laugh. Tomorrow morning I plan to wake up with a smile on my face, and Cory totally pushed out of my mind."

"Good, because tomorrow night we're going to a clambake, and if you're lucky, I might just take you out to see the most magical place on all of Nantucket."

Even though Jamie was intrigued by that comment, even though she asked questions, Sam didn't tell her anything about Misty Harbor Inn. Giving her something else to focus on was a good way to push Cory Lippincott straight out of Jamie's mind.

Caroline was in the kitchen when her niece walked in later that afternoon with her strawberry blonde hair wrapped in a towel.

"Is that what I think it is?" Jamie asked.

"Sure is," Caroline said, taking a couple of dessert plates out of a cabinet and grabbing forks and napkins. "Your grandma's prune cake. I was dreaming about eating a piece and when I woke up this morning, your mom was here in the kitchen whipping it up."

Caroline cut into the dark, moist cake. The buttermilk glaze shimmered on top, and the scents of cinnamon, nutmeg, and allspice wrapped around her. She scooped up an extra-large piece and put it on a plate and handed it to Jamie, along with a fork. "How about a big glass of milk too?"

Jamie tilted her head, studying Caroline. Caroline recognized the gesture. It was the same way she'd always analyzed anything she'd been curious about. "Mom must have told you I called it quits with Cory, but really, Aunt Caroline, I'm okay. You don't need to treat me extra special."

Caroline smiled warmly. She might have told her that that hadn't been her plan, but Sam and Gracie came bounding in the front door, their arms full of groceries.

"You aren't eating my cake already, are you?" Sam said, frowning when both Caroline and Jamie took their first bites. "I just bought ice cream to go with it and—"

"I know Grandma always served it with vanilla bean ice cream, Mom, but really, it's better all by itself."

"And if you skip the ice cream," Caroline added, "you can have seconds on the cake and not feel the least bit guilty."

"I don't think you should ever feel guilty about having seconds on dessert," Gracie stated. She opened the refrigerator and put away a half gallon of low-fat milk, a head of romaine, a bag of deep red tomatoes, as well as celery hearts, and cucumbers. That meant they'd be eating salad tonight. Which also meant Caroline needed to eat maybe three pieces of cake. Salad, she'd always believed, was for rabbits.

"What's all this?" Jamie asked, as she picked up the Misty Harbor Inn sales flyer lying on the kitchen counter.

Gracie glared at Caroline for one short moment, once again raising her brow. "That, Jamie, is a sales flyer for the inn your Aunt Caroline wants to buy."

Jamie looked from Gracie to Caroline, frowning. "Really?"

"It would be a big venture," Sam said, cutting a slice of cake for Gracie and for herself, "and nothing's etched in stone yet. We don't know the first thing about permits, or financing—"

"There wouldn't have to be any financing," Caroline reminded Sam, "if we pooled our inheritance money." She glanced at Gracie. "Which is one very touchy subject at the moment."

"That's because I don't want to buy the inn," Gracie said. She picked up her plate and sat down in one of the overstuffed chairs in the living room, just across from the kitchen. Max was instantly at her side, his tongue hanging out in anticipation. "Your mom and Aunt Caroline both think I'm a stick-in-the mud, but I'm not sure I want to own an inn."

Jamie looked at the flyer again and scanned it quickly, and at long last Caroline saw Jamie's gaze hit the bottom line: the price. Jamie let out a long, high-pitched whistle. Her eyes were wide in disbelief when she looked from Caroline to her mother. "You can't seriously afford this place, can you?"

"Seriously?" Sam said. "Maybe. But we have to look at the whole picture first. Which reminds me." Sam opened her purse and pulled out a sealed envelope. Caroline could see the Deborah Greenleaf Realtor logo on the upper left-hand corner. "I picked up the construction estimates." Sam dropped the envelope on the counter and took a bite of cake.

Before Caroline could grab the envelope, Jamie said, "Construction estimates?" She picked up the flyer again and more carefully studied the colored pictures of the inn. "It says something here about it needing a little tender loving care. Why do I get the feeling 'little' really means a lot?"

Gracie nodded. "It's rundown," she said. "Very run down."

"It's not nearly as bad as Gracie says," Caroline stated, scooping up a second piece of cake and putting it on her plate before heading for a comfy chair in the living room. "A new roof, I'm guessing. Paint, wallpaper—"

"New electrical. New plumbing." Gracie shook her head and turned to Jamie. "Your mom and Caroline don't see the flaws."

"But I do, Gracie," Caroline said, pinching off a piece of cake and feeding it to Max, who'd just licked Gracie's plate clean. "I see every speck of dirt and dust. I felt every creak in the wood and every loose floorboard, but I also can see past all of that. I think you can too. You just don't want to admit it."

Gracie kicked off her flip-flops and curled her legs up on the sofa. "Okay, I admit it, I couldn't help but notice all the beautiful antiques and the stained glass, and maybe, if I were thirty-five again, maybe even forty, I'd consider going in on it with you and Sam. If Sam's even interested."

"I am. Most definitely."

"You are?" Jamie frowned. "It's a big house for three people."

"It's been an inn for over sixty years," Sam said. "It wouldn't be just our home, it would be a B and B too."

"But you'd have to work again," Jamie said, her eyes narrowed, her hair still wrapped in a towel. "I thought you were enjoying retirement."

"I have endless amounts of free time," Sam said, "It's something I've never had before, and as much as I hate to admit it, I feel useless. That's not a good thing at fifty-two." Caroline had been surprised when Sam announced she was planning to retire a few years back, but careful planning, saving wisely, and the alimony checks she'd received from her ex had allowed her to squirrel away more money than her sisters had realized. "I've got too many good years left to sit around doing nothing."

"You don't do nothing," Jamie said. "You cook. You cross-stitch."

"Hobbies. I need something more to fill my days."

"What about the townhouse?" Jamie said. Caroline could see she was uncertain about the idea of giving up the house where she'd grown up.

"You've lived there since Jamie was little," Gracie said. "You couldn't possibly give it up."

"Why not?" Sam asked. "Jamie's not there any longer."

"I could never feel that way." Gracie looked aghast. "All of my memories of Art are in my home—our home. When I'm there, I can still feel him at my side. When I'm in the garden, I can see him pulling weeds or planting his beloved sunflowers. He painted the walls. He built the addition onto the back." She sighed heavily. "It's been my home since I moved away from Mom and Dad. I could never leave it."

"Aren't you all jumping the gun?" Jamie said, sitting down cross-legged on the floor. She fed the remnants of her piece of cake to Max. "I mean, do you even know how to run an inn? Shouldn't you think about that before deciding to buy the place? Right now all I see are two, maybe three women who think they can walk into that inn and have guests magically appear. You need a marketing plan."

"A restoration plan too," Sam added, "and restoration isn't cheap, believe you me, especially here in Nantucket. Of course, the costs for labor and material that I saw in the estimates could be inflated, and I don't know the first thing about the contractors who gave Deborah Greenleaf those prices. They could be high-end builders, when we could probably find someone who works more in the world of reality."

"Are you going to tell us how much the estimates are for?" Gracie asked. "Or do you plan on keeping that information to yourself?"

"Oh…" Sam shrugged, smiling uncomfortably. "I imagine we could very well double the sales price of the home before we were done. Depending on how much we'd want done."

Gracie coughed.

Jamie whistled.

Caroline groaned. She shut her eyes and sighed, seeing nothing but dollar signs twirling around and around. Would it really cost that much to make Mom's Misty Harbor dreams come true?

CHAPTER
Twelve

*I*s the Misty Harbor Inn the magical place you said you wanted to show me?" Jamie asked, stopping beside Sam to peek through the window of a Nantucket souvenir shop on Main Street. The sun was lower in the sky, and it had cooled off a bit after the midday heat, but the air was still warm and pleasant.

"That's the magical place, all right," Sam said. "I know the price seems high—"

"More like astronomical, Mom."

"That's pretty typical for Nantucket. Everything here's expensive, but it's beautiful, isn't it?"

"A little rich for my blood. But who knows? It might grow on me while I'm here."

Jamie dragged Sam into the shop so she could try on ball caps, beginning with a pink one with a rhinestone skull and crossbones on the front. "What do you think?" Jamie asked, modeling it for Sam before looking at herself in the mirror.

"Not bad, but I don't quite see you as a rhinestones kind of girl."

"Me neither." Jamie tugged off that cap and looked around for another one. "You must have liked vacationing here when you were a kid," Jamie said, settling a black cap on her head. The hat was embroidered with a pale blue whale. "I'm surprised we never came here when I was growing up."

"I liked the cross-country road trips we went on. And you were the one who always wanted to hit up every tourist mecca along the way and eat all that junk food"

"And you always managed to find the tackiest motels."

"Tacky, my eye. I looked for places that were modest and clean, and you always had a pool to swim in after a long day in the car."

Jamie pulled off the latest cap, tucked it away with hundreds of other souvenirs, and tugged Sam out of the store, back into the sun-dappled shadows beneath the canopy of trees lining Main Street.

"Remember our trip to Disneyland, when you got lost driving on the LA freeway? We ended up halfway to the Mexican border."

"Oh, I remember all right. You were eight and you were crying because you wanted to see Mickey Mouse and you just knew he'd be gone from the park by the time we got there."

They walked down Main Street, past cafés and clothing boutiques and sweet little gift shops. Sam knew that if she had the rest of her life, she couldn't get tired of poking around in all these stores.

"Somewhere in all my junk, I've got the photo you took of me and Mickey in front of the Matterhorn." Jamie winked at Sam. "You were a pretty good mom, I guess."

Sam laughed.

"Want some ice cream?" Jamie asked as they approached Sweet Dreams, the best ice cream shop on the island. Sam nodded. They had just had cake, but right now, as Jamie was healing her broken

heart, she'd indulge her every whim. They joined a line that snaked
out the door and a ways down the block.

"Want to see the inn tomorrow?" Sam asked. The line inched
forward, and they passed people settled on little bistro tables outside
the shop. Sam eyed the paper cups mounded with mint chip and
cookie dough ice cream and the homemade wafer cones piled high
with hot fudge sauce and sprinkles. She couldn't decide.

Jamie's eyes lit up. "Could we?"

There was only one way to find out.

Sam dug into her bag, pulled out her cell phone, and dialed
Deborah Greenleaf's number, which she'd already programmed in.
She talked with the broker for a few minutes. "By the way, could you
have the shutters opened or removed? We'd really love to see the
view from inside."

Sam winked at Jamie.

"Actually," there was an edge of hesitancy in Deborah's word,
"the owner has told me he won't remove the shutters until he has an
offer in hand. I'm terribly sorry, but—"

"But the view's one of the biggest selling features of the inn,"
Sam said. "Could you talk with the owner again?"

Sam could almost see Deborah shaking her head. "No. I'm afraid
not."

Sam tried yet again and then finally confirmed a time and told
Deborah she'd see her tomorrow.

"We're on for noon tomorrow." Sam smiled, although the owner's
refusal to throw open the shutters left a sour taste in her mouth.

"Gracie's going to have a fit that I made an appointment to go
out to the inn again, but I'm sure down deep inside she'll be excited.
Caroline will be thrilled."

"Do you really think this place is worth all this trouble?"

"Just you wait and see."

At long last, they ordered a banana split loaded with nuts and whipped cream, and they asked for two cherries on top. They grabbed a just-vacated table outside where they could talk and people watch.

"Hey, look at that, Mom."

Sam followed Jamie's finger to an old car stopped in traffic.

"That's got to be the most awesome car I've ever seen." Jamie turned her camera toward the dark blue vehicle with big, bug-eye headlights, spoke wheels, a ton of chrome, and massive tires with rims that were painted pale yellow and cream.

Jamie snapped a few more photos of the car, before it disappeared, heading toward the harbor. "You know, Mom, if I were going to get married—which is really the furthest thing from my mind right now—and I did it here on Nantucket, I'd want to ride to church in a car just like that."

"Well…if, and that's a big *if*, Aunt Caroline—or maybe all of us—were to buy the Misty Harbor Inn, would you settle for riding to the church in a cherry red Packard station wagon?"

"I don't even know what a Packard station wagon looks like."

"Remind me to show you a picture of one when we get back to the cottage. And if you're really lucky, tomorrow you'll get to see a Packard, because there's one pretty much hidden in the carriage house, and it comes part and parcel with the inn. And just wait until you see the antiques, especially the piano."

"You're started to sound just like Aunt Caroline." Jamie licked hot fudge off her spoon. "Are you really serious about buying the inn? Could you really move here, give up your townhouse, your friends?"

Sam had to think about the last part of that question. She had a wide circle of friends. She had her counted cross-stitch club. The townhouse association. It was sometimes too contentious, but they had great progressive dinners. There were always students who remembered her and stopped her on the street to say hello. But she didn't have family in Upstate New York. Jamie was on her own, and she loved living in Brooklyn. She'd never move back to Saratoga Springs.

"You know, Jamie, I think I could give all of that up. Not my friends, of course. But we can call each other. We can get together a couple of times a year. I just want be closer to Caroline and Gracie. And owning a B and B was one of Mom's dreams. It would be nice to make that dream come true for her, even now."

"But you've never worked as a waitress or housekeeper—"

"I kept a spotless house. Well"—Sam smiled—"nearly spotless. Maybe a little cluttered, but your books were always dropped on the nearest flat surface, and your backpack and shoes—"

"I know, Mom, I've never given much thought or time to housekeeping either, but do you really want to devote your retirement years to entertaining people? Washing other people's sheets and towels? Cooking for strangers?"

"Don't think I haven't given those things a lot of thought. The cooking's no problem; that's something I'd adore. Cleaning?" Sam shrugged. "Not exactly my cup of tea, but there are trade-offs in everything. Just wait until you see the inn. It just grabs on and doesn't want to let you go."

"You know, Mom, it sounds like you're already made up your mind to go in on it with Aunt Caroline. Maybe you should stop worrying so much about all the logistics and just do it."

Sam scraped the last little bit of hot fudge from the bottom of the bowl. "You've spent the last fifteen minutes questioning my motives and my real desire to do something absolutely crazy, and now you're pushing me to move forward. What's with you, Jamie?"

"You always pushed me, Mom. That's how I made it through school. That's why I'll soon have my master's. That's why someday I might have a job that pays good money, or at least have a job that I absolutely love. Right now, Mom, it seems like you need a little push, and I'm just the one to do it."

It didn't seem right holing up in her bedroom, but Gracie needed some alone time. Time to think. She stretched out on the bed as she had as a little girl, lying on her stomach, knees bent, bare feet wagging in the air. The blue striped comforter on the little twin bed was a bit scratchy, but the sunlight streaming through the window made it feel warm and comfortable. She thumbed through one of the old photo albums she'd brought with her.

Smiling softly, she ran a fingertip lightly over her husband's face. It was one of those rare candid photos when you catch a person totally off guard, and can see them—forever—in the way you really remember them. Not posed. Not showing off. Art had been on the high school football field, running his guys through their drills. It was hot that day, and she'd stopped by with fresh, ice-cold lemonade, enough for the team, if their coach would give them a break. Art wasn't big on breaks; he was big on discipline, but the guys loved him.

"Hey, coach!" The team's best wide-receiver—Jake Moore—yelled. "Your wife's here."

Art spun around, a slow smile touching his face. That's the picture she'd caught. That's what she was looking at now. "I miss you," she whispered. "A lot."

She blew him a kiss and hesitantly flipped through more pages of photos. Brandon turning cartwheels in the backyard when he was four years old; Paige looking gawky in her ballet tutu at three. She'd hated ballet. She'd preferred going fishing with her dad, keeping score for the high school wrestling team, dishing out Gatorade to the guys during football games.

It wasn't like Gracie to do things on a whim, but she grabbed her cell phone and let it automatically dial Paige's number. It rang and rang, and Gracie let it, knowing Paige might be busy. If she didn't answer, eventually it would roll over to voice mail, and she'd leave a message. She didn't know what she'd say. She just wanted to talk to her daughter.

She flipped over another page in the scrapbook and found a picture of her mother. Rosalie Marris had been so pretty, so sweet. She looked lovely in the picture, standing on the beach in a modest navy blue and white polka-dot bathing suit, her blonde hair pulled back with a light scarf. She was laughing in the photo. *Mom always loved to laugh*, she thought. Gracie didn't remember putting this picture in this photo album, but she must have done so at some point in the last few years. In the background, Gracie could see herself building a sand castle. It was something she still enjoyed doing.

Gracie was maybe seven or eight. Sam was just a toddler, hanging on to Mom's legs. Caroline was farther down the beach, a little way away from the rest of the family, doing a handstand. And far in the background, on top of the bluff, she could see a hint of yellow—it was the Misty Harbor Inn, and Mom was pointing to it. Probably saying to the photographer—Dad, more than likely—"Someday I'll buy that place. I'll run it the way I think an inn should be run. Wouldn't that be fun?"

Dad probably would have said yes. He'd been crazy about Mom. The same way Art had been crazy about Gracie. Some people just got lucky.

"Hey, Mom, what's going on?" Paige answered at last. She sounded concerned. "Everything okay?"

"Everything's fine. I'm not interrupting anything important, am I?"

"I've got a group of tourists climbing rocks, binoculars in hand, looking for peregrine falcons and hawks. Tomorrow I'm doing the puffin tour." Paige laughed. "Never a dull moment in Acadia National Park."

"There haven't been many dull moments here on Nantucket either."

"You're having a good time then? You're relaxing?"

It was Gracie's turn to laugh. "I talked Caroline and Sam into climbing to the top of the Unitarian church bell tower. Ninety-four steps, and oh my, was I exhausted when I got to the top. Not that I'd ever let my sisters know that."

"You should come out to Acadia and stay with me for a week or two. I'd show you what a real hike is like."

"I just might do that, once I get away from here."

"You say that like you're anxious to leave. I thought you'd love being there."

"I do. I just miss home, that's all. It's weird not to be taking care of the yard, making sure the roses don't get all spindly and that Mrs. Turner's dog doesn't dig under the fence and leave messes all over the backyard. And I'm sure your brother and Stacy are finding it tough not having me there to babysit the little ones, and—"

"You've only been gone a few days. Stacy doesn't have a job other than being a housekeeper and mom—"

"That's a tough job, Paige, especially with three children."

"I know that, Mom, but you're always there for them. And please don't get mad at me for saying this, but I think sometimes they take advantage of you."

"I love watching Evelyn and the twins. We cook and garden and fingerpaint, and sometimes we go to the park and swing on the swings, and—" Gracie suddenly realized how lonely she was. She forced herself to hold back her tears.

"Hey, Mom, you're not okay, are you?"

Gracie drew in a deep breath. "It's been three years, Paige. I shouldn't still miss your dad so much, but I do. There are times when I'm sure I'll never be totally happy again."

Paige was silent a moment and then Gracie heard her calling out to someone, one of the tourists, more than likely. "Sorry, Mom, I've got a teenage kid getting a little out of control. Thinks he can fly like a falcon, and I've got to keep him from breaking his neck."

"That's okay, hon. Go."

"I can take some time off and come to Nantucket."

"No, Paige. I'll be fine. Jamie's here, and Sam and Caroline, and Caroline's friend George will be here soon, and, well, I love you. Don't worry. I'm a big girl. I'll get through this."

"I love you too, Mom. But call me if you need me. No matter—" Paige sighed. "Gotta go, Mom. Bye."

Gracie held the phone to her ear long after the connection had ended. Where had this sudden melancholy come from? She'd kept her emotions in check for so long. Through Art's cancer and death, through her mother's. She'd wanted so much to spend this time with her sisters, but now Caroline was trying to pull her away from everything she'd known and loved for nearly forty years. Would she ever really be able to leave it all behind?

"Here we go, ladies."

The teenage host at Bernie's Boathouse on the Wharf seated Caroline first, making a big show of pulling out a chair for her. Obviously, she was starting to look her age, or at least older than her sisters. Unfortunately, the days when she'd looked under forty were definitely gone.

They were seated at an outside table, on the deck overlooking the water. A cheery linen cloth was topped with a piece of white butcher paper, and a low vase was filled with pink cabbage roses. The sun was starting to set over the water, and a tea-light candle flickered gently in the soft breeze. Caroline spread her napkin in her lap and leaned back in her wooden chair, listening to the sound of water lapping gently against the pilings and watching boats of all shapes and sizes bob on the water. Seagulls hovered nearby, waiting patiently for any scraps the generous diners might throw them. It was absolutely lovely, and not for the first time she realized how easily she could live on this island. Nantucket was a glorious place to fall in love with.

Over appetizers of scallops wrapped in bacon and mushrooms stuffed with shrimp and crab, Caroline told her sisters and niece about the travel article she'd worked on all afternoon. "I know it seems odd writing about German Christmas markets in June.

But over a tall glass of ice-cold lemonade—thank you, Gracie, for making that for me"—she smiled at her sister—"I've been writing about gorgeous little villages decked out with greenery and old-fashioned candles, and about eating roasted chestnuts, *Lebkuchen*—gingerbread cookies—and marzipan, and about strolling through stalls in a Christmas market filled with old-fashioned toys, wood carvings, and marionettes."

"Sounds heavenly," Gracie said, "I, on the other hand, ventured out to the library and brought home a number of books on the history of Nantucket, several of them written by one of the Macys back in the 1800s." She wagged her fork at Jamie, before stabbing it into another mushroom. "I wouldn't be at all surprised if there were some myths and legends that might be of interest for your thesis."

"You didn't by any chance find anything new on the Montague family, did you?" Sam asked, and briefly explained to Jamie that they were the original owners of what was now the Misty Harbor Inn.

"I was looking for generalized information on Nantucket, not on any one thing in particular," Gracie said a little stiffly, "but you're welcome to look through the books to see what you can find."

"Mom told me there are rumors about secret rooms and passageways in the inn," Jamie said. Her eyes had been terribly red this afternoon, but they now showed far more signs of life. "Can you imagine how interesting that would be if it was true?"

"We'll only find out the truth if we buy the place," Caroline said, cutting a scallop in half. "Before we go see it again—"

"Are we going to go see it again?" Gracie asked.

"Of course you're going to see it again, Aunt Gracie. Mom's already called the agent and told her we'll be there tomorrow at noon. I'm dying to see what it's like and besides"—Jamie grinned—

"you obviously can't make a decision to buy or not to buy until I give my stamp of approval or a flat-out reject."

"George wants to see it too," Caroline told them. "If only he could be here tomorrow, we could all ogle the furnishings—and that fabulous old Packard—together."

Caroline took a bite of scallop, its buttery flavor so delicious she wished she'd ordered the entire appetizer simply for herself. Lifting another scallop with her fork, she looked at Sam. "When you talked with Deborah, did you ask her if she could have the shutters opened?"

"I asked." Sam shook her head, pursing her lips. "She said, unfortunately, no. And that was an emphatic no."

"That's ridiculous," Caroline said. "I can't imagine anyone buying the inn without seeing everything it has to offer, which means not only the view, but every nook and cranny in the full light from the sun."

"She doesn't seem to think we're serious," Sam said, buttering a thick, warm piece of French bread.

"I can understand where she's coming from," Gracie said, wiping her mouth with a red cloth napkin. "Even *I'm* not sure we're serious."

"Mom's pretty serious," Jamie said. "In fact, we went to the building department this afternoon and tried to get a handle on all that's involved with fixing up a historical property."

"My head was spinning by the time we left," Sam said. "Just getting the permits will take weeks, maybe months."

"We got a checklist," Jamie added, "showing the order in which everything needs to be done. We also got a list of approved exterior colors, and found out there's a class on restoring historical homes."

"You could indulge your artistic side," Sam said to Gracie, "learning all about the decorative aspects of Nantucket's old houses and how to re-create what many of the artisans of the eighteenth and nineteenth centuries produced."

"I imagine we could all indulge in something like that," Caroline said, itching to get her hands on the inn and return it to its once grand state. "I just wish we could learn more about the inn's history. Right now, if I were to hazard a guess, I'd say it's bound up more in gossip and myth—Jamie's favorite topic—than any true historical fact. Did you learn anything at the building department?"

"Nothing but recent history again," Sam said. "But I got some more information from the woman we talked with about the problems with the current owners."

"They lobbied for changes in restoration restrictions," Jamie said, swirling her glass of iced tea around and around so the ice clinked against the side of the glass. "They wanted an exemption from having to use the approved colors, claiming the inn isn't in the historical district, but that was a no-go."

Caroline nodded. "Mrs. Addison—Shirley, the lady who lives next to the inn—told me all about that. They wanted to paint it a candy-apple red and make it look like a barn."

"Were they out of their minds?" Gracie asked, shaking her head. "I'm rather fond of the yellow it's already painted."

"It's called Main Street Yellow," Jamie stated. "It's the only yellow on the list, and that list is very short."

"As it should be," Gracie continued. "If it wasn't, there's no telling what horrible colors people would come up with to paint their homes. Heavens, twenty years or so ago, my neighbor painted the trim on her home a ghastly purple. Art and I were sick about it, but there was absolutely nothing we could do because we didn't

NANTUCKET DREAMS | 130

have any rules about it in the community. Restrictions are sometimes annoying, but they're often put in place for a reason."

"Well, I can tell you right now, I wouldn't repaint the inn anything other than Main Street Yellow and white," Caroline said, trying not to laugh at Gracie's outburst. "The outside needs some screws and nails, maybe some new siding here and there, and some freshening up of the paint."

"Wait a minute." Gracie set down her fork. "You're talking as if this is a done deal. As if we're going to head to Deborah's office after we look at the inn tomorrow and put in an offer. I'm still not convinced."

"Of course not," Sam said, calming Gracie with a smile. "We know that, and it's okay. It's all talk right now."

Gracie's forehead was creased, and her cheeks looked pinched. "My whole life is in Portland."

Caroline put her hand on Gracie's. A decision like this had to be made on her own terms. "I'm sorry," Caroline said, squeezing her sister's fingers. "Maybe I've pushed too hard on this."

"Why don't we talk about it tomorrow, after Jamie's taken a walk through the inn? We don't have to make any decisions now. Would that be okay with you?" Sam asked Gracie.

Gracie toyed with a speck of crab that had fallen out of one of her mushrooms, pushing it around and around on her plate. At last she looked up. "I need to talk to Brandon and Paige before I make a decision one way or another." She smiled. "No matter what I decide though, I'm not giving up my house. Art and I worked too hard to make it a home."

Caroline sipped her iced tea, watching a sleek sailboat tacking back and forth across the wind. The waiter brought their main courses, setting a plate of fettuccini with grilled prawns in front of her.

They chatted and laughed, and it was fun to hear Jamie and Gracie go at each other about which baseball team was the best—Yankees or Red Sox. The gulls hovered about, screeching, diving, soaring high and low. The horn on an incoming ferry blew. Caroline just barely heard her cell phone ring. She dug it out of the deepest recesses of her large golden leather tote.

She was thrilled to hear George's voice. She hadn't expected to hear from him for a couple more days. "I've decided to fly into Nantucket rather than sail. It's been too busy around here to take off for more than a couple of days."

"Are you sure you want to come?" Caroline asked. He'd been there for her so many times, but she hated to pull him away from his work.

"Of course I want to come. I'm eager to see this inn of yours, so I'm flying in tomorrow morning."

Caroline grabbed a pen from her bag and jotted down George's arrival time on the white butcher paper covering the tablecloth. "Come prepared for a busy day tomorrow," she told him. "We're going to the inn at noon, and we've got a clambake to go to in the evening. How does that sound?"

"Like a great time. It's been too many months since I've seen you."

It has been a long time, she thought, after closing her cell phone and putting it away. Not that they saw each other regularly. She'd always been off in one part of the world or another, and he'd been working in Annapolis. Somehow they'd stayed good friends, the best of friends. If she lived on Nantucket they could see each other more often. She liked that thought.

Of course, at this very moment, buying the inn was totally up in the air. It didn't seem to matter how much she loved it or how much she wanted it. She could probably buy it on her own or just with Sam, but she really wanted it to be a family thing—something for all of them, a cherished memento of their mother.

Right now, though, everything hinged on Gracie. That didn't make her optimistic.

CHAPTER
Thirteen

"Feels awfully good to get off that plane."

George dropped his one carry-on bag onto the floor inside the terminal and wrapped Caroline in a bear hug. It seemed forever since she'd seen him, since she'd felt the strength of his arms around her. He was the best friend she'd ever had, and she'd missed him.

"I'm awfully glad you're here. There's so much to do, and so much to see. And you're finally going to have the chance to get to know Gracie and Sam. Jamie too."

"I should have done that months ago. It just didn't feel right coming around shortly after your mother passed away."

George swept a hand though his wind-blown, salt-and-pepper hair, picked up his bag again, and Caroline linked her arm through his. "The worst of that's over. Now's the time for memories, and"—Caroline smiled—"I can't begin to tell you how many memories we've shared. We've watched old movies, put together jigsaw puzzles, cooked—"

George's left eyebrow rose. "You cooked?"

"Well, no, Sam's done most all of that, and I've eaten. But I have listened to her talk to herself while she's working in the kitchen. She reads the ingredients out loud, so you could say I pretty much know all her recipes by heart."

"Does that mean you'll cook for me one of these days?"

"Not if you want to rise and shine the next morning. You know good and well that most everything I try cooking comes out burned or too salty or—"

"We could go through the whole litany of meals you've tried to kill me with, but why don't we climb in the car and head wherever it is you're going to take me."

The airport wasn't very large, and it took only minutes to reach the parking lot from the terminal. George stowed his bag in the trunk and hopped in the passenger seat of the rental car. "Do you want to take me to the marina first? I'm going to stay on a friend's sloop, since he's in Europe for the summer. I figured you wouldn't have room for me at the cottage, and I definitely don't want to intrude too much on girl time."

"You wouldn't be in the way, trust me. Sam's been planning a fabulous meal and she's dying to try her cooking skills on someone other than me, Gracie, and Jamie. But right now, why don't we head out to the inn. I'll take you to the marina later."

George fidgeted in the seat, trying to get comfortable, but the car was about two sizes too small for his six-foot-one frame. His shoulders were broad, his arms muscular from trimming sails, and tightening lines, tacking, and jibing. Since he sailed so often, he kept in shape. He was sixty-six, but he loved to sail, and he planned to do it for at least another twenty years.

"How's Gracie feeling about buying the inn?" he asked. "Still hesitant?"

"That's a bit of an understatement. But I'm sure she'll come around in time."

"Sure, or just hopeful?"

"I'm always hopeful. You should know that by now."

George wasn't a man of many words, but she had always been able to read how he was feeling by the change of expression on his face or the tone of his voice. She hoped he could understand her passion when he saw the inn.

Caroline turned the car off the highway and onto the crushed-shell-and-gravel road, heading west toward the ocean, the dunes, and the Misty Harbor. They hadn't gone all that far when George leaned forward in his seat and stared. "It's not quite as big as I imagined."

"It's big enough. There are a few spacious guest rooms upstairs, each with their own bath, and the two owners' bedrooms are downstairs. And wait until you see the library. It's Gracie's favorite room, and it doesn't take much to understand why."

"Do you have a favorite?"

"The entire place. Of course, I'm in love with the parlor—it's huge, just wait until you see it—and the attic, although you can't see a thing inside, because it's stuffed to the gills with boxes and furniture, and oh! the gardens! The roses and hydrangea and—"

"Anything else?"

"If we could open the shutters—"

George pivoted his head toward her and frowned. "You mean I'm not going to see a view? I'm not going to see the sun shining into the rooms?"

Caroline shook her head. "I'm not any happier about that than you are. The owners don't want the shutters opened or taken down. They want to protect the house."

"That's insane. How can you possibly think of buying a place this big and for this much money if you can't see the whole thing? And the view is all a part of that."

"Sam asked, and she was told no."

"Then I'll ask."

"George, it's not that important."

"Do you want to see the view?"

"Well, yes, of course, but—"

"I'll take care of this." George rarely caused problems, but he was good at getting what he wanted.

Caroline pulled the car up next to Deborah's Mercedes. Deborah had picked up Gracie, Sam, and Jamie, and probably expected to have a rather nice and uneventful jaunt through the inn and the carriage house. George might be a salt-of-the-earth kind of guy, but he was also a good businessman, and if he wanted to see the view through the windows, he'd find a way to get Deborah to jump through hoops to get the shutters removed.

He was out of the car before Caroline, and started marching toward the stairs. He looked awfully big and imposing when he was playing the role of businessman, even dressed in khakis, a polo shirt, and white running shoes.

Caroline caught up with him in the foyer. He stood there listening for voices. He wasn't paying a bit of attention to the stunning woodwork, the bronze chandelier, or the peeling wallpaper. "They must be upstairs," Caroline said. "But why don't I show you around down here before we join them?"

"Running from trouble never got anyone anywhere."

Not for the first time, Caroline realized that George didn't make waves, but he found a way to conquer them, and he did it all with that gentle spirit and charm that she loved so well.

He linked his arm through hers and led her up the stairs. He attempted to shake the banister, and thankfully it didn't wobble or creak. She so wanted him to like the inn, to give her his blessing. He looked at her with a raised eyebrow when the staircase curved, and he spotted the crack zigzagging up the wall.

"That's not the only crack," Caroline said nervously, "but I haven't seen too many."

"Cracks can be fixed, as long as the foundation's good. You'll have to keep an eye out for sagging ceilings too. But"—he tugged her close—"I can see why you've fallen in love with the place."

"Can you?"

"I've bought run-down yachts that have been in dry dock for decades. I've been told they would sink like a ton of lead the instant they touched water again. But some of the worst of those boats are now sailing the world." George's stunning blue eyes twinkled when he smiled. "If I hadn't seen something special in those boats, they would have ended up sold as scraps. There's something special about this old house too. I can feel it."

After George's words made her worries scurry away, they made their way to the second floor. She told George the real estate agent's name, and tried to breathe easily, calmly, when they confronted her in the first room to the right of the stairs. It was the pink bedroom room they'd seen the other day.

"You must be Deborah Greenleaf," George said, walking straight to Deborah, holding out his hand, and shaking hers when it was offered.

"Good afternoon."

"It's a beautiful afternoon. I'm sorry we're late, but my plane was delayed in New York."

"You're from the city?" Deborah asked, giving George her full attention. He had that effect on women—of course—he was dashing, daring, and handsome, like Peter Lawford, who Caroline had had a bit of a crush on after first seeing him ages ago in *Little Women*.

"From Annapolis, actually."

"You're in the Navy?"

George shook his head. "Wright Custom Yachts. I'm George Wright." He smiled. "The owner."

From a lot of other men, that statement might have sounded pompous. With George, it merely sounded matter of fact. He rarely told anyone who he was or what he did. They might get the impression that he had money. Of course he did, but he donated the biggest portion of it to charities, and except for sailing and traveling, he lived a modest life in a townhouse not far from his business. But here he was, letting Deborah think he could end up being another one of her wealthy clients.

Sam, Gracie, and Jamie stood near the big four-poster. They'd heard nothing but wonderful things about George—that he was humble, courteous, a man who'd give you the shirt off his back. Now they looked a bit shell-shocked by the exchange between George and Deborah. They had no idea what was going on, and there wasn't much of anything Caroline could tell them right this moment. She hoped they'd figure out soon that he was playing a role, determined to get them a view from inside.

"Will you be investing in the inn along with Caroline and her sisters, should an offer be made?" Deborah asked. George gave her the hint of a smile, enough to make Deborah believe that it was a possibility, yet he remained noncommittal.

"Actually"—George walked to one of the room's oblong windows, parted the yellowed lace curtains, and stared at the wood that blocked his view—"it's rather difficult to make a decision on a property like this when you can't see it in its best light."

"I'm sorry, I don't quite understand." She looked around and then blushed. "Oh, the dust and, well, the condition of the building. It is a shame that the inn hasn't been kept up. The owners—"

"Dust and dirt and a few loose floorboards can be fixed. What I am concerned about is the view. You know," he said, pointing to the window he stood next to, "I can't tell what there is to see from this window. The garden? The ocean. Or the drive leading to the highway? Do you know?"

"I believe it's the garden." Deborah laughed uncomfortably. "If I had a compass—"

"I rest my case. If you don't know what's outside these windows, how can you possibly expect Caroline, Gracie, Sam, Jamie, or me, for that matter, to imagine the view? I've heard it said time and time again that the principal selling point of a property is location. Right now, I don't see a location at all. I merely see boarded up windows."

"The owner prefers we keep them boarded up, to keep vandals and vagrants out."

George nodded slowly. He frowned, taking his time to respond. "Does the owner want to sell the inn, or not?"

"Of course he does."

"Then please, would you have the shutters opened. Caroline tells me they're nailed or screwed down, but I'm sure you can find a few locals to come by here immediately and take them down. We really would like to see the view. "

"I can't possibly make that happen immediately."

"Then"—George sighed, turning to Caroline—"I'm sorry, Caroline. I think we should go. I can't possibly give you my blessing on the inn, not without seeing the view."

Caroline was flabbergasted. She didn't want to lose her chances of owning the inn, but George had made his stand. If Deborah didn't give in, she was going to have to walk, and her heart would sink. Her dreams would go up in a puff of smoke.

"Actually," Deborah said when George took Caroline's arm and headed for the bedroom door, "I do know a few young men who I can call. It shouldn't take long. Perhaps—"

"That'll be great," George interrupted. "While you're taking care of the shutters, I understand there's a carriage house I should take a look at." Caroline had already told him about the magnificent Packard (a 1941 model, from her Internet search) hidden beneath boxes and far too many odds and ends. Businessman George wouldn't hint at his curiosity about the car; he'd do everything possible to help get the price down on the inn. Showing immense excitement, he'd tried to tell Caroline, was not the way to proceed in a deal of this magnitude.

"Why don't you stroll around in the garden while I make a few phone calls, and then I can open the carriage house for you. I'd be happy to let you look on your own, but—"

"Perhaps you could give me the key, and I'll unlock it for us. Caroline tells me the lock is a touch rusty and difficult to open, and I'm sure you'd like to get as many workmen here as you can, as quickly as you can." George gave her a winning smile.

"I shouldn't, really, but"—Deborah handed the key to George—"I trust you won't abscond with anything."

George crossed his heart. "You have my word."

Again George took Caroline's arm and headed out of the bedroom, with Gracie, Sam, and Jamie trailing along behind. When they were in the hallway, they heard Deborah on the telephone.

George winked at Caroline and then turned back toward her sisters and niece. He smiled. "Nice to see the three of you again."

"Nice to see you too," Gracie stammered. Jamie and Sam winked back. They seemed to know what George had been up to, thank heavens! Caroline wouldn't have to explain his behavior.

When they stood on the back porch and surveyed the garden, George, with his hands clasped behind his back, said, "You're right, it is overgrown, but the scent is amazing. The perfume of the roses and all the other flowers mixed with the salty air off the ocean is wonderful."

George drew in a deep breath, his deep chest rising and falling.

"Thanks for making arrangements to get the shutters removed so we can see the view from inside." Sam leaned against the back porch's slightly loose railing, looking out toward the ocean. "I think you actually unnerved Deborah."

"That wasn't my intention. Well, that's not quite true," George said. "There are still salespeople who think it's perfectly okay to pull a fast one on women. I'm afraid Deborah has been taking the easy way out in trying to sell this inn. She doesn't want to expend any more money or effort than absolutely necessary, especially since it's been on the market for such a long time."

"Exactly," Gracie declared. "I'm sure she's given up on finding a buyer, and I imagine she sees us as simply lookie-loos."

Caroline wondered if she detected a slight thaw in Gracie's attitude toward the inn.

"Let's go look at the carriage house," George said, and took off down the stairs, heading toward the rooftop that could be seen past the jungle of hydrangea. They ducked under the drooping vines and twisted and thorny stems of a climbing red rose that weighted down one of the arbors.

George grabbed his cell phone from the pocket of his khakis and snapped several photos of the carriage house, clearly fascinated by its position on the bluff, where it overlooked the ocean, and to the roses that grew haphazardly over its windows and walls. The rosebushes covered the walls in a riot of pink.

"What do you think?" Caroline asked, linking her arm through his, smiling as she was again struck by the beauty all around her.

"I think the view alone is worth the asking price." George faced the ocean and snapped a few more pictures, the light breeze toying with his hair and making his navy blue polo shirt billow around his chest. "The market's still down and might be for quite some time. I rather imagine you could make an offer far less than the asking price and strike a good deal."

"You think so?" Sam asked.

George nodded. "It's obvious the current owners have lost interest and are probably at the breaking point, ready to dump the inn and all that's in it to the first person who comes in with a viable offer."

Without another word, George headed for the carriage house door, worked the key into the lock, and twisted a few times before it opened. A moment later all five of them made their way through the doors and into the dust and clutter.

"We've heard rumors that there's a secret passage from here into the house," Jamie said, clearly drawn to the mysteries of the inn, "and maybe a hidden room too, although you'd probably have to clear everything out of here before you could find it."

"That could take months," Gracie grumbled. "It seems as if this place has been used as nothing more than a storage shed for years."

"Since before World War II, from the looks of it," George said, thumbing through the box of *National Geographic* magazines Caroline

had opened before. "Caroline tells me you're interested in history."
George turned to Gracie, offering an infectious but reserved smile.
"You must be excited about getting your hands on these old magazines.
There must be a treasure trove of stories that were written seventy or
eighty years ago about all the different places in the world. Imagine
how those places have changed since these were first published. There
may even be articles about animals that are now extinct."

"You think so?" Gracie asked, moving closer, peeking inside.

"I wouldn't be surprised. But"—he started to squeeze through
the narrow passage that led back to the car, his shoulders brushing
against the boxes on either side—"you'll never know, unless Caroline
buys this old place. Now... Let's take a look at the car. I'm fascinated
by old vehicles."

"He means boats as well as cars." Caroline laughed. "If it has a
motor, he's intrigued."

"Well, well, well." George stopped abruptly, and Caroline bumped
into his back. He'd reached the Packard and flung its protective cover
off the hood. He walked to the back of the car, thoroughly studying
its curves and chrome, and tugged the cover the rest of the way off.
"Definitely a forty-one Packard, just as you thought."

"If the car's in decent enough condition and drivable, and if we
did buy the inn"—Caroline turned around and winked at Gracie—
"we could tote guests around town in it, take them on tours of the
island, or pack them a picnic lunch and drive them down to the beach
for the day."

"We'd be the envy of every other B and B on Nantucket," Sam
said, squeezing through the boxes to get close to Caroline.

"What do you think?" Caroline asked George. "With a little
cleaning and polishing, could it look good as new?"

"Hard to tell just yet," George said.

Jamie struggled to get past Caroline and Sam to catch her first glimpse of the Packard, and when she did, she oohed and aahed, her eyes bright, even in the dim light from the one overhead bulb. Jamie ran her hands over the dusty red steel, the chrome, and glass. "I can't wait to ride in it."

"Now, now," Sam admonished and then laughed. "We're not even sure—"

A loud, metallic creak interrupted Sam's words.

"Well, you're in luck," George said, holding up the massive hood. "It looks like everything's intact. It'll need new hoses and belts and probably a complete overhaul just to get it to run, but at least no one has taken the engine."

"Could you do the work on it?" Caroline asked George, whose head was buried under the hood. He was already getting his hands greasy. "Or do you think we'd have to hire an expert on old automobiles?"

"If you end up owning it, I'm sure I could find the time to tinker a bit, as long as you promise to let me drive it every once in a while."

Outside, Caroline heard the first hint of hammering. She heard a man shouting, another responding. Deborah was having the shutters opened and boards removed from the windows. Caroline couldn't wait to stand in the library with a slice of sunshine streaking across the hardwood floors. It would glint off the bronze sconces, brightening that beautiful room and all the others. Everything looked better in sunlight.

"If I could climb under this thing," George said, grunting as he got down on his knees to look beneath the car, "I'm sure—wait a minute."

"Are you okay?" Caroline called out. "There's no need to look at the undercarriage right now."

"It's not the undercarriage I'm looking at. It's some loose boards under the undercarriage."

"A secret passage?" Sam sounded excited.

"It might just be loose boards." George coughed as dust rose around him. "I don't think anyone should browse around here without wearing a mask and gloves, and the boxes should be taken out before you attempt to get a really good look at the car. But I do think this is one special vehicle."

Caroline smiled. *I knew it!*

Slowly, Caroline turned and led the search party out of the carriage house and back out into the sunlight. It was so lovely to hear the sound of the surf again, to breathe Nantucket's salty air, to at last see the sun's rays bouncing off the inn's windows. When George finally stepped out of the carriage house, he was a dusty mess and wearing a crown of cobwebs, but she linked her arm through his. "What do you think?" she whispered close to his ear.

He smiled fondly. "I think you've found a winner here. The inn, the car, your family. It's what you've wanted for a long time."

That it was. It wasn't just her mother's dream after all. It was her dream too.

CHAPTER

Fourteen

Gracie sat outside on the rental cottage's patio, basking in the warmth of the sun, while everyone else was out with George, taking a tour of the Whaling Museum. She wished she could make up her mind about the inn. She had loved seeing it again this afternoon, especially once the shutters had been taken down. It truly was gorgeous with the sun streaming in, and the view of the ocean out the back was breathtaking. The whole place had seemed brighter and newer. There was so much inside and outside that was wonderful, and she knew it could look even better with the touch of a loving hand. She just wasn't sure she could be the one to do it.

Again she wished it had never become an issue, so she wouldn't be required to make a decision one way or another. Why couldn't things simply remain the same?

Around the edge of the patio, potted geraniums and pansies bloomed in the warm summer sun. There were also small vegetables pots—tiny tomatoes and green beans—as well as bunches of fragrant herbs. It was like a miniature garden out here. Art would have loved it.

She stared at her cell phone that rested on the patio table. It looked as lonely as she had been feeling since Art passed away. It wasn't a constant emotion. She certainly hadn't felt all that lonely on this trip, not with Caroline buzzing about full of bright ideas, and Sam asking her for thoughts on dinner menus, needlework projects, and for help putting together yet another puzzle. There'd hardly been time to sit down in a quiet corner to read.

Brandon and Stacy and the kids must be missing her. She felt rather selfish leaving them on their own when they needed her help so often. "Could you pick Evelyn up at school today?" one or the other of them would ask. "She needs to come up with a costume for the fall festival. Do you have any ideas, Mom? Do you think you could whip something up for her?"

Stacy had tried to work part-time, but she wanted to be the World's Greatest Mom, so she ran herself ragged trying to make everything perfect for Evelyn, Jacob, and Zachary. When she couldn't do it all, she or Brandon would call Gracie and ask for help, and Gracie was always there for them. She'd do anything for her kids or grandchildren. She loved them. Besides, Art wasn't around for her to tend to any longer. It was nice to have someone who needed her.

Gracie didn't know what Brandon might think about her buying one-third of a fairly ramshackle old inn. He'd talked about buying a cabin in the mountains, or traveling—to Scotland, mostly. She'd thought about giving some of the money she'd inherited from her mother to the kids so they could take a trip. She smiled at the thought of him out on a boat in Loch Ness, binoculars in hand, searching for Nessie the Loch Ness monster.

She wondered what Art would think of the Misty Harbor Inn idea. She chuckled lightly, only to have Max pull his nose out from among the blue hydrangeas to gaze at her. Max trotted over to her and rested his head on her knee, his big brown eyes full of love and adoration. "I don't have a thing to eat, boy," she said, scratching behind his ears. "But if you're good"—he suddenly stood on his hind legs and danced around in a circle—"we'll go into the kitchen and rummage through the fridge. I know I've told Caroline endless times that you shouldn't eat table scraps, but I don't think a little something would hurt."

Max bumped the leg of a chair, which bumped the table, and Gracie's cell phone slid off and landed in her lap. She laughed again, knowing that was a sign. She had to call Brandon and get it over with.

"Go find your chew bone," she said to Max, sweeping a hand down his silky back, before he scurried off across the lawn. She drew in a deep breath, popped open her cell phone, and dialed Brandon's number. It was a little after four, and if her son was on schedule, he should be home from football practice by now. Soon he'd have the barbecue fired up on the patio so he could grill steaks or chicken that he'd been marinating all day. They were always tender and juicy and—

"Hey, Mom! What's going on?" His greeting was always the same. It was just like Paige's, quite often breathless, as if he'd been in the middle of something important. And she almost always said the same thing.

"I'm not disturbing you, am I?"

"Actually"—oh, she hated to hear her son use that word—"we were just getting ready to head out to a ball game, and Stacy's frantic because the babysitter's late. She should have been here ten minutes ago so we could show her around and tell her about the emergency phone list, and"—Brandon sighed—"it's not quite the same with you away from home. But you are having a good time aren't you?"

"It's beautiful here. The cottage is perfect and—"

"Hang on, Mom, the doorbell just rang."

Gracie heard the phone drop on something. His desk, maybe? The dining room table? The bathroom countertop?

Gracie found herself drumming her fingers on the patio table, waiting…waiting. At long last Brandon came back on the line. "Sorry, Mom. That was the babysitter, and we've got her all set up in the family room with the kids, ready to watch a movie. They miss you, by the way."

"I miss them too. It seems ages, but it's been just a week."

"You're still coming home in another week, aren't you? Stacy's hoping the two of us can sneak off for a weekend away, and we couldn't possibly leave the kids with anyone else."

"Yes, that's my plan."

"Good." He sounded so relieved. "Hey, Mom, I hate to rush, but if we don't get out of here now, we'll get caught in a traffic jam on the way to the game."

She hadn't had a chance to ask him about the inn. "Are you sure you don't have another minute or two?"

"I wish I did, Mom, but we have to get going. Can I call you back later? Oh, wait, we won't be back until late. Tomorrow's not going to be all that good either. *Hmm.* Maybe I could call Monday night. Would that be okay?"

She refused to let him hear her sigh. "Yes, that would be lovely, Brandon. Now you and Stacy go off and have fun and don't worry about the kids. I'm sure Stacy's found just the right babysitter."

"Okay, Mom. Love you."

A short tone sounded, signaling that the connection had been broken before she could get out her "I love you too."

If it had been the other way around, if Brandon and Stacy needed something, even if they only needed to talk, she would have been there for them. She'd never hang up, no matter how busy she might be. Even if she was at the very end of a movie, she'd flip off the television to talk to her children. They were far more important than anything else.

The generations were all so different.

Once again she sighed. She knew Brandon was thankful for what she did to help out, but sometimes she felt extraneous unless her services were needed. Even still, she could see how difficult it was for them to function with her gone. If she moved to Nantucket, what would they do?

She pushed out of her chair, clapped her hand to get Max to come to her, and gave him a generous rubdown. He started to pant, and she kissed the top of his head and took him inside. They'd raid the refrigerator. After that, she'd eat another piece of Sam's prune cake and dive into those history books she'd picked up at the library to see if there was anything at all about the Montagues or the Misty Harbor Inn.

Brandon needed her, but so did her sisters. And at least her sisters would show they were grateful.

"I've made up my mind," Sam said, carrying a bowl of fat red grapes, fresh-cut watermelon, and honeydew to the kitchen table. It was just a small snack before they headed off to the clambake, and her sisters and niece waited eagerly. "Jamie and I talked it over, and I want to go in on the inn."

Caroline's face broke into a smile. "Will you sell your townhouse?" Caroline asked, popping a grape into her mouth.

"Not right away," Sam said. She picked through the fruit salad and spooned mostly watermelon onto her plate. "I'll rent it for a while. There's always a high demand for nice rentals, and I should be able to get top dollar for it. But we probably should discuss a few things first."

Gracie remained silent, toying with the few pieces of honeydew on her plate, plucking an occasional grape and popping it in her mouth.

George had gone to rent a van, a vehicle they could all fit into, but she knew he'd also wanted to get out of their hair. Sam had overheard him telling Caroline, "If you're going to have a serious discussion with Sam and Gracie about buying the inn, I want to stay far away. I can't see Gracie doing it without a fight."

Caroline hoped he was wrong, but considering the expressions flitting across Gracie's face, it looked like George might be right.

Sam opened the notebook sitting off to the side of her plate. "I've gone over the three bids Deborah had on refurbishing the inn. As I'm sure you can guess, they're all over the map, from extremely high to just plain high. One contractor suggests a completely new foundation, another says all new plumbing and wiring, and the third recommends tearing it down and building something new."

"The woman Mom and I talked to at the building department told us that that is impossible," Jamie said. "The inn isn't on the register of historical buildings, or whatever it's called, but the last person who wanted to buy it and tear it down was turned down flat by anyone and everyone in power in Nantucket."

"I wouldn't do that in a million years," Caroline said. "The inn might not have any great historical interest, but I like it as is, nooks, crannies, peeling wallpaper, creaky floors, and all."

"There might be other options," Gracie said, "if we owned the inn."

"Such as?" Sam asked, encouraging her sister to say more.

"Doing the work ourselves, for one. Hiring someone like Bill Dekker—"

"Who's Bill Dekker?" Jamie asked.

"A jack-of-all-trades we met a couple of days ago," Gracie said, laughing lightly.

"But he seemed trustworthy," she continued. "He invited us to the clambake. And Bill's a not only a licensed building inspector, but his card says he's also a contractor. We'd have to check his references, of course, but he might work for us a lot cheaper than some of the bigger, more prosperous builders on the island."

Sam was frowning at Gracie now; so was Caroline. Had they heard her right? Had she said, "He might do the work for us..."?

"There are several other things you haven't mentioned," Gracie said, taking her small notebook out of her pants pocket. "Did you factor in the cost of new linens? The guest rooms could possibly need new mattresses."

"Shirley Addison told me guests had complained to her about the quality of the beds," Caroline said, "so new mattresses might need to go close to the top of any priority list."

Gracie gave a quick rundown of the items she'd thought of over the past few days. "I wasn't giving the inn any serious thought, of course, but my mind's been working overtime, and whenever a thought about the inn popped up, I wrote it down. You know me. I hate to forget things."

"Does this mean," Sam said, pushing her plate back and folding her arms on the table, "that you've decided to go in on the inn with Caroline and me?"

Gracie nodded ever so slightly.

"Aunt Gracie?" Jamie said.

Gracie sighed heavily, but she was smiling. "But if we are able to buy it," she said quickly, "I'm not going to sell my home, and I'm not going to rent it out either. I can stay here until the end of summer, till school starts, and then I'll have to go home." Her mouth set into a momentary frown. "Neither one of you could possibly clean up that inn without my help. I know every secret and shortcut in the book for getting out stains, patching holes in rugs—if any of those old rugs can be saved, and, and, well—"

"So you're in?" Caroline said, her eyes wide. She was practically bouncing in her chair.

"I'll be an owner, and I'll come here as much as I can, but I'll still live in Maine most of the time. We'll have to work out how that will affect the inn's finances and how we divide up the day-to-day work to run it, but—"

Gracie didn't have a chance to say anything more. Caroline had already jumped up from the table and wrapped her in a gigantic bear hug. A moment later Sam joined them.

"Oh," Gracie exclaimed, her words almost strangled. "We'll need a Web site. That's going to cost money too, and—"

"We'll talk about all those other things later," Sam said, thinking she just might burst out in tears of joy. "Right now, it's time to celebrate."

CHAPTER
Fifteen

Caroline was the first one out of the van after George found a parking spot at Madaket Beach. Already she could see the hint of a sunset, with a strip of orange trailing through some low-lying white clouds. Gracie, Sam, Jamie, and George joined her, and they started to walk down to the beach. The heavy surf roared against the sand, and she spotted a few surfers riding the waves in the last bit of evening sun.

Flames from the makeshift bonfire—which appeared to be barbecue grills set into pits in the sand—leapt about, all bright orange, red, and yellow, and puffs of white smoke drifted on the breeze. Caroline inhaled deeply. It smelled like roasting corn and seafood. Her mouth began to water.

"Lobster," Sam said, taking in the aromas. "And sausage. And maybe scallops? I've got to find out what they're cooking." She clutched the peach pie she had spent the afternoon baking.

"Hey, you guys made it." Megan Folger-Wildes was walking toward them, waving. "I'm so glad you came."

"Thanks for inviting us," Caroline said.

"Come on. I'll introduce you to some folks," Megan said, gesturing for them to follow her. "And I'll show you where you can drop off that pie," she said to Sam. They all started to follow, but Caroline saw the flash of a camera and spotted a slim man with knobby knees and bare feet, wearing plaid shorts and a Harvest Chapel T-shirt. Caroline decided to catch up with the others in a minute and headed toward the photographer to introduce herself.

"Hi there," Caroline said, holding her hand out to the man. He had a kindly face with a Bob Hope ski-jump nose and curly, salt-and-pepper hair that just barely waved over the tips of his ears. "I'm Caroline Marris."

"Nice to meet you, Caroline." He pumped her hand up and down, his grip strong and tight, his smile friendly and warm. "I'm Stan Wildes, but most everyone calls me Pastor Stan."

"My sisters and I"—she pointed them out—"are vacationing here, and we can't thank you enough for inviting tourists like us to your clambake."

"The more the merrier, I always say. The book of Job put it another way. 'Anyone who withholds kindness from a friend forsakes the fear of the Almighty.'" He grinned. "And lucky for you, you're about to see one of the most beautiful sunsets in the world."

Caroline turned and saw the clouds were now stained a bright, warm orange, and the sun was just starting to slip beneath the horizon. Stan Wildes began snapping pictures with his small digital camera. "Every travel guide will tell you that the best sunsets on Nantucket are seen right here on Madaket Beach. That's why we hold our clambakes here. It's a good reminder of God's bounty, as well as the beauty He has graced us with."

"I couldn't agree more," Caroline said. The clouds were splashed with pink, orange, and lavender now, and as they watched the sun moving lower in the sky, those colors brightened. Golden flecks dotted the waves out at sea. It almost looked like the ocean was on fire. It was truly a sight to behold.

"I've seen some of the most gorgeous sunsets in the world," Caroline said. "In Egypt, with the pyramids in the background; in the Serengeti, with the animals roaming around; and the Taj Mahal. But this is probably one of the most beautiful I've ever seen." Caroline clutched the Celtic cross at her neck, one she'd bought on her first trip to Ireland.

"God definitely lavished more than our fair share of beauty here on Nantucket."

Caroline was rarely tongue-tied, but didn't know how to answer. He was right, of course. Beauty like this made it easy to remember that God was bigger and more amazing than she could ever understand. She couldn't understand how someone could look at a sunset like this and not believe that God was still working in the world today.

They stood there in silence, watching the sun slowly vanish beyond the horizon. Shades of blue, silver, and purple slowly spread across the sky. Then, just as the last light disappeared into the sea, Pastor Stan linked his arm through hers. "Now, why don't you introduce me to your sisters and friends, and then I believe we should say grace, grab a bowl of chowder, and get this clambake started."

"How do you like the lobster?"

Gracie looked up from the beach chair she'd been sitting in, enjoying the feast that seemed to be never ending, to see Bill

Dekker hunkering down next to her. He was wearing khaki pants and a light cotton sweater. Gracie was struck again by how familiar he seemed.

"It's delicious. A little hard to eat without a table in front of me, and it's a bit messy"—Gracie gestured toward the drips of butter that had landed on her pants—"but I have to say, this is the best lobster I've ever eaten. And the scallops. Oh my goodness. If someone had told me seafood could taste this heavenly cooked over seaweed and seawater, I never would have believed them."

"I take it this is your first clambake?"

She nodded. "And not the last, I hope."

Bill was quiet for a minute. Gracie could see that he was looking at something down the beach.

"I met my wife on this beach nearly forty years ago at a clambake just like this," he finally said. "Back then, of course, we could have an actual bonfire on the beach."

"Oh, I'd love to meet her," Gracie said. She set up straighter and started looking around. "Is she here?"

Bill shook his head. "I lost her four years ago."

Gracie could see the sadness still in his eyes, a misty-eyed look she knew all too well. "For years and years she'd tried awfully hard to get me to go to church with her, and I finally relented. I sat in one of the front pews listening to her sing in the choir and couldn't help but wonder why I hadn't come before. Pastor Stan—you've met him, haven't you?"

Gracie nodded. "A little while ago."

"Well, I found myself completely caught up in his sermon. He made the Bible verses I'd been reading for years actually come to life. He was mesmerizing; so was the choir. After church, right after

Dora—my wife—introduced me to Pastor Stan, she gripped my arm, told me her head hurt, and then she was gone."

"A brain aneurysm?" Gracie asked, surprised that he'd tell her the story, but it seemed to connect them somehow. She knew the pain of losing someone you loved.

He nodded slowly. "I haven't missed a Sunday since then."

"I would have thought you'd stay away, that you'd never want to go back."

"No. No. Call me crazy, but every time I get close to the church, I feel Dora's spirit lingering there. Not like a ghost, of course." He chuckled. "I don't want you thinking I've lost my mind. It's just a good feeling that comes over me when I see Pastor Stan, when I walk into the sanctuary. Dora's heart and soul are inside that church."

He slid a finger beneath his glasses and didn't seem the least bit embarrassed at wiping away a tear. "Don't know what possessed me to tell you all of that. I don't usually open up so easily."

"I lost my husband not all that long ago too." Gracie was surprised she'd said it. She never talked about Art with strangers. She liked to keep him all to herself, tucked in close to her heart.

Bill seemed to sense that she didn't want to say anything more. They sat in comfortable silence for a minute. Gracie watched some children load marshmallows onto skewers and hold them out over the coals. Paige had never wanted to get too close to campfires, but Brandon used to get right up near the flame and light his marshmallow on fire. He always said it tasted better burnt. Gracie chuckled.

"How are you enjoying your first trip to Nantucket?" Bill said.

"Oh, it's not my first trip," Gracie said. "My sisters and I came here every summer when we were kids."

"Is that right?" Bill studied her face and then looked at Caroline and Sam. "When was that?"

"Oh, it's been over forty years." She laughed. "It feels just like yesterday in some ways."

Bill was still watching her, a strange look on his face.

"What did you say your maiden name was?"

"Marris?"

A slow smile spread across his face. "I knew it! You looked so familiar, but I couldn't figure out why. But it was you. I used to play with you and your sisters on the beach back when we were kids."

Gracie felt the air rush out of her lungs. It couldn't be...

"Does this help?" Bill ran his fingers through his hair and made it stick out in crazy patches.

She laughed. Little Billy Dekker. How could she have missed it? They used to play together every summer. "You used to help us build sand castles on the beach."

"And taught you my special technique, if I remember correctly."

Gracie nodded. It had something to do with the right amount of moisture in the sand. She'd never really mastered his style, but she remembered Billy making magnificent creations that he'd carve out carefully.

He was watching her intently. The way he studied her face made her cheeks burn. Had he remembered the kiss he'd given her when they'd been just nine or ten? It was only on the cheek, but Gracie had been aghast and told him to never, ever do that again, and he hadn't. But that hadn't kept him away. He trailed after her wherever she went that summer.

"Hey, you guys, Grandpa Folger's about to start telling his stories," Megan called.

"Be right there," Bill said. He pushed himself up and brushed the sand off of his pants.

"It's funny running into you again after all this time," he said, holding out his hand to help Gracie out of her chair.

"It definitely is." Gracie let him pull her up, and he started to lead her toward the makeshift fire. She stood still, watching him for a second, and then followed.

Sam huddled close to Jamie, wishing she'd brought a windbreaker along for the evening. Even though the dying embers made an attempt to keep everyone warm, a cool breeze had blown in off the sea, hitting her back and chilling her to the bone.

Megan Folger-Wildes sat at Sam's other side, cuddling Addison, her red-headed four-year-old in her arms, while seven-year-old Micah sat beside his mother, rubbing his eyes and yawning.

Sam was dying to tell Megan—to tell everyone—that they were going to buy the Misty Harbor Inn, but she'd promised her sisters not to say a word. They were going to wait until it was a done deal, and then they'd tell their friends, issue a press release, find a listing of past guests, and let nearly the entire world know that the Misty Harbor Inn was under new ownership and would be reopening a year from now. It was all so unbelievable. She was actually going to own a B and B. She tried not to think of all the permits and money and the entire business side of making their mother's dream come true.

"Well, shiver me timbers…" Grandpa Folger shared a mischievous grin with the two dozen or so people gathered around what remained of the fire. He winked at Megan, Addison, and Micah, and then the grizzled old man began to speak in most dramatic fashion. "'Twas a long, long time ago, nigh on two hundred years, when the whaler *Essex* sank to the dark and eerie bottom of Davy Jones's Locker."

Sam had heard something about the sinking of the *Essex*. The tragedy was part of Nantucket's whaling past, and she had seen a plaque about it the other day.

"She was a beauty of a ship who plied the oceans from Nantucket to the South Pacific to the Hawaiian Islands, in risky pursuit of the great sperm whale and the dollars that would line the coffers of many a man."

Sam could see Grandpa Folger had told this story many times, and he had dramatized it quite a bit. It was almost like watching theater. She looked at Jamie, who laughed, and then turned back to the old man.

"It was the year 1820, a good year for whalers. Captain George Pollard and his crew had sailed the world and were at last in the Pacific, throwing their harpoons and capturing their prey. Yet it was a fateful year." Grandpa Folger closed one eye, narrowed the other. His thick and bushy white eyebrows knit together as he looked at each individual sitting around the fire. "Fateful, that is, for Captain Pollard, because that's when he and the *Essex* met their match. A whale like no other refused to be taken. The beast was annoyed with the harpoons being thrown his way. He was angry and mad. So mad, in fact, that he attacked the *Essex*, tearing it apart from stem to stern, until the mighty vessel was destroyed by the whale. Down, down, it sank, never to be seen again."

Sam saw Micah snuggle in closer to his mother. She longed to reach out and pull Jamie close to her like that, like she used to when Jamie was little, but she knew her grown daughter would not appreciate it.

"Ah, but if you think that's the end of the tale and the end of Captain Pollard, you'd be wrong. Many a man, including the good captain, survived that awful calamity. For three months—three very, very long months—Captain Pollard and his crew floated in their lifeboat. Many men starved; many went mad. Only a few survived, rescued at last by another Nantucket whaler, the *Two Brothers*.

"'It's a miracle!' people claimed. 'It's amazing they survived!' There were headlines in all the important papers! Captain Pollard was hailed as a hero, and not long after was given another ship, another chance to ply the oceans in search of the daring and valuable sperm whale. The ship he was given: the *Two Brothers*, the very ship that had saved him. And lo and behold, on Captain Pollard's return trip out to sea, the *Two Brothers* sank. Sank, I tell you. It seemed impossible. How could one captain be so unlucky?"

"Did he survive?" Micah asked. He crossed the sand and climbed into his great-grandfather's lap.

"Aye, he did, young fellow. And one day you can read all about his exploits, although Herman Melville took liberties with the story."

"What story's that, Great Grandpa?"

"Have you ever heard of *Moby Dick*?"

The little boy nodded. "My Dad said he had to read that book in school, and he hated it. I don't really have to read it, do I?"

"Every boy should read it. It's a tale of revenge and derring-do, and it's based on the true story of Captain Pollard."

The little boy frowned. "Do you know any ghost stories, Grandpa? That was okay, but whales aren't as spooky as ghosts."

Grandpa Folger laughed, and his audience joined in.

"Tell our guests what you know about the Misty Harbor Inn," Megan said. "They've been doing research on the place. They might even buy it."

Oh dear. Megan had let the cat out of the bag. Sam nearly groaned.

"I've heard stories about a woman who vanished from the inn." Megan continued. "Maybe she haunts the place. If so, just think how many more guests they'll get, and I'm sure they'll send a little business my way."

"All right. A good old-fashioned legend. Now we're in my territory," Jamie whispered to Sam.

"Maybe you can count this trip as thesis research," Sam answered.

"Now, now, Megan," Pastor Wildes said, grinning at his daughter-in-law, "you'll drive up the cost of that old place if someone thinks they can capitalize on it by telling tales of ghosts walking around the place and going bump in the night."

"So there's no ghost?" Micah's bottom lip stuck out.

"I doubt it." Grandpa Folger laughed. "But it seems to me that I did used to know something about the woman who'd lived there who disappeared."

"We read that it was the second wife of the man who built the house," Sam said.

"Her name was Hannah. Do you know anything at all about the disappearance of Hannah Montague?" Caroline asked.

"Let me see." He looked down at the sand. "I don't know how much of this is true—"

Jamie laughed. "After that last story, it's a strange time to be caring about facts," she whispered.

"—but I remember hearing that the woman was much younger than her husband, and that she was forced into the marriage."

"Do you think her husband might have had something to do with her disappearance?" Sam asked.

"I wouldn't know."

"Did she run away? Was she kidnapped? Killed?"

"I suppose it could have been any of those things." Grandpa Folger shrugged. "As far as I know, she could have been hidden away in one of the secret rooms that supposedly exists in the inn."

"Then there are secret rooms?" Jamie asked, looking clearly intrigued. Sam could easily imagine her daughter spending most of her time at the inn hunting for secret rooms and hidden passageways.

"I think we've all heard rumors about secret rooms," Pastor Stan said, "but how could they possibly exist when the inn has been remodeled several times?"

"Those remodels might have looked extensive on the outside," Bill Dekker said, "but from what I've heard, none of the owners has ever done much more than a down-and-dirty update on the place. I've even heard that the attic and carriage house haven't been touched since I was a boy."

"Be that as it may, Bill," Pastor Stan continued, "my guess is, it's all gossip. Complete speculation. Rumors like that are sometimes spread to increase the price of a property."

Sam could see Jamie listening closely, taking it all in. Sam wanted to make sure to ask her about what she thought later.

"Do you think there could be other secrets surrounding the place?" Caroline asked. Sam could see her sister was so wrapped up in the possibilities she probably wouldn't sleep tonight just thinking about them.

"Could be," Grandpa Folger nodded. "There very well could be, but there's no telling if anyone will ever know what really happened to Hannah Montague. Some stories just aren't meant to be told."

CHAPTER
Sixteen

Caroline had barely slept a wink. She'd lain awake most of the night listening to Max snoring in his basket on the floor next to the bed and to fog horns out on the ocean. She'd lain on one side, twisted over to the other, and tucked her hands under her head, under her pillow, and behind her neck. Nothing worked. All she could think about was Hannah Montague's disappearance. It gnawed at her. The poor woman, gone, just like that, and no one knew what had happened to her.

Caroline pounded her fist into her pillow, tried to find a more comfortable position for her head, and asked herself why it mattered so much to her what happened to Hannah Montague. It had happened well over a hundred years ago and had nothing to do with their buying the inn. It was merely a part of the house's history.

But that was it. That was why it mattered. It was a part of the house's history, and that made it important to know more about what had happened to Hannah Montague.

She rolled over again, staring at the curtains ruffling in the breeze. *Hannah Montague.* Caroline smiled wistfully. Won't we have fun trying to learn more about you once we've bought and moved into the inn?

"You've reached the voice mail for Realtor Deborah Greenleaf. I'm either out of the office or on another call. Please leave your name, phone number, and a detailed message after the tone, and I will return your call as soon as possible. Thanks."

Sam huffed out a sigh, still holding the cell phone to her ear as she looked at her sisters and shook her head. She waited and waited for the tone, and when it sounded, she cleared her throat and said in her most businesslike voice, "Deborah, this is Sam Carter. You can reach me at—" Sam paused for a moment, trying to remember her cell phone number and then added it to her message. "My sisters and I would like to make an offer on the Misty Harbor Inn. Please call as soon as possible."

"I hope she isn't out of town," Gracie said, sliding out of her dress shoes. Gracie and Caroline had made Sam promise to wait until they got back from church to call and make the offer, and she had done as they as asked, but barely. The moment they'd stepped back inside the cottage, Sam had grabbed the phone.

Sam couldn't miss the skeptical glance that Gracie cast at Caroline. "She'll probably call back at any moment. But wouldn't you know it. Now that we've finally made one of the biggest decisions of our lives, we can't get in touch with the real estate agent."

"Calm down, you two," Jamie said, lying on the sofa with her laptop open in front of her. "The inn's been on the market for nearly five years. It's not like someone else is going to come along and sweep it out from under your feet."

"And I'm not going to change my mind about buying it, Gracie," Caroline said, pouring a tall glass of lemonade for George, who'd come to church with them. He had to catch a flight back to Maryland in another two hours, and had to head back to the boat to pack up his things soon. "I know you're worried about my flaking on you, but that's not going to happen."

"I'm just nervous," Gracie said, pushing a lock of hair behind her ear. She sat down in one of the dining chairs. "We're spending a lot of money and we don't even have a game plan yet. I just feel like we're putting the cart before the horse."

"I've done that dozens of times," George said, taking his glass of lemonade from Caroline. "If my heart was truly in the deal, if I wasn't just making a bid on something for the sake of making money, and it failed, well, I didn't really feel like I'd lost anything at all."

"You mean if we're buying the inn more for the love of it, rather than as a business venture, we can't go wrong, no matter what happens?" Sam clarified when Gracie looked a little confused.

"Exactly." George took a sip of lemonade.

"Well I, for one, am madly in love with the place," Jamie said, tearing her gaze away from her computer screen. "There must be thousands upon thousands of stories about the old place. It just staggers the imagination." Max butted his nose under Jamie's arm, and she reached over to pet him. "And of course, the idea of hidden rooms in that place doesn't hurt either. It sounds crazy, but just think of all the hidden rooms that we know existed. Anne Frank was hidden away for all the best reasons, and Corrie ten Boom and her family created a secret room where they could help Jews escape the Nazis. Who's to say there couldn't be one at the inn?"

"Suddenly you're an expert on secret rooms?" Sam teased. She sat down across from Gracie and started to flip through a cooking magazine, even though she was totally engaged in her daughter's words.

"You wouldn't believe all that I've managed to find on the Internet about prisoners of war escaping their captors and would-be kings hiding from the chopping block. And then there are subterranean escape routes, hidden doors, mini hiding holes for valuables..." Jamie closed her laptop and sat up. "I don't know about you, but I can think of all sorts of places inside the Misty Harbor Inn where there could be secret doors. As soon as it's yours, you can start searching for good old Hannah Montague. As far as we know, she could have been walled up somewhere. Buried alive."

"Jamie." Sam shook her head at her daughter. "Please."

"It's possible. Grandpa Folger even said so."

"I don't mind the inn having a few intriguing stories, but I'm not all that crazy about finding a skeleton beneath my bedroom floor." Gracie shuddered.

"Now there's a thought." George grinned.

The phone rang, making them all jump.

Sam grabbed her cell phone quickly and was excited to hear Deborah Greenleaf's voice at the other end. "I'm so happy to hear that you want to make an offer on the Misty Harbor," Deborah said. "I can meet with you on Tuesday—"

"Tuesday?" Sam frowned. "Not today?"

"Unfortunately, I was called out of town unexpectedly and won't be back on the island until Tuesday around noon. That's the earliest I can write up the offer. I'll need a check for a thousand dollars to show good faith, but please, Sam, don't worry. I will call the owners after I hang up and let them know I'll be faxing an offer to them that afternoon. I'm sure they'll be quite excited."

Unfortunately, Sam's immediate excitement had rather fizzled.

"Are you one hundred percent positive you want to give up the chance of living in Chipping Campden?" George asked, as he and Caroline waited for his plane to board. "And you're just as positive that you want to buy the inn?"

"I'm positive." Caroline brushed an errant strand of hair from her face. "There's going to be a lot for me to get used to. Living with other people instead of by myself. Keeping regular hours. That might be one of the hardest things for me to get used to."

"Not hopping on a plane at a moment's notice to fly off to who-knows-where."

"I really am tired of traveling all the time," Caroline said. "But if I get desperate, you can always come to the island and take me sailing for the day so I can feel free and easy for a little while."

"Something troubling you?" He studied her face. "I've known you for thirty years, Caroline Marris. You get antsy if you stay in any one place too long." He chuckled, a soft smile at last touching his face. "You have trouble finishing one thing before you start another. None of that's ever bothered me, but I can see that it worries Gracie. I just want you to be sure of what you're doing before you commit to this, because you won't be able to back out once you've bought the inn, especially if you go in on it with your sisters."

"I am committed. And I'm not going to hurt Gracie."

George touched her arm with one of his warm, strong hands. "That's my girl."

He kissed the top of her head, as he'd done so many times over the years, and when his flight number was called, he picked up his bag and smiled. "Call me if you need anything."

"I will."

"And as soon as that Packard's out of storage let me know. I'm eager to get my hands on it."

"We're going to have the time of our lives, George," Caroline said, smiling as she waved good-bye.

"What do you think of this?" Gracie asked her sisters, lifting a soft floral bedspread in pretty shades of lavender and green.

It wasn't at all what Caroline had in mind for their very own inn's guest rooms, but she wasn't about to tell Gracie that she wanted something simpler. She ran her fingers across a quilted matelassé in a pretty shade of pale aqua. It was simple and clean. She hoped to keep the fabrics and the wall treatments simple and let the furniture and the architecture speak for itself.

"It's pretty, Aunt Gracie," Jamie said. She'd spent her last day on Nantucket following her mother and aunts around from store to store, creating lists of decorating possibilities, but she didn't seem to mind. She had seemed a bit better every day, and she hadn't mentioned Cory in a couple days. Caroline knew it would be a long time before Jamie was over the breakup, but clearly coming here had been good for her.

"I like this," Sam said, pointing to a nautical striped duvet.

Caroline looked at Sam, and then at Gracie. They were going to have to come to a compromise on the décor, and she guessed it might not be easy. She hadn't thought about how different their tastes were, and how that might make this difficult.

"What are you thinking of doing for pillow shams?" Jamie asked, making a note in her notebook.

"These are pretty," Gracie said, pointing at a gingham set that coordinated with the floral bedspread.

"Oh, I think we should go with no pillow shams," Caroline said. "I was thinking we could have a simple coverlet like this for spring and summer, with crisp white linens and plump pillows, at least three or four per bed."

Gracie didn't look convinced. "But you need shams to make a bed look finished. And then, with the bed skirts—"

"Actually, since the beds are made of such beautiful cherrywood and are high off the floor, I bet we could forgo any kind of bed skirt," Sam said. Caroline flashed her a quick smile of thanks, but Sam didn't seem to notice.

"Not only will that show off the wood, but it'll keep the room fresher looking," Caroline said.

Sam nodded. "It'll keep our costs down too. Goodness, the price of bed skirts can be staggering."

Gracie fingered a plush down comforter in the same floral pattern. "We could use these in the winter."

"I was thinking we should reserve winter for family," Caroline said.

Sam squished the corner of a pillow. "But we may need to stay open all year to cover our costs."

"When I talked with Megan at the clambake, she told me that Nantucket's usually dead quiet from the first of November and right through Christmas."

Caroline took a deep breath. Of course they were going to have to work things like this out. That didn't mean buying the inn was a mistake. It would just take time to get it all sorted out.

Gracie tugged her notebook out of the straw handbag she was carrying and jotted down a few notes.

"That would give us time for a little R & R," Sam finally agreed. She looked at each of her sisters and smiled. It managed to ease the tension. "I'm sure we'll need that after our first season."

"You'll probably need a whole lot of R & R after your first week of cleaning and rehabbing the place," Jamie said, laughing. "Thank goodness I'm leaving before that starts."

They walked out of the linen area and toward dining. "The first thing we're going to have a do is take a complete inventory of everything in the house—"

"Especially the kitchen and dining room," Sam added. "I should have checked out what kind of serving pieces are stored away, but I didn't."

"Considering all the wonderful decorative pieces that were left behind," Caroline said. "I imagine we're going to find a whole host of intriguing dishes in the kitchen."

"We could do mix and match." Sam absently fingered through a stack of lacy place mats. "Different china patterns, or stoneware, as long as they have at least one thing to tie them together, like a certain color. The possibilities are endless."

"I saw a few thrift stores here in town," Jamie said, "if the inn doesn't already have enough dishes, you could probably pick up the perfect mix-and-match items for almost nothing."

"We can haunt antique stores for the right pieces too," Gracie added. "I can see our breakfast table—or tables!—now, with the morning sun shining in." It wasn't exactly how Caroline pictured it, but it would work, and she wasn't about to start raising more tension now. "And crystal water goblets and delicate china sugar bowls and creamers—"

"With the shutters thrown open so our guests can see the view of the ocean." Sam drew in a deep breath, smiling with satisfaction and excitement.

Sam reminded Caroline so much of their mother. Of course, Caroline realized, as she wandered off to look at plush cotton bath towels, both of her sisters had mentioned things she'd barely thought about—cleaning and inventorying, for starters. She was an idea person, but had never been good with the practical matters. She would have to change. She'd soon have to be a waitress too, and dishwasher, and housekeeper.

Not for the first time in the past twenty-four hours, Caroline hoped she hadn't gotten into something totally over her head.

Two hours later, they were back in the cottage again, all four of them sitting around a table covered with endless stacks of paper: Gracie's lists, Jamie's lists, and Sam's cost estimates. Sam imagined Caroline's ideas were all stored away in her head—but that was okay; Caroline's ideas were always spot on.

"So we're firm on what we want to offer up front?" Sam asked, broadly underlining, again and again, a dollar amount that staggered the imagination. She already had a thousand butterflies fluttering around in her stomach. "And we're firm on how much higher we're willing to go before we decide enough is enough, that the owners want way too much money, and that we're just not going to break our bank to give it to them?" She looked from Gracie to Caroline.

"I could put in a little more if necessary," Caroline said, and for the first time since they'd come to the island, Sam thought her oldest sister looked a little harried. Caroline wasn't the kind to get stressed out, but buying this inn was a new ball game for her. So was staying in one place. Buying the inn meant she'd be staying on Nantucket and living in the Misty Harbor Inn probably for the rest of her life.

"No. We don't want you to put in more," Gracie said. "We're splitting this three ways. No one else pays more or less."

"Gracie's right," Sam said. "We talked about this already. Our inheritance is paying a hundred percent for the inn, and on top of that we're each putting equal shares into a bank account to cover expenses."

"And Mom's doing all the accounting, since she—fortunately—has a head for that kind of thing," Jamie added, piling her duffel bag and backpack next to the front door, ready to take off for the ferry ride back to the mainland.

"My head's already swimming in the details." Sam threaded her fingers through her hair. She was thinking she just might have to cut it shorter once they moved into the inn. She might need something totally wash and wear, because she had the feeling that for quite a while there wouldn't be great amounts of time to fool with her hair or makeup or clothes. "I was sure I had a good handle on everything we'd need as far as finances go, but somehow I forgot insurance," Sam said, pulling a sheet out from the bottom of her stack. "And oh my word, is there a lot involved with that. It's not just homeowners' insurance anymore, it's—"

As she talked about the insurance, Sam could see that Caroline's eyes were glazing over. "Am I throwing way too many details out?"

Caroline shook her head. "I just wish it was a done deal. I wish we didn't have to worry about moving out of this place in a few days and into a temporary hotel if we don't have a signed contract in hand."

"Even if we do agree on a deal, we'll still have to go through escrow," Sam said. She didn't want Caroline to stress out over the business end of things, but she needed to realize that that they wouldn't be moving into the inn and opening it up to guests in a matter of days. "Escrow's going to take at least a couple of weeks, more likely thirty days, unless Deborah can get things moved along faster."

"Maybe we can get the key before escrow closes," Gracie offered. "I know buying a home or a hotel or anything else takes time, but we are paying cash, so that should account for something. And I'm with Caroline. I'd move in tomorrow if we could. I want to get my hands on the place, start cleaning, talk to Bill Dekker and a few other builders about renovations."

"I think you all need to take a deep breath," Jamie said. "It's all going to happen in its own good time, and once it does and you're in the inn working your fingers to the bone, you're going to wish you had some carefree time to kick back and enjoy life."

Caroline smiled. "You raised an awfully smart kid," she said to Sam. "I have to admit, I for one could use a break from thinking about insurance and building contractors and marketing plans."

"Then my suggestion is," Jamie said, "all of you climb into the car and take me to the ferry and then go down to the beach and have a picnic. It just might be the last time in a long time that you're going to have an evening to call your own."

CHAPTER
Seventeen

Gracie watched Caroline's pen tapping on the table. The noise was maddening, and Gracie wanted to rip the pen from her sister's hand, but she resisted. "We'll need a contingency plan," Caroline was saying to Deborah Greenleaf.

The fact that Caroline thought they needed a contingency plan made Gracie more than a little nervous too. "Not that we have any plans for backing out of the deal, you understand," Caroline continued. "We just want to be safe."

"As you read through the offer, you'll see that I've already included a clause stating that your offer is contingent upon the inspection, plus another based on the three of you being able to obtain insurance," Deborah said.

"Is that common?" Sam asked. "The insurance contingency clause, that is? Do you think there could be some difficulty obtaining insurance on the inn?"

"It's a safeguard," Deborah said. "That's all." Deborah leaned forward in her chair, writing up the details of the offer on the legal-sized offer form. "Since you're paying cash, we can't make this offer contingent upon your obtaining a loan. Asking for a contingency based on your obtaining insurance seemed reasonable. Now, let's talk about escrow costs, title fees, and..."

Gracie concentrated on each and every word. Buying a home back in the seventies had been so much easier than this. She didn't remember much at all about that process, except that Art had done all of the negotiating, and she'd pretty much just signed on the dotted line.

Gracie found herself almost holding her breath. She wished this was over and done with, before something fell apart.

"We'd like to specify that the owner pay all other costs associated with the transaction," Sam said. They'd discussed this already, deciding that this was one item they wouldn't budge on.

Deborah frowned. "Perhaps you'd consider going fifty-fifty on some of those costs? That might make your offer, which is much lower than the asking price, appear more reasonable to the owners."

Sam shook her head. "No, Deborah, we don't want to go fifty-fifty on any fees. We want the owner to pay those. You've given us comps to show what other properties are going for. Most of them are similar in size and location, but are in much better condition structurally. We believe our offer is more than fair."

Gracie felt her stomach tumble. This whole experience verged on being more than she could take, but Sam was the negotiator in the family. Gracie hoped she could work some magic now.

Deborah opened her mouth, as if she were going to offer up another solution, but finally she wrote out the offer and had each sister sign, pledging their very lives, it seemed.

Deborah smiled at last. She rose from her chair. "Because the owners are sometimes difficult to contact, I appreciate your giving them seventy-two hours to respond. I will, however, fax this to them immediately and follow up with a phone call. With any luck, I'll have an answer for you before the end of the day."

It was done. Now the wait began. There were only seventy-two more hours—fewer they hoped—to worry about Caroline's backing out, catching a plane, and flying off to Timbuktu, leaving Sam and Gracie totally in the lurch.

Twenty-four hours dragged by. Twenty-four hours of piecing together jigsaw puzzles with Sam and Gracie, trying to read, and taking long walks on the beach to distract themselves. Gracie seemed to spend the time making a lot of lists, and Sam somehow seemed totally at peace working on her cross-stitch. But Caroline knew they were all on pins and needles wondering when Deborah would call and let them know if the owners would accept their offer.

Caroline paced the floor. She felt as if the walls inside the cottage were closing in on her. She tried writing a travel article about an elegant riverboat cruise through Peru's rain forest. She allowed herself to picture the black lakes, slow-moving sloths, shaggy-tailed monk saki monkeys, the endangered scarlet macaw, and the infamous piranhas. She worked on her computer until well after midnight, when her eyes were too blurry to see the monitor. Gracie and Sam had already gone to bed, so she disappeared into her own room, crawled under the covers, and tried to turn off her mind. She didn't want to think or worry any longer.

It was the cell phone that woke Caroline in the morning. Sunlight sliced through the curtains, straight across the room and into her eyes. She jerked up in bed, trying desperately to remember where she was. She blinked her eyes rapidly until they were finally wide open and able to focus.

She grabbed for her phone, wishing she'd turned it off before going to bed, and noticed that it was already 7:30 on Thursday morning. There were still twenty-four hours before the owners had to make a decision, but maybe they had. Maybe Deborah was an early bird and wanted to start the sisters' day off right.

The number that appeared on the cell phone didn't look at all familiar, and it wasn't local. It was an overseas number. London. She cleared her throat, pressed the talk button, and said, "Hello?"

"Is that Caroline Marris?" The accent was thick and terribly upper-crust British.

Her mouth was dry. She needed to brush her teeth and have a cup of coffee, but somehow Caroline managed to utter, "Yes."

"Caroline! It's Paul Lambrick." It was her landlord in Chipping Camden. "I hope I haven't called too early. I have a devil of a time remembering the difference in time between here and the States."

Then it was definitely a good thing she wasn't in California, where it would only be 4:30. "I was just about to crawl out of bed, Mr. Lambrick, so no, you didn't call too early. I hope everything's fine at Briar Rose. The vicar and his wife have been keeping an eye on the place while I've been over here."

"Everything's fine, Miss Marris. Actually, as far as you're concerned, it might be more than fine."

He paused for the longest time. Was she supposed to know what he was talking about? "My wife and I have made the decision to sell Briar Rose."

Caroline's throat knotted. She could barely breathe.

"I know we've told you for years that we'd never sell. After all, the cottage has been in the family for several hundred years. It's part of our heritage, you know. But neither of us is getting any younger, our children do not want to be bothered with it, and, as much as we hate to part with the cottage, we simply need to let it go."

This couldn't be happening. For ten years now she'd wanted to buy the cottage. For ten years she'd scrimped and saved so she could pay the price. She could do it easily now, especially with her inheritance.

"You're certain, Mr. Lambrick? I know how much you and Mrs. Lambrick adore Briar Rose."

"Yes, yes, we lived there during the first forty years of our marriage. It's a beauty of a place, and you're the only one we know who has loved it even half as much as Mrs. Lambrick and I. That's why we'd like to offer it to you, at a price that should certainly be fitting. Nothing outrageous, you know, not like most other homes in the Cotswolds. After all, you have lived there and paid us rent for ten years."

Caroline was still completely stunned. She dragged in a deep breath and let it out slowly. "I'm absolutely stunned, Mr. Lambrick. As much as I'd like to tell you yes, I'll buy it, right this very second, I'll have to call you back later today. Or, more than likely, tomorrow."

"I understand completely. There are financial matters to consider. You do have our phone number?"

Caroline nodded and then said yes when she realized he couldn't see her. She was in a near state of shock. Total elation. She couldn't believe it. After all these years, she could finally buy Briar Rose.

She was out of the bedroom before she'd even closed her phone. The scent of frying bacon met her. And cinnamon. Was Sam making her cinnamon sticky buns this morning? Or maybe she was making baked French toast with pecans and real maple syrup. Suddenly she was hungry. Famished. She felt...goodness, she felt amazing! She had so much to tell her sisters and Jamie and George, and she wanted to run on the beach with Max and shout out thank-yous to God for answering her prayers.

At long last, Briar Rose was hers. The view of St. James was hers. She could take her walks through the ancient cemetery again without worrying that when she got home there might be a message waiting for her telling her to move out.

She would be the owner of Briar Rose now. It would be all hers.

At last.

And then...reality hit.

The inn.

A sudden pain throbbed near her right temple and behind her right eye. It made her dizzy. Her fingers flew to her head, and she tried desperately to massage away the pain, but it didn't seem willing to leave. It was going to plague her, as was the decision she had to make.

She walked out into the kitchen and saw Gracie pouring milk into a steaming mug of coffee. Sam was peering into the oven. The whole place smelled sweet and comforting.

She'd been in love with the Briar Rose for ten years. For ten years she'd desperately wanted to buy it. And now...there was the Misty Harbor Inn. She wanted it too. It has tugged her into its warm and waiting arms and hugged her close. It was magical. Hypnotic.

She wanted them both; but she had money for only one.

No matter what decision she made, she'd end up hurt. And one decision would hurt her sisters.

Caroline looked at them now. Sam opened the oven door and took out a casserole dish bubbling with her French toast topped with brown sugar, maple syrup, butter, and pecans. Gracie carried a mug of steaming coffee toward her.

Caroline swallowed hard.

"Is something wrong?" Gracie asked when Caroline took the coffee mug into her shaking hand. "You look awful. Was that your phone ringing earlier? Who on earth calls at this time of the morning?"

"I feel fine. Really." Caroline took a sip of coffee. It was extra strong this morning, and Gracie had loaded it with extra sugar and milk, just as she liked it. It burned her throat on the way down and settled hard in the pit of her stomach.

She pulled out a chair at the table and sat. Setting the coffee cup on the table, she folded her hands in her lap. Her whole body was trembling now. She took yet another deep breath. "That was my landlord who called," she managed to say, even though her throat was terribly parched, "the man who owns Briar Rose."

"Is there a problem?" Sam asked, a worried frown touching her face. "There wasn't a fire, was there? You haven't lost anything?"

"There wasn't a fire. Nothing's wrong with the cottage. In fact"— she sighed—"they've decided to sell it. To me, if I'm still interested."

Sam stared at her. Gracie glared.

"What did you tell him?" Gracie asked, her voice tight. Her gaze was frozen with pent-up anger.

"I didn't tell him anything. Well, I did, I said I'd call him tomorrow."

"Why didn't you just tell him you've had a change of plans?" Sam asked. "Why didn't you tell him about the inn?"

"The inn didn't even cross my mind while I was talking to him. I was too excited. You have to understand," Caroline almost stammered. "This is something I've wanted for ten years."

"And you've only wanted the inn for a week," Gracie said, her voice icy.

"That's enough, Gracie," Sam said. "Caroline didn't expect this call any more than we did. What would you do if you were in her shoes?"

"I certainly wouldn't back out on a deal I'd made with my sisters."

Sam stepped toward Caroline. She put a hand on her shoulder. "I'll understand if you change your mind about the inn." She sighed. "I haven't made any real plans yet. Nothing needs to change. I've got my townhouse and, well—"

Caroline looked up to see Sam biting her lip, more than likely fighting back tears. "I'm sorry, Sam." She looked at Gracie. "I'm sorry."

"Does 'I'm sorry' mean you've made your decision?" Gracie asked. "Is it all that cut and dried? You get a call and five minutes later you know that you're going to buy Briar Rose?"

"It's not that easy, Gracie."

"It is easy. You have two choices. Yes or no."

"Neither choice is easy." Caroline looked at both her sisters. She was ready to cry, and wished she could see a touch of understanding in either of their faces. But she didn't. "I told the owner I'd call back later today or tomorrow with my answer."

"As far as I'm concerned, you can call him back right now and give him your answer. Tell him yes, you'll buy Briar Rose, because—" Gracie dragged in a deep breath. "I've had it, Caroline. If you want it to be an easy decision for you to make, I'll make it easy for you.

I'm out of the deal for the inn. Sam, call Deborah and withdraw our offer."

"I can't do that, Gracie," Sam said, and Caroline couldn't miss the tears that slid down her sister's face. "I don't want to do that."

"Then you'll have to do it alone," Gracie said, a moment before throwing open the front door, ready to storm out of the cottage. "I've had enough."

Caroline didn't need to sit inside a church to talk with God. She could have curled up under the covers in her bed and had a conversation with Him there, but she'd needed to get away from the house. She needed a place of refuge—a sanctuary. She found it inside Harvest Chapel, sitting on a wooden pew in the old church building.

She'd called George, tearing him away from an important meeting, and as she talked, she could almost feel him holding her hand. He'd said very little when she'd told him Briar Rose could finally be hers. He'd always be her shoulder to cry on, her rock if she needed someone strong. But he wouldn't and couldn't interfere. "This is your decision," he'd said. "Only you know what's in your heart."

Unfortunately, her heart and head were overflowing with confusion. She had to make a decision, she just didn't know what that decision should be. *Please, God*, she prayed. *Show me the way.*

She hurt inside, not for herself, but for what she'd done to her sisters. Her uncertainty—her selfishness?—had put a wedge between herself and Gracie. Sam hadn't been able to look at her either; she'd left the house, taking Max with her, and headed who knows where.

Caroline shivered. She knew all too well that she was destined to suffer, no matter what choice she made. But Gracie and Sam didn't deserve to suffer too. She'd prodded them, coaxed them, talked about the magic of the inn until they, too, fell under its spell. Then wham! She'd burst their bubble.

I don't want to hurt them, Lord, but how can I give up my dream?

She pulled a hymnal from its rack in front of her and let it fall open. She wasn't looking for anything in particular. She hoped any words would bring her comfort.

> *When peace, like a river, attendeth my way,*
> *When sorrows like sea billows roll;*
> *Whatever my lot, Thou has taught me to say,*
> *It is well, it is well, with my soul.*

Right this moment she didn't feel like all was well with her soul. She could either hurt her sisters or hurt herself; it didn't seem like much of a choice.

"Good morning, Caroline."

She looked up from the hymnal and saw Pastor Wildes standing at the end of the pew, smiling warmly, the light beaming through the stained-glass window sprinkling colors over his khaki pants, his pale blue polo shirt, and the gold cross he wore on a leather chain around his neck.

Somehow she smiled. "Good morning."

"Mind if I join you?"

Caroline shook her head, and Pastor Wildes slid down the pew and sat at her side. "You look a little troubled. Anything I can do to help?"

"Oh, I don't know." She shrugged. "Probably." She sighed deeply and told him her tale.

"St. James is, indeed, a lovely church, and Chipping Campden is far and away one of my favorite hamlets in the Cotswolds."

"You've been there?"

"On a vacation a few years ago. One of those bus tours with thirty or so other baby boomers. Next time I'll be bold and rent a car and risk driving on those narrow lanes that wind through the English countryside." He chuckled, the sound echoing about the hallowed halls of his church. "Nice people on those tours, but once they set to bickering, you feel like the devil's taken over and is wending his way toward the underworld."

"I've been on a few of those trips myself. They're not all that way, but every once in a while, you get stuck on a real doozie."

"And a doozie appears to be what you're caught up in now, I'd say."

"I don't remember ever feeling so miserable. I just wish I knew what to do."

"There's a little something I like to remind my congregants of when they get into a pickle like this. A little something from Matthew that you've probably heard more than once in your lifetime."

"What is it, Pastor?"

"'In everything, do to others what you would have them do to you.'" he said, his voice filled with warmth and compassion. "It's the good old Golden Rule, and wise words to live by."

"I told you this would happen," Gracie said. Sam and Gracie were walking along the beach. Max ran in and out of the surf, chasing seagulls and tugging on seaweed that had washed up on the shore. "I knew this pipe dream would burst."

"It hasn't burst completely," Sam said, feeling so downhearted she could easily bury her head in the sand for the next few days and hide from the world. But she was trying to hold on to the faith she had in Caroline. "First off, I didn't call Deborah and tell her to pull our offer. Second, Caroline hasn't decided that she's moving back to England."

Gracie sighed. "I was angry when I told you to call Deborah. I'm glad you didn't. But Caroline will go back to England. You didn't know her the way I did when we were growing up. I've tried to tell you, Sam, but you refuse to look at the side of Caroline that causes chaos when you least expect it."

"Chaos might be a bit too strong of a word, don't you think?"

Gracie kicked at the sand. "Possibly." She grabbed a small piece of driftwood and threw it out for Max to retrieve. "But as far as I'm concerned, she should buy Briar Rose and go back to England."

"I don't believe you."

"We do nothing but argue."

"That might be all you see, but I see something else completely. I've watched the two of you grow closer in the past two weeks. I've watched you laugh and cry together, over big things and small, even over an old black and white movie."

"That's only natural. We're sisters, but we've never—"

"Don't you dare tell me you've never been close." Sam dropped down on the beach, drew her knees up to her chest, and wrapped her arms around her legs. Gracie sat beside her, a little slower, her knees creaking slightly. "Do you really want her to go back to England?"

"Heavens no. I want to be a family again." Gracie sighed heavily. "That's why this whole thing is making me mad. She claims she wants to be around family again too. She claims she's missed us, that she wishes she hadn't been away so long. If that's the case, why didn't she tell her English landlord to get lost?" She brushed the palms of her hands sharply. "Just like that."

"Because it's not easy to lose something—or someone—you love. You know that."

"Oh, Sam. It's a cottage in the Cotswolds. It doesn't have a heart and soul, not like Art."

"But you don't want to give up your home in Portland. Art's still in every room. You feel him when you're there. That house is almost like one of your children. That cottage might feel pretty much the same way to Caroline. You shouldn't judge her so harshly, Gracie, unless you've walked in her shoes."

"She's had an easy life."

"You don't know that any more than I do."

Gracie shrugged. "I suppose I don't. I just don't want to see you hurt, and every day I've seen you become more and more attached to the inn. If Caroline doesn't stay here, if she doesn't put in her third of the cost, there's no way you can buy it on your own. There's no way even you and I can buy it. We need Caroline."

"She'll come around," Sam said, gazing out over the waves. "Just wait and see."

Gracie wished she had as much confidence in Caroline.

CHAPTER
Eighteen

Anyone want to put together a jigsaw puzzle?" Caroline said when Sam, Gracie, and Max returned. The cottage had been empty when she'd gotten back from her visit to Harvest Chapel two hours earlier. Neither Gracie nor Sam had left her a note saying where they'd gone. She'd spent the last couple of hours alone, and something told her that even though her sisters were back, she was going to feel even more alone.

"This puzzle is right up your alley, Sam. Two thousand pieces and nothing but parrots in all different colors. It could be a challenge to put together."

"Thanks," Sam said, heading straight for the cabinet in the kitchen where they'd stored a bottle of aspirin, "but I've got a horrendous headache. Think I'll just close my eyes a bit and see if it'll go away."

Caroline flopped down on the sofa. "It's awfully pretty outside," she said, aiming her words toward Gracie, who'd already picked up a book she'd been reading and curled up in a chair beneath the sunny window. "Would you like to go for a walk with me? A bike ride? Or maybe go down to the beach and build a sand castle?"

"Not right now," Gracie said, without looking up from her book. "I want to finish this before dinner tonight. Sam and I decided to try a place called the Lobster Claw. You're welcome to join us if you want."

All of a sudden she felt like a fifth wheel. A pariah. It was pretty much the same way she'd felt when she'd left home the first time. Her parents couldn't give her their blessing. They'd wanted her to go to college, to get married, to have babies, and she wanted none of it. She just wanted to experience life. They'd barely said a word to her the day before she left with all her important belongings in one small bag. That was over forty years ago, and that day still hurt.

"I guess Max and I will go for a walk." Caroline hoped someone would say something, but Gracie had clammed up and Sam sat in her chair, her eyes closed, massaging her temples. "Why don't you go ahead and do dinner without me tonight. There's a deli on Main that has chicken salad sandwiches, and I've been craving one. Max and I might drop by there. They might even serve doggie cookies."

Still nothing. No comment. No smile. No acknowledgement whatsoever.

Caroline tried to swallow the knot that had formed in her throat, but it seemed permanently stuck.

"Come on, Max." Caroline grabbed the leash that hung just inside the coat closet door and snapped it on to his collar. "I think we'll head over to the wharf and check out the shops. Is there anything you guys need or want?"

"Can't think of a thing," Gracie said, her nose still in her book. "Have fun."

Caroline didn't bother to say good-bye. She didn't have the heart to hear nothing in return.

She kept her eyes on the slate sidewalk as they made their way past the row of shingled cottages. Max stopped to sniff the flowers bursting out from behind a white picket fence a few houses down, but Caroline tugged his leash and kept walking toward the corner.

She was halfway down the block, with Max scampering at her side, when Sam caught up with her. "Gracie's a little upset right now."

Caroline felt tears stinging her eyes. "And you?"

Sam shrugged. "Still a little shell-shocked."

"I can't blame Gracie for being mad at me, and I know you're worried, but really, Sam, I haven't made a decision yet. It's sort of like that song 'Torn Between Two Lovers.' I really do feel like a fool, but I just don't know what to do."

Sam smiled her wonderfully soft smile, the one that made her so easy to love. "You need to do what will make you the happiest."

"At the risk of hurting you and Gracie?"

"She'll get over it eventually, and I understand where you're coming from. You love Briar Rose."

"I love the inn too. I love you and Gracie more, but I'm afraid if I stay here I'll end up doing something wrong. That I'll disappoint you both."

"You could never disappoint me," Sam said, wrapping her arms around Caroline. "No matter what you do, I'll always be your biggest fan."

She stood in the back garden and looked out over the waves. The surf pounded against the sand, its gentle roar calming her tense nerves. Briar Rose sure didn't have a view like this. Then again, Briar Rose didn't have peeling wallpaper or dirt, dust, and who knows what living in places where you'd never expect. At Briar Rose she could curl up in her favorite overstuffed chair in front of the fireplace and read until she was bored silly; at the Misty Harbor she'd have to work day and night, dusting, cleaning, and washing bed linens. At Briar Rose, she could live just as she'd always wanted to—doing just as she pleased every day. Here in Nantucket, she'd have her sisters.

She would have put out both hands and pretend to weigh the two on a scale, but she didn't think there was much of a comparison at all between the two places. If you put the two side by side...oh bother! The two houses would never be side by side. One of them had to go.

She turned away from the ocean and meandered along the crushed shell path. The garden was beautiful this time of day, so peaceful and serene. She took her time smelling the roses, and she plucked a dark pink bud from one of the bushes and tucked it into her hair.

All of a sudden she was assailed by a familiar scent. Chanel No. 5. Her mother's favorite. It was strong and powerful. She tried to remember if Sam had been wearing the perfume when she'd hugged her. Maybe she had, and it was clinging to her now. But it seemed to be in the air. It was everywhere, as if her mother were walking with her now, admiring the flowers, trying to tell Caroline how to care for them. But Caroline didn't want to have a green thumb. She simply wanted to enjoy the beauty around her, however it grew.

When she reached the front of the house, she climbed the steps and peered through the leaded glass in the front door, and could see all the way to the back of the house. If she really strained her eyes, she might even see the ocean.

The dust covers were off everything now. The shutters were opened, and the boards that had covered other windows were gone. The house looked like it had more of a soul now. It looked almost happy, as if it knew a family might soon be living in it again.

A family.

"Come along girls, we don't want to be late for tea."

Rosalie's voice came to her so clearly, and she could see her mother now, dressed in her flowery Easter dress with a pink coat over it. She'd dyed her shoes to match and wore her own Jackie Kennedy pill box hat so she and her girls would look like a matched set.

Oh, how she'd wanted to hide that day. She had felt strange, a teenager dressed like an Easter egg. But Mom had been so proud. She'd ushered them into the inn and once they were in the parlor, she breathed deeply, as if she wanted to absorb the atmosphere inside and carry it with her always.

Her mother's spirit was in this house. Her laughter, her smiles. None of those things were in Briar Rose.

Caroline breathed deeply. She'd made her decision.

"You didn't tell me the Lobster Claw was in 'Sconset. It's a good thing I asked a local how to find this place, or I would have been totally late for dinner."

Gracie looked up from the dowdy window table inside the charming café housed inside an old fisherman's shack. Caroline was standing there, all smiles. She looked awfully pretty in her purple gauze blouse, her khaki shorts, and a seashell necklace she'd told them had been made for her by some kids in the South Sea islands of Vanuatu. With Caroline, there was always a story.

Gracie couldn't help but wonder what her story was now.

"Table's awfully small," Caroline said, gesturing at the scarred wooden square between them. "I can pull up a chair. Or maybe we could find another table." She looked at Gracie. "Or maybe I can sit by myself."

"Let's just pull up a chair," Sam said, scooting her chair closer to the multipaned window. She was practically sitting in the white linen curtain. "If we'd known you were going to come—"

"You had no way of knowing." Caroline borrowed a chair from a nearby table and pulled it up close to Sam. The café was so small, there wasn't much room for the waiter to walk around, "Have you been here long?" asked Caroline.

Gracie could only hope they weren't causing a problem.

"We'd planned to be here at seven, but we ended up haunting every art studio and pottery shack we found along the water," Sam said. "We even found a place called Dekker's, but it was closed."

"Do you think it was Bill Dekker's place?" Caroline asked.

"It's just a guess, but yes," Sam said. "He did say he's an artist, and what better place for an artist to work than here in 'Sconset."

"I wish we'd been able to see through the windows," Gracie said, trying to act something close to normal around Caroline. She only wished her sister would tell them she'd made a decision, so she could stop playing a guessing game in her head. "I'd like to know what kind of artist he is. For some reason, I can't picture him sitting out on the beach with an easel and palette full of oil paints or watercolors."

"I see him as more of a sculptor," Sam said, "standing over a flaming forge pounding out bronze or steel."

They all tried to laugh, but it seemed forced. The waiter came and took their orders, starting off with hot baby brie en croûte. Each of them followed up with boiled live lobster—the only way to go, Gracie had thought—and they ordered a combination of onion rings and fries, coleslaw, and a lot of cheesy biscuits on the side. They chatted with the waiter, who looked like he had a couple of years to go before graduating from high school, and it helped ease the tension at the table. But Gracie still felt nervous.

Caroline took a sip of her iced tea and kept looking at something or someone across the room, as if she didn't want to look at her sisters. Sam tried making light conversation. Gracie couldn't stand it any longer.

"Have you made a decision, Caroline? If you're going back to England and buying Briar Rose, please tell us now and get it over."

Gracie wasn't sure, but she thought Caroline's eyes sparkled. For some reason she didn't see that as the best of news. It seemed to mean Caroline was going to go back to England, and the sip of water she'd just taken lodged in her throat. It wasn't the loss of the inn that was bothering her so much; it was the loss of her sister.

"I don't want to give up Briar Rose," Caroline said. Her eyes started to water, and she used the corner of her paper napkin to wipe a tear away. "But I can't give up the two of you. I left you once a long time ago. I'm not going to leave again."

Gracie, too, wiped a tear from her eye. So did Sam.

"I'm staying here," she said. "For good. Now let's just hope and pray we get the inn."

Caroline paced from one end of the living room to the other, back and forth, over and over. If the room had had carpeting, she would have worn it out.

"Haven't you ever heard the saying 'A watched pot never boils'?" Gracie asked, from her sunny spot in the cottage's living room, where she pretended to be reading a book. Sam knew better. Gracie had never been so anxious in her life. Even Max's antics couldn't calm them down enough to laugh.

"Their seventy-two hours is almost up," Sam said, staring at the jigsaw puzzle pieces spread haphazardly across the dining room table—a parrot claw here, a feather there. "The offer was simple. One hundred percent cash. An offer doesn't get better than that."

"But we offered almost twenty percent less than they were asking." Caroline continued to pace. She checked the clock on the wall. She paced some more. "They're probably making us sweat because we slapped them in the face with such a lowball offer."

"They slapped themselves in the face," Gracie said, looking up from her book, "by letting the inn get so run down. If they'd cared for it, even a fraction of the way we care for it, they would have taken a few precautions to keep it and all the beautiful things inside from nearly getting swallowed up by the environment. They don't deserve full price. They don't deserve us worrying about whether or not they're upset about how much we offered. At least we made them an offer; that's far more than anyone else has done."

"What if we don't get it?" Sam said, trying to be the voice of reason. "What will you do then, Caroline? You won't have a home in England, and you won't have a place here."

"I refuse to think anything negative, Sam. It's going to be ours. I can't imagine God giving us the opportunity to make Mom's dream come true and then ripping it out from under us."

The phone rang, and Sam jumped. Every nerve in her body tensed.

"That has to be Deborah," Caroline said. "You get it, Sam. You've done more work than anyone else to put this deal together. You're the one who deserves to hear the news first."

"What if it's bad news?" Sam said. She stood up and moved toward the phone. She tried desperately to stop her heart from racing, but she couldn't.

"It won't be bad news," Caroline said. "Think positive."

Easier said than done, Sam thought. She took a deep breath. Her voice stuck in her throat, and she could just barely say "Hello" when she answered the phone. She cleared her throat a couple of times. She breathed hard as she listened to Deborah go on and on and on. If only she'd get to the point.

"Thank you, Deborah," Sam finally said when Deborah told her the sellers' answer.

Sam hung up the phone. She set it on the table and clutched her stomach, which was tumbling over and over.

"What did she say?" Gracie asked. "Spit it out, Sam."

Sam swallowed and swallowed again, trying to get rid of the lump that felt permanently lodged in her throat.

"Please, Sam. Tell us."

Slowly Sam smiled. "It's ours."

CHAPTER
Nineteen

Y ou look just like Mom."

Caroline sat at the bottom of the curving staircase and watched Sam at work with her feather duster, stirring up a hurricane of soot, cinders, sand, and dirt. Her hair was wrapped in a red bandanna that looked just like one their mother had worn when she cleaned house back in the fifties and sixties. Sam had been at it all day. For the past two days, actually—ever since they moved lock, stock, and barrel into the inn. Just two weeks after they signed the escrow papers and wrote their massive check.

Caroline hadn't stopped smiling since that wondrous moment. Even Bill Dekker's less-than-perfect inspection report hadn't dampened her smile. There was a lot of work to be done—a little wood rot, a busted pipe in one of the upstairs bathrooms—but nothing critical, nothing that would kill the deal. The Misty Harbor Inn was in business, or would be as soon as it looked like its old grand and glorious self.

Sam struck a pose for Caroline, aiming her can of lemon wax toward the banister and shaking out at least the twentieth dust rag she'd used so far this morning. "Mom would have had this place spic and span by now."

"I doubt that." Caroline laughed. "Considering where we started, I'd say we're making good progress. As far as I know, she never had to get rid of an abandoned wasp nest inside the oven, or have to take the stove apart piece by piece to make sure she got out every creature that had crawled inside and died." Caroline smiled at her little sister. "Try to put things in perspective. In reality, we're making great progress."

"At least we'll have a place to sleep tonight."

"Thank goodness! It was nice of Megan to loan us sleeping bags and air mattresses, but I'm eager to get the bedrooms cleaned up so we can sleep inside instead of out on the back porch." Caroline swished her dust mop into the corner of a stair tread.

"I would have thought you'd be used to sleeping under the stars."

"I outgrew my love of that a good ten years ago. Now that I've grown up, I long for comfort. We have to buy top of the line mattresses for all the rooms."

"We'll get the best we can afford," Sam said mildly.

Using her dust mop for leverage, Caroline pushed up from the stairs, feeling every one of her sixty-one years. The aches and pains in her back, knees, shoulders, elbows, and hands made her want to give up, but there was still so much to clean, and so much more to fall in love with.

"I hope Gracie doesn't mind sharing a room with me. I toss and turn and—"

"She'll be going back and forth to Maine so much, it probably won't matter." They had decided that when Gracie was in town, she would split the larger bedroom that looked out over the back garden and the beach with Caroline, while Sam took the smaller room toward the front of the house.

Caroline applied the mop to another step, working her way up to the second floor. "I really wish she'd decide to stay full time."

"She'll be here for the rest of the summer," Sam said. "There's no telling how she'll feel when it's time for her to head back to Portland. She might decide it's okay to sell her home—or rent it out like I'm going to do—and stay here permanently."

There's still so much to be worked out, Caroline thought as she leaned the mop against the banister at the top of the stairs. They weren't sure how they would split up the chores once they had guests when Gracie gone much of the time. She guessed they would cross that bridge when they came to it.

The loud thump on the front door took them both by surprise. Caroline whipped around when the second thud hit the door. She stared at Sam. "Are you expecting company?"

Sam shook her head. On the third thwack, Caroline bounded down the stairs and tugged. Still swollen from the elements and age and neglect, it didn't open on the first try or the second. Through the leaded glass window Caroline saw the wavering image of someone short, with white hair. It could only be Mrs. Addison—Shirley, she'd call her, and why not, since she was of an age? On the third tug, the door flew open. Shirley held her cane at an angle, on the verge of banging the door once again. She had a paper bag clutched in her hand.

"Thought you'd never let me in." She stepped into the foyer.

"I'm so sorry about that, Mrs…Shirley." Caroline smiled. "The outside doors are all tough to open, but we'll have that fixed in no time."

Shirley looked around, taking in the faded wallpaper and the layers of dust that still covered the fine woodwork in the foyer. Her lips were set in a thin line. "I hear you've hired Bill Dekker. Good man. He's done work for me on occasion. Doesn't try to rob you blind like some of the newcomers to the island. He's been here forever, but I'm sure you know that already."

"Actually—"

Max charged through the door, a streak of buff-colored flying fur, and almost knocked Shirley off to one side. Caroline instantly grabbed Shirley's arm, keeping her upright. "Hold it right there, Max."

"I've got him," Sam called out, wrapping her fingers around Max's collar. "What on earth have you got in your mouth?" Sam asked the pooch. She tried to yank the white Styrofoam package from his mouth and ended up in a game of tug-of-war.

"Oh my goodness! What have you got there, Max?" Caroline asked, letting go of Mrs. Addison and taking the package from Sam's hands. Caroline's eyes widened. She felt a bit sick to her stomach. "Naughty dog! Where did this come from?"

Max looked at Caroline with innocent eyes, as if he hadn't a clue what she was talking about.

"This wouldn't by any chance be yours, would it?" Caroline asked Shirley, holding out the one-pound package of ground turkey. The plastic and Styrofoam were covered in teeth marks.

Mrs. Addison's lips pursed. Her already pink cheeks turned nearly scarlet. "I was wondering where that got to."

"I'm so terribly, terribly sorry." Caroline swallowed hard. "If he got into your house—"

"I believe he got into the trunk of my car while I was taking groceries into the house. I didn't buy all that much, but I had intended to make myself some turkey burgers for tonight. It appears that won't be happening now."

Sam stepped forward. Smiling, she stuck out the hand that wasn't holding Max's collar. "We haven't formally met yet. I'm Sam Carter, Caroline's youngest sister."

Mrs. Addison took Sam's hand reluctantly and gave it a perfunctory shake.

"I'm making my mother's maple-glazed chicken Sunday night. The inn won't be spic and span by then, but we'd love to have you join us."

"That doesn't exactly make up for my pound of ground turkey."

"Oh, we'll replace that as soon as we get to the store," Caroline said. "We'll be going every day for a while, since we're waiting for a repairman to come out and look at the refrigerator, and it's nearly impossible to keep much of anything cold in an ice chest this time of the year."

Shirley nodded. "Thank you very much for the dinner invitation. I'll bring dessert. I make a mean cranberry cobbler." Caroline met Sam's eye. Apparently Shirley liked to do things her way. "And don't use an ice chest. I have an extra refrigerator in my garage. As long as your dog"—she aimed tightened eyes at the pup—"doesn't get it in his head to rob me blind again, you're welcome to use it. The last thing I want is to come here for dinner this weekend and end up eating spoiled chicken. If I die from salmonella, it won't be good for your fledgling B and B."

"We're so glad you'll come," Sam said, graciously ignoring her comments. "Come by around seven, and if you don't mind, we'll come by this afternoon and put a few things in your fridge. Thank you so much for your offer."

"Don't mind at all. Now"—she leaned on her cane—"I did come over here for a reason, not that I can remember what that was." She frowned. "Oh, yes, I wanted to welcome you." She held out the crinkled paper bag.

Caroline took the bag from Shirley and reached inside. She pulled out a heavy rectangle. It was wrapped in paper that was dotted with angels, and it was rather bent and faded, like it had been used many times over the years. The bow was made from one stringy piece of curly ribbon that didn't have much curl left in it. Of course, as Rosalie Marris had always taught her girls, it's the thought that matters.

Caroline was careful with the paper, making sure she didn't tear even one little corner. She'd regift it to Shirley someday. She could tell from the feel of the gift that it was a book, and when she finally had the paper removed, all she could do was stare. It felt almost holy in her hands.

"What is it?" Sam asked.

"A hymnal."

"Look inside," Shirley said. "Read what it says."

Caroline opened the cover almost reverently and read the elegant cursive writing.

> *For my daughter Hannah on the occasion of her tenth birthday.*
> *May you never disappoint our God.*
> *Your Father, Isaac Elliott (May 22, 1864)*

Caroline looked at Shirley. "This was Hannah Montague's, wasn't it?"

"I believe it was. Before she was Hannah Montague, obviously. She must have brought it here with her when she married."

"This is beautiful, Shirley." Caroline flipped the book over in her hands and felt the smooth leather of the binding. "Thank you."

"Well, since you were asking about her, I thought you might like it. It's a part of this house's history."

"How'd you come by the hymnal?" Caroline asked, handing it over to Sam to examine.

"The artists who owned the inn before selling it to that hotel chain—Ezra and Mabel Fortescue—sold off quite a bit. This was tossed in a pile of odds and ends and I paid a dime for it. I thought I might learn to play the piano someday, but I never did, so it's just been sitting around this whole time."

"Thank you so much, Shirley," Caroline said. "It'll have a place of honor on the piano."

Caroline thought about the inscription as Shirley started back down the path toward her house. "May you never disappoint our God." It was quite a thing for a father to write to his ten-year-old daughter. She wondered about their relationship, about what it was like to grow up with a father like that. She wondered if Hannah resented him, or if she hated him for making her marry a man she didn't love. She wondered if he was still alive when Hannah disappeared. Was it possible he knew something about her mysterious disappearance?

"Let me back my truck up to the porch," Bill Dekker said, using his shirtsleeve to wipe perspiration off his brow, "and I'll put those old mattresses in the bed and haul them off to the dump."

"Are you sure it's okay for us to pay you once a month?" Gracie asked, standing next to the stack of old and utterly awful mattresses they'd hauled out of the bedrooms that morning.

"Sam suggested once a week, but once a month works better for me. I've got bill-paying down to a science. Money comes in on the first, and all the bills get paid on the fifth. I'm a creature of habit and kind of hate getting my system fouled up."

"Then we're two of a kind." Gracie found herself laughing. "By the way, there's lemonade and iced tea in the refrigerator. I've got to get back to work, but if you get thirsty, help yourself."

"Will do," Bill said, easily lifting a twin mattress under one arm and walking out through the open kitchen door. They'd been awfully lucky to meet him again after so many years. In just a couple of days he'd repaired some faulty wiring, put a new toilet and sink in the owners' quarters bathroom, and fixed the leaky showerhead. He'd also programmed his phone number into all their phones and told them to call at any time, day or night, if they had an emergency. Not that they expected any emergencies to pop up that they couldn't deal with on their own, but it was nice to know that Bill Dekker would be available.

Gracie headed for the dining room to start stripping the wallpaper but, she couldn't miss the sound of "Chopsticks" coming from the parlor. Her sisters were goofing off in the middle of the day. But then, maybe it was okay to take a break. Lighten up! Caroline would say, and she'd be right. They'd worked almost nonstop for a couple of days. They really did deserve a rest.

"Mind if I join in?" Gracie walked into the parlor.

There really wasn't room for a third sister on the piano bench, but Sam and Caroline scooted close to each other, leaving just enough space for two-thirds of Gracie's derriere.

The music sounded great, except for a few flat notes and one stuck key that didn't play any tone at all. When Gracie put her index fingers on the F and G keys and the three sisters plunked out the tune together, it resonated throughout the parlor and sounded rather glorious.

"I really think we should entertain our first guests with 'Chopsticks,'" Caroline said. "Somewhere in all of Mom's photo albums, I think there's a picture of the three of us when we were little sitting at the piano together. Wouldn't it be great if we could find that, frame it, and put it on top of this grand old lady?"

"Perfect," Gracie said. "I always dreamed of having a grand piano with pictures of all my family sitting on top. This old thing isn't exactly a Steinway, and it isn't all shiny and black, which was what I dreamed of, but you know what? I think it's better."

"You and me both," Sam said. "And to think we got it for such a steal."

Gracie laughed. "I wouldn't call the price for this place a steal, but—"

Her next words were cut off by a loud and resounding knock on the front door.

"Were you expecting someone?" Gracie asked her sisters, only to have both of them shake their heads.

"It could be Shirley Addison again," Caroline said, "What if Max—"

The loud barks coming from the top of the stairs and the skittering sound of claws on the hardwood steps told them that Max was inside the inn, where he was supposed to be.

"I'd get the door," Caroline said, "but I'm rather trapped between the two of you."

"I'll do it." Sam played a little trill on the piano keys as she stood. Caroline and Gracie did the same and then followed along behind Sam. After three tugs, Sam finally pulled open the front door. On the porch was a pair of man's legs and a giant bouquet of summer flowers: roses, lilies, and daisies in a multitude of colors, with sprigs of baby's breath and spikes of fern.

"Mind if I come in?"

"George?" Caroline said, before he peeked around the bouquet.

"Hope you don't mind my dropping in on you unannounced, but I somehow found myself with a few unscheduled days on my hands, and I figured you could use a strong back around here."

"Come in. Come in!" Sam took the bouquet from George, Caroline threw her arms around him, kissed his cheek, and started chattering a mile a minute, telling him everything they'd accomplished so far.

"What?" George grinned, when they settled down in a set of old white wicker chairs they'd found in the basement and put out on the porch that overlooked the ocean. "You haven't hired anyone to clean out the carriage house yet?"

"I hate to admit this," Gracie said. She felt awfully comfortable around George, as if he were the big brother they'd never had. "But I haven't given a moment's thought to the carriage house. There's already at least a year's worth of work inside the inn."

"Then it's a good thing I'm here, because I want to get my hands on that Packard."

Caroline frowned. "I suppose I could be dragged away from the jobs Gracie and Sam have assigned me and help move boxes out of the carriage house."

"And where are we going to put them if we move them out?" Gracie asked. "The attic's full to the brim, the basement—well, I hate to even think about the basement."

"Why don't you let me worry about the carriage house," George said. "A couple days of sorting and clearing, and—who knows?—I just might find one of those secret rooms."

CHAPTER
Twenty

"Secret room, my eye." Caroline backed out from under the Packard, her hands and knees coated with dust and dirt. When George helped her to her feet, he was grinning.

"Don't tell me there's nothing down there," Sam said, standing next to Gracie. Both of them were watching eagerly.

"Oh, there's something down there all right," Caroline said, waving around the flashlight she'd taken with her under the car. "It looks like the last resting place of everything having to do with the Misty Harbor Inn's horse and buggy days. Old horseshoes, an anvil, a pair of bellows that's seen better days." She shook her head at George, clearly frustrated with his antics. "You told me you made a real find under those loose boards, and I believed you."

"What you didn't do was let me finish my sentence. This is a real find. People like old stuff like that. They'll pay a pretty penny for it."

"Well, if you've got the stamina to exhume all that junk, and if you want to put it up for sale on eBay, or wherever, be my guest. As for me, I have to get back to the kitchen."

"You mean you don't want to see the box with the leg sticking out of it? It could be Hannah Montague."

Caroline flashed an evil, don't-you-dare-tease-me-again frown at George. "Come on, you two," she said, turning to Gracie and Sam, "we've got work to do."

"Next time we go into town, we need to invest in numerous boxes of industrial strength rubber gloves," Caroline said to Gracie. Her back was tired, her neck ached, and she felt a little claustrophobic. Who wouldn't? She hadn't set foot out of the house in twenty-four hours, not since she'd climbed under the Packard hoping to find buried treasure. "I'm sure if I wash one more dish or strip one more bit of wallpaper the skin on my hands is going to dry up and fall off."

"Here, try this." Gracie handed her a tube of lotion that she'd tucked inside the pocket of an old apron she'd picked up at a thrift store in town. "It's the best thing I've ever found for dry skin."

Caroline squeezed a generous portion of cream onto her hands and worked it into her parched skin. Gracie puffed at the lock of hair that hung in her eyes. The dining room table was loaded with stacks of plates, bowls, cups, and saucers in all shapes and sizes and colors. Some were stoneware, but it was mostly china, and nearly all of it was now sparkling in the sun that poured in through the freshly washed windows.

"Looks like we have enough table service to feed a hundred," Caroline said, as Gracie started to sort and take pictures. Gracie had already begun to create a computer database so they could keep track of what they had and what they would need. It seemed like overkill;

Gracie surely wouldn't run her home that way. But this was business, and she wanted to do everything right.

"I'm sure we don't need nearly all of this," Gracie said. "We might have to weed some of it out, especially if George finds more dishes in the carriage house. And who knows what all we'll find in the basement and attic."

"Maybe some of this china belonged to Hannah Montague," Caroline said, applying the steamer to yet another piece of wallpaper, hoping it would pull down easily. "I wonder if she and Jedediah sat around this very same table on a hot summer's evening, talking about the events of their day."

"You dream too much."

"And you don't dream enough." Caroline grinned at her sister, who kept her head buried in the pages of her inventory.

"I think we could be working on this wallpaper for the next week," Gracie said, nodding at the stubborn strip Caroline was working on.

"Well, we're not working tomorrow. Don't even try to make us work on the Fourth of July."

"I haven't forgotten," Gracie said. "Although I really hate the idea of giving up a day's work around here."

Gracie really needed to take a page from Caroline's book of how to live life—she needed to relax, at least a little bit.

Gracie was quiet a moment, studying the myriad dishes and then looked up, holding a saucer. "This one's chipped. Think we should throw it away?"

"Goodness, no!" Caroline snatched it from Gracie's hand. "It'll be perfect for the garden."

Gracie frowned. "A chipped saucer?"

"Of course. I saw a do-it-yourself article once that showed you how you make bird feeders and miniplanters out of old cups and saucers. I'd planned to do it in Chipping Campden. I even haunted thrift shops looking for the perfect cups and saucers, but somehow I never got around to finishing the project."

"What makes you think that if I set this chipped saucer aside you'll get to the project now?"

"Oh, Gracie, you have no faith at all in me."

"Have you started working on the Web site yet?"

"It's on the very top of my to-do list but I really think we should come up with a logo first. We'll need one for the inn, so I've sketched out a few ideas."

"What about the ideas you have for our marketing brochures?"

"They're at the top of the list too, but really, Gracie, we can't do a lot of those things until we get the wallpaper and hardwood floors stripped.

Gracie grinned. "I rest my case. So let's buckle down and get our work done."

"You know, Gracie, sometimes you're just no fun at all."

"How's it going out here?" Caroline called out to George shortly before dinnertime. He'd been messing around inside the carriage house for two solid days now. He'd barely said a word to anyone, except when he came inside to eat and when he said good night before heading off to his friend's sloop in the marina. She'd tried to talk him into staying in the inn, but he reminded her that he liked the rock of a boat on water. It had a magical way of lulling him to sleep.

"Did you hear me?" Caroline said again as she squeezed through the boxes still cluttering the inside of the carriage house. She could hear George tinkering with something, but she couldn't see him.

"It's going great. I found a light hidden behind a couple of boxes that works really well under here."

"Please don't tell me you're under the car digging up all those old horseshoes?"

"I got those out last night. Today it's the Packard that's calling me, and I figured I'd better see what's going on underneath."

"Have you found anything interesting?"

"A lot of grease. A lot of grime." She could just barely hear him, but she recognized the excitement in his voice, even when he uttered the words grease and grime. She supposed it was a man thing. "I've already started taking pictures of some of the parts I think will have to be replaced. I can look them up on the Internet and see what you're looking at cost-wise."

"Think it's going to set us back more than a pretty penny?"

"It's the labor that costs the most, and I come pretty cheap." He slid out from under the Packard, grease on his nose, his chin, and his clothes. "Actually, you get me for free, so it's only the parts that'll come at a cost, and I should have connections that can help us get them pretty cheap."

"Has anyone ever told you you're an awfully nice guy?" Caroline said. She pulled a dust cloth out of the pocket of her jeans and wiped the grease off his nose.

"I think you might have said that a time or two."

Out of the corner of her eye Caroline saw George wink, but at the moment she was far more interested in a box she saw on the far side of the car, one that George had mentioned yesterday. She looked at George and frowned. "You were serious, weren't you? There really is a box over there with a leg hanging out?"

George winked again. "I don't think it's a real live—or dearly departed—woman, and definitely not Hannah Montague, but maybe a rather old doll."

"Do you have any idea how much really old dolls can go for?"

George shook his head slowly. "How long have you known me? Thirty years?"

Caroline nodded.

"Have I ever expressed an interest in dolls?"

"No, but there's a first time for everything." Caroline slipped past George, trying to get around the car. "If they're in good condition, they might look nice in the guest rooms."

"Be careful climbing around back there."

"I've climbed pyramids."

"You're no longer thirty or even forty. The last thing you need to do is fall and break a hip or anything else."

"Are you calling me old?"

"I'm just speaking the truth, Caroline Marris. So please, be careful back there."

She climbed up on one box and, from there, onto another. The boxes were like stair steps, each one carrying her higher and higher. One more. Another. Another. Her foot caved through the top of the next. "Oh no!"

"Caroline!"

She heard the fear in George's voice, and she felt the stack of boxes begin to crumble. She stretched her arm out, knowing she couldn't steady herself. It was much too late for that. But she did latch on to the box of dolls…and then she tumbled, boxes and all.

"Caroline! Are you okay?"

"I'm fine," she called back. Her backside was a little sore from landing hard on the floor, but at least it was her derriere that hit first, and not her head or hip or arm. George was right—she didn't need to break anything.

"You'll be happy to know that there's a big open area back here," she muttered. "No boxes whatsoever, which means if you stop playing around underneath the Packard for a day or two, you should be able to shift all the other boxes back into this space so you can get the car off its blocks and out of here."

"Sounds like a plan."

"A very good plan, I'm sure, but right now, I need to figure out how to get out of here."

"You don't see any trapdoors, do you? Any secret rooms?"

"I see a box full of dolls looking at me through glass eyes. They have beautiful bisque faces, and dresses made out of taffeta and lace. And they're thinking the same thing as I am: Start moving boxes, George, so we can get out of here."

CHAPTER
Twenty-one

I can't believe you've talked me into getting my face painted."
Gracie wrinkled her nose at her sisters, trying not to laugh at the red
and white stripes painted across Caroline's face or the blue square
dotted with white stars painted around her right eye. The artist had
done a really good job, but should a woman of sixty-one really be
walking around looking like the "Star-Spangled Banner"?

And Sam! Fireworks exploded across her face in shades of
blue and white. They were awfully pretty, but again, what on
earth were they doing here? Little kids got their faces painted, not
grandmothers!

"You're looking good, Gracie," Caroline said, her arm tucked
through George's. He was the only one who hadn't succumbed to
Caroline's crazy scheme.

"The least you could do is tell me what's appearing on my face."

"It's a surprise," Sam told her. "Just smile and enjoy it."

"All I ask is that you promise not to take a picture of the three
of us together to put on top of the piano for all our future guests
to see."

Caroline beamed. "I hadn't even thought about that. Thank you so much for the idea, Gracie. It'll be perfect for next year's Fourth of July decorating."

Gracie wanted to groan, but she was afraid if she did so, it might mess up the painting. It was bad enough to be embellished with bright paints, but bright paints that were messed up in the process would be a tragedy. She'd sit still if it was the last thing she did.

At long last, the artist smiled at Gracie. "Done!" She handed her a mirror. "Want to see your work of art?"

"I'm rather afraid to, but let's do it."

Gracie held up the mirror. She stared for long seconds, and at last she smiled. "Not bad."

"What do you mean 'not bad'?" Caroline said. "Yours is the absolute best. You're the Statue of Liberty—and you're beautiful."

Gracie grinned. "Okay, I admit it, it looks rather good."

"Now that you ladies are through getting all painted up for the day," George said, "can we go check out the pie-eating contest?"

"Are you going to enter?" Sam asked.

"Not on your life, but I can cheer with the best of them."

Gracie couldn't believe she was having such a great time. It seemed forever since she'd simply let down her hair, relaxed, and gone along with the crowd. She cheered on both sets of firefighters—volunteers and regulars—as they competed in their annual water fight. The hoses were attached to an antique fire engine and hand pumper, and the spray splashed everywhere, nearly soaking Gracie to the bone. Sam talked her into trying out the potato sack race, and the two of them beat out the team of George and Caroline. She ate corn dogs and cotton candy and barbecued chicken and corn on the cob, served up by Bill Dekker and Megan Folger-Wildes for one of Harvest Chapel's yearly charity fundraisers.

The fireworks shot high into the sky, hissing and crackling, their bright colors ricocheting this way and that. It was all rather glorious, Caroline thought, especially with Beethoven's *Fifth* playing in the background, thanks to an old CD player they'd found in a closet, and some music George had downloaded off the Internet that morning. John Phillip Sousa, the Boston Pops, and Beethoven's canons sounded out loud and clear until they were ready to call it a night not long after the last explosion of color filled the night.

"See you tomorrow," George said, hugging Gracie the same way he hugged Sam and Caroline, although Caroline received a lovely kiss on the top of her head. She was one lucky woman, Gracie decided. George was a good man, kind of like her Art. Some relationships were rather magical, and she saw that between Caroline and her friend.

Less than half an hour later, the porch was cleaned off, the dishes were washed and put away, and Gracie climbed into the shower. The spray wasn't quite as warm as she'd like, but it still felt great to wash the salty air out of her hair and the painted Statue of Liberty from her face. The shower sputtered a few times, and the water turned tepid, making her shiver. The plumbing in the walls groaned. It had been doing that all week.

Climbing out of the shower, she towel-dried her hair, combed out the tangles, slipped into a light nightgown, and crawled under the covers. She burrowed into the comfort of the crisp, cool sheets, turned off the light, and noticed the bisque doll with a taffeta dress and long blonde hair sitting on the chair next to her bed.

"The dolls are pretty," Gracie whispered to Caroline, who was lying on her side in the twin bed next to hers. "I'm glad you brought them in from the carriage house."

"I thought they'd look nice in the guests rooms, but I don't know, I think I could get rather attached to them and, really, when you think about it, we've already planned to put so many other antiques in the guest rooms, we should keep something for ourselves."

"Definitely." Gracie yawned again. "I had a great time today."

"The face-painting didn't bother you too much?"

Gracie shook her head. "Only at first. After I got used to it I rather enjoyed the stares. No one laughed, and a couple of women around our age said they wished they'd had the guts to get a face-painting too."

Gracie yawned again. She tucked her hands under her pillow and closed her eyes. She wanted so much to talk with Caroline, to share the events of the day, but she couldn't keep her eyes open. She could barely retain any sense of reality. She just wanted to sleep, and slowly she drifted off, dreaming of fireworks and rousing music, the clang of cymbals, the blast of canons.

The blast?

Even in her subconscious, she knew there was something not quite right about those canons.

Gracie jolted up in bed. "What was that?"

"You're dreaming, Gracie," Caroline said, her words drowsy—a little grumpy. "Go back to sleep."

"Dreaming, my eye. Something just blew up."

"You've got the sound of fireworks stuck in your head," Caroline said, as if she'd shared Gracie's dreams. "And the canons in Beethoven's *Fifth*. It's all in your—"

Caroline jumped when the canons—or whatever—shot off again. With moonlight shining through the window, Gracie could see Caroline's eyes widen, "What on earth was that?"

"I don't have a clue, but I'm glad you finally believe that I wasn't dreaming."

Gracie sprang out of bed and—water splashed beneath her feet. "Oh dear! We're flooded."

"You're kidding."

"Climb out of bed, get wet up to your ankles, and maybe you'll believe me."

"I'm not exactly crazy about the idea of climbing out of bed," Caroline said, "but I believe you, and unless we want to risk the chance of floating out to sea during the middle of the night—"

"It's already the middle of the night, Caroline. It's two o'clock."

"Okay, no need to get picky, let's just figure out what's going on."

"It has to be the shower." Gracie groaned. "I knew there was something odd about the noises I heard when I took my shower. I should have known the plumbing was going to explode."

Gracie jumped again when the bedroom door opened and Sam trudged in, slogging through the water. "Something tells me the shower's on the fritz."

"Do either of you have any idea how to fix plumbing?" Gracie asked, trying to stay calm. "Art always took care of stuff like that, and I haven't had any problems since he passed away."

"We could always call Bill Dekker," Sam said. "Or George."

"We own an inn now," Caroline said. "It's a big place and one of our guests could run into electrical or plumbing problems in the middle of the night. We won't always be able to get other help. My suggestion is we try to figure this out on our own."

Chaos erupted. With no clear idea where the water came from, Gracie ran to the bathroom, Sam ran to the kitchen, and Caroline grabbed towels and sheets and anything she could get her hands on to build dams to keep the water at bay in the owners' quarters.

"Do you see any leaks?" Sam asked Gracie, who had the doors flung open on the cabinets beneath the bathroom sink.

"These pipes are dry as a bone," Gracie said, on her knees now, kneeling in several inches of water that soaked through her pajamas.

"Think we should turn off the water?" Caroline asked, peering into the bathroom.

"I already turned it off under this sink" Gracie stated. She was breathing hard And her knees hurt from kneeling on the hard tile.

"I turned it off under the kitchen sink too, although I'm not all that sure how good a job I did. I couldn't get the knob all that tight, so it could still be leaking."

"Anyone know where there's a wrench?" Caroline asked, taking charge, even though Caroline probably knew less about plumbing than she or Sam. "If we could find one, we might be able to tighten up the knob and make sure the water's off completely."

"Bill probably has one in his tools," Sam said, "but I haven't a clue where he keeps it."

"In the back of his truck," Gracie added. "Which isn't going to help at all."

"I'll try the basement. He was working on the washing machine yesterday. It might still be there." Caroline slipped in the water as she raced from the room. "Be back in a jiff."

"We could have gone the next thirty years without something like this happening." Gracie plowed her hands through her hair.

"Better now than when our first guests are here." Sam sopped up water with one of their new white towels and rang it out into the sink. "I wish we knew where the water was coming from. I don't hear any drips. I don't see any."

"Drips?" Gracie was incredulous. "It's more like a deluge. A monsoon could have hit us and we'd have less water in here." Gracie grabbed another towel to soak up water. "Is the kitchen as bad as this?"

Sam frowned. She shook her head. "Something tells me the house is a little off kilter. This bathroom must be the lowest point in the house, and—"

Gracie threw a hand up to halt her sister's words. "Don't say anymore. I don't even want to think about having to do work on the foundation or shoring up this part of the house to make it level with everything else. That could cost us a small fortune."

"Found it!" Caroline burst back into the bathroom, a big wrench in hand. She nudged Gracie aside. Her knees creaked as she knelt down on the floor, and she stuck her head under the sink. You could hear the grinding of metal as Caroline turned the knob. "I found what I think might be the main water valve—or whatever it's called—in the basement too. I've got that turned off, so it shouldn't make much difference if we're unable to tighten down this one and the one in the kitchen or not."

"You're sure?" Gracie asked.

Caroline stuck her head out from under the sink and hit Gracie with a sideways glance. "Of course I'm not sure. I'm as much a novice at this as you are, but I don't see the water continuing to rise. I don't hear any more drips or groans in the pipes."

"She has a point, Gracie," Sam said, still sopping up water with the towel. "But I think tomorrow we'd better ask Bill or George— or someone—to give us a quick, down-and-dirty course on home plumbing."

"Quick's perfectly fine," Gracie said, looking at the white towel in her hand. It used to be thick and pristine, but now it was now a candidate for the dump. "But I'll forgo dirty, thank you very much. Right now, I feel like I've seen and smelled and wallowed in enough muck to last a lifetime."

Just then they heard the wail of another set of pipes. Something inside the walls began to groan. And then they heard the very first pop, and then the explosion.

"Well," Caroline said, "at least our first Fourth of July inside the Misty Harbor Inn is going out with a bang."

CHAPTER
Twenty-two

*H*eard you had a little problem in the middle of the night."

Gracie looked up from the middle of the overgrown weeds by the birdbath to see Bill Dekker. There was a carpenter's tool belt wrapped around his waist, and his white T-shirt was smudged with dirt and grime. Somehow she worked up a smile.

"I wish it *had* been little."

"You and me both, since I'm the one who inspected the house and told you the plumbing looked good. Sure doesn't do much for my credibility."

Gracie stood, pressing her hands against the small of her back to stretch out her muscles. She was achy after the middle of the night debacle. "Did you find the problem?"

Bill nodded. "Something simple, thank heaven. The good Lord must have been smiling down on you, because it turned out to be nothing more than a pipe bursting loose behind the bathroom wall. Of course, I had to tear down the wall—and part of the tile—to find it."

Gracie tried to keep the sound of her groan hidden. She hoped this would be not only the first disaster, but the last. Too many catastrophes and their money would run out fast.

"You really should have called me. I meant it when I said I'd be here in a heartbeat if you ladies needed anything."

"At least we showed ourselves—and hopefully you and George and our families—just how resourceful we can be."

"Let's just hope you don't have to show that side of yourselves too often."

"From your mouth to God's ear."

Once Bill had hopped into his truck and took off for town to get plumbing supplies, Gracie strolled around the garden. The last place she'd wanted to be that morning was inside the inn. She needed the fresh air, and it seemed high time that someone tackle a bit of the garden. This was her domain. When she wasn't in church, she felt the closest to God was out among the flowers. When she was in the garden, she felt Art beside her too.

Grabbing a pair of clippers she'd set on the garden's pretty wrought iron bench, she started to gather flowers for the first dinner they would host in the inn. There were so many to choose from. Roses in every color—climbers, floribunda, hybrid tea, grandifloras. Daisies. Coneflowers. Lavender. Hydrangea. Stock. And that didn't come close to naming everything.

The inn had a lot of flaws, including flaws they never would have guessed, like the uneven floor, but the garden made up for everything.

When her arms were full, she went into the inn, skirting the kitchen where Sam was cooking up a storm. Jamie had come back to the island that morning and would be staying for a week, and she was helping her mother prepare the meal. She headed for the dining room and found Caroline snapping photos of the table and just about everything else in the room.

"What are you doing?" Gracie asked.

"I want to make sure our Web page reflects everything inside the inn—all that we do for our guests, everything people will see. I want to open all their senses when they look at our Web site. I want them to smell the food, to feel the lightness of the china cups and saucers. Well, you get the picture."

Gracie refused to roll her eyes, although she felt like it. "Aren't you taking on a little too much? Do you really feel it's important to go all out like that?"

"Our Web page could be the first view anyone has of the Misty Harbor Inn." Caroline snapped a photo of Gracie with the armload of flowers in her hands. "I want people to fall in love with the inn as much as we have."

"Maybe we should hire someone to do the Web page. Not that I think you can't do it—"

"I know. You're worried I won't get it done in time, and that I'll lose interest before it's finished and move on to something else that's caught my interest, but I won't, Gracie."

Gracie had her doubts.

"Come on, Gracie, put a smile on your face."

It was impossible not to, especially with Caroline aiming her camera at Gracie from every angle. She even posed for the camera and then put the flowers in some water. She'd arrange them later. Right now she needed to get cleaned up for dinner, which meant taking a shower. She only hoped that wouldn't lead to another emergency.

"How does the table look?" Caroline asked Gracie as she placed her flower arrangements on the tiger oak buffet. It was elegantly carved with winged griffins that could scare anyone if they happened upon the piece in the middle of the night. There were already flowers on a mahogany sideboard and in the middle of the mahogany table that seated fourteen. Its mahogany was stunning, even with nicks and gouges from well over a hundred years of wear.

The roses' perfume floated around the room. The windows all through the inn had been thrown open early that morning to let in fresh air. The fragrance inside now was sweet. Everything was simply gorgeous, if you could look past the walls that had been stripped of layer upon layer of wallpaper and now bore only streaks of glue.

Gracie turned away from the cut glass vase she was filling with roses and looked at the place settings Caroline had created with the mix and match sets of china, stoneware, glassware, and silver.

"Perfect." Gracie smiled. "It looks like a page from *Country Living* or *House Beautiful*. I'm sure you took a picture or two?"

"Or three or four. I just wish the washing machine hadn't gone on the fritz." Caroline laughed at the pretty table setting with its rather mundane paper napkins. "We'll probably have to buy more cloth napkins before we open the inn. In the long run, it'll be cheaper to wash them than to buy paper napkins all the time. Besides, they'll look much prettier."

"I'll have to teach you and Sam how to arrange flowers. It'll have to be done every day when the B and B's open, and with so many different things blooming in the garden, you'll have a lot to pick from."

"You mean we can't just cut whatever and stick them in a jar?"

"Not if you want to keep a steady flow of guests." Gracie turned back to yet another arrangement.

"Smells great in here." Bill Dekker walked into the dining room, looking rather spiffy in an aquamarine polo shirt and khakis. His eyes were such a pretty blue behind his little round glasses. If Gracie noticed at all, she sure didn't show it.

"The maple chicken Sam and Jamie are cooking up smells like heaven," Bill said. "I've gotta admit, I've never mastered cooking. The kitchen was always my wife's domain, and unless I wanted to wake up with my head detached from my body, I stayed away when she was wielding a knife or vegetable peeler."

"Art was forever in my kitchen." Gracie turned toward Bill. "He was always taste-testing my food, to the point where he wasn't all that hungry when we sat down to eat. He liked to think he was setting a good example for the kids by not overindulging at mealtime." Gracie laughed. "But boy, oh boy, did he love food, especially my pot roast."

"One of my favorites. Haven't had it in heaven knows how long." He shrugged. "I've got a bad habit of going in to town to eat."

"Well, as long as you're working here," Gracie said, "lunch and dinner are on us."

"Breakfast too," Sam said, walking into the dining room, taking off a frilly white apron she'd bought from what was rapidly becoming one of their favorite stores on Main Street.

"Just don't complain if you get fat," Jamie added as she and George followed Sam into the room. "Mom likes sugar and butter."

"She watches too much Paula Deen," Gracie offered, her laugh filling the dining room at the same time Caroline heard the knock at the front door. Max heard it too, and he was off in a flash, barking at the intrusion, desperate to see who was at the door.

"That didn't sound at all like Shirley's cane hitting the door." Caroline headed toward the foyer, trying to ignore the cobwebs they'd missed when cleaning. She made a mental note to tackle them tomorrow.

"It's Mrs. Addison," Caroline called out behind her. "And she's brought someone with her."

Gracie, Bill, Sam, George, and Jamie had all come into the foyer with Caroline and Max to greet their first guests, and laughed at Caroline as she struggled with the front door. "Stop barking, Max," she chastised her companion, who backed away and quieted down when she was able to throw open the door.

Pastor Wildes was on the verge of knocking again, instead he smiled, and held out what must have been Shirley's cranberry cobbler. "Hope you don't mind my joining you." His smile looked a tad uncomfortable. "Shirley invited me and said she was sure you wouldn't mind."

"We don't mind at all," Caroline said, inviting the reverend and Shirley into the inn. "In fact, welcome. It's so nice to have you both with us this evening."

"Stan has this rather obnoxious habit of calling me every day to see how I'm doing. One would think I'm old and frail! All that aside, he's a good walking partner, and I didn't quite feel like walking over here on my own tonight."

"Shirley has a tendency of waving her cane at the seagulls and any stray person walking along the dunes," Pastor Wildes said. Caroline wondered if she dared call him Stan. "It's never a wise idea to let her out alone, especially in the evenings. She can be lethal."

"I've only been arrested once." Shirley harrumphed. "Handcuffed and everything. A police officer cuffed me, threw me into the back of his car, and hauled me off to jail. He felt he had to put on a show."

"You hit a young man with your cane."

"He threw a bottle of soda on the beach. What was I supposed to do? Ignore it? Not on your life."

"Well, you came out of it all unscathed." Pastor Wildes turned to his hosts and grinned. "They released her into my custody not ten minutes after arriving at the station. No charges were filed."

"No charges were filed against that young vandal either." Shirley looked at Caroline and smiled at last. "So, are we still having maple chicken? I'm starved."

It wasn't long before they were all seated around the table and Jamie and Sam brought out the first course, a chopped shrimp Waldorf salad served on plain white china. The salad didn't need anything special to dress it up. It already looked pretty.

When Jamie and Sam were seated, Pastor Wildes lowered his head and offered a blessing. "Dear Lord, as You look down upon Caroline, Gracie, and Sam in their new home, the home that they will share with loved ones, friends, and strangers through the years, as they are sharing it tonight with us, we ask that You bless them and their home, the Misty Harbor Inn. And as we partake of the food they are generously sharing, as they go about the business of renewing the spirit of this inn, we ask that they be blessed with flowers so their house may always know beauty, bread so their house may never know hunger, salt so it may always have flavor, a candle so the house will never know darkness, and sugar so that life will always be sweet." Pastor Wildes looked up at all those gathered around the table. He smiled warmly. "Amen."

In moments they were eating, laughing, sharing stories of their lives, especially Pastor Wildes, who had endless stories to tell about his days as a preacher. "Here's one I particularly like," Pastor Wildes said. "It didn't happen to me, but I'm sure it happened to someone.

It goes something like this." He cleared his throat. "I was at the beach with my children when my four-year-old son ran up to me, grabbed my hand, and led me to the shore, where a seagull lay dead in the sand. 'Daddy, Daddy, what happened to him?' the little boy asked. 'He died and went to heaven,' I replied. My son thought a moment and then said, 'And God threw him back down?'"

"You get used to him after a while," Shirley said flatly and then allowed a grin to touch her face as everyone else was laughing. "He tells endless stories over dinner, and sometimes on Sunday, he gets carried away. Isn't that right, Bill?"

"I plead the Fifth." Bill winked. "I'd rather stay on the pastor's good side. There are stories around the island that he has an extra special connection with the Man Upstairs, and I don't want him telling tales that might get me in trouble."

"Now would I do that, Bill, my friend? You could always respond to the Man Upstairs and remind Him of some of my less reverent jokes and stories from high school."

"I'm so glad we've moved on from those days, Pastor. I kind of like the you of today. I wasn't so fond of the kid I knew back then."

"God led me to my calling. Kicking and screaming at first, but it seems He knew better than I did what was best for me in the long run."

"Do the three of you go on and on like this whenever you're together?" Gracie asked, looking happier than she had in ages. There was no way for Caroline to miss the bit of a twinkle in her eyes or the lightness in her voice. Gracie just seemed happy here. No doubt about it.

"We show a little decorum on occasion," Pastor Wildes said. He wiped his mouth with the flimsy paper napkin. "But honestly,

Caroline, our world can be somber enough without the Lord's children helping to keep it that way. I believe He prefers having us jolly. Life's too short for anything else, and I fully intend to take my jokes with me when I'm called home. I think God might appreciate an extra laugh or two, especially when He's having to deal with too much tragedy."

They all nodded, and Pastor Wildes leaned back in his chair and let out a contented sigh. "It's nice to have some life in this old place again. I haven't been in here in decades, and I can't wait to see it when you've finished restoring it.

"You were here before?" Caroline asked.

He nodded. "My mom would drag me here when I was a kid."

"That seems to have been a rite of passage here on Nantucket," Gracie said. "You weren't forced to sip a proper English tea, were you? In dainty china cups?"

The reverend nodded. "I certainly was. Didn't like it then, don't like it now."

"And here I've given you iced tea with dinner," Sam said, worry on her face. "You should have said something."

"Ah, don't worry at all about it, Sam. You may have noticed that I haven't touched it. I'm not one to complain about anything—with the exception of Shirley, and possibly Bill. If I don't like something, I simply ignore it. That goes for TV shows, politics, world affairs, and how boys and girls dress these days. Saves a lot of upset that way."

"Good words to live by," Caroline said, wishing she could be that way all of the time.

"I do my best, Caroline. I'm sure we all do."

Later that night, Caroline and George strolled along the beach. It was their last evening together for at least a few more weeks. "Wish I could stay longer," he said, tossing a piece of driftwood for Max to chase after. The waves rolled onto the shore, over their bare feet, and then back out again.

"You've already devoted way too much of your time to help us out."

"I think I've devoted more time to the Packard than anything else."

"That's a part of the inn. A big part. In fact, as soon as it's out of the carriage house and fixed up, I want to take pictures of it in front of the inn. It'll look perfect on the Web site. Sam and Gracie and I think it should be incorporated into the inn's new logo that we're having created."

"I haven't stripped any wallpaper. I haven't—"

"You're going to meet me in England in October and help me clean out Briar Rose. That counts for a lot." Caroline stopped. She turned toward him and gripped his arms. "And you've offered endless amounts of moral support. A lot of other men would have balked at me and my sisters buying the inn, yet you've done nothing but encourage."

"That's what friends do, and"—he swept his hands through her windblown hair, tucking thick locks behind her ears—"the way I see it, friends don't come any better than you."

George kissed the top of her head as he'd done so very often over the years. She was going to miss him…more than she ever thought possible.

CHAPTER

Twenty-three

*W*hat do you think of Bill Dekker? Caroline asked Gracie as they stretched out beneath the cool sheets and lightweight bedspreads on their twin beds. They had painted their room a soft blue, the color of the sky on a winter morning, but it looked silver in the moonlight.

"Bill Dekker?" Gracie asked, rolling onto her side. The new sheets crinkled. "He seems nice. Why?" Suddenly Gracie's eyes widened. "You aren't interested in him, are you? I mean, I always thought you were secretly in love with George, that you just didn't want to tell anyone because, well, just because."

"I'm not at all interested in Bill Dekker. I just find him interesting, and I thought you might too."

Gracie's eyes narrowed and again she rolled over onto her back. "I think he's nice, but that's all. Caroline, a lot of people have tried fixing me up in the last couple of years, and I know they mean well, but I was in love with Art for forty years. I don't think I could ever fall in love again."

"Never?" Caroline couldn't quite believe her ears. Gracie of all people was meant to be in love, to have a man at her side. She'd never lived alone. It just didn't seem right, and she seemed so lonely. "Are you sure?"

"I've never really given it all that much thought but yes, Caroline, I'm sure. That doesn't mean I can't have a male friend—whether that's Bill or someone else."

"You have lots of friends. You have me and Sam and your kids, but that's not the same as having a special friend."

"And you have George. Can you honestly tell me you've never thought about marrying him?"

"If I ever married anyone, I suppose it would be George. But I've never wanted to marry anyone. I like my independence. Always have."

"Well, couldn't I have a relationship like that someday way off in the future? With a male friend?"

Caroline sighed. She gave that question some thought, but it didn't seem likely. "I suppose you could."

"Good. Now that that's settled, could we go to sleep?"

Caroline yawned. "I suppose so."

Caroline turned on her side away from Gracie and listened to her sister's soft breathing. Max was curled up in his basket on the floor next to her bed, snoring peacefully. Through the open window she heard the lap of waves on the shore and felt a cool breeze whispering into the bedroom.

"Gracie?" she asked, trying to keep her voice a whisper.

"*Hmm?*"

"You're still awake?"

"I wouldn't be talking to you if I'd been able to fall asleep."

"It feels good here, doesn't it?"

"These pillows aren't the best. Next time we shouldn't go so cheap. In fact, I think we should invest in some good down pillows and offer our guests a choice. The bed and pillows leave such a lasting impression—and we'll want our guests to return."

"Oh, Gracie, I wasn't really talking about the pillows." She chuckled. "I suppose you've already added pillows to one of your lists?"

It was Gracie's turn to chuckle now. "You know, when we were much, much younger, and we shared a bedroom, you'd talk my ear off most every night."

"I would?"

Caroline could sense Gracie nodding her head.

"You were so much like Mom. Such big dreams," Gracie said. "I remember your telling me that someday, when you were older, you wanted to be rich. You wanted to fly to England, buy a British racing green Triumph sports car, and spend the next year or two touring the country."

"I said that? I made it to England, but I never had a Triumph. But I did spend a week hitchhiking in Scotland."

Gracie rolled over and in the near darkness, Caroline could see her grinning. "Did you really?"

"No, silly. I might have been a nomad for quite a long time, and I might have done a lot of traveling on the cheap, but I was a sensible nomad. Can you imagine what Mom would have done if she'd heard that I'd been hitchhiking?"

"I remember she could give us that look that let you know you were in trouble and if you didn't straighten up and fly right, you were in for it when Dad got home."

"And he was a softie."

This time Gracie yawned, trying her best to cover it up with her hand. "Can we go to sleep now?"

"Just one more thing."

"What's that?"

"I want to find some of the best pictures of Mom here on Nantucket. Some with us, some with Dad, most just of her and frame them. There are a lot of nooks and crannies around here, and a lot of flat surfaces. I'd like to put a little of Mom all over the house; let everyone get to know her, as if she were really here."

Caroline could hear Gracie sniff back a tear. "She'd like that. I'd like that." She sniffed. "I'll put it on one of my lists first thing in the morning."

"Oh, there's no need for that, Gracie. I won't forget. You won't either."

An almost icy wind blew across Caroline's shoulder, and she tugged at the bedspread, which had slipped down past her waist. She shivered and tucked her hands under her pillow for a touch of warmth. Outside she heard the hoot of an owl, and the fluttering of wings.

Max stirred in his bed. Caroline could see the whites of his eyes. She watched his eyelids flutter and then close, and he began to snore again.

She rose just a bit and looked at the clock on the other side of Gracie's bed. It was almost three in the morning, way too early to get up. She closed her eyes again and tried to get back to sleep. She didn't dare try to talk to Gracie again. She was sound asleep, her breathing deep as she rested comfortably.

Caroline's mind raced, thinking about the Web site. She had a lot of time to create it, although she imagined she should try and have it ready before Christmas. Hotels, resorts, and B and Bs filled up fast on Nantucket, and people made their reservations early. With the right advertising and promotion, she might find people wanting to make reservations before the holidays and then surprise a loved one with a Misty Harbor Inn brochure tucked away in a gaily wrapped gift box.

More and more ideas came to her, all sorts of promotions. The annual Daffodil Festival, for one. That would be next May, right about the time to open the inn for the season. She could see a Web page with daffodils in the background and the buttercup yellow—Main Street Yellow, if she wanted to get technical—Misty Harbor Inn at the forefront. Gracie, who simply had to be at the inn when they opened, could arrange daffodils in vases. They would give them away as a special treat for every guest. Tulips would follow. Iris. Then big bouquets of roses and hydrangeas. Maybe even sunflowers.

Max yipped quietly in his sleep. A bad dream, Caroline imagined. She opened her eyes to take a peek at her friend just as his head popped up. "What's wrong, boy?"

Max's ears rose. He stared off toward the closed bedroom door. He growled low, baring his teeth.

Then Caroline heard it. There was a thud upstairs. Was it another plumbing disaster? Footsteps! She swallowed hard. Max stood. He growled deep and low. She heard the sound again. Someone was creeping around upstairs.

Gracie jerked up in bed. "Did I hear—"

"*Sh,*" Caroline put her index finger to her lips. "Someone's upstairs."

Gracie sprang out of bed. She grabbed the mop that Caroline had forgotten to put away before getting ready for dinner and held it like a club, ready to use it on an intruder if necessary.

"Think we should call the police?" Caroline asked softly.

Gracie shook her head. "It could be a raccoon or fox, maybe a skunk, heaven forbid, or—"

"A thief," Caroline finished.

"Don't go getting me all nervous, okay? I'm trying to be the brave one, and that doesn't happen all that often."

"Are we going up to the attic?"

Again Gracie nodded. "Make Max stay here. There's no need of him getting hurt...or in the way."

It took some coaxing to get Max to stay put and to stay quiet behind the closed door while Gracie went into the kitchen for flashlights, but soon they were creeping up the back staircase, the one the servants had probably used when the inn was still called Montague House. They headed as cautiously as possible up to the attic.

Oh, dear Lord, Caroline prayed, and even her silent words trembled, *keep us safe.*

They climbed on and on. Someone was definitely rummaging around in the attic. Caroline's imagination began to run wild. Maybe a homeless person had been living up there, and they didn't even know it. Maybe they were intruding on someone's hiding place. Maybe—

The attic door creaked open. Bright light shone in their eyes.

And suddenly, three people screamed.

CHAPTER
Twenty-four

Sam bolted up in bed. "Jamie," she whispered, but the room was silent, and Jamie's bed was empty. She swung her legs out of bed, and fear snatched away her breath; her heart beat heavily. She could barely think, worrying about her daughter.

As best as she could, she dragged in a deep breath. If someone was in the house, if someone had Jamie, she had to move cautiously. She should probably call the police, but that could be an overreaction. Instead, she grabbed her cell phone, made sure it was on, and tucked it into the pocket of her pajamas before opening the door and slipping quietly out of the bedroom.

At the door to Caroline and Gracie's room, she heard scratching on the door. Her heart skipped a beat. Max was trying to get out. Suddenly Sam was afraid to open the door and look in. She wasn't usually the praying sort, but she found herself asking God for protection, not so much for her, but for her daughter and sisters.

She squeezed the door handle. The scratching grew wilder on the other side. Slowly she opened the door, and Max darted out, barking as if his life depended on it.

Sam peered into the bedroom and switched on the light. The beds were empty. Caroline and Gracie were gone.

"Max, stay!" she whispered, but he was already tearing up the back stairs, and Sam gave up trying to be quiet. She ran too, flipping on the lights so she wouldn't stumble in the dark. It didn't matter now if an intruder knew she was coming; Max was making enough noise to scare the dead out of their graves.

She only wished she had a weapon, a baseball bat, anything, but when she reached the top of the stairs, she threw caution to the wind and barged through the attic door.

Jamie, Caroline, and Gracie spun around.

They all screamed.

Max barked shrilly.

"What on earth are you doing up here? You nearly scared me out of my wits."

"It's my fault, Mom. I couldn't sleep and thought I'd look around up here. Never in my wildest dreams did I think anyone would hear me, or assume I was some intruder if they did, but Aunt Caroline and Aunt Gracie caught me."

"Actually, we caught each other," Caroline said, shrugging her shoulders. "She was coming out of the attic just as we were going in and we scared the living daylights out of each other."

Sam clasped a hand to her heart, hoping the heavy beating would slow. "I sure hope whatever you found up here was worth it."

Jamie grinned and held up yet another nineteenth-century doll, similar to the three Caroline had already found. This one wore a gown of lavender satin and velvet.

"She looks a bit bedraggled," Sam said, shaking her head. She wasn't much of an early bird, and three AM was really too early for anyone of sound mind to be awake.

"You'd look bedraggled too, if you'd been shut away in this attic behind several old chests for a good hundred years or more," Gracie said.

"This thing is kind of creepy," Jamie said. She handed the doll to her aunt. "But I knew you'd want to see it."

"Did you find anything else interesting?" Sam asked.

"How about Jedediah and Hettie Montague?" Caroline lifted an antique gilt picture frame that held a painting of petite, severe-looking Hettie and her even more severe-looking husband.

"How about Hannah?" Sam asked, only to see her daughter, Caroline, and Gracie shaking their heads.

"There's a painting of two boys—maybe the Montague sons, Fitzwalter and Lachlan—at different ages. There's no telling how many other paintings have been stored away up here."

"I found some old toys too," Jamie said. "A rocking horse, a doll cradle. Things you might want to put into the guest rooms for atmosphere. Alas"—Jamie shrugged her shoulders—"I didn't find what I came up here for."

"What's that?" Sam asked.

"A secret room—a concealed door."

"That doesn't mean they're not here," Caroline said, "It may simply mean that they don't stick out like a sore thumb."

As much as Sam wanted to believe there were secret passages or hidden rooms in the Misty Harbor Inn, she was pretty sure they were myth and legend. But she was determined to include those myths—embellished, if necessary, in their promotion of the inn anyway.

"Can I see the doll?" Sam said, taking it out of Caroline's arms. "You know, I wouldn't be surprised if the dolls belonged to Hannah."

"What makes you think that?" Gracie asked. "We don't know anything at all about her."

"The message from her father inside the hymnal was rather telling. 'May you never disappoint our God.'" Sam cringed. "I'm sure it goes without saying that any God-fearing person wouldn't want to disappoint God, but it would take an awfully harsh man to write those words in a note to his ten-year-old daughter. I can't imagine her receiving much love growing up, from her father at least. It could be that the dolls were her only companions."

"Or they could have been gifts to her from Jedediah," Caroline said.

Gracie shook her head. "Unfortunately, I don't think we'll ever know."

Sam held the doll carefully. Just like the other three, she not only looked delicate, but felt fragile too, and the last thing she wanted to do was break her arm or rip her beautiful dress. "I once cross-stitched a picture in which the book *Little Women* was opened wide on a lace-covered tablecloth, with a pair of old-fashioned reading glasses laying atop the pages. There was a doll not too much different from this one sitting beside it, leaning against a vase of flowers."

"I remember that," Jamie said. "Didn't you give it to Grandma?"

Sam nodded. "It must have gotten boxed up somewhere when we were cleaning out her house. Maybe we can find it, bring it here and—" Sam frowned, turning the doll over in her hands, feeling the weight of the dress. "What's this?"

"What do you mean?" Gracie asked.

"I think there's something sewn inside the gown. Look at the stitching." Sam held the doll out for her sisters and Jamie to see the inside of the lavender velvet that was lined with a darker silk.

"The stitching doesn't match and the thread's not the same shade as was used on the rest of the gown."

"You aren't thinking of tearing it apart to have a look?" Caroline asked. "Wouldn't that hurt the value? I don't want to sell her, but you never know. Besides, she's Jamie's since she found her." Caroline winked at her niece.

"That's okay," Jamie said, waving her hands. "You guys should keep her."

"I'm not going to tear her apart," Sam said. "It has to be done carefully. I'll need to preserve the thread that was used, take photos, and make sure I duplicate everything when I stitch it back up."

"You aren't thinking about doing that now, I hope?" Gracie yawned. "Every muscle in my body aches, and I am absolutely exhausted. Couldn't all of this wait?"

"It could," Sam said, "unless you're as excited as I am to see what's inside."

"I am," Caroline said. "We know so little about the inn. Maybe something's been hidden inside the doll that'll answer some questions. Maybe it'll tell us why Hannah Montague disappeared."

Sam saw Gracie roll her eyes. "Oh, all right, if we really must, let's go downstairs," Gracie said. "I'll make some cocoa, and Sam can take the poor doll's dress apart."

Sam smiled, hugging the pretty little doll against her chest as she made her way down the stairs. Her sisters and Max followed. She absolutely loved puzzles, and this one definitely intrigued her.

Gracie ladled cocoa into four tall ceramic mugs and topped each with a handful of minimarshmallows. It was the way she'd made it for Art, Brandon, and Paige. She wished they were with her now, watching the mystery of the antique doll unfold. She hated to see the beautiful gown taken apart, but she'd watched Sam at work, and she'd never seen a seamstress perform her task so meticulously.

"Just a few more stitches," Sam said, "and I think I'll be able to get to whatever's inside."

"I don't know why I didn't do this before, but I've found a doll just like ours on an antique doll Web site." Caroline sat at the far end of the kitchen worktable, her laptop open, her reading glasses balanced on her nose. Gracie set a mug of cocoa next to Caroline, handed one to Jamie, and kept Sam's on the counter, not wanting it anywhere close to the doll. She sat next to Caroline and looked at the screen.

"That definitely looks like her," Gracie said, reading the description beneath the picture. "French bisque *poupée* in costume of l'Auvergne, France, circa 1865."

"What does *poupée* mean?" Jamie asked.

"It's 'doll' in French," Caroline answered.

"Well, stop looking at Web pages and look at this," Sam said. Gracie looked across the table in time to see Sam pull what looked like a postcard from inside the doll's gown. "Well, what do you know. There's an ink sketch of a church on the front."

Jamie leaned over her mother's shoulder. "It looks like the Unitarian church, the one with the clock tower—"

"And ninety-four very steep stairs," Caroline added.

"Someone did a beautiful sketch," Gracie said. "Is there anything written on the other side?"

Sam turned it over, handling the card as cautiously as she'd handled the doll. "The writing's just as beautiful as the sketch, so elaborate it's hard to read, but I can make it out. Just don't laugh. It says…" Sam squinted.

"'My dearest Hannah,

I long for the sound of your gaily ringing laughter. It is music to my soul. Though we are far apart at present, my heart reaches out to you. Until we see each other again.…

Your loving and devoted William.'"

"William?" Caroline lifted her mug of cocoa. "Wait a minute. If the Hannah named on that postcard is our Hannah, what's she doing getting a card from a man named William? Her husband's name was Jedediah."

"It could be anyone," Gracie said, yawning. "Father. Uncle. Brother. Friend. Of course, from his words, it appears he might have been something more. A paramour, perhaps."

"Perhaps, my eye," Caroline said. "I'd definitely say there was something going on between Hannah and William. Otherwise, why would she hide the card?"

"You're assuming that Hannah hid the card," Sam said.

"Who else would hide it?" Jamie asked. "And why?"

"Who knows?" Gracie said. "There could be other postcards hidden away inside the other three dolls."

Caroline's eyes widened. "You think?"

Sam patted her mouth, trying her hardest not to yawn. "That, my dears, is something we'll have to find out, but right now, I think we should call it a night."

CHAPTER
Twenty-five

"*F*ind any ghosts under there?"

Gracie laughed at Caroline's question. The sound reverberated off the bottom of the piano that she'd spent nearly the last hour cleaning. "Only cobwebs and a few dead spiders. No spirits, no treasure maps marked with an X, no architectural plans showing the whereabouts of a secret room, and no more hidden postcards."

Caroline snapped her fingers. "That's too bad. I was so disappointed when we didn't find postcards hidden inside the other three dolls. Of course, that makes the one hidden postcard that much more of a curiosity."

"As if we have the time to spend on figuring out the meaning of a hidden postcard."

"You're not the least bit curious?" Caroline asked. "Don't you want to know more about Hannah and William?"

"Yes. No. Maybe."

"You're being awfully indecisive today."

Gracie sighed inside. What she wanted to do was get the inn cleaned up. Maybe a year from now they could go on treasure hunts, but not right now. Why couldn't Caroline understand that?

Sliding out from under the piano, Gracie brushed her hands off on her already dirty shorts and then ran her fingers through her hair, hoping to give it some semblance of order or at least get rid of any spiderwebs that might have latched on. Looking at Caroline, however, made Gracie realize she wasn't the only one who'd let the inn's dust and dirt get the best of her.

"You're a mess. What on earth have you been doing?"

A look of guilt flitted across Caroline's face. It was a look Gracie had seen many times in the past.

"Actually, I've been doing a lot of things. Stripping wallpaper in the stairwell. Going onto the Internet to look at paint colors. I can't wait to show you what I've found. It's a rich, deep pumpkin. Not a garish orange, don't worry, Gracie, you'll love it."

Gracie could only stare at her sister in utter disbelief.

"And since Jamie's as interested in the mystery of the Misty Harbor Inn as I am, I thought it might be fun to spend some time with her searching the attic for more hidden postcards, or any other clues about Hannah Montague's life."

Gracie bit her tongue. She didn't want to make waves. It wasn't as if Caroline didn't work hard, it's just that she couldn't focus.

All her life Gracie had focused. On home. On her husband, her kids, and now her grandchildren. Staying on top of all that was important meant everything to her. Now she'd added the inn to her list of priorities. She was putting her whole heart into the Misty Harbor, yet Caroline... Gracie sighed heavily. Caroline cared; maybe she just didn't care enough. And that hurt, especially since this whole thing had been her idea.

Tossing the dirty dust cloth on top a pile of others she'd been using all morning, Gracie picked up a clean rag and went back to work on the piano's intricately carved legs. *Be nice*, she told herself. She took a deep breath. "And did you find anything interesting during your adventure with Jamie?"

Caroline grabbed a rag and started to clean another ornate piano leg. "Box after box of old clothes that should have been given to the Salvation Army years ago."

"You don't plan to give away anything really old, I hope. No nineteenth-century dresses or hats or beaded purses, things we can use when we're finally able to decorate?"

"Nothing like that has turned up yet, but Jamie's still—"

The front door flew open, and Max came bounding into the house. He ran into the parlor, hit the pile of dirty dust rags, and went sliding all the way across the room and behind a pair of wingback chairs. His head hung low, as if he was staring guiltily at his muddy paws; he then turned his big, brown pleading eyes toward Caroline and Gracie. *Please, don't tell anyone where I am!* they seemed to say.

The front door was slammed a little harder than necessary to get a point across. A couple of windows rattled in the parlor. Sam stalked into the room, her pale aqua T-shirt smeared with muddy paw prints, her khakis stained green at the knees. Her fists were clenched at her sides. "Where is he?"

"Who?" Caroline asked not so innocently.

"If you can't tell simply by looking at me, you need glasses," Sam practically bellowed, which was so not her style. "I'm looking for Max."

"Looks like he got into something he shouldn't have," Gracie said, looking around the room, pretending she didn't see the pup. "Please tell us it was something here at the inn and not over at Shirley's again."

"Oh, it started at Shirley's." Sam's jaw tightened. "We now have half of one of her hydrangeas in our garden, not that we didn't already have enough. We also have one of her gardening boots. A gardening boot that now has holes in it."

Caroline forced herself not to laugh. "None of that explains the mud you're wearing."

Sam tugged at the hem of her T-shirt. "In his hurry to get away from Shirley's shouting, he came running at full bore, hit the back of my legs, and sent me sprawling into the grass. And then, when I scolded him, he decided we should kiss and make up. That explains the paw prints on my shirt—twenty-five pounds of cocker spaniel standing on my chest, licking my face."

It was all Gracie could do to keep from laughing. "You aren't hurt, are you?"

"The only one that's going to hurt is that dog. So where is he?"

Max poked his head around one of the wingback chairs, a hangdog expression on his furry face. He crept toward Sam, leaving more dirty paw prints on the floor. He came to within inches of Sam's grubby knees, tilted his head up, and whimpered.

"Is that meant to be an apology?" Sam asked, glaring down at the precocious pup. She sighed heavily and then gave in to Max's pitiful face and patted him on the head. "Okay, I forgive you. This time."

Max hopped up on his hind legs and danced around for a moment or two, until what could only be a cane rapped at the front door. Max dropped down on all fours. He tilted his head toward the sound of the second thud and then took off, his claws scrabbling on the floors as he raced to the parlor and up the curved stairs.

"I'm the one who needs to apologize since he's my dog," Caroline said, heading for the foyer. "Something tells me Shirley's not going to be in the best of moods."

The elderly woman stood on the front porch, half of a blue-flowered hydrangea caught in a hand covered with a gardening glove. She glared at Caroline before dropping what was left of the bedraggled hydrangea on the doorstep. "I believe this belongs to you now. I'll expect my new one—planted in my garden—within a week."

"I'm so sorry, Shirley. We're trying to keep an eye on Max, but—"

"If you're not careful, I'll invest in a bull mastiff to keep guard on my garden."

Caroline grinned. "Bull mastiffs are awfully sweet. I'm sure Max would love having a friend to play with."

Shirley's back stiffened as she rose to her full height of five foot two. "Any dog of mine would be much better behaved."

"Would you like to train Max?" Caroline asked in all seriousness. "I've tried, with little luck. He even had a trainer in England. Sadly, he's just a tad incorrigible."

Something told Caroline that Shirley Addison had been incorrigible as a child too. She certainly was feisty now. But Caroline could see she needed to placate her elderly neighbor.

"Would you like to come in for a bit?" Caroline asked. "Have some freshly squeezed lemonade?"

Shirley fanned her face. "Well, now that you ask, it is a tad warm out here and a glass of lemonade would be nice."

Shirley made her way slowly into the foyer. "That dog isn't around, is he? The last thing I need is for him to mow me down and I end up with a broken hip. Can't risk going to the hospital. You get pneumonia there, and people my age, well, let's just say I want to stay far away from hospitals."

"He's upstairs, probably seeing what kind of mischief he can get into." Caroline took Shirley's arm, only to have her hand gently slapped away.

"I may be old, but I'm not feeble. I get along quite well with my cane. Just tell me where you want me."

"Come on in here," Sam said, leading Shirley and her sisters into the parlor. "We're still cleaning and we have a lot of updating to do, especially here in the parlor, where we hope our guests will want to spend a lot of time."

Sam led Shirley to an overstuffed chair. "Have a seat, Shirley, and I'll bring you some lemonade."

Shirley knocked her cane against the upholstery and coughed when a speck or two of dust floated into the air. She offered her now familiar harrumph, at last lowering herself into the chair. "If you have cake or cookies, I'll take those too. The walk over here takes all the starch out of me."

Caroline couldn't help but notice the way Shirley looked around the room with a critical eye, and with the sunlight now pouring in through the windows, it was all that much easier to find things to be critical about. Shirley's gaze settled on the pile of cleaning rags and then the piano. "You aren't using water to clean the wood on that piece, I should hope."

"No," Gracie said. "A little lemon oil is all."

"You might want to clean it first. You can pick up a good wood cleaner at Malcolm's. Ask Bill Dekker to get some for you. He's usually in that neck of the woods every day. If you haven't worked with antiques before, talk to Bill. He'll steer you right. And whatever you do, don't use water, at least not a lot of water. Loosens the glue and the veneer. And don't allow anyone to tell you it needs to be stripped down. Nothing ruins an antique more quickly than getting rid of color that comes with age."

"Thank you," Sam said, setting a glass on the table at Shirley's side, along with a dessert plate filled with snickerdoodles Sam had made that morning. "Gracie's knowledgeable about antiques, but I'm a rank amateur."

Shirley looked pleased as punch. "If I didn't tell you, Quincy Court, my home, was built in 1799. We've been fortunate enough to keep it in the family since the very beginning, but there have been a few generations that let the place slip. One of those generations had the house before me." Shirley clucked her tongue several times. "Took me and Mr. Addison a good year to get it looking as it should. Nowadays I polish everything once a week."

"Sounds a bit overwhelming," Caroline said, glancing at all the woodwork in the parlor. "Exhausting too."

"Not when it's a labor of love." Shirley nibbled at the edge of a snickerdoodle, looking slyly from one sister to another. "By the way, there was something more I remembered about that woman."

"Hannah Montague?" Caroline asked, pulling a dusty ottoman up close to Shirley. "Something about her disappearance?"

Shirley nodded slowly. "I heard she drowned. Of course, I also heard she was a thief," she said, her voice low. "Heard that from an old-timer when I was just a kid. Also heard that she was a spendthrift, that she'd squandered all her husband's money."

"But it's still just rumors, right?" Gracie asked. "There's nothing in writing about any of this, is there?"

"Could be, but I don't know. Of course," Shirley's voice turned conspiratorial, "if she was a thief, if she got involved with a bad guy, she might not have drowned. She might have been killed, and who knows where the body was dumped."

Caroline hoped that wasn't the case. But they'd never know the truth until they learned more about Hannah's life.

"I know it was a long time ago when you bought the hymnal," Caroline said, hoping Shirley's memory was good enough to stretch back over sixty years, "but did you buy anything else at the same time? Antique toys? Dolls?"

Shirley gazed off in the distance for a moment, and then she said, "Well, yes, there was a doll. Prettiest thing I'd ever seen, and I just had to have her."

"You bought her?" Caroline asked, growing more intrigued by the moment.

"For a dollar. My mother thought the doll was ugly, but not I." She took a sip of lemonade. "I still have her, and I'd hate to part with her."

"Would you mind if we looked at her?" Caroline asked. "We've found several other old dolls that we think might have belonged to Hannah, and last night we found a little something hidden in one of the gowns."

Shirley's eyes brightened. "Money? Jewels?"

Caroline smiled. "An old postcard."

"A postcard?" Shirley white brows knit together. "Hidden away in the lining of a doll's dress, you say? Sounds quite odd. I suppose you could look at Jezebel—that's what I call her, from the Bette Davis movie, because she has pretty much the same eyes—but I'd hate to part with her."

"You can keep the doll, Shirley," Caroline said. "We'd just like to look at her. See if her gown was used as another hiding place."

"Do you want to look at her now?"

Boy, did they ever! Who would have thought that their feisty next-door neighbor might hold the answers to many secrets?

Quincy Court was pure Nantucket. Its exterior was boxy, with gray shingles crawling with pink roses. The garden was neat as a pin, Sam thought, except for the hole where the blue hydrangea bush had been. Now there were heaps of dirt splattered about the neatly mown lawn, and there were flower petals and leaves scattered about. Max had created one terrific mess.

"Take your shoes off," Shirley ordered, when they stepped into the foyer. "No need tracking in dirt needlessly. Just makes more for me to clean.

Caroline slipped out of her flip-flops. Gracie and Sam did the same, before Shirley led them into the parlor, a quaint and charming room that enveloped Sam in the sweet scent of the roses sitting atop a coffee table. "Did you decorate this yourself?" Caroline asked, realizing as soon as the words came out of her mouth that they might have sounded insulting, as if it seemed impossible for Shirley to create such a room. She quickly added, "It's beautiful. I love all the nautical pieces."

"I haunt estate sales and thrift shops. None of those excessively expensive antiques stores for me. Megan Folger-Wildes' shop is different, of course, but even she's been known to inflate a price or two."

"Sam saw a ship's masthead not long after we arrived on the island and she just had to have it," Gracie said, "until she saw the price tag. Changed her mind right away."

"I originally thought it would look good inside the inn. I had these grandiose plans to decorate the rooms just like yours," Sam said, "with a ship's wheel here, a harpoon there, but the inn doesn't really lend itself to that."

"There's nothing that says you can't decorate one of the bedrooms to look like this. You could move furniture around too," Shirley said. "Nothing says you need to keep that heavy furniture in the parlor. And really, girls, mixing styles can work, if you do it well. I don't have much time, but if you need any guidance, I'd be happy to steer you in the right direction."

Using her cane for balance, Shirley lowered herself into one of the white chairs. Its upholstery had bright blue, yellow, and green flowers on a white background, with throw pillows made from striped fabric in matching colors. It worked beautifully. It wasn't as clean and simple as she had been envisioning, but Caroline could certainly see the inn's parlor looking bright and cheerful like this. Looking at her sisters, she could see they were thinking the same thing.

"I'm sure you ladies have more to do than stand around here talking to me all afternoon, since you really came over just to see the doll."

They hoped that wasn't an admonishment. Besides the dinner, they'd had Shirley over for the Fourth of July fireworks, and she'd already been over a couple of other times just to complain or offer her opinion. But maybe she just enjoyed the attention.

Sam seemed to sense that too. "Do you like putting together jigsaw puzzles?" she asked. "If I'm not doing cross-stitch or watching cooking shows, I like to put together puzzles. I think I'm driving Gracie and Caroline crazy asking them to join me all the time."

"I've done a few in my day."

"As soon as we get a bit ahead on our cleaning and redecorating," Sam said, "I'll have you over. We can have a girls' night and work on a puzzle."

"Buttering me up will get you nowhere." Shirley grinned. "But I'd enjoy that. The kids and grandkids don't come much anymore, and I don't think the great-grandkids even know who I am. Getting old can be rather sad. But that's neither here nor there." She wagged a finger toward a picture perfect Wedgwood blue cabinet in a far corner of the room. "Open the doors carefully. I have some delicate china in there, but Jezebel's there too. As much as I'd like to keep her out and on display so I can see her all the time, I don't want dust or the sun getting to her. I'd like to keep her aging gracefully."

Caroline felt her fingers shake as she approached the china closet. She didn't know if the one postcard they'd found meant anything at all, but why else had that one seemingly innocent postcard been secreted away inside the lining of a doll's gown? And who was William? Oh, how she hoped there'd be another postcard inside Jezebel.

Slowly, cautiously, she opened the glass-paned doors on the top of the cabinet. The china inside clanked together, but thank goodness nothing fell. Jezebel sat on one of the shelves, and the beautiful smile on her bisque face seemed to say, *Thank you for rescuing me. I've hated being stuffed away.* Sam held her gently, taking her from her hiding place, while Gracie closed the doors.

"Feel anything?" Gracie whispered, as if their current adventure was totally hush-hush.

"Not yet," Caroline said. "She feels even more fragile than the other dolls and the fabric her dress is made from could shred if we're not careful."

Caroline put the doll into Sam's loving hands. She could see her sister breathing shallowly. Sam moved at a snail's pace. She appeared to be testing the weight of the fabric, trying to determine if there was a postcard inside. "I feel something," Sam said, "but I'm not sure if it's a stiffening agent or—"

"A what?" Caroline said.

"A stiffening agent. Another piece of fabric that was used to give the gown more body. Or it could be something else entirely.

And then…Sam smiled triumphantly. "There's something here."

"A postcard?" Caroline asked.

"I'm not sure yet."

"Would you mind terribly if we took the doll back to the inn?" Sam asked Shirley. "I have a big magnifying glass there that I use with my cross-stitch, and I have a good pair of scissors that'll help me take the stitching out of the gown and sew it up again. I'll make it look like it's never been touched."

Shirley was clearly hesitant. She heaved a sigh. "Well, all right, but I want her brought back tomorrow. Understand?"

Sam didn't know just exactly what possessed her, but she gave Mrs. Addison a kiss on the cheek, and the elderly woman blushed. She shooed them off. "Be gone with you now. I've had just about enough of you for one day."

Once again Sam hunkered down with scissors and a needle, staring at the intricate stitching through the lighted magnifying glass. Caroline paced, eating one snickerdoodle after another, waiting for the doll's surgery to end.

"Just a few more stitches," Sam said, hoping her sister would get the message, "and I should be able to work my fingers inside and pull it out."

Gracie leaned against the kitchen counter, biting her lip. "You know, this could all be a waste of time. We don't know anything about Hannah Montague other than she existed and she had a father who was a...well, not a nice man. No one can give us a definitive answer about anything else. For all we know, she could have been an elegant woman who died happy in her bed upstairs."

"Which bedroom do you think would have been hers?" Jamie asked, She grabbed a snickerdoodle, popped half into her mouth, and fed a piece to Max.

"Periwinkle, I'm sure," Caroline said. "It's the biggest one and it has that lovely marble fireplace with seashells etched into it."

Sam knew which room she was talking about, but they hadn't even started working on the guest rooms yet. And they had planned to strip off that faded blue wallpaper.

"Since when is that room named Periwinkle?" Gracie asked. "I don't remember talking about guest room names."

Sam looked up from the doll's pretty royal blue velvet gown in time to see Caroline shrug. "I thought it sounded nice. Did you have some other thoughts?" Caroline asked Gracie.

Sam braced herself. Part of the reason they hadn't done much with the guest rooms was that they still hadn't agreed on what the rooms should look like. Her sisters' decorating tastes had never been the same, and the disagreement had to come to a head at some point. She focused on the doll dress.

Gracie plopped down in the chair next to Sam. "Actually, I kind of like the name Periwinkle."

"Me too," Sam said hesitantly. After all this, was it really going to be that easy? "We could use blue as the main color in that room." She looked back up to see her sisters nodding.

"We could replace that dusty old wallpaper with a pretty floral print," Gracie said. "I bet we could find some with flowers that look like periwinkles."

Caroline looked hesitant, but she nodded slowly. "If we keep the bed linens clean and simple. Just a nice white duvet, maybe with some light blue pillows for accent."

"With the dark furniture, that would look nice," Sam said, looking from one sister to the other.

"Let me go get my notebook. I want to write this down before we forget it," Gracie said, pushing up from the table. A moment later, she was back, and she wrote down Sam's idea of matching the towels in the bathroom to the wallpaper.

"I think this might work," Gracie said. She chewed on the end of her pencil. "What about the other rooms? What should we call them?"

"That pink room could be Amaryllis," Sam said, looking up from the fine stitching in the doll's gown to give her eyes a break. "We can make the room rosy pink, I think, the colors variegated from light to dark."

Gracie flipped a page in her notebook and wrote it down. "It's a pretty name and a pretty flower. Think we can find just the right wallpaper?"

"Heaven only knows." Sam pulled another stitch out of the gown. "I have an idea. Let's take a break from all the cleaning and go into town tomorrow or the next day and look at wallpaper. That might give us more ideas for the other two rooms."

"My aching muscles think that's the best plan I've heard in days." Caroline flexed her neck, tilting her head from side to side, front to back, stretching out her muscles. "I vote for—"

"Got it!" Sam drew the postcard out of its hiding place in the gown, her hand shaking again. She didn't know why she was so excited about this. They could simply have been part of a game Hannah played with—who? Her husband? Her friends? The mysterious William?

Once again there was a masterly ink sketch on the front of the postcard. "What's this?" Sam asked, holding it up for her sisters and Jamie to see.

They studied it intently. "Why couldn't it be something simple like the Old Mill?" Caroline asked. "It's impossible to look at the mill and not know what it is. But this...it's a house."

"It looks just like dozens, maybe hundreds of other houses on Nantucket," Sam said.

"Maybe we're trying to read too much into the picture," Gracie said. "The first one was a church we recognized. This one's a house and it could be anywhere. Whoever drew it—William, I guess—could simply have a fixation for buildings and drew whatever suited his fancy. So what's written on the back?"

Sam turned it over slowly, only to see a series of numbers. 7 17 22 21 8 2 8 18 26 19 2 23 26 21 2 23 15 11 5. She sighed heavily, setting the postcard down on the table. "Numbers. That's it. We don't even know who this one's from."

Caroline leaned in over Sam's shoulder to get a better look. "Where's the other postcard?" Caroline asked. "I want to look at something."

"I put the doll and postcard in the china cabinet in the parlor," Sam said. Caroline went to get it.

Jamie collapsed on an old wooden stool. Max sat at her feet, looking up at her, his tongue lolling. She rubbed her eyes. "This is all rather intriguing"—she yawned—"but maybe we're obsessing too much over this Hannah Montague thing."

"As much as I hate to say this, I have to agree," Gracie said. "We should store both postcards away and get back down to business. If we squander too much time dreaming up conspiracy theories, we won't be ready to open next June."

"You're right," Sam said, setting the doll aside. "This whole thing's giving me a headache."

Caroline came back into the kitchen, holding the first postcard they'd discovered. She picked up the second, looking at the pictures, at the writing. At last she looked from Jamie, to Gracie, to Sam. "These were both mailed from the same place. Boston. The ink looks the same, and Hannah's name and address are in the same handwriting. This second postcard has to have been from William."

"But it's nothing but numbers." Gracie said. "What could they mean?"

Caroline looked at Sam. "You're the princess of puzzles, Sam. What do you think?"

Sam rubbed her eyes. "I think I'm getting awfully tired and all I want to do is climb into bed."

"Me too," Gracie said.

"What about you, Aunt Caroline?"

Sam couldn't miss the hint of misery that flooded Caroline's eyes. "I don't want to give up. I'm certain there's more to the postcards, but we really do need to buckle down and work on the inn." She sighed heavily. "There's always tomorrow to follow the mystery and see where it leads."

CHAPTER
Twenty-six

Gracie pressed her hands against her lower back and wished away the pain and the strain. It had taken most of the summer, but the garden was finally starting to take shape. It didn't seem possible, but it was already the first of September. Labor Day was just around the corner.

In a few more weeks, the trees would shrug out of their summer wardrobe and change into their fall colors...and she'd be gone. Of course, they'd all be gone. She was headed back to Maine to hug her grandkids, and she would stay there for much of the fall. Caroline was heading off to England to say good-bye to her beloved Briar Rose Cottage, and Sam would return to Upstate New York to pack up all her belongings and put her townhouse up for rent.

Gracie leaned against the railing on the back porch and looked out at the flower beds, the meandering paths, and the arbor she'd walked through every afternoon on her way to the beach. It was really starting to look nice. She could get used to this.

But then she thought about her grandkids. She thought about how much Brandon and Stacy depended on her, and she remembered again why she couldn't come back and live here year-round the way Sam and Caroline wanted her to. She couldn't give up the home she'd known and loved for so long. Not for good.

The day after tomorrow, she'd be back in her old routine, helping to chauffeur her grandchildren to and from schools and activities, responding at a moment's notice to her son and daughter-in-law's calls for help. It would feel good to get back to that routine.

She walked down the steps and along the path to the arbor and turned back to look at the inn. It didn't look at all like the place they'd visited that first day on the island. It now had a fresh coat of Main Street Yellow paint. The trim was so white it glistened. The snowy white shutters had been thrown open, and the windows gleamed.

The inside still needed a lot of work, but they'd gotten the hard parts done: hardwood floors stripped, chimneys cleaned, new water heaters installed, new commercial-grade washer and dryer. They'd sanded down the cabinets in the kitchen and repainted them a soft cream, and when they'd torn up the old, dilapidated kitchen linoleum, they had found hardwood floors beneath. They had accomplished so much.

When they came back a month from now, they could work on the fun stuff. As much as she was looking forward to being home, she couldn't help but look forward to coming back and getting started here again. She felt torn.

"The three of you have done a mighty good job fixing up this place."

She turned. Bill had walked up from the beach, wearing his usual smile. The temperature was dropping every day, and he was wearing jeans now instead of shorts. Undoubtedly, before long, the thermal underwear would come out of the drawer, and the real islanders, the ones who lived here year-round, would be wearing flannel and wool, and lots of layers to keep warm.

But not today. Today, it was still beautiful, warm, and sunny with a clear blue sky.

Gracie looked back at the inn. "You can add yourself to the list of people who've made this place look pretty again. I was just thinking about all we've accomplished in such a short time."

Bill had been here nearly every day, tackling the projects that required more skill than the sisters possessed. She's seen him most Sundays at Harvest Chapel too, and Bill had become a big part of their lives here in Nantucket.

"Should be a lot more done by the time you get back."

"We seem to be abandoning you when it's time to do the really hard work."

Bill chuckled. "Tearing up the downstairs bathroom will be a lot easier when the three of you don't have to use it every day. And the plumbing in the basement—" Bill thrust a hand through his shaggy gray hair. "—I can't apologize enough for not catching some of the problems before you signed your name on the dotted line for this place."

Gracie hated to see Bill apologize for something that most anyone could have missed. "The roof could have been missing and it could have had an army of mice living in the attic," Gracie said. "It could have been gutted on the inside, and Caroline and Sam still would have insisted on buying it anyway. And you know, I've gotten used to the idea of being part owner, even when the old place creaks at night and startles me out of a sound sleep."

"Does that mean that one of these days, we can anticipate your sticking around permanently?" Bill studied her face.

Gracie stared at the inn for a moment. "Oh no," she said, finally tearing her eyes away. "Portland, Maine, is home. Always has been. Always will be."

"Any regrets?" Caroline asked Gracie and Sam as they stood in the foyer, waiting for Bill to show up and give them a ride to the ferry.

"Not a one," Sam said. "In fact, I think I've lost five pounds in the past three months."

"Certainly not from lack of food." Gracie wrapped an arm around her sister. "I always knew you could cook, but I had no idea you cooked all the time. In spite of all the work we've done, I'm pretty sure I've gained the five pounds you lost."

"I'm going to miss you two." Caroline already felt the tears building in her eyes. "Suddenly England seems a zillion miles away and a lifetime ago."

"I could say the same about Upstate New York." Sam picked up the duffel bag she'd placed on the floor about an hour before. She slipped the strap over her shoulder, as if she anticipated Bill arriving any moment. "In just three months, Nantucket's become home. I never would have expected that to happen, but it has."

Gracie grinned. "Listen to you two. You'd think you were leaving for good instead of just one month. We'll all be back here before you know it, and once we start working again, you'll wonder what ever possessed you to buy this place."

"Who are you trying to fool?" Caroline asked Gracie. "You're pretty attached to this place too."

"Okay, maybe I am. But I'm eager to get back to the kids, to my book club, and my church. I've missed that life."

A horn honked outside, and Caroline could see the wavy form of Bill's pickup through the etched glass window in the front door. Thank goodness it was such a short drive to the ferry, because Sam would have to sit on her lap so they could all fit in the cab.

Gracie and Caroline grabbed their bags. They weren't taking home as much as they'd brought with them three months ago. There was no need to. They'd be back soon.

CHAPTER
Twenty-seven

Caroline paused for a moment on the walk of the Misty Harbor, breathing in the crisp salt air of the Nantucket autumn. October had arrived, clad in glorious hues of gold, russet, and burnt orange. She strode to the temperamental Nantucket Blue front door, turned the doorknob, and applied the customary shove of her hip—and practically flew into the inn. It had sprung open with absolutely zero resistance. She was halfway across the foyer before she was able to stop.

The door must have been one of Bill's projects while they were gone.

"I'm back!" she shouted near the top of her lungs, listening to the echo of her voice reverberating through the rooms. She was pretty sure she was the last one to arrive. Sam had brought her minivan to the island, and it was already parked out front.

Caroline heard footsteps pounding down the stairwell before she saw Sam and Gracie, both clad in jeans and boots and the Fair Isle sweaters. They could almost pass for twins. Caroline suddenly felt out of place in a long chocolate brown corduroy jumper, a creamy turtleneck, a pair of sheepskin-cuffed Uggs, and a bulky sweater—a going-away gift from the vicar's wife.

Sam and Gracie threw their arms around Caroline, and suddenly she felt totally at home again. The Misty Harbor Inn was where she belonged.

"When did you get here?" Caroline asked.

"Hours ago." Sam grabbed Caroline's hand and dragged her into the parlor. "Look."

"Oh my." Box upon box lined one wall in the parlor. They'd all been opened. "What's in them?"

"Wallpaper. Linens. Upholstery fabric." Gracie crossed the room, opened the flaps on one of the boxes, and pulled out a plastic bag full of upholstery nails. They'd chosen them over a month ago, using only the pictures on numerous decorating Web pages to make their choice. "I haven't inventoried everything yet. I hope everything we ordered is here, but I can safely say that we're going to be busy the next couple of weeks."

"Only a couple of weeks?" Caroline frowned. She was so hoping Gracie would have decided to stay for good, but it sounded like she'd made up her mind.

"As much as I want to stay—"

Sam held up her hand to halt Gracie's words. "No excuses necessary, Gracie. We knew when we bought this place that you'd come when you could. We can't expect you to be here all the time."

"It was really nice to be home this past month," Gracie said, pulling bag after bag out of the boxes, as if she was afraid to look her sisters in the eye. "The two of you were away from the inn too, so I didn't need to feel guilty about not being here. But it's probably going to feel different when I go home the middle of the month."

"We'll just have to find some work for you to take home with you," Caroline said, although she had no idea what that would be. Gracie couldn't very well hang wallpaper or upholster furniture from Maine, and working on a Web site was not her sister's forte. But Sam was right—they'd gone into this with their eyes wide open. Gracie would not be here all the time, and they simply had to deal with it.

"What were you doing when I arrived? Wait! Let me guess." Caroline grinned. "You were running around the second floor looking for secret rooms."

"Close." Sam crossed the room and sat on the piano bench. She played with the keys. The notes were flat. Caroline made a mental note to call a piano technician. "We were checking out the bathrooms."

Caroline's brow furrowed. "The bathrooms? Why? Did something happen with the plumbing again?"

"Nothing like that. Bill left us a note." Sam pulled a piece of lined paper from her back pocket and read, "'Sinks and toilets replaced, upstairs bathrooms. Downstairs plumbing fixed—no more 2:00 AM floods. Floor in downstairs bath shored up.'" Sam looked up at Caroline. "The list goes on, but you've got to see this."

She grabbed Caroline's hand again and dragged her back to the curving stairs and up to the second floor. Max and Gracie scurried along behind.

Caroline laughed as they raced down the hallway, acting like schoolgirls out for a good time. The Periwinkle Room looked nearly the way they'd left it. Wood-frame bed and mattress covered with dust sheets. Antique dresser covered with dust. Rocker stripped of paint and ready for a new coat, plus upholstery. Nearly threadbare carpet rolled up and pushed against one wall.

Caroline's eyes widened. "There's still so much work left to do."

"Except in here." Sam pushed Caroline toward the bathroom. "Look."

Light filtered in through the window, but it was dim until Gracie switched on the antique bronze sconces on either side of the big oval mirror. Her gaze skimmed over the new, old-fashioned pedestal sink and matching toilet, but she couldn't skim past the tile work around the combination tub and shower. It was stunning. A work of art. It was a mural of a basket made of seashells and overflowing with blue periwinkles.

"I don't remember asking Bill to have tile work done while we were gone," Caroline said.

"We didn't," Gracie said. "He's an artist, remember? My guess is he did this on his own. The periwinkles are just like the ones in the wallpaper we selected, right down to the colors."

Caroline's mind was reeling. "But how can we ever repay him?"

"You can tell your guests to come to 'Sconset and visit my workshop." Bill's deep voice literally boomed through the room. "Hope you don't mind. I let myself in."

Gracie was the first one to hug him, Caroline the last, and she didn't want to let go. He'd done so much for them. "Goodness, Bill, this is the best homecoming present I've ever had."

"It wasn't much. We had a big storm, and my place got rained out, so I stayed here for a few days. This is what a guy like me does when he can't get outside."

"Okay, so if you couldn't get outside, where did you get the tiles?" Caroline grinned, not falling for his act.

Bill looked sheepish. "You caught me. I'd been planning this since you showed me the wallpaper. It turned out better than I expected."

"This is going to put the rest of the bathrooms to shame," Gracie said, shaking her head.

"I've got drawings worked up for those rooms too. If you're interested, I can get the tiles at cost and the labor—well, I'll give you a discount, and maybe you can show my work off on your Web site."

"I knew there had to be a catch here someplace," Caroline teased. "But if it works for Gracie and Sam, it works for me."

"Speaking of the Web site, how is it coming along?" Gracie asked Caroline later as they worked together in the foyer, hanging the pastel blue- and yellow-striped wallpaper above the dark cherry-wood wainscoting. She'd worried for days now, wanting to ask that question when Caroline hadn't found the time or had the inclination to give them an update, but she couldn't wait any longer. They simply had to have the site up and running at least by the first of November, since they were running ads in the December issues of several travel magazines and would be featuring the Web site address prominently. It wasn't uncommon for guests to make reservations six months in advance in Nantucket, so they had to be prepared.

"Well," Caroline said, handing a strip of paper to Gracie, "the home page is complete, but I'm still working on some of the detail pages."

Gracie thought for sure her neck and face had turned red, considering how the heat of anger was rising in her body. "Do you mean to tell me you have only one page ready?"

"It's not as bad as it sounds. I have notes and all my photographs and—"

"You promised to work on it while you were in England."

"I had to empty out an entire cottage. Ten years of living in one place. That took time, Gracie. I've been here for three days now, and I've hung wallpaper until I'm blue in the face. And you know what? I'm going to be hanging wallpaper and upholstering furniture and decorating two weeks from now and long after you've gone back home, so don't look at me as if I've been doing nothing."

Gracie swallowed hard and squeezed back hot tears. She finished applying the piece of paper Caroline had handed her, smoothing it out, making sure it was perfect. Then she climbed down from the ladder and walked out the front door. It slammed behind her.

Gracie headed for the wrought iron bench in the middle of the garden. Yesterday, she'd planted burgundy, gold, red, and yellow mums in all the planters and urns scattered around the garden. She'd made a lot of headway on the overgrown jungle during the summer, and there was going to be even more work next spring, but right now, it seemed to be the perfect place to cry.

She heard footsteps crunching on the shell-and-gravel pathway and saw Caroline coming toward her. Tentatively, Caroline sat down beside her.

"I'm sorry," Gracie said. She pulled the sleeves of her sweater down over the heels of her hands. The view was still stunning, but the autumn breeze was chilly. They wouldn't be able to sit out here much longer.

"Me too."

"I'm awfully critical, aren't I?"

"Sometimes," Caroline said softly. "But I have trouble keeping focused on one project. You know I've been that way all my life. I mean, I wish I could be more like you. Organized—"

"—to a fault."

"That's not so bad."

"Sometimes it is, Caroline. I don't have much spontaneity, not like you, and I've always wanted that." Gracie sighed heavily. "You might wish you could be more like me, but I wish I could be more like you."

"Then nothing would ever get done around here."

"That's not true. You do work hard."

"I just get distracted easily."

"Gracie! Caroline!"

Gracie and Caroline both sprang to attention, turning toward the house. Sam was hollering at them from one of the attic windows.

"Come up here! You've got to see what I found."

Max's head popped up from the spot by the arbor where he'd been sleeping in the sun. He took off in a flash, heading for the kitchen door. He waited somewhat patiently for Gracie and Cardline to open the door and then bolted through the kitchen and up the back stairs.

Gracie moved a little slower. She was also glad she and Caroline had finally gotten a bit of hurt out of their systems. They were bound to argue again, but it would never last for long. Maybe they just needed to talk more, to be truthful about what bothered them.

Gracie hadn't been up in the attic since the end of the summer, but it looked like nothing had changed. Dust motes danced serenely in the sunlight from the window, and boxes were still stacked sky high. Someday there might be time to tackle the mess, but that would be well into the future.

"This'd better be good," Caroline said, laughing when Sam appeared before them, covered with dust and cobwebs.

"Oh, it's good all right." Sam smiled. "It's an old sampler, and it's beautiful. And here's the best part of all: I think it was stitched by Hannah Montague."

Sam had been hugging the dark wood frame to her chest. She slowly turned it around for Gracie and Caroline to see. "Down here"—she tapped on the glass—"beneath the Bible verse, are the letters 'H.E.' That's got to be Hannah Elliott. It's dated 1864, the same as the inscription inside her hymnal."

Gracie moved in closer for a better view. "If that's really hers, she did awfully good work for, what, a ten-year-old?"

Sam nodded. "I was thinking the same thing, although some of the letters are uneven, and some are darker and thicker than others."

"Girls back then were always so precise." Gracie added.

"What does it say?" Caroline asked.

Gracie read the verse the little girl had so lovingly embroidered:

"Let the word of Christ dwell in you richly in all wisdom;

teaching and admonishing one another

in psalms and hymns and spiritual songs,

singing with grace in your hearts to the Lord.

Colossians 3:16"

Caroline looked at it closely. Pink, white, and pale reddish-brown seashells zigzagged along the border, with musical notes scattered among them. "What do you think the seashells and musical notes mean?" Caroline asked.

Gracie laughed. "Here we go again, trying to find a meaning in something that might have no meaning at all. It's highly possible that Hannah might have thought the seashells and musical notes would look pretty together."

"Well, I prefer to think there's more to it," Caroline said. "I have the feeling Hannah was a little girl who didn't like to take orders from her father, bucked him at every opportunity."

"And what makes you think that?" Gracie asked. She thought her sister must be projecting her own personality on Hannah.

"Just a hunch," Caroline said. "All we really know is that she married beak-nosed Jedediah Montague, who had to have been much older than she. An arranged marriage—no doubt one she didn't want."

"That's totally made up, Caroline," Gracie said. "We don't know the first thing about her."

"But I want her to have a story. I want to bring her to life," Caroline said. "If I have to make up a life for her"—she shrugged—"so be it."

Gracie shook her head, grinning. "You're as incorrigible as Max."

From somewhere in the attic, Max barked.

Gracie coughed, fanning away the dust motes in front of her face. "You know where the sampler would look good? In the library."

"Should we hang it now?" Caroline asked.

"We could do that," Gracie said. "The room's painted and papered, and we really need to start filling it with odds and ends to give it a homely feel. We can set out some of the knickknacks of Mom's that the two of you brought back to the island, and—"

"Was that a knock at the door?" Sam asked. "I could have sworn I just heard a cane tapping away, trying to get our attention."

The sisters heard a whimper. Max peered out from his hiding place, his brown eyes wide. He was doing his best to look innocent. "Oh dear," Gracie said. "Now what has Max done?"

CHAPTER
Twenty-eight

ince you didn't come over to say hello when you got back, I figured
I'd just have to come say hello to you."

Shirley Addison strode through the foyer and into the parlor.
Her cane tapped on the hardwood floor with every other step.

"We're glad you did, Shirley," Caroline said. She wondered when
Shirley would lower the boom and tell them what Max had messed
with this time. "But we've been a little busy since we got home. What
do you think of all the work we've done?"

Shirley made her way to one of the sofas that would be
reupholstered in the next few weeks and gave it a whack with her
cane. They were relieved to see only a little dust puff out and into the
air. Using her cane for balance, she sat down. She looked around. "I
see you copied my parlor."

Sam set Hannah's sampler on top the piano for now. They had
drawn inspiration from Shirley's parlor. Their parlor had the same
nautical theme, and they had used stripes and flowers to bring the
theme out, just like she had. The walls were a light, calming blue.
They had found and framed an old mariner map and hung it over

the couch, which they were recovering in a cheery floral fabric. They planned to use pillows of blue and white stripes to set it off. They'd set a mirror in a bronze ship porthole by the piano, and there was an antique wooden buoy perched on a steamer trunk they planned to use as a coffee table.

"You know what they say, imitation is the greatest form of flattery." Caroline smiled.

"In writing, it's considered plagiarism, but"—Shirley finally allowed herself to smile— "the color is a tad different. Perhaps a little softer." She frowned. Her lips twitched back and forth as she looked about the room. "Actually, I rather like it." She smiled. "Good choice, girls."

"Could I get you some hot chocolate?" Caroline asked, hoping to make amends before Shirley had an opportunity to chew them out for whatever Max might have done. "Some tea? Gracie and Sam brought some lovely flavors with them. Passion fruit, mango, pomegranate."

"I'm a Lipton fan, myself. Just plain old black stuff. With caffeine. Made with a tea bag."

Caroline swallowed hard. Their neighbor was in rare form today. "Is everything all right, Shirley? Has something happened? Did Max do something?"

"Why, no, what makes you ask that?"

"Oh, no reason," Caroline said. "We sometimes worry about him going over to your place and getting into something he shouldn't."

Shirley harrumphed. "Not today, as far as I know, although I'm sure he'll pay me a visit before the week's out. What about our Jamie? And George? Will they be visiting soon?"

"Jamie should be here in a little while. She has fall break this week. And George this coming weekend."

"Then I suppose you'll invite me for dinner to celebrate your homecoming?"

"How about Saturday night?" Sam said, but before Mrs. Addison could reply, Max bolted through the parlor, sliding across the floor. He had something big and oddly shaped in his mouth, and Caroline went after him.

"Max! What are you trying to hide?"

Max growled as he ran from the parlor into the dining room and then into the kitchen, with Caroline hot on his trail.

She found Max standing at the kitchen door, begging to go outside. He wasn't going anywhere until he handed over his bounty, though. "What have you got?" Caroline asked, holding out her hand. Max growled. "Bad boy! You know you're not supposed to growl at me. Drop it!" Max turned his head the other way, completely ignoring her. "You heard me, Max. Don't pretend you didn't. If you want to go out, you've got to hand over your toy."

Caroline latched on to the slobbery mass of color. "Give!"

Max wasn't about to let go. The tug-of-war lasted for a good ten seconds, until Max tore away from Caroline and made a mad dash up the back stairs. Caroline followed, knowing exactly where he was heading—his favorite place. The attic.

It was way too dim in the attic to see much of anything well. They really did need to install better lights. If it hadn't been for Max's panting, she might not have found him.

She peered around several stacks of boxes. "What are you hiding back here?"

Even in the murky light, she could see a pile of toys, an old bone, some uneaten dog cookies, and…an old puppet theater. She parted the dusty curtains behind the stage and found Max peering up at her with innocent eyes. She wanted to laugh but didn't, not when she saw the puppet clenched in his jaws. It was Punch—a headless Punch. Judy lay on the floor beside Max, a little worse for wear, one arm chewed almost beyond recognition. "Shame on you, Max. There's no telling how old these puppets are, and you've destroyed them."

Caroline shook her head in frustration and reached down to grab what was left of poor Punch's body. She looked at him closely. One leg had been ripped off. His clothes were wet with slobber. "Goodness, Max, have you been using Punch as a chew bone?"

She wrested the puppet from Max's mouth and looked to see if she, or rather, Sam could put the puppet back together again, when she noticed something wedged inside ornery old Punch. She poked her finger in and dug around inside, and—

Oh my!

"How many do you think there are?" Sam asked.

"A dozen or so," Caroline said as they huddled around the dining room table. It was cluttered with piles of their mother's linen and lace tablecloths, napkins, and doilies, which Gracie had brought back to the island.

Caroline worked at untying the pink silk bow wrapped around what had to be more postcards. Sam wanted to tell her to hurry up but bit her tongue.

"Be careful, young lady." Shirley hovered close, watching Caroline, Gracie, and Sam's every move. "If more of those old postcards are inside, the last thing you want is for them to turn to dust."

"It would be nice to have a historical preservationist with us right now, someone who knew the best way to handle old documents,"

Sam said, "but I'm too eager to see if they are postcards and what's on them."

Gracie drummed her fingers on the dining room table. "I can't even imagine what would have happened if Max had ripped Punch completely apart and taken the packet outside."

"He would have buried it somewhere," Caroline said. "They'd probably be lost forever, and we'd never learn more about Hannah."

"You're being a little too hopeful," Sam added. "Finding more postcards—if that's what's inside—doesn't mean we'll learn more about Hannah. If they're like the other ones, they'll just confuse us more."

"Oh, come on, Sam. You're the bright one in the family. The school teacher and puzzle solver," Gracie said. "You should have been able to figure out what those numbers meant on the last card."

It seemed to take forever, but at last the packet was free of ribbon, and the calico was unfolded to reveal more of William's postcards. A few of the edges were stuck together, but when Caroline handed them to Sam, she worked at them carefully, wedging them apart, until she had seven postcards sitting atop the table.

"That's the Brant Point lighthouse," Sam said, pointing to one of the cards, but being careful not to touch it. "That's the Atheneum."

"This is the Three Bricks, and this one"—Caroline tapped the table next to the postcard with an eerie depiction of a gravestone—"this could be any number of cemeteries."

"There's a name on one of the stones." Sam moved in for a closer look. "I'd have to get a magnifying glass to read it, but it looks a little like Montague."

"What's the postmark date?" Caroline asked.

Sam turned it over carefully, her fingers barely touching the edges. "I can't see all of it, but the year could be 1879."

"May be 1878? That's the year Jedediah Montague died," Gracie stated. "Do you think that's his headstone?"

"It could be," Sam said. She wished Jamie was here to help figure things out. She always had good insight. "But what does finding a picture of Jedediah Montague's headstone prove? That William was a little morbid?"

Caroline sighed heavily. She gently turned each postcard over to see what was written on the back. "Numbers again," she said as she flipped one over. "What on earth could those numbers mean?"

"Who knows? But let's not ignore the rest. Look at this one."

Sam read the words out loud:

> "Millions of happy spirits live
>
> On thy exhaustless store;
>
> From thee they all their bliss receive
>
> And still thou givest more."

"This William fellow was rather a jokester." Shirley *tsk*ed. "It's beginning to look more and more like he and Hannah were having a bit of a fling."

"Possibly," Caroline said, "although I don't want to believe it. I don't know anything about her, but I don't see her as a floozy. I think she was just unhappy."

"So what cryptic message did our William write on the next postcard?" Shirley asked. "Wish you were here?"

Caroline shook her head. Shirley could be awfully sweet when she wanted to be, but right now wasn't one of those times. Caroline turned over another postcard and read:

> "Come, Lord, Thy love alone can raise
>
> In us the heavenly flame;

Then shall our lips resound Thy praise,

Our hearts adore Thy name."

And yet another:

"My dearest Hannah,

Red Caps beat White Stockings 10–1.

Great day for Boston!

Wish you'd been at South End Grounds with me.

Must prepare Sunday's sermon.

Your servant and fond admirer,

William."

"There aren't any numbers on that one," Caroline said. "No verse, or Scripture. Just the note."

"What's the postmark on that one?" Gracie asked. "The others are postmarked in 1880, but this one could have been written earlier—or later. There might be a reason why there weren't any numbers written across the top."

Sam turned the card over to look at the postmark. "*Hmm*, you're right. It was earlier. Two years earlier, 1878—that's around the time Jedediah died."

"And now that you mention it," Sam said, "he died before most of the other postcards were sent."

"So why hide them?" Caroline asked. "It doesn't make any sense."

"Personally, I think you ladies are trying too hard to find something where there's nothing," Shirley said, pushing up from the chair. "Those numbers are probably nothing more than doodles, scribbled by a man who had nothing better to do with his time."

"You're probably right," Gracie said. "They're nothing more than postcards. No secret code. No secret alliance. Just a big joke between two old friends."

"I hope you're wrong," Caroline said. "Though I am beginning to suspect that the joke's on us."

"Please tell me you've done this before," Gracie said, sitting cross-legged on the floor watching Sam tear apart one of the sofas. "Covering one cushion on a simple French Provincial chair is one thing. Upholstering an entire sofa is another."

"I watched Martha Stewart do this once. It was a piece of cake."

"I certainly hope this piece of cake doesn't end up wasting yards and yards of expensive upholstery fabric—"

"I got this upholstery fabric for a song. I'll have you know." Sam held up a length of cheerful blue, green, and yellow fabric against the side of the couch and nodded.

"Stop being such a fuddy-duddy," Caroline called, laughing at Gracie all the way from the dining room. Caroline was working on the Web site, while poor Jamie was studying the postcards, a task she'd been at off and on for days. She wasn't going to discover anything, Gracie wanted to tell her.

"How's it going?" George sauntered into the parlor, looking for Caroline, no doubt. There were smudges of grease on his nose and forehead.

"If you're asking me and Sam," Gracie said, "I suppose it's going as good as can be expected, considering that two novice upholsterers are trying to perform miracles."

"Jamie and I are in the dining room," Caroline called out. "But stay there. I need a break before I go blind staring at this computer screen."

"In case Caroline hasn't told you," Sam said to George, looking up from her work, "she's putting the finishing touches on the Web site, and it's looking awfully good."

"I just hope we can get the bedrooms completely decorated before we go live," Gracie added. She would be leaving in a little over a week, and she hoped they could finish before then.

"They'll be done, not to worry." Caroline walked into the parlor and, with a tissue she pulled from her pocket, wiped the grease from George's nose. He'd been working on the Packard nearly nonstop since he'd arrived on the island the day before, and Gracie was beginning to feel as if he was as much a part of the inn as she and her two sisters.

"The Packard should be done before we know it too," George said, sitting on the piano bench . Caroline took a seat beside him.

"Any luck with the gauges?" Caroline asked.

"I was afraid I'd ordered the wrong ones." George combed his fingers through his hair. "I had a terrible time getting the old gauges out of the dash, and I thought the new ones wouldn't go in, but just when I was about to give up—well, I won't bore you with the details. But the first time you drive that old car, you'll know exactly how fast you're going, how much gas you've got, and you'll even be able to play your favorite CDs. Of course, all that depends on whether or not I can find all the engine parts to get the motor running."

"Is it that difficult?" Sam asked. She placed the old fabric she'd taken off the sofa over the new upholstery as a sort of pattern.

"Not really. There are a lot of parts dealers around who specialize in Packards, plus there are any number of clubs across the US. Fortunately, most everything on your car is in good condition. It's just a matter of taking all the pieces apart, cleaning them up, getting rid of any rust or corrosion, and then putting it all back together again."

"That simple, huh?" Gracie helped Sam stretch the old piece of fabric over the new and then started to pin it down.

"I take pictures along the way. First time I restored a boat, I thought I could remember each step I took when taking it apart. Big mistake. Somehow I ended up with parts left over and had to hire an expert to help me out. Live and learn."

"I'm thinking we might have to hire an expert to help us figure out William's postcards to Hannah," Jamie said, coming into the parlor with Max hot on her heels, both of them munching on oatmeal cookies. "They're frustrating, to say the least. However, I've been trying to look at them analytically."

"Often a dangerous undertaking," Caroline said, adding, "for me, anyway."

Jamie rolled her eyes. She looked so much like a taller, thinner, strawberry-blonde version of her mother. "I've entered the postmark date on each card on my chart. I was hoping there'd be some rhyme or reason to the dates, like William sent them every third Tuesday, or something, but the dates are random. There are six weeks between the date the first and second postcard were sent, but it was nearly two years before he sent the next one—or at least the next one that we've found—and that was after ol' Jedediah kicked the bucket. After that, there were four weeks between the next two cards, three between the two after that, and just two between the final two."

"As if it were becoming more urgent," Caroline said.

"Exactly," Jamie said, dropping down on a still-dusty club chair. "But why?"

"I think maybe your schoolwork is getting to you," Gracie said, smiling at her niece. "As Festus said to Paul in the Bible, 'much learning doth make thee mad.'"

"Hey now," Jamie said, playfully tossing a pillow toward her aunt. "There are plenty of myths and legends here on Nantucket. My adviser was thrilled when I suggested coming here to do research. And this is a legend if I ever saw one."

"And what happens if you don't unravel this particular legend before class starts again next week?" Sam asked her daughter.

"Then I'll just write about one of the old whaling stories." Jamie waved a dismissive hand. "I can do that in an afternoon."

"Do you think the pictures on the front mean anything special?" George asked. "Were they places that had some special meaning to Hannah or to William? Places he'd like to visit again?"

"Could be either one," Gracie said, "not that we'll ever know for sure."

"What about the numbers on the backs of some of the postcards?" Caroline asked. "Have you figured out what they mean?"

Jamie shook her head and took another bite of the cookie. "I tried comparing them with the date on the postcard, to see if there was some correlation, but I'm still baffled."

"I think they weren't supposed to be understood by anyone but William and Hannah," Sam said. "Some secret code between the two of them."

"It would be nice if we knew more about William," Jamie said. "We're guessing he was a minister, but he might not have been."

"Yet that seems pretty reasonable," Sam added, "since he said he had to write a sermon."

"True." Jamie broke off a piece of her cookie and fed it to Max. She brushed the crumbs from her hands. Gracie bit her tongue as they fell on the floor. "We can also say with pretty much certainty that he lived in Boston, since that's where all the postcards were mailed from."

"Too bad he didn't have an unusual name like Hezekiah or Thurston," Caroline said, "That would have made it easier for us to try and find mention of him in Boston historical records. We'd never in a million years be able to nail down a William."

"I hate to be a nag," Gracie reminded them, "but none of us has time to do a lot of historical research on anything right now." She was tired of this never-ending talk of Hannah and William. "Our number one priority is getting the inn up and running by the middle of May. I know a lot has been accomplished, but there's still so much more."

"We have the logo from the designer, and it looks great," Caroline pointed out. "And the wallpapering downstairs is finished."

"But we have a whole lot of furniture to reupholster and most everything to do in the guest rooms," Gracie said, hoping she could get her point across. "And let's not forget, we have to have almost everything ready by Christmas. I want Brandon and Stacy and the kids to see it finished. I don't want them to think we made the wrong decision to buy the inn."

Sam put down her scissors. She took the pins out that she'd held clamped between her teeth and stuck them in her pin cushion. "You know what I think?"

"What?" Gracie asked, knowing Sam was trying to change the subject.

"I think we need a break."

"I couldn't agree more," Jamie said. "In fact, I know exactly what we should do."

"Which is?" Gracie asked. She wanted to continue on with the upholstery projects, but was sure she'd be outvoted.

"I want to take a look at the places William sketched on the postcards."

"We've been by each one dozens of times," Gracie said. "I don't see how paying each one a visit will help figure out if there's a secret code hidden in the messages."

"Maybe not," Jamie said, "but it might put all of us in a different mindset. Make us think a little more creatively. Besides, it will help me with my paper. What do you say?"

"It's educational," Sam said. "How can you say no?"

"You know me," Caroline said, "I'm always open to a bit of sightseeing."

Always open to a bit of goofing off is more like it, Gracie thought. But maybe she needed to goof off a bit too. Life really was too short to always be the stuffed shirt in the family.

CHAPTER
Twenty-nine

ny luck?" Sam asked Caroline and Gracie when they climbed
back into Sam's van. They'd split up, with Gracie and Caroline
visiting the Unitarian church, which had been sketched on the
earliest postmarked postcard they'd found, while Jamie and Sam
had visited the Methodist church a few blocks away. They had been
hoping to accomplish as much as they could in a short amount of
time.

"Not really," Caroline said, putting on her seat belt. "They have
records going back as far as 1808, but we didn't find anything of use.
No mention of Hannah Elliott or Hannah Montague. No Jedediah,
none of his family members, and no minister named William. How
about the two of you? Did you find anything?"

Sam shook her head. "Not a thing, other than several very helpful
people. No Jedediah Montague. No Hannah. No Hettie. No Elliott
listed as a congregant, and the only nineteenth-century pastor whose
first name was William died from consumption in 1862."

"Please tell me you don't think we should visit every church on
the island and look at their historical records," Gracie said. Caroline

could tell the hunt for information about the elusive William and Hannah was wearing Gracie out.

"There were a lot of churches here in the late 1800s," Sam said. "And we don't know how many have old records."

"Personally," Gracie added, "I think we should assume that William simply drew pictures of places that intrigued him."

Caroline knew Gracie didn't want to be out on this seemingly impossible mission. She wanted to be back at the inn working. Caroline couldn't help but wonder how much of that had to do with her drive to stay focused, and how much had to do with guilt, with wanting to get most everything done before she returned home, so most of the burden would be taken off Sam's and Caroline's shoulders.

They really had needed a break, though, and Caroline, for one, wasn't about to make Gracie feel guilty when she returned home. Something told her that Brandon, bless his heart, was making his mom feel guilty enough about being here and leaving him and Stacy in the lurch when they needed a babysitter.

"So, where do we go next?" Sam asked.

"The Quaker Meeting House."

Visiting each building or location William had sketched on his postcards had seemed like such a good idea in the beginning, but as they went from place to place—the Old Mill, Brant Point Lighthouse—they began to feel like they were spinning their wheels. The only thing they learned by visiting the cemetery where Jedediah Montague was buried was that his grave was next to that of his first wife, Hettie, and his sons, Lachlan and Fitzwalter. There was no sign of Hannah's grave anywhere nearby.

They sat in the Brant Point Light parking lot. The structure was blindingly white against the clear blue autumn sky. A few tourists milled around them. "You know," Jamie said, looking over the chart she'd printed out, "we—or I—could be overthinking all of this. The postcard with the church sketched on the front was postmarked April 20, 1880. I probably should have looked at church records to see if anything significant happened right around that date."

"You mean something like a robbery?" Sam asked. "Remember Shirley's telling us that there had been rumors that Hannah was a thief? Maybe she and William were up to no good, and—"

"I can't believe that about Hannah," Caroline said, interrupting her sister. "I just don't see her doing anything illegal."

"We don't know anything at all about her," Gracie pointed out. "There are no pictures, no diaries, nothing but a few old dolls and some postcards."

"And the sampler." Sam closed up another button on her light coat. "And her hymnal with that horrid message from her father written inside."

"I think they were old friends, and William was trying to keep up their friendship," Caroline said.

"Via very cryptic messages?" Sam asked. "That's just too strange, Caroline. There has to be more to it."

But what?

"I think I might have the Packard running by Christmas," George said, taking a second helping of the mashed potatoes. Sam had made them with garlic, heaps of butter, real cream, bits of bacon, and sunflower seeds, and they were decadent and delightful. "The engine's in a lot better shape than I thought, and I ordered a new alternator while you four were out playing sleuth."

"Failed sleuths," Gracie said. She wished they'd never discovered that first postcard. "It seems that the more we think about all our so-called clues, the more questions we end up with."

"How's the meat loaf?" Sam asked, serving Jamie another slice of the savory gourmet version of the traditional comfort-food favorite. She seemed to be steering the conversation away from Hannah before Gracie's irritation boiled over into something more.

"Such as?" George asked, ignoring Sam's question.

"Well, we're assuming—and it seems to be a pretty good assumption—that William was a man of the cloth," Gracie said, trying to remember all their questions. "Would he travel from Boston to Nantucket for cloak-and-dagger meetings with a married woman?"

"She was married when he first started writing the postcards. She was widowed later on," Caroline reminded her. "William may or may not have been a minister at one time. Why he wrote, we may never know, but I'm beginning to think he wrote to console her, that there was nothing romantic involved."

"Why do you say that? That's a big stretch of the imagination," Gracie said. "Think of some of the wording he used in his postcards. 'Once more with great pleasure I embrace a few moments to write you a short letter.'"

"That could very easily have been written by a minister to a former congregant," Sam said.

"Okay, how about this one," Gracie said, remembering many of the words quite well. "'Though we are far apart at present, my heart is with you every moment.'"

"Sounds rather endearing," Jamie said. "It wasn't all that long ago that I was plagued by a man whose heart was everywhere but with me, whether we were apart or together." It was the first time Gracie had heard Jamie mention Cory since she'd come back, and it was good to see her joking about him. Time, plus, no doubt, the business of the fall semester, had done wonders for her niece's heart.

"I can't get over thinking that the numbers mean something," said Jamie.

"Like what?" George asked, a forkful of potatoes close to his mouth. "A date and time, maybe? Code for a meeting place?"

"Do you really think they were meeting each other?" Caroline asked. "There aren't any dates and times, no mention of meeting."

"But that makes sense," George stated. "Hannah hid the postcards, which means she didn't want anyone seeing them. Maybe William was someone she'd been told not to see or communicate with."

"If that's true," Sam said, "it makes sense that he wouldn't have mentioned any dates and times for a meeting—outright, at least. Hannah could have gotten in trouble if the postcards were found."

"So maybe he did include some type of code in the postcards, but I don't know how to figure it out. I thought the numbers written on the back had something to do with dates and times, but there are too many numbers, and they make no sense."

"This is all giving me a headache." Gracie pressed her fingertips to her temples. "I'm only here for another few days. Couldn't we put those postcards aside for now? If we have time at Christmas, maybe the whole family can join in on the guessing game."

"Penny for your thoughts," George said, as he settled down on a deck chair on the back porch. Caroline was looking out at the vast black expanse beyond the sand. They were bundled up in bulky sweaters and jackets, listening to waves crash on the shore, watching stars skitter across the sky.

"Just thinking how much I love it here."

"I like it too. And it's a lot closer to Annapolis than England was, which makes it easier to see you. Those visits every three or four months were getting kind of old."

Caroline couldn't help but agree with George. Being with him here felt more relaxed than those visits had, in spite of all the time he had spent working on the Packard.

"One of these days, you might be able to visit and not have to work."

"I told you before, Caroline, that putting that Packard back together doesn't feel like work. Real work is sitting at a desk in my office, making sure bills are paid. It's hounding customers to get them to pay their invoices and making sure we have the right materials on hand for every job. Sometimes it means taking a phone call at three in the morning from a client who wants to lynch me because his boat is on the fritz, even though the problem is that he didn't maintain it properly. That gets old."

"I've never heard you talk like that before."

He sighed. "It's been building up. I've got to say that some of the best times I've had in the last six months have been right here on the island. I've liked spending time with you and your sisters, getting to know Bill Dekker and Pastor Wildes, and—"

"And working on the Packard." Caroline smiled. "I'm beginning to think you might want to take it away with you once it's totally refurbished."

"No, what I think I need to do is retire so I can spend more time here on the island and drive it whenever you think it's okay. See you when I want. Not have to catch a flight away from Nantucket, like I have to do in the morning."

"You told me once you'd never retire."

"A man can change his mind, can't he?"

"I suppose." The night air was crisp, but it was refreshing, carrying the scents of salt and damp leaves. "I just can't picture you happy unless you're working."

George pushed up from the chair, drawing Caroline up with him, and walked to the edge of the porch. "There are other jobs besides building and selling boats. Who knows? I might find a job with a tour company. Take little old ladies on scenic drives around Scotland. Or maybe I'll start a tour company for hearty souls who want to brave the less-than-peaceful parts of the world."

"That last option's out. I may not have any say in what you do or don't do, but I'd have to put my foot down on the brave-souls tour. I'd rather have my best friend alive than, well, the opposite."

George pulled her close. She'd always felt comfortable standing beside him, and sometimes she wondered why they'd never progressed beyond friendship. *Sometimes*, she supposed, *more intimate relationships aren't meant to be.*

He kissed the top of her head as he always did when he said good-bye. She started to slip away from his arm, to let him go, but this time he turned toward her. He looked into her eyes, smiling softly. His fingers slipped under her chin and tilted her face up to meet him. And then he kissed her. So warm, it took her breath away, made her question every sane thought she'd ever had. And then he was gone.

Gracie climbed in bed and pulled up the soft blankets. It was cool enough now that they had piled down comforters on all the beds, and she snuggled under the covers. They smelled like the special lavender soap Sam used in the laundry. It was early to go to bed, but she needed some time to think. She couldn't get her mind off the postcards. She kept thinking about Hannah and William and Jedediah. Who was William, other than a minister from Boston? And what about Hannah? What was she to William?

Gracie punched her pillow, closed her eyes, and tried to sleep. She didn't need to think about the mystery of the Misty Harbor Inn. She had so little time left at the inn, and there was so much left to do. She couldn't leave without doing her fair share.

Again she tried to doze off, thinking about the list she'd compiled before going to bed of all of the things that she needed to do before heading back to Portland, when her cell phone rang. She grabbed it off the nightstand and saw that it was Brandon.

She found herself sighing. The thought of talking to her son, whom she loved with all her heart, didn't bring all that much pleasure at the moment. He was bound to ask her if she could come home early because the kids needed her, or to make sure she wasn't planning to stay in Nantucket longer than she'd originally planned.

Gracie held the phone under the blanket. She didn't want to answer it. Didn't want to hear it. She wanted the ringing to stop—and at long last, it did.

Guilt tore through her. How on earth could she ignore her son? She quickly punched in his number.

Brandon picked up on the very first ring. "Hope my phone call didn't wake you, Mom."

"No, no, I was just…preoccupied." She hated to lie. Preoccupied was an honest enough excuse for not answering before. "Everything okay?"

"Fine. Of course, the kids miss you."

She missed them too, but she didn't want to fall into Brandon's trap, his roundabout way of making her feel in the wrong for not being home to take care of them.

"Did you talk with Stacy yet about coming here for Christmas?" Gracie sat up and adjusted her pillows to support her back. "Caroline and Sam are making plans, and we're all hoping to have the entire family here."

"It's a long trip, Mom. It's been a long time since you traveled any distance with toddlers and a seven-year-old. Maybe you've forgotten how rough it can be."

She'd forgotten nothing. "You just fill the car with lots of games, play I Spy a thousand times, and before you know it, you're in Nantucket. Evelyn's asked me dozens of times about the ferry ride and if she'll see whales or seals, and really, Brandon, it's a lot closer than Scotland. I know you're making plans to take the family there in the next couple of years. I think you should plan this trip too."

What had come over her? She never made her children feel guilty. It didn't seem right, but she had asked him about Christmas several times already. He had to make a decision, and the sooner the better.

"I'll talk to Stacy about it. Football season'll be over and I do have two weeks off."

"The kids will love it here."

"I'll try to let you know when you get home. You're still coming home day after tomorrow, aren't you? Stacy wants you to help her make a Halloween costume, and you've got to be here for the harvest festival."

She thought about saying no. There was so much more to do around the inn. She wanted to plant more chrysanthemums and prune the roses. She wanted to buy old books to fill the library shelves. But Brandon and Stacy needed her. The children wanted her around. Reluctantly, she said, "I'll be home day after tomorrow."

She disconnected and let out a sigh. Was she living her own life or letting her son tell her how it should be lived?

"Well, I guess this is it." Caroline stood with Sam, seeing Jamie and Gracie off. Both of them were ready to leave the island and would not return until shortly before Christmas.

"Yep. And I've decided to free my mind of every thought I ever had about Hannah Montague," Jamie said, standing next to Gracie's small car. "I have my thesis to finish and two part-time jobs and I just don't have the time to think about some mysterious woman who died well over a hundred and thirty years ago."

"You and me both," Gracie said, the keys to her car dangling from her fingers. "So you decided to write about whalers instead?"

"I finished my paper last night." Jamie patted her bag.

"That's good to hear," Caroline said, "because I've put her out of my mind too." That wasn't exactly the truth, but she had to stay focused. Gracie had been hammering that into her head for months now. Thinking about Hannah Montague was pulling her away from her responsibilities. She wouldn't let that happen anymore.

Gracie cocked her head to one side, looking at Caroline with a look of skepticism.

"Really," Caroline protested. "In fact, I've put away the postcards. Not where I can't get to them, but into the china cabinet, where they won't get carried off by a precocious pup."

"And I'll keep her away from them too," Sam said. "We've got most of the hard stuff done at the inn, but we need to keep on top of things. Advertising. Promotion. Going to chamber of commerce mixers. Getting to know more people in town, so they'll recommend the inn to their friends."

"All the things I dislike doing," Gracie said. "It's probably a good thing I'm leaving, or you'd have me giving a speech in front of the Rotary Club."

"We'd rather have you here, even if you did nothing but sit in the library and read all day," Caroline said. She was going to miss Gracie, even the cantankerous Gracie. "But when you're back here for Christmas, we should be able to do nothing but kick back, and that goes for the entire Marris clan."

"And George too?" Gracie asked.

"George too," Caroline said, once again remembering his kiss. It had felt so right, but she didn't want things to change between them. Their relationship had worked perfectly for ages; why stir up something that could easily lead to problems?

Off in the distance, Caroline heard the ferry sounding its horn. There weren't all that many this time of the year; there'd be even fewer come Christmastime. Caroline didn't want to wave good-bye to her sister and niece. She was going to miss them terribly. All she could hope was that someday Gracie would decide to stay.

That would be an awfully nice Christmas present, she decided. If not this year, then maybe next.

CHAPTER
Thirty

Caroline ran from one end of the inn to the other, checking every last detail. Candles stood in each of the house's front windows. The fudge was made—thanks to Sam. Christmas sugar cookies decorated. A tiny tree had been decorated in each guest room. Cinnamon sticks, pine cones, dried orange peels, and whole clove potpourri—the Misty Harbor Inn's own special mix—filled many of their mother's Christmas bowls and were scattered about the inn.

The Misty Harbor Inn had to be perfect. It was Christmas, after all, and the entire family would be there.

"Is the wreath on the front door?" Caroline called out to Sam, who bounced between the kitchen and the dining room, setting out candied nuts, toffee, and peanut brittle that she'd stayed up late last night making. Caroline had strung popcorn for the big Christmas tree in the parlor. Gaily wrapped presents were scattered all around.

"Where's your mind, Caroline? I've already answered that question at least three times, and the answer's still yes.'"

"Well, in answer to your question, Sam, my mind is gone. I think I lost most of it last June when we bought this place, but the good Lord has promised to return it to me someday soon."

"Thank heaven!"

Caroline stood in the foyer checking out the evergreen garland wrapped around their curved stairway. Red velvet bows she and Sam had made added a touch of extra color to the garland. At the Misty Harbor Inn, the holidays would always be done up right.

"Mom would be so proud," Sam said, slipping an arm around Caroline's waist.

Caroline nodded. She drew in a deep breath. "Sometimes it's hard to believe that it's all really ours."

"When I think how sore my back has been since June and how little sleep we've gotten at times, I definitely believe it's ours," Sam said.

Caroline took a deep breath. "Well, should we head to the ferry to pick everyone up?"

Sam nodded. "Gracie's going to be so surprised when she sees how much has happened to the inn."

"She will, and she might even wonder why she balked at buying it in the first place."

They had accomplished a lot in the two months since Gracie went home. The guest rooms were just about ready now. They'd hung the wallpaper in the Periwinkle Room and the Amaryllis Room, and with simple bed linens, the furniture shone. They'd chosen dark green for the walls of the other room, and had added a few modern touches like contemporary lamps to blend the old and the new. They had decided to call that the Emerald Room. And for the suite, they'd decided to make the smaller room child-friendly, with a synthetic rug and gray and green striped washable wallpaper.

Caroline wrapped her thick wool scarf a little tighter around her neck and opened the front door, and she and Sam stepped out onto the front porch. The Packard was waiting, its bright red paint spit-polished and shined, looking as it probably had the day it was driven off the showroom floor.

"Your carriage awaits." George opened the back passenger door and did a little bow. He looked handsome in his black wool trousers and his green cashmere sweater, with his blue eyes sparkling. He'd come a week early to make sure the Packard was in pristine shape for this day—Christmas Eve—and Caroline gave him a quick kiss on the cheek before climbing into the car.

Bing Crosby was singing "White Christmas" as they drove to the ferry terminal. The sound came out sweet and low through the speakers George had discreetly installed. He'd tossed a red afghan over one row of backseats and a green afghan over the second row to keep all his passengers—three children and seven adults, plus himself—snug and warm. The Packard would hold them all perfectly. Next June, it would hold their guests too. What a year they had to look forward to.

At the ferry terminal, George, Sam, and Caroline huddled together, watching for Gracie, Jamie, and the rest of the family. At long last they appeared, bundled up in coats and jackets, walking down from the ferry as sprinkles of snow floated down.

Gracie practically flew into Sam's and Caroline's arms. Had it really been only two months since they'd seen her?

Caroline hugged nieces and nephew and grandniece and-nephews—the twins and seven-year-old Evelyn, who was the light of Gracie's life—and in only minutes, they were winding their way down icy streets, heading for the big old mansion sitting atop the dunes.

When they had settled in, Jamie took her cousins on a tour, and George went into the kitchen to make hot apple cider. Caroline, Sam, and Gracie stood arm and arm in the foyer.

"I'd almost forgotten how beautiful it is." Gracie's eyes sparkled as she took it all in.

"It's far more beautiful than it was the last time you were here," Sam said. "The upholstery work's done, and the pictures are hung—including old Jedediah and Hettie."

"Oh dear! I hope the little ones don't see that pair and have nightmares."

"We could always cover them with a sheet," Sam said.

"Or hang a wreath over them," Caroline added.

"No, I suppose we just have to get used to them," Gracie said firmly. "After all, they've pretty much become a part of our family."

"Speaking of family, look at this."

Sam held out a picture, and Gracie stepped closer to see it. Sam had worked on it for more than two months now. She'd even given up sleep to finish her masterpiece—a sampler not unlike the one Hannah Elliott Montague had created.

Caroline studied the Misty Harbor Inn sampler. All around the edge, Sam had embroidered sailing ships and whales. She'd worked in shades of blue, with hints of pale to dark gray and white. The stitches were so small that the blue sky and puffy clouds seemed real, as if they were floating across the sky. At the center was the inn, but Sam had tried to envision it as if Hannah Montague were stitching the sampler well over a hundred years ago. She'd even put Hannah in the picture—a young woman on a bench in the garden.

"It's beautiful, and such a nice tribute to Hannah." Gracie's eyes were wide, full of admiration. "I said I wouldn't think about her when I was gone, but I did. Of course, I've come to realize that we don't know truth from fiction about her any longer. We've made up so many stories about her."

"Caroline and I have made up even more while you've been gone, but let's not talk about Hannah right now. You have to see what all we've done."

Sam grabbed Gracie's hand and led her from room to room. There were pine wreaths and garland everywhere and a sprig of mistletoe just for fun. Out on the back porch stood a flocked tree decorated with seashell ornaments and a starfish on top.

"Wait till you see it at night," Caroline said. "It's covered with tiny twinkling fairy lights, like most everything else in the garden."

"Let me guess," Gracie said, "George did a lot of the decorating."

"Most all of the outside," Caroline admitted, proud as punch. "But there's one more thing you have to see."

"You're going to love this," Sam said, leading Gracie to the library.

Gracie's eyes brightened when she entered the room. They sparkled. "We still need a few hundred more books to fill the shelves, but we wanted to get started."

Gracie walked slowly toward the bookcase on the far wall. She touched the leather-bound books gently. "Alcott, Dickens, Austen, Byron." She turned with shining eyes and smiled at her sisters. "Even a copy of *Moby Dick*."

"We wanted to pick books we thought Hannah might have read."

"You did a great job," Gracie said, running her finger along the spines. "A perfect job. I wish I'd been here to help."

"We do too," Caroline said, "but only because we missed you."

"O, star of wonder, star of light, star with royal beauty bright, westward leading, still proceeding, guide us to Thy perfect light."

"Good heavens, Brandon!" Gracie put a loving hand on her son's arm. "You're as off-key as our old piano."

"And he sings so loud." Evelyn—still in the red taffeta Christmas dress she'd worn to the Christmas Eve service at Harvest Chapel—sat on top of the piano bench, alongside two-year-old Zachary and Jason. "Mom and I think he sounds like Smokey Bear, especially at church. It's kind of embarrassing sometimes."

"Hey!" Brandon grinned as he glared at mother, daughter, and wife. "At least I sing. And I know the words too. That's more than a lot of guys."

"Just don't sing on the football field," his wife Stacy said, slipping an arm around his waist. "Your team will tease you from now until doomsday."

"And these kids of ours will be upset if Santa Claus doesn't come tonight, so off with you now." Brandon lifted the twins down from the piano bench. Evelyn jumped off and wrapped her arms around her grandmother. "Did you put cookies out especially for Santa?" he asked.

"Lots and lots of cookies." Evelyn ran across the room and held up the fancy plate. "And Aunt Sam promised to put a glass of milk out before she goes to bed. She says Santa likes it best when it's ice cold."

"Just like your dad." Stacy winked at Brandon. "Come on now, let's get upstairs and get into your pajamas. Daddy'll be up in a little bit to say good night."

Max ran up the stairs with the little ones, yipping once or twice, no doubt having been stepped on or squeezed too tightly by one child or another.

"It's been a lovely night," Sam said, when the parlor was quiet. "But I for one can't wait until morning."

"Mom's still a kid at heart," Jamie said, slinging an arm around Sam. "She likes to find her stocking filled with goodies, and if I don't keep an eye out, she'll unwrap presents on the sly and then rewrap them again."

"I really do hate to wait until Christmas morning," Sam smiled. "I think I learned the unwrap and rewrap trick from Caroline."

"Okay, I admit it. I was never much good at waiting either. Tomorrow morning's going to be so much fun."

"But we've already received the best Christmas present possible," Gracie said, looking around the room, not just at her son and daughter, but at the beautiful inn. "The chance to buy this old place, and then not have it fall down around us." Everyone laughed.

They talked around the piano until Brandon went into the dining room for a cup of hot cider. Gracie followed after him.

"I have to read *The Night Before Christmas* to the kids," he said to Gracie as he ladled the steaming cider into a cup.

"Your dad always read it to you and Paige when you climbed into bed on Christmas Eve." She pulled down another mug and held it out.

"It's a tradition I wanted to keep."

"Maybe we can start a new tradition, with you and the family coming here each Christmas. We have plenty of room, and the ocean's right outside. I would have loved staying at a place like this when you and Paige were young."

"I didn't expect it to be even half this nice." Brandon filled her cup with cider and handed it back to Gracie. "You kept telling me that it was a ramshackle old dump."

"I don't think my words were ever that appalling."

"Pretty close, Mom. You told us Aunt Caroline was crazy to want to buy the place and even crazier to think she could fix it up."

"Maybe I overreacted. I like things neat and orderly, and the inn was anything but that when we first saw it."

"But you didn't see anything good about it."

"I did, though. Didn't I tell you about the garden, about the flowers and how much your father would have loved getting his hands in the soil?"

Brandon shook his head. "No, Mom, you didn't. Honestly, you made it sound like you hated the place and just wanted to come home."

Gracie couldn't believe she'd given that impression to Brandon, but maybe she had. Six months ago she had wanted nothing to do with the inn. "I really wanted to see the inn through Caroline's eyes. She saw nothing but beauty; I saw nothing but work. I guess I let that influence everything I said to you."

Brandon chuckled. "So you're telling me now that you really love this place and you don't mind being here?"

"I don't exactly want to give up my home, but I do like being here. Caroline and Sam would love for me to live here permanently, and when you stop to think about it, it isn't all that fair for me to leave and let them do all the work." She leaned back against the counter and took a sip of the cider. It was sweet and spicy, warming her as it went down.

"But what about the kids? Evelyn would be devastated if you weren't around all the time."

"I love them. You know that. It's just that—oh, I don't want to hurt you, Brandon. But"—she didn't want to say it, but it was high time Brandon knew the truth—"I guess I'm tired of feeling taken advantage of. Last summer I wanted to stay longer, but you and Stacy needed me. You said I just *had* to come home. Then the same thing happened this past fall. Remember? You told me Evelyn needed a Halloween costume, and you went on and on about cornucopias and school projects at the harvest festival."

Brandon placed his mug on the counter. "I told you those things so you'd have an excuse to leave here. I knew you'd stay if Aunt Caroline and Aunt Sam asked you to, whether you wanted to or not."

Brandon's words stunned Gracie. "You mean you contrived all those reasons for me to come home?"

"Not exactly contrived. They were real reasons, but Stacy and I can handle things on our own. After Dad died, we did it so you'd feel needed."

Gracie laughed. "I did feel needed." Her eyes traced the grain on the hardwood floor. They hadn't been taking advantage of her. They tried to keep her busy and give her a purpose. And they had done that for her. "Thank you."

"But once you came here, well…" Brandon thrust his fingers through his hair. "Obviously, we read the situation wrong."

"No, you didn't." Gracie put a hand on her son's cheek. "You did it so I wouldn't have to make the hard decisions on my own. You wanted me to be happy, and I didn't have a clue what I really wanted. I still don't."

"So you don't want to come here for good?"

"I'm not sure." She took another sip of her cider and looked around the kitchen. The cabinets were worn but cozy. The new counter was a gorgeous flecked granite. The hardwood floors gleamed under a fresh coat of varnish.

She and her sisters had done this, the three of them. And they'd done it together.

CHAPTER
Thirty-one

What are you up to in here? Escaping the noise in the parlor?"
Sam asked Jamie. Jamie was holed up in the library late Christmas
afternoon. William and Hannah's postcards spread out on the desk
in front of her. "I thought we'd all agreed to put the postcards behind
us. You already turned in your paper about whaling myths."

"Got an A too." Jamie laughed. "But don't tell me that you haven't
thought about them."

"I haven't had time to think about them or anything other than
getting the inn up and ready to run."

"Well, I have."

"And what have you found? Anything?" Sam pulled a chair up
next to her daughter and sat down.

Jamie moved the postcards around on the desk, putting the
pictures in a different order. She continued to stare at the cards.

"It seems like I've been working on my thesis forever," she said.
"When you're talking myth and legend in American history, there's
a lot to cover."

"Such as?"

"I've been thinking about the dollar bill."

Sam cocked an eyebrow at her daughter.

"You know, there are all these repeated references to the number thirteen. That's the number of steps in the unfinished pyramid, the number of stars in the constellation over the eagle's head, the number of arrows in the eagle's claw, and the stripes on its shield. No one is sure why that number is repeated so many times, but there are conspiracy theories about why the images are like that. Is there any truth to these theories? No one really knows."

"Okay." Sam nodded. "What does that have to do with Hannah and William?"

"I'm not all that sure," Jamie said, rearranging the cards again. "But as I worked on my thesis, I thought about how it doesn't matter if they're true or not, because either way, the fact that they exist influences the way we think about the images. I haven't looked at a dollar bill the same way since my professor pointed out all the thirteens. And I started wondering if we'd let the myths and legends we heard about Hannah influence our thinking. We heard she was a thief. We heard she'd disappeared. We heard she was buried in a secret room in the inn. We heard she was a spendthrift who squandered her husband's money. That's all just legend. In my classes, I've learned that when you're looking into a legend, you should always start with what you know for sure. And the only proof we had of anything was that William—whoever he was—sent Hannah postcards with cryptic messages on them."

"Cryptic messages that lead us absolutely nowhere."

"But if there is some way to find out what really happened, it will be here, in these postcards. I've been thinking ever since I was here in the fall that we need to look more closely at them. I'm more convinced than ever that there's some secret code hidden in them."

"Once intrigued, always intrigued."

Sam looked up to see Gracie and Caroline walk into the room, shutting the library door behind them, and effectively silencing the sound of video games and remote control vehicles racing around the parlor's hardwood floors.

"That certainly doesn't mean I've solved anything, but…" Jamie pulled Hannah's hymnal out from beneath a stack of papers. "I got to thinking about the verses William had written on the postcards. At first I thought they sounded like they came from the Bible, and then I realized they're stanzas from hymns. Not just any old hymns, but ones from Hannah's hymnal."

"Are you sure?" Caroline sat on the edge of the desk.

"Look at this card," Jamie said, lifting a postcard bearing William's sketch of Nantucket's famous Old Mill. "It reads:

'Come, Lord, Thy love alone can raise

in us the heavenly flame;

Then shall our lips resound Thy praise,

Our hearts adore Thy name.'"

"It's pretty," Caroline said, "but—"

"I found the hymn it's from. *It's The Desire of All Nations*. In Hannah's hymnal, that's hymn number sixty-four, page twenty-five, stanza two."

"And?" Sam asked. She wasn't sure where Jamie was going with this.

"It's a convoluted puzzle, Mom, but look at the date on the postcard. June first. It probably took two, maybe three days at the most for the postcard to travel from Boston to Nantucket, which would mean it arrived on June third, or maybe fourth. I'm guessing the hymn number—sixty-four—signified the date."

Caroline, too, looked baffled. "That's a big stretch, Jamie, if you're saying that number sixty-four stands for the sixth month and the fourth day."

"That's exactly what I'm saying. That theory works on every postcard. On each postcard containing part of a hymn, I've compared the postcard's postmark date with the number of the hymn and the verse it's from. A postcard postmarked July 29 has a verse that comes from hymn number eighty-one, or August 1, just three days after the postcard was mailed. A postcard postmarked May 10 has a verse that comes from hymn number 513. There can't be that much coincidence, Mom. Those stanzas have to reflect the date William and Hannah were to meet."

"It does seem plausible," Caroline said, picking up one of the postcards. She frowned as she looked at the hymns. "But what about the time? Where is that reflected?"

"Page number and verse number," Jamie said matter-of-factly. "There are rarely more than four stanzas. 'Come, Lord, thy love alone can raise' appears on page twenty-five and it's stanza two."

"And what time is twenty-five and two supposed to represent?" Gracie asked.

"My guess," Jamie stated, "is 2:52. Probably AM, not PM because if William and Hannah went to that much trouble to hide their meetings from her husband—or whoever—they'd want to meet in the middle of the night."

"Wouldn't Jedediah hear Hannah getting out of bed?" Gracie asked.

Jamie laughed. "I have two theories on that."

Caroline grinned. "Spit them out."

"Either Hannah and Jedediah slept in separate rooms, which very well could have been the case, or he wasn't home during the night."

"And where would he have been?" Sam asked.

"I can think of all sorts of theories. So could the three of you, if you put your mind to it. But they'd just be theories."

"But Jedediah died before a bunch of these were sent," Gracie said.

"Once he'd passed away, she might have had to slip out at night to hide her liaisons from Jedediah's sons."

"Since we're talking theories here, how on earth could Hannah and William come up with these codes?" Sam asked. "He lived in Boston; she lived in Nantucket. It's not as if he would have sent her another postcard telling her how to hide a secret code."

"Maybe just like you, Mom, they liked puzzles. Maybe they knew each other as children or teens and created puzzles."

"It's all conjecture."

Jamie nodded. "Just like the theory on the dollar bill." she said. "No one knows if it's true, but someday, someone might find proof that it's correct."

Gracie laughed. "That is the most convoluted—"

"Maybe it is convoluted, Aunt Gracie, but I've looked at every other possibility, and that's the only thing I can come up with. And like I said, the postmarks and the verse numbers are constant."

"So—" Caroline flipped over the postcard in her hand. It showed a finely rendered pen and ink drawing of Brant Point Light. "Are we guessing the picture on the front is where they were supposed to meet?"

Jamie shrugged. "That seems the most likely option. It appears they're all right here on Nantucket."

No one said anything for a moment. Sam wasn't sure what to believe. It seemed impossible. But then, so much of what had happened this year seemed impossible, and yet here they were, all three Marris sisters together, reopening the Misty Harbor Inn. Finally, Sam spoke.

"This is quite an elaborate system they had for communicating. They must have really wanted to make sure no one figured out what they were up to."

"But it still doesn't tell us what happened to her," Gracie said. "We still don't know where she went when she disappeared."

"I suppose we can only hope and pray," Caroline said, "that something good happened to her when she disappeared. And that someday we'll figure out the truth about that too."

CHAPTER
Thirty-two

Caroline was in the garden with her sisters, tending flowers in the spring sunshine, willing them to bloom in time for their open house to introduce the inn to the community. The distinctive diesel whine of a delivery truck met their ears as it made its way over the shell-and-gravel drive.

The brand-new signs—one for the top of the steps leading up from the beach, one to hang at the front of the house—were scheduled to be delivered today, and the sisters dropped what they were doing and raced to the front of the inn.

Sam signed for the box, hands shaking with anticipation. They thanked the driver, who'd become a regular face over the months, and set the box on the front steps. They used Gracie's flower clippers to cut the heavy tape.

"What if they're not right?" Gracie asked. "What if the paint is smudged or they misspelled *Misty* or *Harbor* or left one of the *n*'s out of *Inn*?"

"Gracie," Sam said patiently, "we were sent a proof before they made the signs. This company has been making signs for a good hundred years. They'll be fine."

Quickly, they opened the box, anxious for what they would find. They tugged away the shrink wrap and the paper surrounding the signs, and removed the one on top.

"Wow!" Sam exclaimed. "It's fabulous. Exactly what we wanted."

The oval sign was painted Nantucket blue and Main Street yellow to match the yellow of the inn and the blue of the door. The sign showed an open doorway, a symbol of welcome. Pink roses rambled around the entryway. It wasn't an exact depiction of what guests would see when they arrived, but it was close. It spelled out home and comfort, and that's exactly what the sisters were trying for. And off to one side was the long cherry red hood of an antique car. The words Misty Harbor Inn were at the top. At the very bottom: Est. 1852.

The date was a bit of a stretch. The inn itself was established a hundred years later, but the history of the Misty Harbor was important, and the sisters had wanted to give credit to the year the old mansion was built.

"I'll call Bill and ask him if he'll hang them for us," Gracie said. "I don't want to chance messing them up."

"Anyone want lemonade and maybe some lunch?" Sam asked, holding one sign. Gracie carried another, and Caroline tagged along up the stairs with the now-empty box. "Jamie's probably hungry too."

They followed Sam toward the kitchen, but stopped short when they heard Jamie calling out to them from the library. "We—or I should say you—have your first reservation!"

Food was completely forgotten. Sam was the first into the library, pulling a chair up next to Jamie, who sat at the desk with her laptop open wide. "Oh my," Sam said, her words a near whisper, "it's for the week of July Fourth. Two people. And they want the Periwinkle Room."

"Cause for celebration!" Gracie said, smiling widely. "Dinner out tomorrow night."

"Don't get so antsy for a celebration," Caroline said, sounding unusually practical. "The open house is just a few days away. We can celebrate then. As much as I like to eat out, we really need to economize. It's cost us far more to get this place up and running than any of us ever dreamed possible, so—"

"All right, Miss Stick-in-the-Mud." Gracie sounded gleeful at the role reversal. "No going out to celebrate. But maybe Sam will make Mom's prune cake for dessert tonight."

Sam nodded, her smile bright. "One of these days I really need to teach the rest of you how to cook. What will you do if I ever get sick when we have guests?"

"Wheel your bed into the kitchen so you can give us step-by-step instructions on how to do everything," Caroline said. She stood behind Jamie to peer at the computer over her shoulder. "I don't have my reading glasses handy. Did they say anything else? Do they have any special requests?"

"Let's see here." Jamie scrolled down on the online reservation page. "Here we go. 'The Misty Harbor Inn looks enchanting. My husband and I spent our honeymoon there, and now we're celebrating our fiftieth anniversary. We loved the Misty Harbor Inn then. I know we'll love it next summer.'"

"We'll have to do something special for them." Gracie said. "We'd all better put our thinking caps on. There's no time like the present to start planning the future."

It all sounds so wonderful, Sam thought. A July Fourth reservation. By this time, she'd been hoping they'd have the inn completely reserved for the full month of June, but it would take time. No doubt they'd have a few guests before then, and when July Fourth rolled around, they'd no longer be novices at running an inn.

They could even give their guests all sorts of ideas for what to do on Independence Day. They could even suggest getting their faces painted.

CHAPTER
Thirty-three

"How much time do I have before the open house starts?" Caroline hollered, running through the kitchen. There must be at least a couple things she'd forgotten in her haste to finish up her share of open house chores.

"Fifteen minutes," Gracie said, arranging last-minute tulips and dahlias and lilies—their garden's April bounty. She was placing a vase in every room in the inn.

"Those look beautiful, Gracie."

"Thanks." Gracie tried to sound calm, but Caroline knew better. She was just as nervous as Caroline. "Where's Sam?"

Sam plowed through the kitchen door, looking even more harried than Gracie and Caroline. "I was out retrieving a platter of canapés that Max ran off with. The canapés are history; but this is my favorite tray. Honestly, Caroline, we've got to do something about that dog." Sam blew out a huff. "If anyone shows up early, I can whip up something else and get another tray of goodies on the table just in time."

"Need any help?" Caroline asked. The inn was spotless. Sam had the food under control. Gracie had nearly finished putting out the flowers. George was outside, parking the Packard in front of the house so everyone would see it. He had wanted to get another coat of wax on it before the guests started to arrive. "Oh, wait," she said. "Never mind. I nearly forgot something I have to do."

"What more could need to be done?" Gracie asked. "I mean really, Caroline, we've done more than enough already, don't you think?"

Caroline shook her head. "This is definitely necessary."

She raced up the back stairs to the attic, threw open some boxes, and found the exact dress she was looking for. It might have been white at one time, but age had mellowed it to a warm ivory. It was a stunningly beautiful long Victorian gown of satin and lace, with fold upon fold of fabric that created a bustle. The cuffs were a mass of pearls that that formed something like a wide bracelet. Pearl buttons raced up the back to the very top of the high, stiff collar. The waist couldn't have been much more than eighteen or twenty inches. The woman who had worn it must have stood barely five feet tall. A tiny thing, for sure.

Could it have been Hannah?

No matter who had worn it, Caroline knew it would look perfect lying softly across the bed in the Periwinkle Room. It would be the perfect complement to the Battenberg lace canopy that draped over the high four-poster cherrywood bed.

Caroline shook out the gown. It had been wrapped in once-white tissue paper, as if someone had been readying it for a trip. A wedding trip, maybe? An elopement? It was wrinkled, but she was sure most of them would shake out. She headed down to the second floor and walked into the Periwinkle Room. She shook out the gown again and then laid it on the bed and smoothed out the sleeves, the bodice, the skirt. It was so incredibly beautiful. If she'd ever married… But no, that would never happen.

Downstairs she heard a familiar rapping on the door. Definitely a cane. Leave it to Shirley Addison to be early.

Caroline dashed out of the room, swept up a piece of newspaper she spotted on the floor, and made it to the foyer at the same moment as Gracie. They both took deep breaths, smoothed their hands over the simple pastel spring dresses they'd chosen for the event, and opened the door.

"About time you came to the door." Using her cane, Shirley made her way into the inn, all the way to the parlor, where she spotted her favorite chair and sat down.

"We're so glad you came, Shirley," Caroline and Gracie said in near-perfect unison.

"Wouldn't miss it for the world."

Max came running then from out of nowhere, skittered across the parlor floor, and came to a dead stop next to Shirley's legs. She pulled a dog cookie from out of her purse, told Max to sit, and then held out the treat. Max took it gently and lay down on the floor to eat it quietly next to Shirley. Caroline and Gracie exchanged incredulous looks.

"Hope you don't mind if we slip out for a bit to help Sam with the last of the hors d'oeuvres?"

"Of course not. Be off with you now."

When they reached the kitchen, Sam was placing the last of the fresh batch of canapés on the tray.

"Anything we can help you with?" Gracie asked.

Sam shook her head. "No, I think it's all under control—at last. I just wish Jamie could have been here."

"And I wish I didn't have to go back home in a couple of days," Gracie said, "but I'll be back for the Daffodil Festival in May, and the rest of summer. At least this time I don't feel like I'm abandoning you. Not when the place looks so wonderful."

"It does look good, doesn't it?" Sam said, lifting the tray, ready to take it into the dining room.

"I can't wait to hear what our guests have to say." Gracie looked at her watch. "They should start arriving at any moment."

"Then let's get—" Caroline stopped, looking at her hands. "I've got to wash my hands first. Max must have dragged an old newspaper out from the attic or something. I'm glad I found it before our guests start roaming around."

Caroline tossed the piece of paper into the trash can, but before she could turn away, she saw the headline staring up at her: Robbery at Brant Point Lighthouse. Hannah Montague Disappears.

Caroline grabbed the piece of newspaper out of the trash and scanned it quickly. "This is impossible," she said. "Our Hannah was a thief after all."

"What are you talking about?" Sam asked.

Another knock sounded at the door. "I'll tell you later. We've got to get going," Caroline said, looking up toward the front door.

"We can give it one more second," Gracie said. Caroline glanced at her sister to make sure she was serious, but then turned back to the newspaper. "Is that article really about Hannah?"

Caroline looked at it again. She nodded. "It looks like it's from 1880 and . . . I can't read it all right now, but it insinuates that Hannah Montague was a thief. That she stole money from the Brant Point Lighthouse—and then she disappeared."

"Not our Hannah."

"I don't want to believe it either," Caroline said. "But that's what it looks like."

"One mystery down," Sam said sadly, "And another mystery begins."

"You've done a wonderful job restoring the inn," Rex Lansdowne, the editor of one of the island's online newspapers, told Caroline and Sam. He had been wandering throughout the inn, taking pictures here and there. "I hope my article and photos, not to mention the ad you placed, will help fill your rooms this summer and fall."

"I love reading your newspaper," Gracie told Rex. "It was one of the first places we thought of when we were deciding where to place advertising."

"I was afraid I might have to exaggerate a bit about the facilities when writing my article, but that won't be necessary. The food alone is worth bragging about." He took a bite from a canapé.

"Our sister Sam will be thrilled to hear that," Caroline told Rex before he walked away to talk to some of the other business people on the island. They'd issued an open invitation to all the members of the press and the chamber of commerce as well as the folks from Harvest Chapel. They knew they wouldn't all show up, but for the past two hours there'd been a steady stream of people from the church Gracie and Caroline had come to call their spiritual home, plus friends and friends of their friends. It was spring, and Nantucket was still rather quiet, so people here were locals. It would be nearly a month before tourists started to arrive. They had one more month to prepare menus, test recipes, and maybe even catch a little bit of rest before the hoped-for summer rush began.

Bill Dekker, Pastor Wildes, Grandpa Folger, and Megan Folger-Wildes had arrived near the beginning of the open house, and each of them had helped in their own special way. They'd all become great friends these past few months, as had Shirley Addison. In fact, they were becoming some of the best friends Caroline had ever had.

Other than her family, she could only think of one person who'd been there for her more than their newfound Nantucket friends: George. Caroline looked across the room and saw him chatting with a few ladies in the choir at Harvest Chapel. He seemed perfectly at home and had made sure everyone got a good look at the Packard on their way in.

The open house was nearly over when Pastor Wildes stood near the beautiful old piano and drew the attention of all the guests. "It's a pleasure to thank Gracie, Caroline, and Sam for their wonderful hospitality today."

The gathering of guests and friends poured into the parlor, and the sisters moved toward the piano, linking arms, as they'd finally linked their lives. Caroline felt tears welling up behind her eyes, in spite of the happiness and warmth she felt.

"I hope you'll all join me in blessing our friends and their lovely inn. Proverbs 24 says, 'By wisdom a house is built, and through understanding it is established. Through knowledge its rooms are filled with rare and beautiful treasures.' Our friends Gracie, Caroline, and Sam are treasures themselves, and they have breathed new life into the treasures that they found within these walls." Pastor Wildes folded his hands in prayer. "Lord, we ask that You fill the Misty Harbor Inn and all who dwell within with Your spirit. Bless this new venture, and prepare for our friends a path filled with new friendships, new experiences, and new joy. And we ask, Lord, that You make this inn a safe haven, filled with Your love, now and always."

"Thank you, Pastor," Caroline said, taking his hands and then giving him a hug. Gracie and Sam did the same. They chatted for quite some time, and when they found Shirley asleep in her own special chair, with Max asleep at her feet, Pastor Wildes woke her gently, helped her up, and accompanied her home. It wasn't long after that everyone was gone and the inn was quiet at last.

CHAPTER
Thirty-four

*L*ater that night, after the sisters had cleaned up and put away the dishes and straightened all the rooms, Caroline and George went down to the beach. It was such a calm and peaceful night, with the moon sparkling down on the ocean. A light breeze blew. It should have been chilly, but she felt rather warm inside. She'd always felt that way when she and George walked side by side.

They talked about how many people had attended the open house and the good feedback they'd heard. Caroline was particularly gratified that so many people had commented on how nice the Periwinkle Room looked, and George had entertained Pastor Wildes for a half hour showing him the new, modern features he'd installed in the Packard.

"I can't believe you're going back to Annapolis again tomorrow," Caroline said. "I wish you could stay longer this time."

"I wish I could too, but I've got a huge project ahead of me. I'll have to make a couple of trips to London to work on the plans for an eighty-two-foot sailboat." He tucked an arm through Caroline's, and pulled her closer to his side as they walked. "Retirement's starting to sound better and better all the time, although I am looking forward to building this boat. My client wants a throwback to the fifties and sixties, with a lot of wood inside."

"It'll be kind of like working on the Packard again."

George nodded. "I have to admit, working on that car for so long has made Nantucket feel more like home than my boatyard."

"This place feels like home to me too. I actually feel almost settled, and never in my wildest dreams did I ever think I'd feel that way."

"I never thought you'd settle down either. You've seemed different here. You're happier."

"Really?"

Again George nodded. "Really."

They turned and walked back toward the inn. The sea grass, illuminated by the moon, swayed in the light breeze. George seemed to grow serious, thoughtful. He was never a laugh-a-minute kind of guy, but now he seemed to have something on his mind. Something weighing heavily on him. She wished he'd open up and let her be a part of whatever was troubling him.

The waves rolled up onto the shore, lapping softly, and George led her toward the steps they'd built to take visitors from the inn to the beach. From where they stood, they could see the inn, its windows lit up against the night sky. It was hers, and it was beautiful.

Caroline sat on one of the steps, looking out at the ocean. The moon still hung high in the sky, casting moonbeams across the water. George tucked his hands into his coat pockets, and then he knelt.

On one knee.

Caroline thought for sure her heart had stopped.

He drew his hands out of his pockets, and in the starlight, she could see the small velveteen box. He opened it slowly. The ring was a simple band of diamonds. Nothing fancy. George knew her too well for that.

He looked up into Caroline's eyes. "I've been in love with you longer that I thought it was possible to love someone. I didn't even know it was possible to love someone as much as I love you." He swallowed hard. "We've been together for thirty years, and I'm hoping for at least another thirty." Again he swallowed. "Caroline, will you marry me?"

She couldn't take her eyes off his. There was so much love there. She loved him too, but—

"I love you," she whispered, hoping he could hear her words over the roar of the ocean and the heavy beating of her heart. "I've loved you since that first day we met. There's no one else in my life who could ever make me as happy, who—"

"You're telling me no, aren't you?"

Caroline drew in a deep breath. "I've never wanted to get married. You know that. You've always known it."

He turned again to look at the ocean. "I thought that might have changed. I've long hoped it would change. But"—he drew in a deep breath and let it out slowly—"I just couldn't be here any longer unless I knew. I don't want to leave, but—"

"You don't have to go, George. Why can't we just keep on as we have?"

"That's not what I want, Caroline."

She wiped a tear away from her eye. For a moment, the only sound was the waves crashing against the shore.

"Why don't you go back up to the inn," George said. "Tell everyone I had a great day, that I'm sorry I couldn't say good-bye, but I really need to go."

"Can't we talk?"

He shook his head. "We have. You want one thing; I want something else." He thrust a hand through his thick gray hair. "I'll watch you until you get back to the inn."

"You don't have to."

"Yes, I do. That's who I am, Caroline. You know me well enough to know that."

She did know him well, and as she walked up the stairs, knowing he watched her every move, she wondered if she'd ever see him again.

Caroline walked inside and shut the door behind her. She leaned against the kitchen counter and drew in a deep, ragged breath. She couldn't believe what had just happened. She had just lost her best friend. She had let him just walk away.

Caroline put her hands on the counter to steady herself. She knew she had done the right thing, but that didn't make it hurt any less.

"Is that you, Caroline?" Sam called from the parlor.

"Yes," she said weakly. "I'll be in there in a moment." She took a deep breath and pushed away from the counter, and tried to compose herself. She took a glass down from the cabinet next to the sink and filled it with cold water. She drank it down in one gulp and then refilled it, and slowly started toward the parlor. She hoped they wouldn't be able to see that she'd been crying.

"What happened, Caroline?" Gracie asked as soon as she appeared in the doorway.

There was no hiding something like this from her sisters.

"George just proposed." Caroline set her glass down on the mahogany table by the door.

"Finally!" Sam dropped her needlework into her lap and clapped her hands. "It took him long enough. Tell us all about it!"

"Oh, Caroline, that's wonderful!" Gracie jumped up and came toward Caroline, as if to give her a hug.

"I said no."

Gracie stopped dead in her tracks.

"But...why?"

"Caroline, you've always loved him," Sam said. "Even if you won't admit it to yourself, it's true."

"I don't know." Caroline grabbed on to the back of one of the newly upholstered club chairs. "I don't think I do. Not like that."

Caroline couldn't explain it. She knew that from the outside, she and George had seemed like an old married couple for years. But actually marrying him was something that had never really entered her mind. How could that work? Could she really learn to think of him like that? She was grateful her sisters didn't ask her any more. Instead, Gracie gently stepped forward and wrapped her arms around her. A moment later, Sam did the same, and her sisters held her as she cried.

She cried for George, for how horrible it felt to break his heart. She cried because her relationship with her best friend could never be the same. She cried because she honestly couldn't imagine this place without him.

They stood there, all three Marris sisters together, until Caroline didn't have any tears left. Slowly, she pulled away.

"I'm sorry," she said. Gracie pulled a tissue from her pocket and handed it to her, and she swiped it under her eyes. "I don't know how to thank you."

"Of course." Sam steered her toward the sofa and sat down next to her. "We're your sisters. We're here for you." Max got up from his place by the fire and climbed up next to Caroline. He spun around in a circle, looking for the most comfortable position, and then settled down against her leg. "We'll always be here for you."

It sounded trite. And yet, Caroline knew as she looked around the parlor at the grand old piano, the rich upholstery, the ornate wallpaper, it was true. Her sisters would be here for her. They were in this together now. She, and Sam, and even Gracie—poor, uptight Gracie—had given up everything start a new life together. They were now linked together in ways she could never have imagined a year ago. The inn had done that.

No, Caroline thought, *it wasn't the inn that brought us together. It was Mom who did that.*

Running this inn had always been their mother's idea. Even though they'd lost her, they had fulfilled her dream, just like she'd always wanted.

"Mom would be so proud to see us here like this," Caroline finally said.

Gracie and Sam nodded.

"She would have sat in that chair, right by the fire," Gracie said, pointing to one of the club chairs by the mantel. A warm orange glow radiated from the fire dancing on the hearth, and the room smelled faintly of cedar smoke.

"And she would have been reading," Sam said. "Or working on a crossword puzzle."

"Or telling stories," Caroline added. She held the tissue to her damp cheeks and wiped the last remnants of the tears away. "She always loved to tell us stories." She looked at the empty chair by the fire. It was easy to picture her mother there.

"I'm sorry she didn't live to see it," Gracie said. Caroline knew she didn't just mean what they'd done with the inn. Their mother's greatest wish had always been to see her daughters together like this.

The fire danced and spun. Max laid his head on her lap, and she stroked his soft fur. She looked at Gracie and then at Sam, their faces illuminated in the soft firelight. No matter what challenges the sisters faced, they would face them together.

And Caroline knew that no matter what happened in the future—no matter what happened with George, or with her travel writing, or how things went when they welcomed their first guest— she was home. "Mom would have wanted us here together like this. And as long as we own the Misty Harbor Inn, she will be right here with us."

A Note from the Editors

We hope you enjoy Nantucket Dreams, created by Guideposts Books and Inspirational Media. In all of our books, magazines and outreach efforts, we aim to deliver inspiration and encouragement, help you grow in your faith, and celebrate God's love in every aspect of your daily life.

Thank you for making a difference with your purchase of this book, which helps fund our many outreach programs to the military, prisons, hospitals, nursing homes and schools. To learn more, visit GuidepostsFoundation.org.

We also maintain many useful and uplifting online resources. Visit Guideposts.org to read true stories of hope and inspiration, access OurPrayer network, sign up for free newsletters, join our Facebook community, and follow our stimulating blogs.

To order your favorite Guideposts publications, go to ShopGuideposts.org, call (800) 932-2145 or write to Guideposts, PO Box 5815, Harlan, Iowa 51593.